James Freeman Clarke

Memorial and Biographical Sketches

James Freeman Clarke

Memorial and Biographical Sketches

ISBN/EAN: 9783337009724

Printed in Europe, USA, Canada, Australia, Japan

Cover: Foto ©Raphael Reischuk / pixelio.de

More available books at **www.hansebooks.com**

MEMORIAL AND BIOGRAPHICAL SKETCHES.

BY

JAMES FREEMAN CLARKE.

BOSTON:

HOUGHTON, OSGOOD AND COMPANY.

The Riverside Press, Cambridge.

1878.

RIVERSIDE, CAMBRIDGE:
STEREOTYPED AND PRINTED BY
H. O. HOUGHTON AND COMPANY.

CONTENTS.

JOHN ALBION ANDREW.

JOHN ALBION ANDREW.

JOHN ALBION ANDREW, the great War-governor of Massachusetts, the pilot who weathered the storm, the twenty-first governor of the State after the adoption of the Constitution of 1780, was born in Windham, Maine, May 31, 1818.

When I was about twenty years old, I took my first journey. I went to Portland, and thence by stage along the eastern shore of Lake Sebago, and the lakes adjacent to it. At a certain point, in the town of Otisfield (now called Naples), I was struck by the picturesque situation of a farmhouse on a hill, which looked down on two lovely sheets of water, and on a valley through which ran a stream out of one lake into the other. Dark and lofty pines and distant mountains made a background for this lovely landscape. The sweet valley was like that described by Spenser : —

"A pleasant dale that lowly lay
Between two hills, whose high heads overplaced,
The valley did with cool shade overcast.
Through midst thereof a little river rolled,
By which there sat a knight with helm unlaced,

Himself refreshing with the liquid cold,
After his travel long and labors manifold."

Taken with the beauty of the scene, I asked the
driver of the stage, by whose side I was sitting, if
he thought the people who lived in that farm-house
would be willing to take me to board for a few
days. " I guess they will," said he; " they don't
see folks very often, and they'll like well enough
to hear the news from outside. They 're nice
folks, the Chutes are; if they take you, they'll
do well by you." So I dismounted with my bag,
and found the driver's prediction correct. They
gave me a room, from one window of which I
looked up to the head of a lake, twelve miles
long, bordered by the primeval forests of pine
trees, some of them a hundred and fifty feet high,
without a limb except at the top. From the other
window of my chamber I beheld another clear ex-
panse of water, and " the little river " running
into it. I saw no knight sitting there then, but
only Andrew Chute, the son of my host, catching
trout for my breakfast. But had I possessed the
spirit of prophecy, I might have beheld a very
chivalric knight there. For about thirty years
after that time, I was describing the scene to
my dear friend, John A. Andrew, and he cried out,
" Why ! that must have been Uncle Chute's house
in Otisfield." And then he told me that, at the
very time I was there, he was a boy, some twelve
years old, living at his father's house in Windham,

near by, and that both then, and later, he had often gone to that very house, and sat by that very stream, enjoying the beauty of the scenery, resting himself from " his labors manifold." And surely never was there a knight in all Spenser's roll of chivalry who bore a whiter shield, or struck a more gallant blow on behalf of the oppressed and the defenseless, than he.

Amid this romantic scenery of forests, lakes, and mountains, the boy grew up, his soul fed with the kindly influences of nature. The forests, where the white pine, pitch pine, and Norway pine grew together, and where the lumberers were only then beginning to build their winter camps, stretched in silence and solitude around. The people lived on large farms, containing two or three hundred acres, divided into pastures for sheep and arable land for corn, potatoes, and wheat. At Mr. Chute's they seldom had meat. Their chief food was bread, butter, milk, and potatoes, but the cooking was excellent, and the people were intelligent and good. The women of the family did the work of the house, and usually got through by noon, and then sat together sewing and reading. In the winter, the men went into the woods, and passed several months in the lumberer's camp, felling, hewing, and hauling timber. Around the camps the snow would often lie ten feet deep, and the son of my host, Andrew Chute, took me to see the log-house where the lumber-

men slept. One whole side of this house was a
fire-place, made of stone slabs, on which an immense fire of logs burned day and night. Though
the thermometer often fell to 20° or 30° below
zero (F.), yet, as no wind could reach them in
these forest recesses, the men were comfortable,
warmed by their exercise during the day, and at
night sleeping with their feet to the fire and their
heads to the air. I, a youth who had never seen
trees more than thirty or forty feet high, and only
hills and ponds, never lakes nor mountains, was
filled with delight at the sight of these novel wonders. And, afterward, I fancied I could trace in
John Andrew the influence wrought on his soul
by such scenes. They helped him to dignity, self-
possession, elevation; in short, character.

These country people, though having small means,
usually contrived to save enough to send one son,
at least, to college. Andrew Chute was a student
at Waterville, and John Andrew was sent to
Bowdoin. I have heard little of his college life,
except that he was a favorite there, as elsewhere,
because of his joyous, kindly, and helpful disposition. How much he studied, I have never
learned. But we have one striking proof that
when only eighteen years old his heart already
was warm with a generous philanthropy and a
sense of religious obligation. This appears from a
sentence written in the album of a classmate,
Richard Pike, afterward a clergyman in Dorchester, Mass.

PIKE! — May you ever be the poor man's friend, the champion of the slave, a preacher of righteousness, and a son of God.   JOHN ALBION ANDREW.

May 31, 1836.

After graduating at Bowdoin College, Andrew came to Boston, and studied in the office of Mr. Henry H. Fuller, an uncle of Margaret Fuller. After he was admitted to the bar, he continued to practice for a time with Mr. Fuller, but afterward was law-partner, for many years, with Mr. Theophilus P. Chandler, at the corner of Court Street and Washington Street, Boston.

In March, 1841, the Church of the Disciples was founded in Boston, having, among other methods, one of keeping all the seats free to all comers; another of frequent social meetings, and a form of worship in which the whole congregation could take part. The only condition of membership was faith in Jesus, and a desire to become his disciple. During the first year of the church, on September 30, 1841, John Albion Andrew entered his name on our church book; and continued until his death, more than twenty-five years after, an active and useful member of our body. During a long period, we held weekly meetings for conversation on important topics of religion and duty — and his presence always added interest and value to these discussions. A man of strong religious convictions and warm religious emotions, he was without the least tinge of cant, and so free in his

utterance, that he spoke with the same familiar
confidence of spiritual things as of earthly ones.
He was very fond of the Scriptures, and would
often discuss, at length, the meaning of Paul ;
sometimes bringing out a sense which few com-
mentators, I imagine, had ever suspected. The
first time I saw him, he was presiding over an
adult Bible-class, which met on Sunday afternoons.
Different members of our church would take
charge of it in succession. I, myself, though pastor, had no responsibility about it, but often attended its meetings with the rest of the society.
On this occasion I was struck with the extreme
youthfulness of the presiding member, for he
seemed scarcely more than a boy. His cheeks
were rosy red, and his head covered with thick
curls, and his mouth was quivering with interest.
As he spoke, I soon perceived that he was no boy,
but a person of very clear mind ; and, on inquir-
ing, was told that it was young Mr. Andrew, a
lawyer in Mr. Fuller's office.

As the customs of our church included occasional lay-preaching, it happened that on several
occasions Andrew occupied the pulpit, and con-
ducted the services. And this he did with such
simplicity and earnestness that all were glad to
listen to him.

He was also, at this time, for I speak now of
the period between 1840 and 1850, much interested in a new religious newspaper, of which he

was, for a time, one of the editors, and to which he was a frequent contributor. Any one who possesses the early numbers of the "Christian World," published in Boston by Geo. G. Channing, will find therein many striking articles from the eager and industrious pen of this young lawyer.

He was by nature and education a religious man, fond of the Bible and familiar with it. There was no sentimentalism about him, though much sentiment. He was fond of prayer-meetings and conference-meetings. During many years he attended quite regularly the meeting above referred to, held for conversation on all important questions in religion, morals, and social life ; and he always spoke clearly, strongly, and sweetly. The simple customs of the church suited him. While Governor of the State, and amid the great responsibilities of the war, he would usually stop after church on Sunday, and talk for half an hour with any of the members who chanced to stay, calling them Brother A. and Sister B., as of old. Whatever comes of good manners, — civility to all, an equal attention to all, — that was natural to him. But the mere etiquettes and conventional proprieties of position he never seemed to notice. In this he resembled John Quincy Adams, who once, when presiding over a convention of Unitarians, began his address thus : " Brethren and Sisters." Whereupon, when Father Taylor, the Methodist sailor-preacher, was afterward called upon to speak, he said, " I have heard wonderful words to-day ! I have heard a man, whose arm has wielded the armies and navies of the nation, say to all of us, ' Brothers and Sisters.' But that was right, for all will be brothers and sisters in Heaven. There will be then only ' Brother Christian,' and not any ' Honorable Mr. Christian,' nor ' Judge Christian,' nor even ' Rev. Dr. Christian.' "

John Andrew and Father Taylor were dear friends. For many years Andrew was secretary of the Boston Port Society, which sustained Father Taylor's chapel. Nor did he resign that office when he became Governor, but attended the meetings as before, not to preside over them, but simply to keep the records as clerk of the corporation. He loved to go to Father Taylor's conference meetings and talk with the sailors, and listen to the rough sons of the ocean, when made tender by the sense of God's presence, and by the softening influences of the place and hour. Also when, as he said, he wanted " a good warm time," he would go to the meetings of the Colored Methodist Church, of which Brother Grimes was pastor. And Mr. Grimes always came to Andrew when he needed anything for his people. In that church, with the colored people, John Andrew would often be found, sitting among them, joining heartily in their hymns, or listening with his open sympathizing expression of face to their prayers and exhortations.

One of the occasions, upon which I was struck by his mental and religious utterances, was in 1845, when he spoke earnestly at a meeting of our church, to prevent a secession of members who thought it necessary to leave it on account of an exchange of pulpits between the pastor and Theodore Parker.

"Brethren," said he, "I do not believe in the principle of come-out-ism. I am not a come-outer. I am a stay-iner. I shall not leave this church because the majority differ from me, on this or any other question. You may, indeed, turn me out, but you cannot make me go out of my own accord. This is my religious home; and if you turn me out of your meetings, I will stand on the outside, and look in through the window, and see you. If I cannot do this, I will come the next day, and sit in the place where you have been, and commune with you. I belong to your communion, and must belong to it always." So tenderly did he say this, that many were dissolved in tears. All the elements of the great lawyer and orator were in this argument, delivered to a hundred people in a private house. I can understand from that speech what the Chief Justice of the Supreme Court of Massachusetts meant by saying, that though he sat on the bench when Choate and Webster and other great lawyers of the Suffolk bar had argued before him, he had never been so touched as to be obliged to hide his emotion, except when listening to Governor Andrew.

In our church, Andrew was always foremost in all plans and movements of benevolence and reform. His contributions were large and generous for the freedmen, for the prisoners, for the street-boys, for the poor, for the home for aged colored women. He always did the most for those most forlorn and helpless; his maxim being, "Aux plus déshérités le plus d'amour."

I have a letter from Governor Andrew received near the close of the war, which he wrote one Sunday evening; in which he referred to a suggestion made in church that day, that, at our Wednesday evening meeting, we should attempt an efficient movement in behalf of the suffering freedmen.

I desire to echo your suggestion. . . . . We in the North are in comfort and prosperity. We must intervene for the immediate preservation of the colored people of the South, powerless for the moment to save themselves, and by wise and prudent generosity help to float them over, until a new crop can be made. . . . . I presume I shall not be able to attend the meeting; but I beg the privilege of helping its purpose, though absent. And therefore I write to express the hope that our congregation will move in the most efficient way, and to ask your acceptance of a subscription of one hundred dollars from yours faithfully and cordially,

JOHN A. ANDREW.

It is said that when all the parts of a great building, like St. Peter's at Rome, are in good proportion and perfect symmetry, nothing looks very large. And so when all the faculties of a man are well developed, he does not seem so great a man as when he has some single power developed in an abnormal manner. Such a full, rounded character was that of John A. Andrew. He was no fanatic in any respect; he was not extravagant in any direction; although a reformer, he was not an extreme reformer; although a conservative, he was not an ultra conservative. In every direction his life seemed to flow out easily and happily, and to unfold itself in an entire and perfect harmony. During those twenty years, when he was practicing law in this city, he was already very much interested in the anti-slavery cause. I believe he never became a member of the Garrisonian Abolitionist Society, yet he was intimate and friendly with them, and always ready to defend any person arrested under the Fugitive Law of 1850.

The generation which is now growing up does not, cannot, understand the intense interest and romance of that period. The law of 1850, for restoring fugitives to their owners, was passed hastily, under the impression on the part of Congress that something of the sort was necessary to save the Union. But it was a most unrighteous and unconstitutional law. The Constitution of the United States says, that in all suits in common law, in which the value at issue is more than

twenty dollars, the right of jury trial shall be
maintained; but a colored man living as a free
man in Massachusetts, with the presumption of
freedom in his favor, could, under that law, be arrested and turned into a slave without ever seeing
a judge or a jury. This fugitive slave law was so
opposed to law and to gospel, and so contrary to
the sentiment of common humanity, that it perhaps did more for the anti-slavery cause than anything else, particularly when it was enforced by a
conscientious and honest marshal or commissioner,
who thought it his duty to carry it out faithfully,
as he would any other law. Then it would arouse
against it the moral sense of a large part of the
community. Each time that a fugitive was arrested in Boston, another blow was inflicted on
slavery, and new converts made to the abolitionists. It needed little argument to convince a community educated through many generations in the
principles of the Declaration of Independence, that
a man who had gained his freedom at the risk of
his life, and by means of heroic efforts and a martyr's endurance, had a right to that freedom.
Great crowds in the meetings of the abolitionists,
in Faneuil Hall or other places of assemblage,
were thrilled at the sight of the dark faces and
the broken words of these refugees from that iron
bondage. There might be seen Frederick Doug-
las, soon to become one of the great orators of
the land. Or there might be Henry Brown, who

escaped from slavery in a packing-box; or William Crafts, whose wife, disguised as a young southern planter, brought her husband with her in the capacity of a body servant; or Lewis Hayden, who escaped from Kentucky with his family; or Father Henson, whose story equals in romance anything invented by the imagination of poet or novelist. When men like these were in danger of arrest and return to torture and death, no wonder that men cursed those who framed and defended the law by which they were seized, under the shadow of Bunker Hill. No wonder that Blackstone and the Bible and all the noblest records of the race were appealed to, to show that there was a law of supreme justice, higher than any human enactment, which forbade their surrender. These questions stirred the blood of men, agitated their minds, and divided the community into parties. On one side were the politicians; the conservatives; commerce, fearing the loss of southern custom; and good society, which regarded abolition as in bad taste. On the other side was youth, enthusiasm for ideas, "the strong siding champion," conscience, and the deeper religious conviction. To this last company Andrew belonged. In his law-office you would often find these fugitives. They knew that they had a friend there to whom they could always go for advice and comfort.

One of these men, who enjoyed for many years the friendship of Mr. Andrew, was Lewis Hayden.

He had been a slave in Kentucky, and had escaped, many years before, by the help of Rev. Calvin Fairbank and Miss Delia Webster, who were arrested, convicted, and sent to the Kentucky Penitentiary for this act of illegal humanity. Lewis went first to Detroit, and from there came to Boston on a mission to obtain funds for a church of poor colored people in that place. He spoke in their behalf to our congregation one Sunday evening, and thrilled us with the eloquence born out of stern reality, — for " wretched men " are not only " cradled into poetry by wrong," as Shelley tells us, but also into eloquence. I well remember now, after an interval of twenty-five or thirty years, Hayden's description of his sufferings and his escape. He said that he first became desirous of freedom from hearing a fellow-servant read aloud one of the speeches against slavery, delivered in Congress by Mr. Slade of Vermont. " I never knew my misery till then," said he. " I went home, and looked at my wife and my children, as they lay asleep, and said, ' You are my wife now, but you may not be my wife to-morrow. You are my children now, but to-morrow I may have no children, for you may be sold away from me, and I cannot help it.' " Mr. Hayden afterward settled in Boston, and has risen by his intelligence and worth to positions of honor and influence. He was associated as an assistant to Governor Andrew in the State House, and has since been elected to the Legislature of Massachusetts.

In 1851, Shadrach, a colored waiter in a hotel in Boston, was arrested as a fugitive slave, and was forcibly rescued by a body of colored men, " under the lead," as Mr. Wilson says, " of Lewis Hayden." Hayden was arrested, tried, and acquitted. I was residing in Western Pennsylvania at the time, and wrote a note to Hayden, in relation to which I received the following one from John Andrew, which I insert here chiefly for the sake of the concluding sentences : —

BOSTON, *5th March,* 1851.

DEAR FRIEND, — Lewis Hayden received a line from you last evening, which he begged me to answer in his behalf, and to express for him the gratitude he feels for the kindness and sympathy you entertain toward him. It gratified him beyond measure, that you should thus remember him. He is bound over to answer to the next term of the U. S. District Court. But I have no idea that he, or any other person, will be convicted. The poorest colored man finds no difficulty in procuring bail at a moment's warning. I think there is a reaction commencing. The rescue of Shadrach was a noble thing, nobly done. The thing was the result of the extemporaneous effort, energy, and enthusiasm of an old man, a personal friend of Shadrach, who stimulated by his own stubborn zeal the few with whom he came in contact, to follow him in his determination to save his friend (whose horror of a return to slavery he had always known) from the hands of the law, at whatever

2

personal hazard. That man will never be found. Indeed, all the principal actors are, as I understand, beyond the reach of process.

God grant that no man may ever be sent from Massachusetts into the prison-house of slavery. I hate war, and love peace. But I should less regret the death of a hundred men defending successfully the sacred rights of human nature, and the blood-bought liberties of freemen, alike cloven down by this infernal law, than I should the return to bondage of a single fugitive.

In great haste, your friend,

JOHN A. ANDREW.

Thus it will be seen, that ten years before the war began, John A. Andrew was prepared to choose a war for the sake of human rights and human freedom, before a peace which sacrificed both.

The object of many men, conspicuous in their day, eminent as lawyers, statesmen, or writers, is only personal success; their motive, personal ambition. Such was not the spirit in which Andrew studied and practiced in his profession, during the twenty years which followed his admission to the bar in 1840. His own course is best described in an address made by him in 1864, to the graduating class of the Medical School of Harvard University, in which he thus spoke : —

" There is nothing more practically and simply true than that success, abiding and secure, the happiness and usefulness of a professional career, is proportioned to the purity, singleness, and generosity of the purpose with which it is pursued. No thinking man has lived to middle age who has not seen, with his own eyes, brilliant powers thrown away, capacity for lasting impression on society and for solid happiness as the reward of real good accomplished, made the forfeit of the poor and selfish pursuit of changeful fortune, or uncertain fame, or inglorious ease. What a defeat is such a life ! Will you treat your profession as a trade, out of which merely to make your bread, while you indulge every whim of a mind to which duty is irksome, and fruitful toil a mere fatigue ? Then you sacrifice the hope of honorable competence, of solid reputation, the sweet and infinite satisfactions of a worthy life. Will you use it as the mere instrument of sordid gain? Then you sacrifice your love for Science, who stands waiting to feed you with immortal food, while you dwarf your soul to the worship of the very dust she treads under her feet. . . . . The first duty of a citizen is to regard himself as made for his country, not to regard his country as made for him. If he will but subordinate his own selfhood and ambition enough to perceive how great is his country and how infinitely less is he, he presently becomes a sharer in her glory and partaker of her greatness. He is strengthened by her strength, and inspired by her intellectual and moral life. Standing utterly alone, what man is anything? But associated with his fellows, he receives the instruments, the means, the opportunities, and facilities for action."

In 1859, when the memorable invasion of Virginia, by John Brown, took place, I recollect that brother Andrew came into one of our Wednesday evening conference meetings, and told us that fearing the old Ossawattomie hero would have no sufficient legal defense, he had telegraphed to eminent counsel in Washington to secure them in the case, and had made himself responsible for (I think) thirteen hundred dollars for legal expenses. He gave us an opportunity to contribute a part of this sum, which was done on the spot. Having made himself thus prominent in behalf of the old hero, he was summoned to Washington to appear before the Committee of Congress appointed to investigate the affair at Harper's Ferry. He was there questioned by Jefferson Davis of Mississippi, and Mason of Virginia, as to his motives in being at such trouble and expense. The testimony he gave was exactly like himself, straightforward, open, frank. When they asked him what he had done, he told how he had collected money and sent it on to John Brown, because he thought his hurried trial a judicial outrage. When he was asked whether he did that from his interest in anti-slavery or simply from humanity, he said that although it was difficult for him to sound his own praise, yet he would tell the committee that on one occasion he had gone to Washington to obtain a pardon for a man who was under sentence of death, and obtained it and went back and gave it to him, never having any knowledge of him, nor ever having seen him until he put in his hands the President's message of commutation. The man had no friend, and he accordingly took the trouble for him, without the expectation of fee or reward.

Finally, when Mr. Davis asked him what he thought of the course of John Brown himself, and of his character, he said he thought that the outrages which he had suffered from the pro-slavery men in Kansas had wrought him up to the point of doing what he himself thought was an unlawful attack upon the people of a neighboring State. "And, since the gentleman has called my attention to the subject," he continued, "I think the attack made upon Senator Sumner in the Senate at Washington, which, so far as I could learn from the public press, was, if not justified, at least winked at throughout the South, was an act of very much greater danger to our liberties and to civil society than the attack of a few men upon those living just over the border of a State." It required some courage to say this at that time in Washington, and when he came back to his own State, he was not lowered in the opinion of the people.

Afterward, presiding at a meeting held for the relief of John Brown's family, he said: "Whether the enterprise of John Brown was wise or foolish, right or wrong, John Brown himself was right. I sympathize with the man, I sympathize with the idea, because I sympathize and believe in the Eternal Right."

That same year he was chosen a delegate to attend the Republican Presidential Convention in Chicago, which nominated Abraham Lincoln and Hannibal Hamlin. He, at first, was in favor of Mr. Seward, and voted for him as a candidate. I believe he afterwards considered it fortunate that he did not succeed in his selection of a candidate.

When elected Governor of Massachusetts, in November, 1860, he had seen very little of public life, having been a member of the Legislature only a single session, and this, I think, was the only political office he had ever held. But he had, during that session, easily made himself the leader of the House, and produced such an impression of his ability and force of character, as to cause him to be nominated for Governor, in spite of the opposition of the regular politicians, who had made quite different arrangements. But the people knew well, by that instinct which in serious times seems to lead them aright, that John A. Andrew was the man wanted in the coming crisis.

He was elected Governor of Massachusetts by the largest popular vote ever cast for any candidate, and for five years he was reëlected Governor every year by the general voice of the people, in spite of frequent opposition from the smaller sort of politicians. But John Andrew and the people of Massachusetts knew each other, and they agreed very well together. Of that magnificent record

of the War-governor of Massachusetts it would
take too long to speak adequately, and it is not
necessary, for it is in all our memories, in all our
hearts. We remember his foresight, prophetic of
the coming hurricane, his preparations, his getting
the militia of the State into working order, the
ridicule cast upon the two thousand overcoats and
blankets which we afterwards saw warming our
Sixth Regiment in the storms in the famous days
of 1861. We remember how he thought of everything and put life, courage, and heart into everything; how he did the work of many men in the
State House, tiring out his aids and secretaries,
and after they had done all they could, locking
himself in his room, and sitting there half the
night writing and thinking and preparing for the
next day; how he ordered rifles from England,
armed steamers, fortified the coast, made repeated
visits to Washington, and strengthened Mr. Lincoln and others in their determination to uphold
the Union. We remember how he initiated the
movement of colored troops, and staked his popularity upon the measure; how he attended the
convention of loyal governors at Altoona, and
drew up their address; all this is fresh in all
men's memories. On the very day of his inauguration as Governor of the State, he sent one of his
secretaries to interview Governor Washburn of
Maine, to inform him what, in his opinion, was
necessary for the New England States to put them

in a condition to defend Washington.[1]   I saw him
at Readville present a flag to the Fifty-fourth
(colored) Regiment, which, under Colonel Shaw,
did such work at Fort Wagner; and of that flag,
only the staff came back to the State House.   In
the attack on Fort Wagner, on the 18th of July,
1863, Sergeant Carney, a full-blooded African,
grasped these colors from the dying color-sergeant,
as they were falling from his hands, and bore
them to the parapet; he fell himself, struck by
five bullets, but still held the staff in his hands,
and, as he was carried back, he said, "The old
flag never touched the ground, boys!"   That was
one of the instances of the war which Governor
Andrew delighted to repeat.

All those who had anything to do with him
while Governor, agree in regard to his great
power as a worker.   Colonel Albert G. Browne,
in his extremely interesting memoir of the official life of Governor Andrew, testifies to what he
saw of this in his position as military secretary.
"Almost invariably he was at the State House as
early or even earlier than either of his secretaries,
and his appearance was the signal for fresh work
in every department of the building.   Paying
hasty calls at the offices of the Adjutant-general
and the Surgeon-general, on his way, nine o'clock

[1] This secretary was Albert G. Browne.   The answer returned
by Governor Washburn was: "Wherever Massachusetts leads,
Maine will follow close, if she cannot keep abreast."

rarely found him absent from his own desk; and
there he continued until sunset, and often until
long past midnight, unless some public duty called
him elsewhere. His private affairs were utterly
neglected. His family he rarely saw by daylight,
except in the early morning and on Sundays, and
to a man of so affectionate a disposition this was
the greatest sacrifice. . . . . During the few first
months of the war his labor at the State House
averaged twelve hours daily; and during April
and May, 1861, the gray light of morning often
mingled with the gaslight on his table, before he
abandoned work, discharged his weary assistants,
and walked down the hill to his little house on
Charles Street, to snatch a few hours of sleep before beginning the task of another day. After
his bath and hasty breakfast he would reappear
at the State House as fresh as the morning itself,
without a trace perceptible to the casual visitor of
irritation or fatigue, while perhaps half an hour
later his attendants of the previous night would
come to their places cross and jaded. . . . . He
held every one strictly to the full measure of duty.
Great was his indignation, one dreary afternoon,
the day before Christmas, at finding the office of
the Secretary of the Commonwealth closed half an
hour earlier than usual. There was a severe snow-
storm raging, which suspended business throughout
the city; and the clerks of that office had closed it,
forgetting that there should have been drawn and

forwarded up stairs for the Governor's signature, a pardon which had been granted to a convict in the State Prison, according to a custom which he had of granting one pardon, each Christmas morning, upon the recommendation of the warden. It irritated him that the clerks below should have forgotten such a duty. During his own hard work during the day, the thought of the happiness which the morrow would bring to that convict had lightened his heart, and he felt a positive pain that others should not have shared that feeling. Though unwell, he hastily broke out of the room, walked through the driving snow across the city to the house of one of the officers of the State Department, brought him back to the State House, stood by while the pardon was drawn and the great seal of the Commonwealth attached to it, signed it, and despatched it by one of his secretaries to the prison."

Warden Haynes has said that there was never a governor who took such interest in the prisoners in Charlestown. When he went over there and found that there were men confined in the solitary cells, he would sometimes go into a cell and be shut in with the man. One evening he said to me, " I have been to Westborough Reform School to-day, and this little incident occurred there. After the boys had gone through their various exercises and repeated their lessons, and they had all gone out to their dinner, and the rest of the company were following, I heard a little voice calling, 'Governor Andrew, Governor Andrew.' I looked up and did not see where it could come from. At last I saw, at the upper part of the hall, a gallery, and behind it some closed doors. These were the doors of cells, and in one of these a boy was confined, whose voice I had heard calling to me. I asked who he was, and was told that he was a boy shut up for some offense and not allowed to go out during the day.

" I ordered him to be brought down, and learned that when he was first brought to the school, he had been badgered and teased by the other boys, who had harassed him until, at last, provoked by them, he had told of some offense which one of them did, and got him punished. Afterward, guilty of some offense himself, he was told of, and was suffering the punishment for it. So I ordered all the boys to be called in, and putting the little fellow beside me, in a kind way, told the boys what they had done, and explained to them how much better it would have been if they had used the little fellow kindly. I tried to make them feel the loneliness of this little stranger come among them, and how mean it was to torment him instead of comforting him. They had made a tell-tale of him by teasing him, and then became tell-tales themselves. I made them promise to do differently with the next boy, and said I should ask them about it when I came again." In that

way he always contrived to produce an impression
upon those with whom he was talking.   Father
Finnotti, in a very affectionate article which he
wrote for the " Boston Post " shortly after Governor
Andrew's funeral, told how he had frequently
been to him to get a pardon for some convict, and
how glad Governor Andrew was when he could
grant his request, and how firm he was when he
could not conscientiously do it.   Then he would
say: " No, Father Finnotti, I cannot do it ; my
duty to the State prevents it."   " And," said Father
Finnotti, " I went away feeling a greater respect
for the man than I ever had before."   Once, on
the Sunday after Governor Andrew's death, after
church, a man with tears in his eyes told me how
Governor Andrew once gave his services to him
as counsel, gratuitously, when no one else would
take the case.   Oliver Warner, the Secretary of
State, could not say enough of the personal kindness of which he had been the witness on the
part of Governor Andrew.   To all those who were
friendless he was a friend.

A lady who has taught a school of colored children at Port Royal, S. C., during many years,
described to me her last interview with Andrew
after he had returned to his law office in Boston.
She had consulted him about a claim for damages
for certain articles lost on a vessel burned at sea.
" I found him," says she, " talking with a gentleman on some minor point of law, which Mr.

Andrew explained to him again and again; but the
listener failed to apprehend the idea, and so Mr.
Andrew was obliged to return to it, with that 'But
don't you see?' which must be so disheartening.
When the man left, Mr. Andrew turned to a lady
sitting by, in whom he recognized, I think, some
one who had formerly been a member of his family. She wanted his influence to get a situation
as copyist. He listened and advised, without pre-
occupation or hurry, and with the tenderness and
gentleness of a brother. Then came my turn.
As he shook hands, I said, 'I thought a teacher
required some patience, but I believe a lawyer
needs the most.' He laughed, drew a long breath,
and passed his hand over his forehead with the
same weary look I had seen before; and then immediately began to talk as eagerly as if mine were
the only business in hand. I had written a statement of our shipwreck; and when I reported to
him that an officer of the boat was heard to say,
'There are niggers and nigger-teachers enough on
board to damn any boat!' his face expressed his
indignation. Then he asked many questions about
our work, laughing loud at the negro who said 'he
was just crazy for larn,' and the woman who was
learning the alphabet, and said she 'had been chas-
ing that letter' (meaning B.) 'the whole night,
and couldn't catch him.' As I went away, he gave
me a fervent God-speed in our work."

These little anecdotes will show how genuine

was his humanity, and how natural to him it
always was to think of the wretched, and of those
who had no helper. He acted thus both from
feeling and conviction. It was a natural instinct,
and a sacred principle. Always hopeful, always
humane, the cynicism which some persons regard
as wisdom was intolerable to him. But he was
no blind enthusiast. He regarded what was possible as carefully as what was desirable. He
examined the means as closely as the end. He
saw that most questions have two sides, and that
only by being just to both, can we be of use to
either. Therefore, though a determined anti-
slavery man, he was never able to join Mr. Garrison's party in denouncing the Constitution and
demanding a dissolution of the Union.[1] Though

---

[1] This balanced judgment is well shown in the following statement of General Sargent: "He was as independent of favor
as he was of fear. He had the excellent quality of resistance to
the improper solicitation of those to whom he not only owed a
part of his advancement, but whose sympathies were his own.
In a memorable week of 1861, when the so-called conservative
hostility to John Brown and his supporters was at white heat
and violence was imminent, the Governor was earnestly solicited
to preside at a meeting in honor of John Brown, that the Executive presence might deter the mob from outrage. The solicitation was fervid and eloquent. In the evening that preceded the
meeting at which his presence was requested, the Governor, with
a single staff officer, went by appointment to give a final answer
to the request. A large but solemn conclave of earnest men like
himself awaited his coming.

"After kind greeting and hearing a few words from some of
them, Governor Andrew spoke, with as much emotion as com-

a strong peace man, he was no non-resistant. Though an earnest temperance man, he was not a total-abstinent, nor a prohibitionist. Violent men, on both sides, denounced him for this moderation. He was bitterly blamed by an eminent abolitionist for not bringing the State power to put down a set of noisy gentlemen who made some disturbance in an anti-slavery meeting in Boston. Because he defended the policy of license against that of prohibition, he was accused in temperance meetings of being in the daily habit of drunkenness — though he scarcely ever drank the whole of a single glass of wine at dinner. Because he refused to sign the warrant for the execution of a

ported with firmness, nearly as follows : ' You know, my friends, how dear this cause of anti-slavery has been and is to my heart. You know how we have hoped and prayed and toiled together. You know what I think of John Brown as a man, and how surely I believe that his memory as a martyr will remain when constitutions shall be forgotten. You know how keenly I should feel reproach from you, my coadjutors, for any supposed recreancy to a cause, when official position that I owe in great measure to my advocacy of it gives me, as you think, power to serve it. But perhaps you do not feel, as I feel, how much easier it is to inveigh against a public officer, when we are not responsible for the administration of his office, than it is to properly administer an office which is a trust for all the people of the State. With all sympathy with the anti-slavery cause, and believing all that I have said of John Brown to be true, and with all affection and respect for you, I cannot, as a magistrate, so far forget the trust reposed in me by the Commonwealth as to expose her highest executive office to indignity and reproach by presiding at a meeting convoked to celebrate an act which, as a lawyer, I know is technically treason.' "

murderer, he was accused of being false to his oath of office, and following his anti-capital punishment prejudices. There was great excitement against him through the State for his course in this matter, and he gave no reason publicly for it. I once asked him why he did not take some method of giving his reasons and explaining to the people the grounds of his non-action. His reply was: "If I did this, it would seem as though I were placing myself in opposition to the courts, which would be an evil. I prefer to bear the misrepresentation myself. My back is broad enough for that."

Governor Andrew was opposed, in principle, to capital punishment; but, until it was abolished, he deemed that it should be inflicted when the law required it. He was also opposed to war, and a strong advocate for peace. But when the war became inevitable, he put the whole ardor of his soul to rousing the North, and preparing it for its work.

That this was no abandonment of his old convictions is certain. For I was myself present, years before the civil war seemed possible, and when no such event had been dreamed of, at a peace meeting in Boston. Some of the speakers had maintained that all wars were wrong on both sides; and that no nation should fight, even in self-defense. When Andrew spoke, he denied this doctrine, and, though standing there to defend the principles of peace, he said, "I had rather help carry on a war for freedom, justice, and humanity, than keep a peace on merely mercantile principles, and for merely selfish considerations." These facts I have referred to as showing the equipoise of his judgment, and how well he kept the maxim to preserve an equal and well-balanced mind in all emergencies.

These judicial qualities, this calm, joyous, hopeful temperament, this conscience and industry, we had always known. But not till the great outbreak of the civil war did we suspect the hidden powers of foresight, courage, inspiration, which made him so easily take his place in the very front of northern statesmen. Others doubted, questioned, waited to see what would happen; he never hesitated. He seemed to see at a glance all that was to come, and what was needed to meet it. The fiery trial which palsied so many brains among our eminent men gave to him clear sight, ready decision, and determined firmness. More than any one else he thus realized the description of "The Happy Warrior" by Wordsworth: —

> "Whose powers shed round him in the common strife,
> Or mild concerns of ordinary life,
> A constant influence, a peculiar grace,
> But who, if he be called upon to face
> Some awful moment, to which God has joined
> Great issues, good or bad for human kind,
> Is happy as a lover, and attired
> With sudden brightness, like a man inspired,

3

And, through the heat of conflict, keeps the law
In calmness made, and sees what he foresaw."

From the very day of his inauguration, January
5, 1861, Governor Andrew began to prepare his
State for war. He sent on that day a messenger
to the governors of New Hampshire and Maine, to
inform them that he intended to prepare the active militia of the State of Massachusetts for immediate duty. Accordingly, general orders were
issued to that effect in the same month. Andrew
put himself early into confidential communication
with General Scott, and arranged with him for the
march of troops to Washington, if they should be
needed, and, when the decisive hour struck, Massachusetts and her leader were found ready.

Immediately on the news of the taking of Fort
Sumter by the confederates, the whole South became one frenzy of excitement. President Lincoln
issued his call for seventy-five thousand troops, of
which two regiments were assigned to Massachusetts. Within a week from the issue of this proc-
lamation, Governor Andrew despatched *five* regiments to Washington, beside a battalion of rifle-
men and a battery of artillery. This was done
by means of that wise foresight which led him to
act at once, when action was necessary, without
waiting for the slow delays of legislation, so that
in some of his messages " it is touching," says
Horace Binney Sargent, " to read an allusion to
certain expenditures made ' without authority of

law,' but which he leaves to the candor of the Legislature. The like prescience induced him, in advance of all statesmen, to urge upon the National
Government the then astonishing enrolment of six
hundred thousand men."

On the morning when the first telegram for aid
reached Boston from Washington, the State House
was in great excitement. Companies were being
selected for the service from different regiments,
which were heard of as being most ready. As Governor Andrew was passing through Doric Hall
he heard a strong voice asking, "Will not the
Governor let us go? We want to go." Andrew
asked what regiment it was; learned it was the
Sixth, from Lowell and the adjacent towns; asked
when they could set out; learned that they could
be ready by nine o'clock the next morning, and
ordered them to be taken. Thus promptly this
civilian decided, when suddenly called to take the
helm in a hurricane.[1]

Thus Andrew himself speaks of those thrilling
days: —

"I may testify to the impressions stamped forever on
our memories and our hearts, by that great week in
April, when Massachusetts rose up at the sound of the
cannonade of Sumter, and her Militia Brigade, springing
to their arms, appeared on Boston Common. It redeemed the meanness and the weariness of many a pro-

[1] Memorial Address at Hingham, October 8, 1875, by Horace
Binney Sargent.

saic life. It was the revelation of a profound sentiment, of manly faith, of glorious fidelity, and of a love stronger than death. Those were days of which none other in the history of the war became the parallel. And when, on the evening of the anniversary of the battle of Lexington, there came the news along the wires that the Sixth Regiment had been cutting its way through the streets of Baltimore, whose pavements were reddened with the blood of Middlesex, it seemed as if there descended into our hearts a mysterious strength, and into our minds a supernal illumination. . . . . Never after did any news so lift us above ourselves, so transform our earthly weakness into heavenly might. . . . . The great and necessary struggle was begun, without which we were a disgraced, a doomed, a ruined people. We had reached the parting of the ways, and we had not hesitated to choose the right one."

On the afternoon of that 19th of April, 1861, I passed into the Governor's office in the State House, through the ante-room, crowded with the fathers, mothers, and wives of the soldiers just attacked in Baltimore. Telegrams were arriving, officers coming and going, messengers from the adjutant-general's office, from the quartermaster's office, judges, senators, the most influential men in the city ; and poor women came to ask if their sons had been heard from. In the midst of this commotion, the Governor sat at his table, calm in the midst of all, attending to each piece of business in order, hearing and answering all inquiries, considering and promptly deciding every difficult point, and writing the famous telegram which seemed to show, for the first time, that *tenderness* might be an element in war. At all events, I cannot but think that this telegram had much to do with the tenderness afterward manifested. It encouraged women to go as nurses to the hospitals, and to be received in them; it encouraged the sanitary commission in its work, and gave a tone of humanity to what was to follow. And how many days afterward do I recall during the war, when, going to his room in the State House on some special business, I found him always the same, — calm, tranquil, doing such an enormous amount of work, like Goethe's star, " Without haste and without rest." He worked like the great engine in the heart of the steam-ship. The vessel may be rolling and pitching amid frightful seas, her decks swept by successive waves, but there, in the centre of the ship, the engine works steadily on, with tranquil accuracy, but enormous power. Such force, so steadily exercised, was his. There was no jar, no strain, no hurry, no repose ; but constant equable motion, on and on, through all those weary years, to their triumphal end.

One secret of this great working-power was the natural equanimity of his temper. He was always cheerful, sunny, full of anecdotes and pleasant mirth, with infinite good nature, with none of the corrosive element of irritable self-love. If we keep to our image of an engine, this oil of kindness was the lubricating medium which prevented all waste of power by friction. Of this " golden temper of Governor Andrew," Mr. Nason says, " it was the sunshine God sent into his happy heart to bear him through the labors of his life."

Another cause of his executive force was that, both by conviction, instinct, and habit, he never stopped to lament over the past, or to anticipate with anxiety the future. I recall one illustration of this in 1854, on the occasion of the rendition to slavery of Anthony Burns, from Boston. The excitement in the city was intense. The streets, from the Court House down Court and State streets, and on to the ship, were densely packed with a crowd, not noisy, but whose faces gathered blackness as the fatal procession drew near. Attentive observers were very apprehensive of a bloody collision between the soldiers and the people. A posse of many hundred constables and policemen, the marines from Charlestown, cavalry, infantry, and a light battery with shotted guns, were thought necessary to get this one poor fugitive through the streets. The escort was hissed, the soldiers greeted with shouts of " kidnappers! kidnappers ! " and various emblems were hung from the windows. John Andrew's office at the corner of Court and Washington streets was the centre of the excitement, and filled with people. Some of his friends were draping it in front with black cloth.

On the opposite corner swung a coffin, under which the escort must pass. But Andrew sat quietly at his desk, writing, the only calm man in the room. He had done all he could to prevent the rendition before, — now, he could do no more, and sat at his desk as serene as if no such events were taking place around him. His perfect good sense revolted from the folly of wasting strength and time in mourning or raging about the inevitable.

In like manner he had an instinctive aversion to worry or anxiety about evils which might never arrive. I recollect once being present with him at the graduating exercises of a State Normal School. When called upon, as Governor of the State, to address the class, he referred to the fre-quent recurrence in their essays and addresses of a tone of anxiety in regard to their great coming responsibility as teachers. "That is all wrong," said he. "You have no occasion to be anxious at all. You have been well prepared here, and if you try to do your best, trusting in God, your responsibilities will be not a bit greater than you can meet. You are too solemn about it. Look forward cheerfully to your work. You will find it, I have no doubt, a very happy one. Do not trouble yourselves beforehand about any difficulties, but wait till they come. Remember what Abraham Lincoln said when he was asked what he would do, if such or such perils intervened: 'I never cross a river till I come to it.'" As the Governor thus

spoke, his own face beaming with cheer and good-
nature, I observed the light come back to the faces
of the pupils, and have no doubt they long remembered this kind and judicious advice which Governor Andrew always followed himself, thus avoiding
much unnecessary trouble.

Another secret of his executive ability was the
rare faculty he possessed of applying his mind at
once to each question as it arose, and deciding it
on the spot.   He did not say, " I will think about
it, and let you know to-morrow."   He knew that
to-morrow would have to take thought for the
things of itself, and that thinking at once is the
easiest way.   Thus have I seen him in the State
House, when question after question was submitted
to him, looking at each man in turn, making some
shrewd inquiry, giving his decision, and turning
to the next subject.   Moreover, and especially,
his eye was single, and that filled his whole body
full of light.   There was no prejudice to blind, no
vanity to mislead, no private aims to be gratified,
no passions to weaken and betray.   He took no
time in asking, before he made his decision, what
would be its effect on his own popularity or his
own fortunes.   There never was a man who had
less of the politician's habit of watching public
opinion and its tendencies in order to see if it will
be profitable to be just.   Here again I recollect a
story he was fond of telling of Andrew Jackson,
who was asked whether some course he proposed

would be thought Democratic by his Democratic supporters. " What do I care what they think?" shouted the old general. " If I want to know what is Democratic, I do not ask Tom, Dick, and Harry. I ask old Andrew Jackson." " *He* (slapping his breast), *he* is a Democrat, and if he thinks it Democratic, that is enough." [1]

---

[1] No doubt his natural humor and love of merriment also supported him amid his labors, as these same qualities upheld Lincoln. I quote the following from Gen. H. B. Sargent's address at Hingham : —

"And yet through all the grief and shame that attended our first shock of arms, his high-hearted hope and cheerful ways inspired us all. His voice and laughter were a defiant cheer to fate.

" His sense of fun crops out even in grave discussions. One smiles for instance in reading a long law argument in a veto message to the Senate, 'in relation to Jurors,' at his suggestion that the returned bill might operate to exclude from that bulwark of liberty, the jury — as persons unfit to serve on juries ' by reason of being engaged in pursuits made criminal by statute ' — all who fish ' out of season ' or sell ' nuts except by dry measure.'

" Even on this occasion the memory of his witty words, laughter that was almost articulate with mirth, and his cheery shout of merriment at some pronounced absurdity, reminds me how much his sunshine lightened labor in these early days of the rebellion ; when matters were so hurried that the aides would follow the soldiers of moving regiments down the steps, to tighten some buckle of belt or knapsack, or to thrust percussion caps into the pocket ! In the offices, crammed to suffocation with every applicant and contrast — the charitable and the selfish, the sublime and the grotesque — there was food for mirth as well as sadness. There were sutlers seeking an outfit, and saints with bandages and lint ; English officers tendering their service, and our regulars giving good advice ; inventors of new-fangled guns, pistols, and sabres, only dangerous to their possessor, and which the inventors threatened to sell to the Confederacy if we did not buy them ; gen-

One example of this moral independence I may mention. At the time that the Unitarians were preparing to have a national convention in the city of New York, some one said to me, " Will Governor Andrew consent to preside over that convention? " " I do not know," said I, " whether he will or not, but I will ask him." I did so. He inquired where and when it was to be held, and told me to say that he would preside. I thought that many public men if they had been asked in that way to preside over a meeting of a religious body, unpopular throughout the country, not very influential compared with the great religious bodies of the land, would have waited and considered what the effect upon their personal popularity would be. He did not hesitate for a moment. It never entered his mind to think of the effect of such an action on his position. He simply considered whether he had time to go and preside, and when he saw that he had, he said at once that he would go.

tlemen far gone into consumption, desiring gentle horseback exercise in cavalry; ladies offering to sew for us; needlewomen begging us not to let ladies take the bread from soldiers' wives; philanthropists telling us that confederate workmen, in our arsenals, were making up cartridges with black sand instead of powder; saddlers proposing sole leather cuirasses shaped like the top of a coffin; bands of sweet-eyed, blushing girls bringing in nice long night-gowns 'for the poor soldiers,' or more imaginative undergarments 'fearfully and wonderfully made,' redolent of patriotism and innocence, embroidered with the Stars and Stripes, and too big for Goliah."

Another instance occurs to me of the power which Governor Andrew possessed of throwing his mind into any subject, and of thinking it through. In the midst of the war, being at church one Sunday morning, I asked him a question after the service which led him to speak of Harvard University. In answering the question, he went on to consider the whole subject of university education, and as we walked he developed a complete theory of the ends to be kept in view and the methods to be adopted by the college government. "If I were appointed president of the college," said he, "this is what I would do," — and then, for nearly an hour, as we walked round Boston Common, he explained his system and the way in which he would try to carry it out. Those who met us and saw his earnestness of manner no doubt thought that he was explaining some important matter connected with the war. This power of concentrating his mind upon any theme and holding himself to it, constituted no small part of his force, and made him capable of filling almost any position with success.

Impatient of pedantry, disliking all formalism, an intense realist, his thoroughly practical mind always kept in view the *object*. The majority seem soon to forget what they are working for. His thought never let go the object to be attained, while examining all the means by which to attain it. The famous case of the "overcoats" illustrates this. Projecting his judgment forward, he saw that when the war broke out it would be sudden, that men would be wanted immediately, that it might be cold weather, that their health and consequent efficiency would depend on their being warmly clothed, that the overcoats would be the garment they would not be likely to have, and which would keep them warm. So he ordered the two thousand overcoats, amid the derision of that class of people who laugh at the propositions of the man who sees further than themselves, and then, when his foresight is justified, forget immediately that they ever laughed at all.

Every one remembers the energy with which he pursued the plan of employing colored troops, till at last he obtained permission from the War Department to do so. In a personal interview with Mr. Stanton, he received written authority to raise volunteer companies of artillery for duty in Massachusetts and elsewhere, and such companies of volunteer infantry as he might find convenient. With his own hand, Governor Andrew added, " and may include persons of African descent organized into separate corps." This was on January 26, 1863, and was a great step forward toward crushing the rebellion. He immediately returned to Massachusetts, and raised the Fifty-fourth Regiment of Massachusetts Infantry, the first colored men admitted as soldiers to the service and defense of the Union. A second colored regiment, the Fifty-fifth, soon followed. But, though consenting to receive their services, the government refused to these men a soldier's pay, and offered them a smaller sum, such as was paid to stevedores and cooks. This they unanimously refused to receive, and so went without pay for more than a year. The Governor summoned the Massachusetts Legislature in extra session, and procured an act to be passed to pay them the full amount from the State treasury, and sent paymasters with the sum to South Carolina, where the troops had gone. But these brave fellows declined to take it, saying, " We will wait till the United States chooses to pay us our just dues." The Governor, though a sweet-tempered man, was capable of a righteous indignation, and on this occasion it burst all limits. He appealed to the War Department, to the Attorney-general, and at last to the President ; quoting in his letter to the latter the opinion of the Attorney-general, and then demanding that they should be paid, showing what had been their services at Fort Wagner and elsewhere, and what were the sufferings of themselves and their families. But the President still hesitated ; and then the Governor turned to Congress, and addressed a letter to Thaddeus Stevens, June 4, 1864, in which he used these remarkable words. " For one, I will never give up my demand for right and justice to the soldiers. I will pursue it before every tribunal. I will present it in every

forum where any power resides to assert their
rights and avenge their wrongs. I will neither
forget nor forgive, nor intermit my effort, though
I should stand unsupported and alone ; nor, though
years should pass before the controversy is ended.
And if I should leave the world with this work
undone, and there should be any hearing for such
as I, elsewhere in the universe, I will carry the
appeal before the tribunal of Infinite Justice."
Under the pressure of threatened legislation, the
War Department at last gave way, and the colored
men were made equal with the whites.[1]

His influence over men was great. He could
convince, persuade, and bring to his views persons
of the most opposite characters, each of them won-
dering how he was able to do so much with the
other. He once told me that he believed he was
personally acquainted with almost or quite every
man of any prominence in the State.

[1] Happening to be in the Governor's office when he was writing
this letter, he read it to me. Not long after, I had the satisfaction
of preaching in the hall of the House of Representatives at Washington, and describing the magnanimity of those colored soldiers
in refusing the money till they could have justice with it, though
they and their families were suffering for need of it. Then I
added, "If this action had been done by Greeks or Romans, it
would have been put in our school books, and we should be
taught to admire its heroism. But because it has been done by
colored people we do not think much of it. For myself I had
rather be one of those colored soldiers, continuing to serve the
country, but refusing his pay till he could have justice, than a
member of Congress, sitting in his comfortable chair and taking
pay regularly, and yet not having the courage to pass a law to
pay those colored men their due."

When he was chosen Governor he was much disliked, on account of his supposed ultraism, his peace principles, his anti-slavery ideas, his plain, sturdy democracy of thought and manner. But in making his appointments he acted independently of cliques and parties, laid aside his own preferences, and sedulously sought out the best man, whoever he was. His opponents soon perceived that he was just as likely to appoint their sons to offices in the regiments as others, — and the sons, going to the war, were sure to bring their parents into a cordial support of the government. " Two years after the war began," says Colonel Browne, " he was not aware in regard to half the colonels of the Massachusetts troops, what had been their political connections, and was quite surprised when he was told one day that, out of the first fifteen colonels of three years' volunteers whom he had commissioned, only one third at the utmost had voted for Mr. Lincoln for President, while more than one third had voted for Mr. Breckinridge."

Wherever he went, the walls between him and those he met melted away. His simplicity, heartiness, steadfast, open purposes, clear, frank statements, kindly spirit, made men easy in his society. They forgot their reserves and their prejudices. Whenever he went to Washington, during the war, he came at once into intimate relations with Lincoln, Stanton, Sumner, Chase, the diplomats, the generals, the politicians of all orders, and the business men who thronged the Capital. Mr. Stanton, so hard and repellant to others, never was able to resist Governor Andrew. " Our representatives in Congress ask me to persuade Stanton to this and that ; I don't understand it. Why are they so afraid of him ? He needs them more than they need him. He always does what I want, and yet he does not need me." But the moral atmosphere of Washington was not agreeable to him.

I once went to Washington with him, at his request, in company with one or two other of his intimate friends. It was at the end of 1861. We went together to Brigade reviews of the troops then in and around Washington, and to a Division review in Virginia, where we saw a skirmish from the top of a hill. We rode home by night through the Virginia woods, the Wisconsin and Pennsylvania regiments marching by our side, and singing

> " John Brown's body is mouldering in the grave,
>   His soul is marching on,"

while the moonlight glittered on their bayonets, and soft rivulets of fire ran down the dried up beds of the streams on the opposite hill-side. These incidents excited all the romance of his nature.

I recall another scene at Washington : Governor Andrew asked me to go with him to see President Lincoln. It was late at night, after ten o'clock; but when we reached the White House the porter said that the President had gone out with Governor Seward. Recognizing Governor Andrew, he added, "Walk in! walk in, Governor!" We went in, and looked into the rooms on the lower floor. All were lighted, but all were vacant. Then Andrew went up stairs, and I followed. He came to a door before which stood two little pairs of shoes. "This is the childrens' room," said he; "I should like to go in and see them asleep." He put his hand on the handle of the door, as if to open it; and then, changing his mind, turned away. But the impulse was such a natural one! In the palace of the nation, in the midst of the great rebellion, the image of these little children, quietly asleep, took his heart for the moment from all the great affairs of the country and the time.

I also recall with much pleasure a visit with the Governor to the home of Francis P. Blair, at Silver Springs, Md., where we passed the evening in very agreeable conversation with Mr. and Mrs. Blair. I recollected the time when all we knew of Mr. Blair was that he belonged to what was contemptuously called the kitchen-cabinet of General Jackson, and was regarded as the most bitter and unscrupulous of partisans. It seemed strange, therefore, to find in him a kindly old gentleman, mild and calm and wise, and in full sympathy with

4

Governor Andrew and the North.   Andrew was
emphatically what Washington Allston once called
himself, "a wide liker."   Of Mr. Blair and his
wife I remember his saying: "When they sit beside their wood fire. and talk anything over, and
agree about it, they are pretty sure to be right,
and there is no use saying anything more on the
subject."

Beside Colonel Browne's volume, to which I
have already referred, the book which gives the
best account of the work done by the Governor
during the war, is "Massachusetts in the Civil
War," by William Schouler, Adjutant-general of
the Commonwealth.   The energy, activity, foresight, courage, which marked Andrew's conduct
during these years will fill any reader of that
book with admiration.   General Schouler, who
was in close relations with him all the time, thus
closes his volume : —

"How well he served his country, and upheld the
dignity and honor of Massachusetts. these pages may in
some degree illustrate.   But we know how much greater
he was than our inanimate words can disclose.

"At a period when the State required its wisest and
best men at the head of the government. John A. Andrew was selected.   We believe this choice to have been
a special Providence of God.   He had walked amid
his fellow men with quiet and heartfelt respect. with a
conscience untarnished, a heart uncorrupted by love of
gain, or vulgar contact with personal strife or mean

ambition. He has passed away; and, with him, the
greatest. the wisest, the noblest of Massachusetts Governors."

Massachusetts, a State containing only 1,200,-
000 inhabitants, furnished for the defense of the
Union, under his lead, 160.000; or more than one
in eight of all, old and young, men and women,
sick and well.

Who can forget that last day in office, when he
made his valedictory address to the Legislature!
He invited to his room a large number of his
friends. It was a remarkable scene. There were
gathered in the council chamber men and women
of all ages, from Levi Lincoln, then eighty-four
years old, to little girls; side by side were old
abolitionists and old conservatives, orthodox men
and radical men, men and women of all ranks and
all ages. It seemed to me to be such a scene as
will take place at the resurrection of the just.
And it was on this occasion that after going.in
and making his address, he stated his views on
reconstruction. They seemed strange to many
persons at that time, but the strangest part of all
was, that he who had been so energetic in the
prosecution of the war should be the first man to
come forward and recommend the most generous
treatment of the South. It was on this occasion
that he declared that there could be no real reconstruction nor lasting peace, until the South was

guided by its natural leaders, the intelligent white Southerners. He had devoted the whole energy of his soul to causing justice to be done to the blacks, now he was willing' to labor that equal justice should be done to the Southern whites. He did not desire to see the Southern States controlled either by selfish carpet-baggers, or by ignorant freedmen.[1]

After he had retired from the gubernatorial chair, Andrew Johnson, who was then acting President of the United States, sent for him, and said: " I want to give you some office; I would like to

---

[1] These words, from this valedictory, have, as General H. B. Sargent said, "a glorious ring:" "Having contributed to the army and the navy, including regulars, volunteers, seamen, and marines, men of all arms and officers of all grades and of the various terms of service, an aggregate of one hundred and fifty-nine thousand one hundred and sixty-four men; and having expended for the war out of her own treasury twenty-seven million seven hundred and five thousand one hundred and nine dollars, beside the expenditure of her cities and towns; she has maintained, by the unfailing energy and economy of her sons and daughters, her industry and thrift, even in the waste of war. She has paid promptly, and *in gold,* all interest on her bonds, including the old and the new, guarding her faith and honor with every public creditor while still fighting the public enemy; and now, at last, in retiring from her service, I confess the satisfaction of having first seen all of her regiments and batteries (save two battalions) returned and mustered out of the army; and of leaving her treasury provided for by the fortunate and profitable negotiation of all the permanent loan needed or foreseen, with her financial credit maintained at home and abroad, her public securities unsurpassed, if even equaled in value in the money market of the world, by those of any State or of the nation."

appoint you Collector of the Port of Boston."
"No," replied Governor Andrew, "I do not wish
to hold any office in connection with the Government. I shall go back to my profession; but, Mr.
Johnson, I should like to take this opportunity to
say something to you. The man who ought to
receive that position is Hannibal Hamlin, and I
shall be most happy as a citizen of Massachusetts
to ask you to offer him this office; for I think that
when the Massachusetts delegation at Chicago, at
the second Presidential election of Mr. Lincoln,
substituted your name as Vice-president, in the
place of that of Hannibal Hamlin, they did what
they ought not to have done. Not that I mean to
say, Mr. President, that Mr. Hamlin would make
a better Vice-president than you, but because I
think Massachusetts should have stood by Mr.
Hamlin."

He was equally broad in his religious views,
and equally free from all religious or sectarian
prejudices. He was the first Governor of Massachusetts who ever went to the Catholic College
at Worcester, with his aids, to attend commencement exercises there. He said: "I wish these
young men to understand that we look upon them
as our fellow-citizens, and that they will have to
consider themselves citizens of Massachusetts."

Though of Puritan origin, being descended on
his mother's side from Francis Higginson, pastor
of the first church in the colony, and though a

Unitarian in belief, he urged the appointment of the National Fast to be put on Good Friday, so as to unite all other denominations with the Episcopalians and Roman Catholics in keeping the same day. Two of his most intimate friends were Father Fenotti, a Roman Catholic priest, and Father Taylor, the Methodist. Father Taylor declined speaking at the funeral, saying, " I cannot trust myself, I can only cry."

Worn out, no doubt, by the incessant labors and anxieties of the war, his iron constitution gave way, and he died suddenly, by a stroke of apoplexy, October 30, 1867. I received a telegram announcing his death, while attending a convention in Vermont. When the news was known in this body, one gentleman rose and said, " Tell the people of Massachusetts there is not an intelligent man, woman, or child in Vermont who will not mourn for this death as for a personal bereavement." On my arrival in Boston, I found the whole city moved as by a public calamity. And surely it was such. This man, less than fifty years old, seemed fitted for a long and great career. He was wanted for all important occasions which might arise ; the one man fitted for any and every crisis and public need. The most valuable man in the community, as we count value, was taken from us — the man who could help us through any coming crisis. And then the loss to his friends, who were so many in all ranks of society, was irreparable. No wonder that a great sadness fell over the community.

The funeral took place November 2d, on the Feast of All Souls — a fitting time, as it seemed to many, to lay in the bosom of earth the remains of one to whom all souls were dear, and who called no man common or unclean. The shops were generally closed, and vast numbers stood along the route of the procession with serious faces. But perhaps the most touching sight of all were the poor colored women who ran by the side of the coffin the whole five miles from Boston to Mount Auburn, to take one last look at the face of their friend.

From the address delivered at his funeral, I select the following passages, which I think no one, who knew the man, will consider exaggerated : —

" Why has this great company assembled here to-day? Why have these magistrates, judges, senators, men of business, men of literature, left their legislation, their work, their study, and come around this coffin? Why does the energy of Boston give this hour to thought and tears? Why, to-day, out of Boston, out of Massachusetts, out of New England, on the prairies of Illinois and the Sea Islands of Georgia, does grief rest on the souls of men and women, thinking of him who lies here before us? A soldier of the West in Louisiana said to a friend of mine, ' I know the whole name of only one Governor — that is John A. Andrew.' It is not merely because

he held the high office of Chief Magistrate.   Others less
widely known have done this.   It was not merely because of his great abilities.   Others, perhaps, with more
shining qualities than his, have passed away with no
such sense of loss as this.   It is not even because of the
work he did for the Union in its hour of danger, or his
services, eminent as they were, during the bitter war.
These are not yet fully understood, not wholly known,
even by ourselves.   We come here to-day, not because
of his office, for he was a private citizen; not because
of his genius, for it was plain, practical, simple; not because of any long and large experience, for ten years
ago he was so little known that his name was not in the
American Cyclopædia, and he had not yet held his first
office, that of member of the lower House of the Massachusetts Legislature.   But to-day, JOHN ALBION AN-
DREW is mourned as no other man in the Union would
be lamented, because of his *character;* because everybody fully trusted him; because he was the oné man in
the Union whom every one knew to be perfectly relia-
ble, unselfish, transparent as a piece of crystal; to be
trusted in any great danger or emergency with absolute
confidence; the one man whom it seems as if we *could not*
spare, because the *one man* to whom this whole distracted,
divided, betrayed nation could look in any coming hour
of danger as a leader in whom all might unite, North
and South, East and West, Radicals and Conservatives.
We mourn to-day because, he being gone, the *Union*
is not so much the Union as it was — that mediatorial
character having been taken away.

   " What a lesson is this of the *power of character!*   It
has carried him up, during ten short years, from ob-

scurity to eminence. Because God gave him originally
the precious gift of such a sweet evenness of temper,
such equality of soul, such joy in simple things, such
modesty and manliness combined; because he began life
with such a sincere purpose of right-doing; because his
aim was not to exalt himself, to win fortune, to get fame,
to hold power; but to do work for God and man; because, all these years when few knew much about him,
he was faithful to daily duty; faithful to unpopular
truth; loyal to freedom, justice, humanity, when the
crowd went the other way; because he pursued without
haste or rest the way upward into truth and right;
therefore did Providence at last thus exalt him to a
great opportunity, such as no man in Massachusetts ever
had before, and give him the strength to fulfill a work to
be memorable through all time.

"His eye was single, and therefore his whole body
was full of light. No mote of egotism, vanity, or selfishness blinded his eye; no prejudice, envy, or hatred
clouded that clear vision. He had no enemies; he
could not have any. People might dislike him, be
angry with him for neglecting this or doing that which
interfered with their pet projects or special interest;
but abuse him as they might, misrepresent him as they
did, slander him for this or that, they never could make
him angry with them. That sweet milk of human kindness no mortal could ever sour. He could not be partial
or prejudiced or unjust: in such stable equilibrium was
his mind maintained by the steadfast gravitation of his
heart to justice and honesty.

"In him was illustrated also the original and deeper
sense of the word integrity. His integrity was the com-

plete balance of soul, making him go wholly into all that
he did, without reserves, limitations, or qualifications —
'the inner substance and the outer face' — all kept in
exact harmony. In that limpid soul all was visible, as
in some of the bays of Lake Huron you can see clear to
the bottom, sixty feet down, and count every agate or
carnelian on the sand.

"But it would be a great wrong to truth and Christianity to omit here, in the presence of death and eternity,
and in these consecrated walls, the fact that John A.
Andrew's character was rooted deep in religion. As
his pastor and friend for more than twenty-five years,
having met him all this time in our weekly conference
meetings when his face would irradiate peace, while he
opened to us the Scriptures, expounded Paul, or revealed to the little group of friends the deeper experi-
ences of his life, I ought to say that I never knew a
more pure, simple, straight-forward piety than his; faith
without narrowness, piety so manly and cheerful. His
heart took in all sects and names. He was at home with
orthodox and heterodox, with Protestant and Catholic.
To-day there sit by his coffin the representatives of some
of this largeness of heart; Father Taylor, who has been
his intimate friend for so long a time; Mr. Grimes,
whose church he so often visited, and who could tell to-
day, had we time to hear, of a thousand acts of good
will to the race whom he has served so well. We had
hoped to have here Father Fenotti, a dear friend of his,
but he has been detained; yet let me read a few lines
of his note: —

"'Trying as it is to me, and exceedingly painful to
refuse the request, I cannot meet you and the other rev-

erend gentlemen to-morrow morning, to perform an act
of love and religion toward the sacred remains of a
friend whom I have loved and esteemed with an in-
tensity of affection not surpassed by that with which I
love my brother. Governor Andrew was dear to me.
His coming to my house always electrified me. During
the long spells of sickness to which I am subjected, his
visits, which were very frequent, did me a heart day's
good. I cannot express what I feel about it.' "

As daylight faded from the skies, we laid him
in his Mount Auburn resting-place. Before the
coffin was closed we looked on his face again.
Was it a fancy, or did I really see a new expression on that well-known countenance — as of one
going calmly but modestly forward to meet a
strange and wonderful scene. Awe and manly
self-respect were blended in that look. Was he
then going up to meet the great kindred souls,
who, like him, had fought a good fight, finished
their course, and kept the faith? And, amid that
noble band, did he also recognize a yet more majestic and more loving friend, saying, " Come,
blessed of my Father! For inasmuch as ye did
it to the least of these my brethren, ye did it unto
me!" I might have been deceived in the outward phenomenon, but I was not mistaken in regard to the inward reality.

The next day was Sunday, and after our memorial services for our brother were concluded,
there was handed to me this message, written on
a scrap of paper : —

"I wish you could know what Massachusetts men, who were in the West during the war, thought of Governor Andrew. I never saw him. Born in Massachusetts, I was in Ohio from 1858 to 1865. I took his proclamations into my pulpit, and read them to the people, weeping the while with grateful pride, that my native State had such a Governor and leader. Massachusetts' sons, away from home, blessed him, and felt that the old Bay State would be kept at the front, under God, by John A. Andrew.   V."

Two years later the remains of Governor Andrew were removed to the cemetery in Hingham, the town in which he had spent his summers for many years, and the early home of his wife. On this occasion his friends and neighbors testified their loving memory of his worth by a general attendance at the services. I will select a few passages from the address on that occasion. Over the pulpit of the church was his portrait, and these immortal words from his address at a Methodist Camp Meeting at Martha's Vineyard, August 16, 1862: "I know not what record of sin may await me in another world, but this I do know: I was never mean enough to despise a man because he was poor, because he was ignorant, or because he was black."

"Two years to-day, on the 30th of October, 1867, the State of Massachusetts, the nation, and an innumerable company of friends, lost the helpful presence and inspired mind of John Albion Andrew.

"And now, after these two years, during which his thought has been so present with us all, you have brought back his earthly remains to lay them in the midst of your homes. And in this you have done well. It seems more suitable that those who have lived together should sleep side by side; pleasant to each other in life and in death not divided.

" Who does not feel the tender charm which lingers around these silent villages where 'the rude forefathers of the hamlet sleep.' It is well that our friend should rest here, for here he loved to come and make his home when he could escape from the care and pressure of business. Here he sat in your church, taught in your Sunday-school, visited you in your homes, and made himself as fully a Hingham man as if he and his ancestors had always lived in this place. And among all the words he said in public, I know nothing which carries with it so much of the charm of the thought and heart of John A. Andrew, as his speech here, when you came to congratulate him on his nomination for Governor. He said — and let me repeat a few of his familiar words : —

" 'This is one of those occasions which come in the course of all our lives, when no poor form of human speech is adequate either to the solemnity or to the gladness of the hour. I confess to you, my old friends and neighbors, associates and kinspeople of Hingham, that I could more fitly speak by tears than by words to-night. From the centre of my being, from the bottom of my heart, for this unsought, enthusiastic, cordial welcome, this tender of your generous sympathy, dear friends, I thank you. . . . . How dear to my heart are

these fields, these hills, these spreading trees, this ver-
dant grass, this sounding shore of yours, where now for
fourteen years, through summer's heat, and sometimes
in winter's storm, I have trod your streets, and rambled
through your woods, and sauntered by your beach, and
sat by your firesides, and felt the warm pressure of your
hands, sometimes teaching your children in the Sunday-
school, sometimes speaking to you, my fellow-citizens,
— speaking to willing ears. . . . . Here I have found
most truly a home, free from the cares and the distrac-
tions, from the turmoil, doubts, and responsibilities of a
laborious and anxious profession. Away from the busier
haunts of men it has been given me to find here a calm,
sweet retreat, where, in the society of private friendship,
I have been able to refresh the wearied spirit and
strengthen the worn hands of toil. Here, dear friends,
I have found the home of my heart. It was into one
of your families that I entered and joined myself in holy
bands of domestic love to one of the daughters of your
town. Here, too, first have I known a parent's joys and
a parent's sorrows. So whether you say aye or no here
to the selection which may cause me to occupy at a
future day the chief seat in the Commonwealth, I now
declare with all the earnestness and honesty of a manly
conviction, that John A. Andrew is forever your friend.'

"And now you receive back, people of Hingham, all
that remains of your friend, and will guard in your midst,
forever, these relics of a just and true man. They will
add a new sacredness to the sacred spot where they lie;
they will invest this ancient town with another interest. When strangers come to visit the place, they will
ask for the grave of Governor Andrew; for

"'Such graves as his are pilgrim shrines,
　Shrines to no code or creed confined,
　The Delphian vales, the Palestines,
　The Meccas of the mind.'

"When you and your children visit the cemetery, your feet will linger near that place, and you will tell them of his great virtues, and they will grow up to be better men and women for the reminder of these ashes. This silent dust will speak, to tell them that, better than wealth, power, or fame, is the life of an honest man. If our nation should be corrupted by prosperity, if its high places should be occupied by ignoble men, if truth should seem about to desert the earth, — go to that spot, men of Hingham, and be assured, by the memory of the good and great Governor of Massachusetts, that virtue is no name and that there is no *such* success as that of purity of heart. As long as WASHINGTON lies in Mount Vernon, LINCOLN in Springfield, and ANDREW in Hingham, the South, the West, and the North, will each have one spot consecrated to patriotism, truth, and honor, — a spot which will help to keep the land to its high traditions, its solemn duties, and its grand future."

In October, 1875, a marble statue of Governor Andrew was placed in the Hingham church-yard, on which occasion a very interesting address was delivered by General Horace Binney Sargent, from which we quote the following sentences. General Sargent was appointed by the Governor his senior aid, and so continued until commissioned Lieutenant-colonel of the First Massachusetts Cavalry.

" How fitting that this martyr to the eternal vigilance
of Liberty should rest in the old town where the first
signer of the Declaration of American Independence —
John Hancock — opened his baby eyes !   When, also, I
remember that during the war of the rebellion, with its
nights of vigil and its days burdened with all the civil
duties of an executive ; seven inaugural and valedictory
addresses, exhaustive of many subjects, before the State
Legislature of five successive years ; thirteen veto messages, many of them with elaborate law arguments ;
ninety special messages ; the patient and critical, verbal
as well as legal, examination and approval of one thousand eight hundred and fifteen acts and resolves ; innumerable speeches and addresses on many subjects and
in many places ; all these civil duties added to the overwhelming cares of a War Minister, as well as ruler —
in war time — when all the offices of the State House
were overflowing with infinite inquiry, complaint, and
diplomacy that were involved in the rapid and constant
recruitment of one hundred and sixty thousand men, the
State House being like a camp with going and returning troops; when I reflect on this, and remember that,
during all these Titanic years of toil which were bearing
Governor Andrew surely to his early grave, he still continued to perform his duty as Secretary of Father Taylor's little Bethel for Seamen — I feel gratified, as by a
divine harmony, that John Albion Andrew, whom I
reverently deem the most Christ-like of all war's ministers, should sleep in the same country grave-yard
where sleeps that old communion-bearing deacon of
your church — that honest, stout, old deacon — who, at
the capitulation of Yorktown, by the order of his friend

as well as commander, Washington, received the sword of Cornwallis! Major-general Benjamin Lincoln, of the army of the Revolution, and John Albion Andrew, twin patriots of the elder and the later time! God grant them rest!

"To me, this Covenanter spirit, this union of conscience and claymore, of sword and gospel, is sublime. So, in the will and inventory of Miles Standish, the great Puritan captain, are recorded 'three muskets with bandaleros' and 'three old Bybles.' Armed thus with faith and courage, men are girded with the sword of the spirit, and become the Xaviers or the Luthers of mankind."

As the years go by, the memory of this great and good man will be more and more appreciated. In all coming time the sons of Massachusetts will gratefully remember and honor the man " who ordered the overcoats and received the flags."

5

II.

JAMES FREEMAN.

JAMES FREEMAN.

ONE of the few remaining antiquities in the city of Boston is the church of old gray stone, known as King's Chapel. Outwardly, its aspect is one of solid strength rather than architectural pretension. Its interior, however, is very striking, and to my mind, superior in its simple elegance to that of any other church in the city. It is said to be modeled on the plan of Sir Christopher Wren's *chef d'œuvre*, St. Stephen's, Walbrook, London. It is one of the few churches which contains marble monuments of the old families of Boston. In my childhood there still remained the state-pew of the colonial governors, higher and larger than the other pews, and with a canopy above it. This building, the oldest Episcopal church in New England, became the first Unitarian church in the United States, in consequence of a change of opinion taking place in the mind of a young man who was chosen as reader and rector by this society, at the close of the American Revolution. This young man was James Freeman.

Dr. Freeman is known to the religious public as the first avowed preacher of Unitarianism in the United States : he is remembered by the people of Boston as one. who. for fifty years. was identified with all the best interests of that community. Though never ambitious of literary distinction. his writings occupy an important place in the literature of the country. both for justness of thought and purity of expression. But the friends of Dr. Freeman forget all these things in remembering his personal qualities. They recall him as the playfellow of children. the friend and counsellor of youth. the charming companion in social intercourse. whose happy sentences were always freighted at once with wit and wisdom. and in whose character were beautifully blended the most austere uprightness and the most generous sympathy. As. however. I cannot speak of these things without appearing to strangers to exaggerate. and to his friends to understate. his peculiar excellence. I shall rather dwell on the events of his life ; adding. at the close. some traits illustrative of his private character.

The first ancestor of Dr. Freeman who came to this country was Samuel Freeman. proprietor of the eighth part of Watertown. Mass.. a place settled in 1630. His son Samuel went to Eastham. on Cape Cod. with his father-in-law. Thomas Prince. Governor of Plymouth. He inherited his father-in-law's estate in Eastham. and the family remained on Cape Cod till Constant Freeman, the father of the subject of this notice, removed to Charlestown, Mass., about 1755. James Freeman was born in Charlestown, April 22, 1759. His father moved to Boston soon after, and he was sent to the public Latin School in that city, then under the care of Master Lovell, a somewhat famous teacher in his day. He entered the school in 1766, being seven years old, at that time the age fixed for admission. Among his classmates were the late Judge Dawes, of the Supreme Court of Massachusetts, Rev. Jonathan Homer, D. D., of Newton, Admiral Sir Isaac Coffin, of the British Navy, and Sir Bernard Morland, afterward a member of the British Parliament. When his friend, Dr. Homer, used to speak of the great men who belonged to their class in the Latin School, Dr. Freeman would sometimes add: "But, Brother Homer, you forget our classmate who was hanged." The name of this unfortunate member of the class cannot now be supplied.

James Freeman entered Harvard College in 1773, and was graduated in 1777, at the age of eighteen. Among his classmates, were Dr. Bentley and Rufus King. The American Revolution dispersed the College, and interrupted for a time his studies. But he must have laid the foundation of good scholarship there. In after years, he was an excellent Latin scholar, a good mathematician, and read with ease the French, Italian,

Spanish, and Portuguese languages. In the latter languages, I recollect his reading for amusement, at the close of his life, the works of Father Feyjoo and Father Vieira. With the writings of Cicero, Tacitus, Lucretius, and other Latin authors, he was thoroughly acquainted. Though he always spoke lightly of his own learning, he was far more of a scholar than many men of greater pretensions.

After leaving College, Mr. Freeman went to Cape Cod to visit his relatives there; and, as he strongly sympathized with the revolutionary movement, he engaged in disciplining a company of men who were about to join the Colonial troops. In 1780, he sailed to Quebec, in a small vessel bearing a cartel, taking with him his sister, in order to place her with her father, then in that city. On his passage, he was captured by a privateer, and was detained at Quebec after his arrival, first in a prison-ship, and afterward as a prisoner on parole. He did not leave Quebec till June, 1782, when he sailed again for Boston, arriving there about the 1st of August. Being a candidate for the ministry, he preached in several places, and was invited, in September, to officiate as Reader at the King's Chapel, in Boston, for a term of six months.

The King's Chapel was founded in 1686, and a wooden edifice for public worship was built in 1690. The present building, which is of stone, and which is still one of the finest specimens of church architecture in New England, was erected one hundred and twenty-eight years ago, — the corner-stone having been laid in 1749. Dr. Caner, the Rector of the church, had espoused the British cause, and he accompanied the British troops, when they evacuated Boston, in 1776. The few proprietors of King's Chapel, who remained in Boston, lent their building to the Old South Congregational Church, whose house of worship had been used by the British army as a riding-school. The two societies occupied the building alternately, each with its own forms and its own minister, — one in the morning and the other in the afternoon. Under these circumstances Mr. Freeman commenced his services as a Reader.

I have in my possession a file of letters which Mr. Freeman wrote to his father in Quebec, from which I will make some extracts, showing his opinions and feelings at this time. These letters have probably not been opened for sixty years.

December 24, 1782. . . . . . " I suppose, long before this reaches you, you will be made acquainted with my situation at the Chapel. The church increases every day. I trust you believe that, by entering into this line, I have imbibed no High Church notions. I have fortunately no temptations to be bigoted, for the proprietors of the Chapel are very liberal in their notions. They allow me to make several alterations in the service, which liberty I frequently use. We can scarcely be called of the Church of England, for we disclaim the authority of that country in ecclesiastical as well as in civil matters. . . . . I forgot to mention in my former letter the sum I receive for preaching. For the first six months, I am to be paid fifty pounds sterling. This is not much, but, when I engaged, the church was small, consisting only of about forty families. It has already increased to nearly eighty. So that I imagine that at the end of the six months, when I shall enter into new terms, the salary will be increased to two hundred and fifty or three hundred pounds lawful money per annum. I wish for no more. Indeed, if at any period of life I knew what contentment was, it is at present."

In the course of the year or two following his settlement, Mr. Freeman's opinions on the subject of the Trinity were so far modified by his studies and reflections that he found it necessary to propose to his church to alter the Liturgy in the places where that doctrine appears. An English Unitarian minister, Mr. Hazlitt, was at that time residing in Boston, and his intercourse with Mr. Freeman may have contributed to this change of sentiment. But only as an occasion — for this change of view lay in the direction of the tendencies of Mr. Freeman's mind and of the tendency of thought in that community, as appears from the ease with which Unitarianism spread in Boston. Mr. Hazlitt was the father of William Hazlitt, the essayist. The latter was born in Boston, and Dr. Freeman used to speak of him as a curly-headed, bright-eyed boy.

Dr. Greenwood, in his sermon preached after
the funeral of Dr. Freeman, thus speaks of the
way in which this change of the Liturgy was ef-
fected. He says that Mr. Freeman first thought
of leaving his Society. " He communicated his
difficulties to those of his friends with whom he
was most intimate. He would come into their
houses and say: ' Much as I love you, I must
leave you. I cannot conscientiously any longer
perform the service of the church, as it now
stands.' But at length it was said to him, ' Why
not state your difficulties, and the grounds of
them, publicly to your whole people, that they
may be able to judge of the case, and determine
whether it is such as to require a separation between you and them or not?' The suggestion
was adopted. He preached a series of sermons,
in which he plainly stated his dissatisfaction with
the Trinitarian portions of the Liturgy, went fully
into an examination of the doctrine of the Trinity,
and gave his reasons for rejecting it. He has
himself assured me that when he delivered these
sermons, he was under a strong impression that
they were the last he should ever pronounce from
this pulpit. . . . . But he was heard patiently, at-
tentively, kindly. The greater part of his hearers
responded to his sentiments, and resolved to alter
their Liturgy and retain their Pastor."

Alterations were accordingly made in general
conformity with those of the amended Liturgy of

Dr. Samuel Clarke, and, on the 19th of June, 1785, the proprietors voted, by a majority of three fourths, to adopt those alterations.[1] In a letter to his father, dated the first of June, he says, after describing the changes which had been made in the Liturgy, " In two or three weeks, the Church will finally pass the vote whether they will adopt the alterations or not. I flatter myself the decision will be favorable; for out of about ninety families of which the congregation consists, fifteen only are opposed to the reformation. Should the vote pass in the negative, I shall be under the necessity of resigning my living." He adds, however, that in this case, he has no fear but that he shall find employment elsewhere. " Thus," says Mr. Greenwood, " the first Episcopal Church in New England became the first Unitarian Church in the New World. The young Reader at King's Chapel was surely placed in peculiar circumstances. It is his praise that he made a right and manly use of them; that he did not smother his convictions and hush down his conscience, and endeavor to explain away to himself,

---

[1] Before this vote was taken, the proprietors had taken measures to ascertain who properly belonged to the church as pewholders, and what pews had been forfeited by the absence of their former owners, according to the letter of their deeds. And, that no ground of complaint should exist, the proprietors engaged to pay for every vacated pew, *though legally forfeited*, the sum of sixteen pounds to its former owner. — *Greenwood's History of King's Chapel.*

for the sake of a little false and outward peace, the obvious sense of the prayers which he uttered before God and his people, but took that other and far better course of explicitness and honesty. By this proper use of circumstances he placed himself where he now stands in our religious history." [1]

The next thing to be considered was the mode of ordination to be received by Mr. Freeman, who was as yet only a Reader. In a letter to his father, dated October 31, 1786, he describes an application made to Bishop Seabury of Connecticut, and Bishop Provost of New York, for ordination, from which the following extracts are taken, which illustrate both the opinions of the time, and the character of Mr. Freeman : —

" My visit to Bishop Seabury terminated as I expected. Before I waited upon him, he gave out that he never would ordain me; but it was necessary to ask the question. He being in Boston last March, a committee of our Church waited upon him, and requested him to ordain me, without insisting upon any other conditions than a declaration of faith in the Holy Scriptures. He replied that, as the case was unusual, it was necessary that he should consult his presbyters — the Episcopal clergy in Connecticut. Accordingly, about the beginning of June, I rode to Stratford, where a convention was holding, carrying with me several letters of recommendation. I waited upon the Bishop's presbyters and delivered my letters.

[1] Greenwood's Sermon after the funeral of Dr. Freeman, p. 11.

They professed themselves satisfied with the testimonials which they contained of my moral character, etc., but added that they could not recommend me to the Bishop for ordination upon the terms proposed by my church. For a man to subscribe the Scriptures, they said, was nothing, for it could never be determined from that what his creed was. Heretics professed to believe them not less than the orthodox, and made use of them in support of their peculiar opinions. If I could subscribe such a declaration as that I could conscientiously read the whole of the Book of Common Prayer, they would cheerfully recommend me. I answered that I could not conscientiously subscribe a declaration of that kind. ' Why not ? ' ' Because there are some parts of the Book of Common Prayer which I do not approve.' ' What parts ? ' ' The prayers to the Son and Holy Spirit.' ' You do not then believe the doctrine of the Trinity.' ' No.' ' This appears to us very strange. We can think of no texts which countenance your opinion. We should be glad to hear you mention some.' ' It would ill become me, gentlemen, to dispute with persons of your learning and abilities. But if you will give me leave, I will repeat two passages which appear to me decisive : *There is one God, and one Mediator between God and man, the man Christ Jesus. There is but one God, the Father, and one Lord Jesus Christ.* In both these passages Jesus Christ is plainly distinguished from God, and in the last, that God is expressly declared to be the Father.' To this they made no other reply than an ' Ah ! ' which echoed round the room. ' But are not all the attributes of the Father,' said one, ' attributed to the Son in the Scriptures ? Is not Omnipotence for instance ? ' ' It is true,' I answered,

'that our Saviour says of himself, *All power is given
unto me, in heaven and earth.* You will please to observe here that the power is said to be *given.* It is a
derived power. It is not self-existent and unoriginated,
like that of the Father.' 'But is not the Son omni-
scient? Does he not know the hearts of men?' 'Yes,
He knows them by virtue of that intelligence which He
derives from the Father. But, by a like communication, did Peter know the hearts of Ananias and Sapphira.'
After some more conversation of the same kind, they
told me that it could not possibly be that the Christian
world should have been idolaters for seventeen hundred
years, as they must be according to my opinions. In
answer to this, I said that whether they had been idolaters or not I would not determine, but that it was full
as probable that they should be idolaters for seventeen
hundred years as that they should be Roman Catholics
for twelve hundred. They then proceeded to find fault
with some part of the new Liturgy. 'We observe that
you have converted the absolution into a prayer. Do
you mean by that to deny the power of the Priesthood
to absolve the people, and that God has committed to
it the power of remitting sins?' 'I meant neither to
deny nor to affirm it. The absolution appeared exceptionable to some persons, for which reason it was
changed into a prayer, which could be exceptionable to
nobody.' 'But you must be sensible, Mr. Freeman,
that Christ instituted an order of Priesthood, and that
to them He committed the power of absolving sins.
*Whosoever sins ye remit they are remitted unto him, and
whosoever sins ye retain they are retained.*' To this I
made no other reply than a return of their own emphatic

Ah! Upon the whole, finding me an incorrigible heretic, they dismissed me without granting my request. They treated me, however, with great candor and politeness, begging me to go home, to read, to alter my opinions, and then to return and receive that ordination, which they wished to procure for me from their Bishop. I left them and proceeded to New York. When there I waited on Mr. Provost, Rector of the Episcopal Church, who is elected to go to England to be consecrated a Bishop. I found him a liberal man, and that he approved of the alterations which had been made at the Chapel. Of him I hope to obtain ordination, which I am convinced he will cheerfully confer, unless prevented by the bigotry of some of his clergy. The Episcopal ministers in New York, and in the Southern States, are not such High Churchmen as those in Connecticut. The latter approach very near to Roman Catholics, or at least equal Bishop Laud and his followers. Should Provost refuse to ordain me, I shall then endeavor to effect a plan which I have long had in my head, which is, to be ordained by the Congregational ministers of the town, or to preach and administer the ordinances without any ordination whatever. The last scheme I most approve; for I am fully convinced that he who has devoted his time to the study of divinity, and can find a congregation who are willing to hear him, is, to all intents, a minister of the Gospel; and that, though imposition of hands, either of Bishops or Presbyters, be necessary to constitute him priest in the eye of the law, in some countries, yet that, in the eye of Heaven, he has not less of the indelible character than a Bishop or a Patriarch. Our early ancestors, who, however wrong they might be in some particulars, were in general sensible and judicious men, were of this opinion. One of the articles of the Cambridge Platform is that the call of the congregation alone constitutes a man a minister, and that imposition of hands by Bishops or Elders is a mere form, which is, by no means, essential. The same sentiments are adopted by the most rational clergy in the present day, who give up the necessity of ordination as indefensible, and ridicule the doctrine of the uninterrupted succession as a mere chimera. I am happy to find many of my hearers join with me in opinion upon this subject."

As might, perhaps, have been foreseen, it was found impossible to procure Episcopal ordination, and Mr. Freeman and his church finally determined on a method differing from both of those suggested in his letter. He was neither ordained by the Congregational ministers of Boston, nor yet did he omit all ceremony of induction, but (as Mr. Greenwood says) he fell back on first principles, and was ordained by the church itself, by a solemn service at the time of evening prayer, November 18, 1787. The Wardens entered the desk after the usual evening service, and the Senior Warden made a short address, showing the reasons of the present procedure. The first ordaining prayer was read, then the ordaining vote, to which the members gave assent by rising, by which they chose Mr. Freeman to be their " Rector, Minister, Priest, Pastor, and Ruling Elder." Other ser-

6

vices followed, among which was the presenting a Bible to the Rector, enjoining on him "a due observance of all the precepts contained therein."

From the time that Mr. Freeman was thus set apart to his office, he sustained the various duties of the ministry till 1809, when the Rev. Samuel Cary was, at his request, associated with him as colleague; after whose death, in 1815, he again served alone till 1824, when the Rev. F. W. P. Greenwood was inducted as colleague. In 1811, he received the degree of Doctor of Divinity from Harvard College. In 1826, his health had so far given way that he was obliged to give up to Mr. Greenwood his parochial duties and retire to a country residence near Boston. Here he lived nine years, surrounded by the affection of young and old, and, though suffering from painful disease, always cheerful, and at length expired November 14, 1835, in the seventy-seventh year of his age.

Dr. Freeman was a member of the first School Committee ever chosen by the people of Boston, which was elected in 1792, the schools before that time being under the charge of the Selectmen of the town. He was for many years on this Committee, and was one of those by whose labors the Public School System of Boston has been brought to its present excellent condition. He was one of the founders of the Massachusetts Historical Society, and, during a long period, one of its most active collaborators, contributing many valuable papers to its collections. He was also a member of the American Academy of Arts and Sciences. His publications consist of a Thanksgiving Sermon, 1784; a Description of Boston, published in the Boston Magazine, 1784; Remarks on Morse's American Universal Geography, 1793; a Sermon on the Death of Rev. John Elliot, D. D., 1813; a volume of Sermons published in 1812, which passed through three editions; and another volume in 1829, printed as a gift for his parish, but not published; besides many articles in periodicals. He printed no controversial sermons, and indeed seldom preached them. His style was sententious and idiomatic, and has often been spoken of as a model of pure English. Though there is no trace of ambitious thought or expression in his writings, their tone and spirit are wise and healthy.

Although Dr. Freeman was the first, who, in this country, openly preached Unitarianism, under that name, he always referred to Dr. Mayhew and others as having preached the same doctrine before. This was no doubt true. Some form of Arianism had prevailed in New England for several years before Dr. Freeman's time; but he was the first to avow and defend the doctrine by its distinct name. This fact necessarily brought him into relations with other advocates of these opinions, and he corresponded with Priestley and Belsham, and especially with Theophilus Lindsey,

whose character he much esteemed. He also had
sympathy from Chauncy, Belknap, and others
older than himself, and among his contemporaries
from men like Bentley, Clarke, Eliot, Kirkland.
And as he loved to "keep his friendships in re-
pair," he was surrounded in after years by multitudes of younger friends and disciples. He loved
the young, and always sought to help them. I
have been told of his urging new married people
among his parishioners to join the smaller and
struggling parish of some young minister — "Go
there," he would say, "and grow up with that
church, and make yourselves useful in it." He
sympathized with young men in their diffident
first efforts, and always encouraged and befriended
them. How then could the young help loving
him? He was no zealot for his own opinions,
but a thoroughly liberal man, and was intimate
with men of all denominations. The good Bishop
Cheverus was one of his best friends. He could
not tolerate intolerance, and disliked Unitarian
bigotry quite as much as Orthodox bigotry. I
have heard him say, "Sterne complains of the cant
of criticism. I think the cant of liberality worse
than that. I have a neighbor who comes and en-
tertains me that way, abusing the Orthodox by
the hour, and, all the time, boasting of his own
liberality." He carried his freedom of mind into
matters of taste as well as matters of opinion.
Bred in the school which admired the writers of

Queen Anne's day, he loved Addison, Pope, Swift, Gay, and in Theology, such writers as the Boyle Lecturers and James Foster. But finding that many young persons were interested in Wordsworth and Coleridge, he patiently read these authors to see if he could find any good in them. I remember his reading Coleridge's " Aids to Reflection," and his " Friend," in the last years of his life, and, when he had finished them, he said, " I find some excellent ideas in him, though I do not understand all his mysteries. He is a cloudy fellow. I leave those parts to you younger folks."

The leading traits in Dr. Freeman's character, which immediately impressed all who saw him, were benevolence, justice, and a Franklin-like sagacity. He could endure to see no kind of oppression, and was always ready to take sides with any whom he thought overborne. He was punctilious in keeping all engagements, and his honesty descended into the smallest particulars of life. A lady said she had seen him once under the following circumstances. " I was riding, with another lady, past Dr. Freeman's house, in the town of Newton, and we noticed a dwelling opposite, which seemed closed and unoccupied, the garden of which was full of flowers. We thought of gathering a few, and while we hesitated, we noticed an old gentleman, with long white locks hanging on his shoulders, slowly walking on the other side of the road. I asked him whether he thought that, as there was no one living in the house, we might gather some of the flowers. He looked up at us with an arch smile, and said, ' They are not *my* flowers, pretty ladies.' Somewhat confused, I repeated my question, to which he replied, — ' I have no right to give them to you, they are not *my* flowers, pretty ladies.' We rode away, not knowing till afterward who it was, but having received a lesson in regard to the rights of others which we were not likely soon to forget."

A few examples taken from his familiar conversation, though trifling in themselves, will illustrate his character and turn of mind.

A lady, who had heard of the Atheist, Abner Kneeland, giving public lectures in defense of his views, said, " What a dreadful thing it is, Dr. Freeman!" " I think it will do a great deal of good," replied he, and then mentioned a variety of facts to show that arguments in support of Infidelity had always brought out so many new defenses of Christianity as to leave religion on a higher and more impregnable basis.

He was a great lover of truth, but his regard for the feelings of others kept him from harshness. To a young friend, whom he thought in danger of carrying independence too far, he said, " It is well to be candid, but you need not say everything which is in your mind. If a person, on being introduced to me, should say, ' Dr. Freeman, what a little, old, ugly, spindle-shanked gentleman you are,' he would no doubt say what was in his mind, but it would not be necessary, I think, for him to say it."

Some one said to him of a book: " It is too long." " All books are too long," he replied, — " I know only one book which is not too long, and that is Robinson Crusoe, and I sometimes think that a little too long."

He related this anecdote of the famous Mather Byles. " I was once walking with Dr. John Clarke, and we met Mather Byles. He took my arm and said, ' Now we have the whole Bible here. I am the Old Testament, you, Mr. Clarke, are the New Testament, and as for Mr. Freeman, he is the Apocrypha.' "

As Dr. Freeman was talking one evening in his family, I took notes of his remarks without his being aware of it. From these I copy the following sentences : —

" Do you see human faces in the coals of fire ? The propensity I have to form the human figure is frequently annoying to me. I make men and immediately put them into a fiery furnace."

" I find I am growing very thin. Some people carry handkerchiefs to wipe away tears which they do not shed, so I wear clothes to conceal limbs which I do not possess."

" Is that Coleridge you are reading ? Coleridge himself reads curious books, — the authors who wrote in Latin at the revival of learning. We have better writers now. To be sure, there were Grotius and Budæus, who were excellent writers, and especially Erasmus. Knox wrote well. But he was an arrogant and rash man. He condemned the French Sermon writers, and said how inferior they were to the English. As an instance, he quoted an Englishman, who had in fact copied from the French. That fellow did not find it out. In his Essays, Knox declares all mysteries and all knowledge, gives advice to young merchants and to young tailors. He was a man of bad manners. He attacked the King of Prussia bitterly. The king stood such things, however, with great fortitude. He was satisfied with possessing absolute power."

"You are reading 'John Buncle.' The author, it seems, was a Unitarian. About Emlyn's days, Unitarianism had not made much progress. Did he get any persecution? They used to put Unitarians in jail. Our ancestors would have undoubtedly done so, or more probably would have put them to death. But none appeared. Dr. Mayhew was the first who cared much about it. There was a certain concealment practiced before about the Trinity. Fisher" (of Salem, I suppose) " had a singular way of satisfying his conscience. He was asked how he could read the Athanasian creed when he did not believe it. He replied, 'I read it as if I did not believe it.' Those are poor shifts. Mr. Pyle being directed by his Bishop to read it, did so, saying, 'I am directed to read this, which is said to have been the creed of St. Athanasius, but God forbid that it should be yours or mine.' As the English rubric orders this creed to be 'said or sung,' another man had it set to a hunting-tune and sang it. These methods, I think, would hardly satisfy the conscience of a truth-loving man."

This is a random specimen of his conversation in the last years of his life. If any one had thought of recording his sayings, a very agreeable book of table-talk might have been easily prepared. But this is one of the things we are apt to remember when it is too late.

I cannot better close this notice than by some further extracts from Dr. Greenwood.

" Dr. Freeman was truly humble, but he was above all the arts of deception and double-dealing; and he could not be awed or moved in any way from self-respect and duty. He made all allowances for ignorance and prejudice and frailty, but arrogance he would not submit to, and hypocrisy he could not abide."

" He possessed in a remarkable manner the virtue of contentment. You heard no complaints from him. He was abundantly satisfied with his lot, — he was deeply grateful for his lot. The serenity of his countenance was an index to the serenity of his soul. The angel of contentment seemed to shade and fan it with his wings. 'I have enjoyed a great deal in this life,' he used to say, 'a great deal more than I deserve.' "

" He loved children, and loved to converse with and encourage them, and draw out their faculties and affections. His manners, always affable and kind, were never so completely lovely as in his intercourse with them. Naturally and insensibly did he instill moral principles and religious thoughts into their minds, and his good influence, being thus gentle, was permanent."

"The mind of Dr. Freeman was one of great originality. It arrived at its own conclusions, and in its own way. You could not be long in his society without feeling that you were in the presence of one who observed and reflected for himself."

"Even when his mind grew enfeebled, it showed its strength in weakness. His memory sometimes failed him, and his ideas would become somewhat confused, in the few months preceding his death; but his bearing was always calm and manly; he fell into no second childhood."

"He looked upon death, as it approached him, without fear, yet with pious humility. He viewed the last change as a most solemn change; the judgment of God upon the soul as a most solemn judgment. 'Let no one say, when I am dead,' — so he expressed himself to his nearest friends, — 'that I trusted in my own merits. I trust only in the mercy of God through Jesus Christ.'"

So lived, labored, and died James Freeman. A man who impressed himself on all his friends, on his community, and on his time, as a pure and true influence, for which we might well be grateful. Many might say, in the words of a French philosopher: "D'autres ont eu plus d'influence, sur mon esprit, et mes idées. Lui, m'a montré une ame Chretienne. C'est encore à lui que je dois le plus."

III.

CHARLES SUMNER.

CHARLES SUMNER.

HIS CHARACTER AND CAREER.[1]

———•———

SINCE the tragical decease of Abraham Lincoln, the death of no man has made such an impression on the public heart of America as that of Charles Sumner. The departure of John A. Andrew was felt as deeply, but not as widely; for our great War Governor had not been so long nor so extensively conspicuous. Far and wide the nation feels the loss of the Massachusetts Senator, and feels it as a great public disaster. The din of political discussion is hushed for a few days; the roar of business is suspended in the great cities, while he is carried to his grave. Public bodies pass resolves expressive of their sense of a general bereavement; men take each other by the hand in the street, and in low tones utter a few words of mutual grief. The friends who have fought by his side during long years, when success seemed hopeless, — whose little barks have sailed attend-

[1] An Address read to the Church of the Disciples, March 15, 1874.

ant on his, and partaken the gale ; younger men, who have chosen him for their leader, and amid the thick of battle pressed where they saw his white plume wave, now clasp hands in silent sympathy. The colored people, whose hearts are always right, though their heads are often wrong, some of whom had allowed themselves to become estranged from him by the arts of demagogues, now recognize in him the best friend their race has ever had — a friend who, with his dying breath, still besought that equal rights might be given to them. Massachusetts, disgraced by an unauthorized act of her Legislature, has hastened to express her undiminished confidence in her Senator, righting the wrong where it was given ; and, happily, her voice reached him in the senate chamber before he left it forever. Even those who have opposed him and criticised him in life, come, as the custom is, to hang wreaths on his tomb. Politicians, speech-makers, and preachers, who had little sympathy with him in his struggles and sufferings, join the mourners at his death, and float in the great current of sympathy. Those who believed his course wrong and his judgments unsound, are now disposed to revise their opinions, and admit that he may have been right, after all. Anger is hushed, hatred is rebuked, the voice of censure is still. Those whose evil schemes he baffled, whose selfish plans he exposed — those who were tired of hearing Aristides called just — now feel, for a moment at least, how poor was their position by the side of his.

In the presence of this striking phenomenon of universal grief, I am disposed to modify a criticism I lately made in this place on the character of the American people. I said then that our idolatry is the adoration of *smartness.* Perhaps it is, but it is now apparent that while we admire intellect, we worship integrity. For this general sorrow means *love.* Smart men are admired, Charles Sumner is *loved.* This indicates that, beneath all its superficial judgments, the American people knows and reveres what is truly good. Smart men may be popular, but the public heart goes out in love only to those whom it can trust. So it was when Abraham Lincoln, so when John Albion Andrew, died; so now at the death of Charles Sumner. For these three were all of the same type of honesty, sincerity, conscience. All had encountered opposition and incurred unpopularity in life; and all three at their death have received the homage of a nation's tears.

Charles Sumner was the most unpopular, perhaps, of all. He was eminently what politicians call an "impracticable man;" that is, a man who cannot be induced to sacrifice his principles to the success of his party, or to silence his convictions for the sake of his own interest. Nor had he that tact which some men, and many women, possess, by which they can express unpalatable opinions

without irritating their opponents. He had the
kindest heart; he would not intentionally hurt his
worst enemy; he never bore malice, though he
deeply felt a wrong; but he was not adroit in the
use of language, and so, often, without intending
it, he wounded the vanity, the prejudices, the
pride, the self-conceit, of his opponents. And
these wounds are seldom forgiven or forgotten.
Therefore, this warm, large heart, longing for
sympathy, prizing friendship so highly, was continually misunderstood, and was very much alone.

People accused him of self-conceit, arrogance,
and vanity. This was partly owing to the child-
like *naïveté* with which he would talk of his own
career and his own accomplishments. What other
men think and conceal, he said. But to me his
narratives were always very interesting; and I
gladly listened by the hour to his account of those
transactions, all of which he saw and a part of
which he was. For the subjects were never un-
important; they related to the most momentous
events, to the most critical times. In those events
he was an important actor; and he spoke of himself and what he did with perfect simplicity, just as
he spoke of what Lincoln and Stanton said and did.
I am afraid there will be nothing nearly so interesting in the books which he labored with so much
care, as in those anecdotes of his daily life, which
probably perished forever. His books, though full
of learning and thought, are a little stately, while

his talk had the charm of spontaneous inspiration, and was illustrated by that sweet smile, radiant of good-will, and coming fresh from the fountain of an uncorrupt heart.

No doubt Charles Sumner was born with a large desire for human approbation. He longed for the esteem of his fellow-men as few long for it. And, therefore, it was greatly to his credit that he made himself unpopular, from first to last, by advocating causes, and announcing ideas, usually in advance of the time. He loved approbation, but he never bought it by disloyalty to a conviction. Some men take pleasure in being persecuted, and are a little uneasy if not engaged in a fight. Sumner loved peace with all his heart, but was obliged, for conscience' sake, to be always in war. He loved the good-will of those around him; but he was obliged to relinquish it. He loved sunshine — and had to live in storms. Therefore, the fact that he was very approbative I regard as an element of his greatness. He would not have been so noble without it, for his fidelity to principle would not have cost him so dear.

Abraham Lincoln and Sumner were always friends, for they were men of the same type. Difference of opinion never estranged them, for they met on a plane higher than that of opinion. But many others disliked Sumner because he kept himself always on that upper level of principle. The air was too thin for them to breathe. He would

7

not come down to the more comfortable platform
of party expediency. They only asked him to be
silent. If he had consented to that, he might
have continued the most powerful statesman in
the country. But he could not be silent in the
face of any question of right and wrong. So it
was decided that he should be crushed, and all the
noxious elements in the political world were combined against him, and he was removed from his
most important place. But he had his consola-
tions. He had the aid of that "strong-siding
champion, conscience," and he found the truth of
the poet's statement that

> "Far more joy Marcellus exiled feels
> Than Cæsar with a Senate at his heels."

When a man dies whose virtues have created
hostility, who has been vilified and slandered,
there often comes a singular reaction. When
death lays its pale hand on the brow, men suddenly forget their prejudices and dislikes, and
recognize the greatness of soul that before was
hidden from their eyes. So, when this nation was
weeping for Lincoln — "in the passion of an angry
grief" — those who had been ridiculing him for
years confessed their wrong, and acknowledged his
greatness. So it is now, in the case of Charles
Sumner. Death, removing him from our outward
eye, enables us to see him inwardly and truly.
Thus have we looked at a mountain, and only seen
the creeping mists and clouds which concealed it;

but when the west wind moved the air, the vapors were suddenly dispersed, and the pure snowy summits came out in sharp outline against the blue sky. Death does the office of that cold wind. After the earthquake and fire and tempest of passionate and godless strife have passed, death comes, and the Lord speaks to us in that still, small voice.

One reason, I think, why the people loved Charles Sumner, is, that they felt how much larger his views were than those of most of his companions in the Senate. They did not, perhaps, say, "He is a statesman, the others are politicians," but they recognized the fact. When any important question came up, other men might consider it in relation to party interests. Sumner always attempted to study it in the light of history and political science. He sought to know and to declare the *truth* in regard to it — the truth as deduced from the past experience of nations and the mature judgments of the wise. The country is in peril to-day, because there are so few statesmen in public life. We send men to Congress to legislate on the currency, on finance, on taxation, who are mere local politicians, who have devoted their lives to the management of parties, who know nothing of political economy, nothing of commerce, who have never studied any work on finance, — men who imagine that by printing a sufficient number of pieces of paper with the word " dollar " on them, we shall make every one rich. And now when the place of a statesman is to be filled, now, when we need in Congress men acquainted with practical affairs, it is proposed to send some other politician. Why not sometimes a man who has never meddled with politics, but who is sagacious and experienced in mercantile pursuits, — some man of business, of whom we have many in Boston, with a statesman's intellect?

Another reason for this national grief at the death of Charles Sumner was his belief in man — his broad humanity. His life was devoted to the service of his race, — high and low, rich and poor, white and black. To him *man* was sacred. He did not feel the cynical contempt which it is the fashion to express for sentiment. His nature was rich in generous and noble feelings, and it was this very thing which gave him such power over the people. A character devoid of sentiment awakens no enthusiasm. The best knowledge is not reached by the cold intellect alone, but by the heart and intellect united. No one has ever gained any deep and lasting influence over men who did not possess something of this sacred ardor, this prophetic vision, a sight beyond sight, which pierces through the veil, and makes everything which is honorable, noble, just, and generous, as real as daylight and sunshine. Sumner owed his hold on the people to his large endowment of noble sentiment. Politicians could not understand it. Men who thought

that the only wires to be pulled were those of selfishness, tried again and again to defeat him here
in Massachusetts ; but they tried in vain. His
anchor went to a depth their sounding-line could
not fathom, and held by the eternal rock of human
nature. During all the long conflict with slavery,
his voice was heard like a trumpet, appealing to
the rights of man. He stood conspicuous in the
nation's eye, a young Apollo —

"In silent majesty of stern disdain,"

and dreadful was the clangor of his silver bow as
he shot his arrows thick and fast into the sophisms
used by slaveholders and their allies. When they
could not reply with argument, they silenced him
with murderous blows. But Sumner did as much
for the cause of freedom by his suffering as he had
done by his speech. When the news of that assault reached Boston, a meeting was hastily called
— I think in the Tremont Temple. Boston then
raised its voice against that cowardly, brutal, and
murderous assault on a Massachusetts Senator.
But many a man who did not raise his voice in
public at that time, took a vow of hostility in his
heart against the institution which prompted that
assassination.

Once, while Mr. Sumner was here in Boston,
still suffering from those injuries, I was passing
his house in Hancock street, and went in to see
him. He was in his chamber, resting in an easy

chair, and with him were three gentlemen. He introduced one of them to me as Captain John Brown, of Ossawattomie. It was the first time I had ever seen John Brown. They were speaking of this assault by Preston Brooks, and Mr. Sumner said, " The coat I had on at the time is hanging in that closet. Its collar is stiff with blood. You can see it, if you please, Captain." John Brown arose, went to the closet, slowly opened the door, carefully took down the coat, and looked at it for a few minutes with the reverence with which a Roman Catholic regards the relics of a saint. It may be the sight of that garment caused him to feel a still deeper abhorrence of slavery, and to take a stronger resolution of attacking it in its strongholds. So the blood of the martyrs is the seed of the church.

Once, when Mr. Sumner was showing me his autograph of John Milton, he said : " Perhaps I have a special interest in that MS., on account of what happened to me one day after my injury. I had tried to go back to my place in the Senate twice, but found myself unable to remain there. The second time, after I returned to my own chamber, deeply discouraged, I said : ' Then this is the end. It is all over with me now.' And I confess that the tears came to my eyes, thinking I could do no more work for my race or my country. But I raised my eyes, and saw before me a volume of Milton. I took it down and opened it mechanically. It opened at his noble sonnet on his own blindness, to Cyriack Skinner, where, he says, that for three years he has not seen sun or moon or man or woman.

> —— ' What supports me, dost thou ask ?
> The conscience, friend, to have lost them, overplied
> *In Liberty's defence, my noble task,*
> Of which all Europe rings, from side to side.'

I read this," said Mr. Sumner, "and I, too, felt comforted and encouraged by the words of Milton."

So it is that nobleness, courage, faith, extend themselves! Not only is the blood of the martyrs the seed of the church, but the thoughts of brave men leap over gulfs of two centuries, and inspire with fresh hope other heroes, fighting other battles of liberty.

Wordsworth, in one of his sonnets, says that England has need of Milton, and that he ought to be living now.

> " O, raise us up, return to us again —
> And give us manners, virtue, freedom, power."

But Milton is living with us still, in his great example and his inspiring words. He stood by the side of Charles Sumner in that hour of darkness, and raised *him* up. And so shall Charles Sumner live, and after two centuries shall *his* example inspire and awaken other souls, in this land and elsewhere, to do their duty, so as to be able to

say with him — "I have fought a good fight, I
have finished my course, I have kept the faith."

Those of us who were so fortunate as to be in
our church hall on the evening in December,
when Mr. Sumner was present, had an example
of his kindness of heart and affability of manner.
I had asked him to come, and he gave no definite
promise, so that I hardly expected him. He was
taking tea in Cambridge that evening, yet he
came to Boston, and found his way by the street-
car to the vestry. It pleased him to see how glad
we all were to speak to him and shake hands with
him. With a good deal of reluctance, he finally
yielded to your requests to say something to us all.
But when he began to speak his heart warmed toward the young people present, and he addressed
himself to them, telling them what great opportunities were awaiting them in the approaching
years. He said no word of the past; nothing of
what he had seen and done; only of the magnificent future which was before the rising generation, and the noble duties which they had to fulfill.
In him, it seemed, then, that —

> "Old experience did attain
>   To something of prophetic strain."

Nothing could be more modest, genial, friendly,
than were his words and conversation at that time.
A happy smile was on his face all the evening,
and I could not but fancy that he felt more at

home among these youthful admirers, than in the
Senate Chamber or among his political associates.
It is a pleasant memory to carry in our hearts.
Once or twice he said that he wished he had been
born later, so as to be able to take part in the
events which are to come soon. In regard to this,
one lady said to him afterward, that "she thought
the Lord knew better than he did when he ought
to have been born." And, indeed, how indispensable has his work been during the last twenty-
three years! Others may have been before him
in originating the anti-slavery movement; others
may have come closer to the common people in
urging the abolition of slavery; some may have
been more fiery; some more adroit. But where
do we find combined in one person so much of
moral sentiment with so much intellectual culture;
so much unity of aim with variety of attainment;
such purity of heart joined to such practiced ability; so much of white-souled integrity and faithful
industry in work; such sweetness and such courage; such readiness to brave enemies, and patience
to endure sufferings, as we find united in the life
and character of Charles Sumner!

In one of Theodore Parker's letters to Charles
Sumner, he says: "I look to you to be a leader in
morals — to represent justice. I expect you to
make mistakes — blunders. I hope they will be
intellectual and not moral; that you will never
miss the right, however you may miss the expedi-

ent. All our States were built on the opinion of to-day. I hope you will build on the Rock of Ages, and look to Eternity for your justification. You see, my dear Sumner, I expect much of you. I expect heroism of the most heroic kind. Yours is a place of great honor, of great trust, but of prodigious peril; and of that there will be few to warn you, as I do now. You see that I try you by a difficult standard, and that I am not easily pleased. I hope some years hence to say: ' You have done better than I advised.' "

Perhaps that time has arrived. When these two noble souls meet in the eternal world, I think that Theodore will say to Charles: " *You have done better than I advised.*"

[I add, below, the selection of Scriptures read on this occasion. These passages seem to describe Charles Sumner as if they had been written for him; and are another example of the fact that the Bible is a mine of thoughts and expressions where may be found the very words needed for all events, and with which to describe all characters.]

Help, Lord! for the godly man ceaseth, for the faithful fail from among the children of men.

Who shall ascend into the hill of the Lord? and who shall stand in his holy place?

He that hath clean hands, and a pure heart, who hath not lifted up his soul unto vanity, nor sworn deceitfully.

Mark the perfect man, and consider the upright, for the end of that man is peace.

He put on righteousness, and it clothed him; his justice was his robe and diadem.

Unto him men gave ear and waited; they kept silence for his counsel. They waited for his words as for the rain, and opened their mouths as for the latter rain.

When our iniquities had separated between us and God, when our hands were defiled with blood, when justice was turned backward, and we spoke oppression,

Then the Lord stood up to plead, and said, What mean ye, that ye beat my people to pieces, and grind the faces of the poor?

Is not this the fast that I have chosen, to loose the bands of wickedness, and let the oppressed go free, and that ye break every yoke?

For ye have not hearkened unto me, saith the Lord, in proclaiming liberty every man to his neighbor, and every man to his brother, but brought them into subjection, to be unto you for servants and for handmaids.

Therefore, thus said the Lord, Behold! Son of Man, I have made thy face strong against their faces, and thy forehead strong against their forehead : as an adamant, harder than flint, have I made thy forehead : fear them not, therefore, nor be dismayed at their looks, though they be a rebellious house.

Those who understood him not shall say : This is he whom we had sometimes in derision, and a proverb of reproach.

We fools accounted his life madness, but now is he numbered among the saints.

For glorious is the fruit of good labors, and the fruit of wisdom shall never fall away.

The memorial of virtue is immortal; for when it is present, men take example of it; and when it is gone, they desire it; it weareth a crown and triumpheth forever.

God hath made of one blood all nations of men to dwell on all the face of the earth ; and God hath shown us that we ought not to call any man common or unclean.

He stood up as a fire, and his word burned as a lamp. He did wonders in his life, and after his death his body prophesied.

Approving himself in all things as a servant of God — in much patience, in afflictions, in necessities, in distresses, in stripes, in tumults, in labors, in watchings, in fastings; by pureness, by knowledge, by long-suffering, by kindness, by the Holy Spirit, by love unfeigned, by the word of truth, by the armor of righteousness on the right hand and on the left ; by honor and dishonor, by evil report and good report ; as a deceiver, and yet true; as unknown, and yet well-known ; as dying, and, behold, he lives; as chastened, and not killed ; as sorrowful, yet alway rejoicing; as poor, yet making many rich ; as having nothing, and yet possessing all things.

Wherefore, seeing that we are compassed about with so great a cloud of witnesses, let us lay aside every weight, and run with patience the race set before us.

THE BATTLE-FLAGS AND CHARLES SUMNER.

[The following extract is from remarks made at a hearing before a Committee of the Massachusetts Legislature, to which was referred the question of repealing the vote of a previous Legislature, which censured Sumner for proposing to have the names of the battles fought in our civil war taken from the United States battle-flags. The resolution was repealed ; and the notice that Massachusetts, on second thoughts, had taken back her words of condemnation, fortunately was placed in Sumner's hand just before his death.]

We have just passed through, gentlemen, a great historic period. We have concluded a long and terrible struggle, in which the deadliest enemy to the peace and prosperity of republican institutions has been at last conquered. Among those who carried on that long war was one who went from Boston to the United States Senate in 1851,— a comparatively young man. He had made himself unpopular here by opposing the men and the measures which were then fashionable. Daniel Webster was then the idol of this community, and every man who opposed him was at once ostracized. This young man was, by nature, very fond of the approbation of his fellow-men; he was not a Luther nor an Elijah, indifferent to public opinion. No man ever felt more keenly than he the opposition of enemies, the estrangement of friends, "hard unkindness' altered eye," unjust censure, false accusation. Yet, during twenty years, he has encountered all these. Like Cato, he could say, "The gods love the triumphant cause — the conquered cause is the one I defend." He began his public career in Congress by attacking, in unanswerable argument, the infamous fugitive slave bill. He opposed with all the energy of his nature, and all the power of his intellect, the repeal of the Missouri compromise, and the introduction of slavery into Kansas, and for this speech was struck down on the floor of Congress. He has always advocated emancipation, and during the war his voice was always raised against all concession or compromise. He is the Abdiel of our day, —

> "Among innumerable false unmoved,
> Unshaken, unseduced, unterrified."

Owing to his labors and sufferings, and those of his noble anti-slavery companions, the United States is now really free and really one. The war has ended in peace and union. Wishing to obliterate the signs of disunion, he has proposed to remove from the army register and the flags of the United States army the names of the battles fought between the North and the South, — to the flags of the States this resolution does not apply. Mr. Sumner has not proposed, and does not propose, to change a single motto on any monument or any flag in the whole North. But the army of the United States is now the army of the whole country. It now recruits its soldiers from every State, and I entirely agree with Mr. Sumner that it would be eminently proper and right that on those national banners no sign of the past conflict shall remain. Yet for making this proposition, so perfectly just and right if the Union is restored, a majority of the legislature of Massachusetts saw fit to censure this patriot, this hero of liberty, this noble and chivalric champion of human rights and human freedom. This was done by men, many of whom owe their position on that floor to what he and his companions have endured and done when they were playing marbles or studying their English grammar. Such a vote of censure will do no harm to our Senator. His reputation and influence stand on too deep a foundation to be disturbed by such an act — an act which will do more injury to those who perpetrated it than to him. Many of them, no doubt, were sincere, and thought they were doing right, and they may be sorry for what they have done, but will not have to blame themselves. But when in a few years the green sod shall be placed over the form of Charles Sumner, and he sleeps where " the wicked cease from troubling, and the weary are at rest," — then, when, as recently in the case of Horace Greeley, and formerly in the case of Abraham Lincoln, all the angry voices of hatred are swallowed up in one grand tide of grateful remembrance, I think that in that day it will not be a pleasant thing to remember that the Massachusetts legislature censured him, after all his years of toil in her service, because he carried the principles of peace perhaps a little too far; because he was a little too generous, too magnanimous, and too ardent in his desire for full and entire reconciliation between the North and the South. Might he not use the same language as Edmund Burke did before his constituents at Bristol, should he want to make an explanation of his conduct: "And now, gentlemen, on this solemn day, when I come, as it were, to make up my accounts with you, let me take to myself some degree of honest pride from the nature of the charges which are brought against me. I do not here stand before you accused of venality or neglect of duty. It is not said that, in the long period of my service, I have sacrificed the slightest of your interests to my ambition or to my fortune. . . . . No! The charges against me are all of one kind; that I have pushed the principles of general justice and benevolence too far, further than a cautious policy might warrant, and further than the opinions of many would go along with me. In whatever accident may happen to me in life; in pain, in sorrow, in depression, in distress, I will call to mind these accusations, and be comforted."

IV.

THEODORE PARKER.

THEODORE PARKER.[1]

WE have, during the last week, heard of the
death of Theodore Parker, — a noble and worthy
soul, known well, honored and loved by most of
us. I cannot let this day pass by without taking
occasion to say a few words, however incomplete
and inadequate, in memory of his worth. And, in
speaking of him, I hope to avoid all extravagance
of eulogy, all indiscriminate praise, all sweeping
generalities of statement. As he to others, so I to
him. He once refused to accept the established
rule of necrology, *De mortuis nil nisi bonum*, —
"Say nothing but *good* of the dead;" and substituted for it this other and better rule, *De mortuis nil nisi verum*, — "Say nothing but *truth* of
the dead." "It is no merit," added he, "to die.
Why praise a man because he is dead?" I will
remember this honesty, brother, in speaking of
thee.

Theodore Parker was the ripe fruit of New
England; baptized in the Lexington Meeting-

[1] A discourse delivered after his death, June 3, 1860.

house; learning his letters in the primary school; taking strength from the granite and gravel below, and from the cold winter winds above; learning freedom of utterance at town-meeting; inheriting strong sense, clear logic, and penetrating insight, in his ancestral blood; of the stock of the Puritans; of the tribe of Massachusetts; a Yankee of the Yankees; a Unitarian also, by inheritance from plain-thinking parents; and as touching all youthful habits of behavior, all moral requisitions of a strict community, blameless. No man more than he, since Benjamin Franklin, has shown those traits of common sense, joined with abstract speculation; sensibility of conscience, poised with calm judgment; the fanatic's devotion to ideas, with the calculating prudence of a man of the world; which make the basis of New England character and its essential strength.

When, on the 19th of April, 1775, the British troops marched to Lexington and Concord, they found at Lexington the militia company of that town — eighty strong — drawn up on the green, in front of the Meeting-house, to receive them. The captain of the company waited till the British troops — eight hundred in all — had reached the green and deployed into line opposite, and till their commander had ordered the Americans to disperse. Then he, too, gave the same order to his men; not wishing to sacrifice life in a useless resistance to overwhelming numbers, but letting the British soldiers, for the first time, look in the face of the American militia. But, while they were dispersing, the British fired; and the green-sward, on that April morning, was stained with the first American blood which fell in the great struggle. Out in Kentucky, the hunters heard of it, and baptized their newly planted town by the name of Lexington. In Europe, the nations heard of it, and dated from that hour the beginning of a new era for the destinies of man. The captain of that militia company was John Parker, grand-father of our Theodore; and his gun was kept by Theodore in his study, to be used, if necessary, in protecting the fugitive slave under his roof.

Born thus, amid New-England life, in a farmer's home; driving the cows to the field, and going to the district school; listening to sermons, and to discussions in town-meeting; studying his Latin grammar by the light of the kitchen fire; harden-ing his body and soul with stern manual labor, and training his intellect by the wholesome stud-ies of the common schools, — the genius of Theo-dore Parker took its flight upward, from its hum-ble nest in the meadow-grass to its singing-place among the stars. It is an honor to our institu-tions when they train up their boys into such men as he.

There is no real greatness where we do not find in a man the three elemental tendencies of Intel-lect, Affection and Will, — all in full and harmo-

nious activity. Either of them alone cannot constitute greatness. We see, among practical men,
some of immense energy, who sweep everything
before them by their resistless will; but they are
not *great* men; for their energy is not directed by
any great thought, and not inspired by any generous love. And there are also men of great intellectual powers, but without any energetic purpose,
any clear aim; whose knowledge tends nowhere.
Like gold locked up in a miser's iron chest, their
intellectual powers and treasures profit no one,
and are useless. And so there may be love, —
saintly love to God, humane love to man; but
because not illuminated by insight, nor directed
by energetic purpose, it stagnates into a merely
sentimental piety, a sentimental philanthropy.

Theodore Parker's intellect was remarkable for
its varied faculties. It was strong in analysis
and synthesis, in marshaling a multitude of facts,
and in ascending from facts to comprehensive
laws. His memory of details was astonishing;
but his power of systematizing those details —
making them drill in companies, and march in
squadrons, and take on the order of battle — was
equally striking. His mind was strong in its per-
ceptions and apprehensions; very able to seize and
retain individual facts. In his childhood, he could
repeat whole cantos of poetry, and could learn by
heart a poem of five hundred lines at a reading.
Before he was ten years old, he had studied bot-

any so as to know all the shrubs and trees of Massachusetts, and the names and habits of the plants in his vicinity. At ten, he began Latin; at eleven, Greek. At twenty-one, he had read Virgil twenty times, Horace nearly as often; besides having made himself master of chemistry, natural philosophy, astronomy, and mathematics. Presently he added French, Latin, Italian, Spanish, and German, and afterward Hebrew.

And all this knowledge was *live* knowledge. There are some men who accumulate facts as the ants gather grains. They are merely the collectors of dry seeds, which never germinate. They are the slaves of their knowledge, — not its masters. There are great scholars who never know what to do with their accumulated stores. Not so with our friend. His mind was not like a forest in winter, when the trees stand close above and the bushes thick below, and where the icy branches rattle together while the cold wind roars through their tops. It was like the same forest when the summer sun has poured life into every part, and the myriad buds and leaves expand; when the blossoms open, the birds and insects flit through the tender foliage, and a soft perfume comes mingled from a thousand flowers.

Theodore Parker possessed a power of acquisition, which few men, out of Germany, have had. He knew the contents of all the books in his library. He could take the substance out of a book in an incredibly short time. On that fatal winter which broke down his constitution and determined his fate (the winter which killed him), he was in the habit of filling a carpet-bag, not with novels, but with works of tough philosophy and theology, in Greek, Latin, German, in old black-letter print, and yellow parchment covers; and would study them, Monday, while riding in the cars, to lecture on Monday night; study them, Tuesday, while riding to lecture at another place on Tuesday night; and so on, studying all day and lecturing every night, till Friday. On Friday he would come home, write his Sunday's sermon on Saturday forenoon, visit the sick and suffering of his society on Saturday afternoon, preach Sunday morning to two or three thousand people, rest a little on Sunday afternoon, receive his friends on Sunday evening, and away again on Monday.

I asked him, " Do you read all your books? and do you know what is in them?" " I read them all," said he, "and can give you a table of contents for each book." During that winter he lectured to about eighty thousand persons, in every part of the free states, from Maine to Wisconsin.

When in Germany he went to see the old theologian, Ferdinand Christian Baur, of Tübingen, and he asked him how many hours a day he studied. The old man replied with a sigh, "Ach! leider, nur achtzehn," — "Alas! only eighteen."

Parker never studied eighteen hours a day, I suppose; but I think he put the twenty-four hours' study of common men into his six or twelve hours a day: for he who studies with an active mind will learn more in a few minutes, than another, studying passively and idly, will gain in an hour. What Parker knew, he knew; and he knew that he knew it. All his knowledge lay at hand, accessible, like the tools of an orderly workman.

But the scholarship and knowledge of Theodore Parker made but the beginning of his intellectual work. He was an original thinker. Very early addicted to metaphysical pursuits, he never relinquished his taste for them. In philosophy, he belonged to that school of thinkers who are called Transcendentalists; who believe that man, as God's child, receives an inheritance of ideas from within; that he knows by insight; that he has intuitions of truth, which furnish the highest evidence of the reality of the soul, of God, of duty, of immortality. He joined, not doubtfully, but with most earnest conviction, that great company of ideal philosophers, at whose head stands the divine Plato, and in whose generous ranks are the chiefest intellects of the race, — Socrates and Pythagoras, Epictetus and Antoninus, Plotinus and Jamblichus, Erigena and Anselm, Descartes and Liebnitz, Cudworth and Henry More, Pascal and Kant, Cousin and Schleiermacher. But his chief powers he consecrated to theology, which he justly regarded as the queen of the sciences. It has become the fashion with many, in these days, to undervalue both philosophy and theology, and to consider them as idle and empty studies, leading to no practical results; while the arts and sciences, natural philosophy, the knowledge of external things, social questions, humanities, philanthropies, and reforms, are the only really solid and valuable studies. Not so thought Theodore Parker. He knew, as well as any, how empty is a great deal that is called theology; but he also knew that every man has, and must have, a philosophy and theology, true or false. He knew that every man's philosophy underlies his theology, and that his theology underlies all his practice. He knew that theological reform must precede all other reform; that as one thinks of God and God's character, so will he form his own. He knew that, while God is regarded as partial, willful, and revengeful, man will continue to be partial, willful, and revengeful too.

Until our theology becomes Christian, we can have no Christian morality nor Christian ethics. Those who believe that God has foreordained some human souls to an eternal hell hereafter, can very easily believe that he has ordained some human races to be slaves forever here. Those who think that God is full of wrath against his enemies will consider it right themselves to be filled with wrath against theirs. Therefore, Theodore

Parker drove the deep subsoil plough of a sound theology under the roots of a false morality and ethics. And, when I say a sound theology, I refer especially to his doctrine of God, — to theology. strictly so called; for his views here were mostly noble and admirable. His Christology, or doctrine of Christ, I think defective; and his Anthropology, or doctrine of man, defective too, in important particulars. He ascribed too absolute moral power to the human will; he did not enough recognize the element of evil which comes to us from the solidarity of the race, — inherited from behind, and caught by contagion from around. He regarded sin as always and strictly a self-originated disease; never as a contagious epidemic, or as an inherited tendency. And all which to me seem his mistakes, theoretical and practical, had their root here.

There was also in the mind of Theodore a poetic quality to which he never did justice. Imagination is too spontaneous a faculty to thrive in a brain which is driven forward in the direction of constant work by so energetic a will. His friend William Henry Channing, writes: " Once I remember telling him that his grand mistake was this concentrated unity of purpose. He was really richer in impulse, imagination, sympathy, and varied power, than he knew himself to be, or allowed himself to be."

The active element in Theodore Parker was

very predominant. It went always abreast, at least, with the speculative. He studied and speculated in order to act. He was a worker in the world; was here to do something, not merely to think something. Hence his interest in all reforms, in all social progress, in all which tends to deepen and heighten human culture. Before him, his life lay planned out like a chart; and his work was arranged beforehand for every year. Indeed, his intense activity, as I just said, seemed often to weaken or repress his intellectual power; for thought needs a resting-time to ripen. Too constant action impairs the sweep and strength of the intellect. Especially is the imagination, that airy faculty, cramped by too energetic a will. It can only spread its wings when allowed perfect liberty and choice of its own time.

But what an amount of work did our brother do, with tongue as a speaker, with pen as a writer, with hand as a helper. First, as a preacher and lecturer, he stood unrivaled in the rare gift of making popular and interesting to thousands the results of systematic philosophy and theology. Before a crowd collected to be entertained by his wit, pointed comments, and sharp criticism, on the persons and things around them, he did not avoid an almost scholastic discussion of first principles; a careful analysis of conduct, character, morality; large generalizations, systematic and exhaustive distributions. Hour after hour, the great audience

would listen ; held by the thread of a masterly
and clear argument ; enlivened indeed, not infre-
quently, by flashes of wit, and touches of poetic
description. But, if he entertained and amused
them, he did not have that for his end, but merely
for one of his means. His end was to revolutionize public opinion ; to beat down, by terrible blows
of logic and satire, the cool defenders of inhuman
wrong ; to pour floods of fiery invective upon
those who opposed themselves to the progress of
a great cause ; to fill all minds with a sense of responsibility to God for the use of their faculties ;
to show the needs of suffering man ; to call attention to the degraded classes ; to raise up those
who are bowed down, and to break every yoke.
He also came in the spirit and power of Elijah.
He was ready to denounce the Ahabs and Herods
of our day, the hard-money kings of a commercial
city, the false politicians whose lying tongue is always waiting to deceive the simple. His fiery indignation at wrong showed itself, in the most terrible invectives which modern literature knows,
against the kidnappers, the pro-slavery politicians,
the pro-slavery priests, and the slave-catching
commissioners. These invectives were sometimes
cruel and severe ; in the spirit of Moses, David,
and John the Baptist, rather than in that of
Christ. Such extreme severity, whether in Jew
or Christian, defeats its own object ; for it is felt
to be excessive and unjust. I cannot approve of

Theodore Parker's severity. I consider it false, because extravagant; unjust, because indiscriminate; unchristian, because relentless and unsympathizing. But then I will remember how bitterly he was pursued by his opponents; how Christians offered prayers in their meetings, that he might be taken away; how the leaders of opinion in Boston hated and reviled him; how little he had, from any quarter, of common sympathy or common charity. I cannot wonder at his severity; but I cannot think it wise. Being so great, I wish he had been greater. Being so loving to his friends, I wish he could also have felt less bitter scorn toward his opponents.

Together with his work as a preacher, he did a great work as lecturer and platform-speaker; and, in addition to this, another great work as writer. Book after book, pamphlet after pamphlet, issued from his busy brain and pen. I think, if anywhere, he failed intellectually here, — in a too great rapidity of production. His early writings are much more rich and full than his later ones. His " Discourse on Religion " — his first printed book — remains his best one. He did not give himself time to 'go down as deeply as he might, and to meditate as fully as he might, before he printed. But his writings were read by tens of thousands throughout America and Europe. Every one in the land knew him. To the farthest prairies of the West, to the remotest corner of

England, his writings have penetrated. They were translated into different European languages. So he did the full work of three men, — first as a preacher, then as a lecturer and platform-speaker, and last as a writer.

As a preacher, I think, he was wanting in the perception and utterance of some of the truths of the gospel, but he did an immense good to thousands by his splendid utterances in behalf of right, justice, and good. He denounced wrong as no others denounced it; he appealed to the sense of responsibility as no others; he called upon the religious element in the soul to assert itself against all that is selfish, worldly, and sensual in man. Thousands were roused by him to see what life was for, — what only makes it really life. It is not necessary for every man to preach every part of the gospel, in order to do good. Having gifts differing according to the grace given them, men are called to preach according to the proportion of their *own* faith.

When Paul preached to Felix, he did not think it necessary to say anything about the doctrine of reconciliation by Christ. He preached "right-eousness, temperance, and judgment to come;" and "Felix trembled." No one can deny that Theodore Parker made many a Felix tremble by precisely the same sort of preaching; and I think that the Master will admit, that, though not doing all the work to be done in the vineyard, he faithfully and nobly did the work which God, by the sincere convictions of his soul, had given to him to do. "Care is taken," says Goethe, "that trees shall not grow up to heaven;" and God does not mean nor require that every man shall do everything. He asks us only to be faithful to our own duty, which is determined by our own insight and conviction.

But head and hand alone, without heart, cannot make real greatness. There must be warm devotion to some person or to some cause, there must be affection, there must be love constantly pouring life into the intellect and will, else the intellect freezes into mere formality, and the will hardens into mere habit or dead routine.

Theodore Parker's soul was a loving soul. He was born with enthusiasm for the True, the Beautiful, and the Good; and the secret of his power over men was, that he was able to retain to the last this enthusiasm. They saw in him one man, who, though a great intellect, could yet love and adore; who, though a great practical worker, could feel tenderly all human woes and wrongs. Therefore they gave him their hearts, and were willingly led by his genius and commanding thought.

He was a man of warm feeling; a man of tender sympathy; a man who felt as sincerely for the sufferings of a poor Irish laborer, or a poor drunkard, or a deserted child, as he did for the great cause of human progress. The humblest never appealed to his sympathy in vain. How often have I heard of his interest in one or another unfortunate! — some exiled foreigners, some poor widows, some orphan children. His time, though so precious, was at the service of any forlorn vagabond and outcast; and I think that He who said, "Inasmuch as ye have done it unto the least of these my brethren, ye have done it unto me," will prefer this practical obedience to his command, and sympathy with his spirit, to the most Orthodox confession which Theodore might have made.

The friends whom Parker loved, he loved with his whole heart. He loved them as Jonathan loved David; his love for them was wonderful, passing the love of woman. A word of kindness, an act of good-will, was never forgotten by him. His noble soul opened itself to affection like the blossoming apple-tree to the balmy sunshine in this early June. His sympathy with humanity inspired his flaming and ardent zeal for the oppressed everywhere; and as, in our land, the colored man is the most oppressed of all, therefore he felt most keenly *his* wrongs, and labored most zealously for *him*. Cold-hearted and selfish politicians, who think that to get office is the only motive in politics, could not understand this. His whole heart, as well as his whole reason and conscience, were in the cause of suffering and enslaved man; and for this that noble heart throbbed to the end.

9

This loving heart, which glowed with such devoted and steadfast affection for his friends, which burned with such ardent interest for the sufferers everywhere, could not be, and was not, wanting in the highest type of love. It rose through friendship to humanity, through humanity to piety. Having loved his brother whom he had seen, how could he *not* love also the invisible but ever-present Father of us all? His piety was tender, filial, reverential; devout as that of Pascal, St. Bernard, or Madame Guyon. It was an instinct of adoration for infinite beauty and perfect love. Those who blamed his irreverent speech toward the outside of religion, toward the letter of the Bible, toward the sacraments of worship, little knew how tender and deep was his reverence toward the Great Father, whom he also loved to call the Mother, — Father and Mother of all men.

In looking for some illustration of this strangely exuberant and varied genius, I have recalled, as its best emblem, a day I once passed in crossing the St. Gothard Mountain, from Italy into Germany. In the morning, we were among Italian nightingales and the sweet melody of the Italian speech. The flowers were all in bloom, and the air balmy with summer perfumes from vine and myrtle. But, as we slowly climbed the mountain, we passed away from this, — first into vast forests of pine, and then out upon broad fields of snow, where winter avalanches were falling in thunder

from above. And so, at noon, we reached the
summit, and began to descend, till we again left
the snow; and so rode continually downward on
a smooth highway, but through terrible ravines,
over rushing torrents, into dark gorges, where the
precipices almost met overhead, and the tormented
river roared far below; and so on and on, hour
after hour, till we came down into the green and
sunny valleys of Canton Uri, and passed through
meadows where men were mowing the hay, and
the air was fragrant, not now with Southern vines,
but with the Northern apple-blossoms. Here we
heard all around us the language of Germany;
and then we floated on the enchanting lake of the
Four Cantons, and passed through its magnificent
scenery, till we reached, at dark, the old city of
Lucerne. This wonderful day, in its variety, is a
type to me of the career of our brother. His
youth was full of ardor and hope, full of imagination and poetic dreams, full of studies in ancient
and romantic lore. It was Italian and classic.
Then came the struggling ascent of the mountain,
— the patient toil and study of his early manhood; then the calm survey of the great fields of
thought and knowledge, spreading widely around
in their majestic repose, and of the holy heavens
above his head, — the sublimities of religion, the
pure mountain air of devout thought and philosophic insight; and then came the rapid progress,
on and on, from this high summit of lonely specu-

lation, down into the practice and use of life, — down among the philanthropies and humanities of being, — down from the solitary, serene air of lonely thought, through terrible ravines and broken precipices of struggling reform; by the roaring stream of progress, where the frozen avalanche of conservative opposition falls in thunder to crush the advancing traveler; and so, on and on, into the human homes of many-speaking men, among low cottages, along the road the human being travels, and by which blessing comes and goes, — the road which follows —

> " The river's course, the valley's peaceful windings,
> Curves round the cornfield and the hill of vines;
> And so, secure, though late, reaches its end."

Out of classic, Roman-Catholic, mediæval Italy, into Protestant Germany; out of the land of organization and authority into the land of individual freedom; out of the historic South, inheriting all treasures of the past, into the enthusiastic, hopeful, progressive North, inspired with all the expectations of the future, — such was the course and progress of his earthly day. A long life, though closed at fifty years; as that day on the St. Gothard seemed to us already three days, long before sundown.

And now, after this survey, I must conclude him to have been a really great man; because deficient in none of the elements which constitute greatness. A great intellect was in him directed

by a great will toward an aim given by a great
heart. The heart of love poured life into his
thoughts and actions. His is a name to stand
always high in the catalogue of New-England
worthies; and, as long as Benjamin Franklin is
remembered, Theodore Parker will not be forgotten. No monument will be erected to his memory at Mount Auburn; at least, not in our day;
but very probably the grandchildren of those who
condemned him most may call on our grandchildren to subscribe for his statue, or to take tickets
for the centennial celebration of his birthday.

I am reminded of the saying of Jesus concerning John the Baptist, in which the Saviour seems
to excuse the harshness and rudeness of his pre-
cursor, on the ground that such a work as he had
to do required a man whose faults would lie in
that direction. A civil and smooth-spoken gentleman, a man of proprieties, would not have
drawn the multitudes into the wilderness to hear
their sins denounced and their wickedness condemned. Nor would such an orator have gathered
crowds into the Music Hall. Theodore was the
John the Baptist of our day, — the prophet of a
transition state, when the law had ended, but the
gospel only just begun. He belonged to the period when the kingdom of God is taken by violence. He was not a reed shaken by the wind,
nor a man clothed in soft raiment; but he was one
of those whom the times require, and who, if es-

sentially different, could not do their work. And
as Jesus apologized for John, and excused his
harshness, on the ground that such a character
was required for such a work, so I doubt not,
that, if our brother failed in the same way, it was
for the same reason ; and I think that our Master
will make for him the same excuse.

And now he has gone ! That brain filled with
the last results and discoveries of the French,
English, and German intellect, has gone ! We
can no more turn into Exeter Place to consult
that encyclopædia. That great worker, who could
swim steadily abreast of the rising tide of events,
keeping always on its topmost wave, always having his word ready for the hour and for each event
of the hour, has gone to sleep under the blue Tuscan
sky. His dust mingles with that of the men of
many ages, — with the Oscans and Latins, with
the Tarquins and old Etruscan chiefs, with Roman consuls and Roman orators, with Carthage-
nian invaders from Africa, with Keltic invaders
from Gaul, with Cimbri and Greek, with Ostro-
goth and Lombard, with mediæval monks and
doctors, with the dust of St. Francis, Dante,
Michael Angelo, Petrarch, and Tasso. And, if
he may not rest in Santa Croce with the illustrious dead of Florence, neither is Dante there,
nor Savonarola. The kindred dust of the great
Italian reformer was dispersed in flame on that
Cathedral Square, near which our brother's re-

mains repose. Let him sleep there after life's
. fevered task, our New-England cosmopolite, in
that cosmopolitan society, — in that soil made up
of the dust of men of all races, all creeds, and all
characters. But we in Boston shall often miss
him. When that great Hall shall stand silent
and empty, Sunday after Sunday; when plausible
rhetoricians utter their sophisms without contra-
diction, because our great critic is not here to answer them; when great national crises come and
go unanalyzed, because he is not here with his
ever ready brain and well-filled memory to give
the immediate judgment which history is afterward to assign, — in such hours as these we shall
remember the greatness and mourn the absence of
our Boston Socrates, — of our gift of God, — our
Theodore.

SAMUEL GRIDLEY HOWE.

THE CHIVALRY OF TO-DAY.

ILLUSTRATED IN THE LIFE AND CHARACTER OF SAMUEL G. HOWE.[1]

AMONG the Romans, courage made the essence of all virtue. The word *virtus*, or manliness, or courage, was the same as our *virtue*.

Courage has not been always considered a virtue among Christians. Not to fight but to submit, was long supposed to be the chief duty of a religious man. The Christ himself was supposed to be made up of passive virtues — patience, submission, non-resistance, meekness, humility. In all mediæval pictures, he was represented as bowing down his head like a bulrush; standing mute like the sheep that is sheared. And through many centuries, the saint, *par excellence*, was the man who retired from the world and its evils to fast and pray, and save his own soul, instead of remaining in the world to fight with its evils, to resist its abuses, to meet falsehoods in battle with honest argument,

---

[1] A sermon preached to the Church of the Disciples, Boston, January 16, 1876.

to make war against triumphant and powerful villainy.

Not such the view of the apostle Paul. To him life was a long battle for right against wrong, for freedom against slavery, for humanity against all that would harm it. "Put on the whole armor, the panoply, of God," says he. "Fight the good fight of faith." "Take the helmet of salvation and the sword of the Spirit." "Stand fast, quit you like men, be strong." "Son Timothy, war a good warfare." He meant every blow to tell. "I do not fight as one who beats the air," said he; when he struck, he struck to hit. But it was a moral strife. He had no hostility to men, except when they represented principles. "We wrestle not against flesh and blood," but against wrong principles, against evil forces, against the influences which darken life, against triumphant wickedness, no matter how highly placed.

Nor was the goodness of Jesus merely or mainly passive. He went forth from the quiet air of his Nazarene home to a conflict with the ruling principles and ideas of his time. The Pharisees were the masters of the nation's mind, the guides of public opinion. He denounced and opposed them. What was harder, he must disappoint all the expectations of the people. They hated the Romans, with their soldiers and tax-gatherers. He went to the house of the Roman centurion to heal his child; he made a Roman tax-gatherer one of his apostles. They hated the Samaritans — he made a Samaritan the hero of a lovely story. They were hungering for a Messiah who should lead them against the Roman power — he told them that his kingdom was not of this world. All the virtues of Christ were active, not passive. His love was active love, going about to do good. His piety was practical piety, resisting and opposing all formalism, all ceremonial worship, and calling on men to worship God in spirit and in truth. The life of Jesus was one long act of heroic courage.

If we distinguish between the essence of courage and its accidents, we shall see what an indispensable ingredient it is in all goodness. It is the power which makes us ready to encounter difficulties, meet opposition, go without delay or hesitation to each duty, attacking every task of life as soon as it presents itself, not shirking the work of to-day, or putting it off till to-morrow; being ready to speak the truth, whether men hear or forbear; standing by our convictions, though custom, authority, and friendship are all on the other side. This is courage; and without it, goodness is a sickly plant, virtue a pale shadow, religion a hollow decorum, exercising no influence and deserving none.

The distinction usually made is between physical courage and moral courage. I prefer a different classification. I should make three kinds of courage, namely: Personal courage, Moral courage, Christian courage.

I do not like the phrase, "physical courage," because this is often only insensibility to danger. In this sense, a stone would have more courage than a brute; a brute more courage than a man; a coarse and brutal man more courage than a man of thought and imagination. But insensibility, which plunges blindly into danger, does not deserve the name of courage. That alone is true courage which sees the danger, knows all the risk it must run, and yet is willing to encounter it. There is no courage in risking a peril to which we are insensible. If a man can truly say, "I never knew what fear was," he must also say, "I never knew what courage was." The capacity of feeling fear is essential to all true courage. To feel fear and rise above fear — that is what we understand by courage.

We have just followed to his grave a man the like of whom has never been seen in New England. In him were united the qualities of Sir Launcelot and the good Samaritan. He was not a saint, in any sense of the word; but he was in some ways better than a saint, perhaps nearer to Christ than most saints. He had his faults, no doubt; he was probably far from perfect. Perhaps his strong will sometimes made him despotic; his determination may have made him intolerant of the tendencies of minds different from his own.

According to the common definition, he was not a religious man, for he made little profession, and cared little for ceremonial worship. But according to the definition of Jesus, he may be called a citizen of Heaven: "Not every one that saith unto me, Lord, Lord, shall enter into the kingdom of Heaven; but he that doeth the will of my Father, who is in Heaven." But even if I were able to point out his defects, I should not care to do so, for to look at faults seldom does us good. What does us the most good is to see the noble qualities of others, for this lifts us towards a better life.

Samuel Gridley Howe, then, as I judge, possessed in a high degree all the three kinds of courage of which I have spoken; and I will illustrate them all by the story of his life.

Personal courage loves danger for danger's sake; not because it is insensible to it, but because it enjoys its excitement and stimulus. What a strange attraction have war and the tumult of battle for many men! This courage of the battle-field is shared with man by his faithful companion, the horse, who rushes with joy into the thick of the fray; not from insensibility to danger, for he is a timid and imaginative creature, but because he is lifted, like man, above all fear, by the strange fascination of the battle-field. Two thousand years ago this had been noticed by the author of the Book of Job, who wrote of the horse:

" He saith among the trumpets 'ha ! ha !' and smelleth the battle afar off."

Dr. Howe, in this respect, was like one of the Knights of the Round Table. When he went to Greece to fight by the side of Byron; when he risked his life and liberty to help the Poles in their insurrection ; when he stood by Lafayette in the streets of Paris in the struggle of 1830 ; there was mingled with his sympathy for human freedom, something also of the " gaudium certaminis " — the delightful excitement of peril. But also there was the conviction that in each case there was a principle at stake, and that here was the eternal conflict for the rights of man ; and so the personal courage of the knight was joined with the moral courage of the hero. He was ready to die, but only in a good cause — *non indecoro pulvere sordidum.*

This marks the difference between personal courage and moral courage. Personal courage gives the joy of conflict ; moral courage adds to this a deeper joy, the satisfaction of fighting for truth, justice, freedom, humanity. It also enlarges the sphere of the battle ; lifting it to the vast field where principles of truth and falsehood contend in the grand struggle of reason with reason. And so, when the antislavery controversy began in this country, it was easy to see where Dr. Howe would be. With his friends, John G. Palfrey, Horace Mann, Charles Sumner, Theodore Parker,

John A. Andrew, Frank Bird, and others like them, his heart, voice, pen, purse, hand, were always given to the cause of the slave. How much he did in that cause few can tell, for he was a man who never spoke of his own past efforts or achievements. But it was always well understood that if any help was needed in that cause, Dr. Howe could be relied upon. I only saw Captain John Brown twice — once in Charles Sumner's room on Hancock Street. The other time it happened thus : I met Dr. Howe in the street one day, and he said, " Captain John Brown — Ossawattomie Brown — is in my office. He has a plan in view, and if you would like to help him, he will tell you something about it." I went to the office, and Captain Brown was there alone. He described to me what he had done in Missouri, carrying away slaves from the frontier through Kansas and Nebraska, and said, " I intend doing the same thing, on a larger scale, elsewhere; but where, and how, I keep to myself. My idea is to destroy the value of slave property along the border, and so drive slavery South." If John Brown, or any one else, had a blow to strike for humanity, he knew that he had an ally always ready in Dr. Howe.

But there is a third kind of courage which carries the soul up still higher. I call it Christian courage, because Jesus Christ possessed it in the highest degree. It is the courage which enables a

10

man to attempt the cure of the worst forms of
human suffering and sin, believing that he can
overcome them. Jesus Christ made himself the
physician to cure the worst diseases of the race.
He had the courage to attack all evil, believing
that he could put under his feet all enemies.

Social science, as popularly taught now, teaches
"the survival of the fittest." Its theory is that
the law of progress consists in the death of the
weak and sickly, and the survival of the healthy
and strong. According to this view, the best thing
that can happen is for all the feeble in mind and
body to die as soon as possible, and only the best
endowed natures to remain to continue their race.
The logic of this system would seem to be that
any one who provides hospitals for the sick, asy-
lums for the insane, houses of reformation for the
vicious, is really an enemy to human progress, by
keeping in existence those who had better be out
of the way.

The Christian theory teaches an exactly opposite view. It says, "If one member suffer, all
suffer." It regards the human race as one body,
and declares that the body can only be in health
when every part is in health. In its large philosophy it, indeed, encourages every attempt at
making the good better, the wise wiser, the
healthy more healthy; but its own special work
is to raise the fallen, heal the diseased, help the
weak, teach the ignorant. This was the sign

which Jesus gave to those who wished to know
if he were the Messiah; that the blind received
their sight, the lame walked, the lepers were
cleansed, the deaf heard, the dumb spake, the dead
were raised up, and that good news had come for
the poor.

To attempt this kind of work requires the highest kind of courage of all. And this is the work to
which Dr. Howe devoted the last forty years of his
life in Boston. He made himself — with all his
high gifts, his rare accomplishments, his knightly
courage — the servant of the blind, of the idiots,
the slaves, of the most friendless and the most forlorn. And I cannot but think that such a life and
such labors must do more to carry humanity forward than efforts exerted at the other end of the
scale. There is an inspiration about such generosity as this which kindles a similar enthusiasm,
and adds to the motive power of mankind. The
real progress of man consists in *giving him more
soul;* and how many souls have been quickened
by the work of our dead hero, who can tell?

One instance I happened to hear of, indirectly,
from a Western gentleman whom I once met.
He told me that a young woman, one of Dr.
Howe's teachers in the School for the Feeble
Minded, went out to Ohio and took charge of a
similar school just established in the capital of
that State. Her salary, paid by the State, was
only $300; but she refused the offer of twice that

sum to go and teach a private school in Kentucky, saying " that they could easily find others to go there, but she was afraid no one else would come to take care of her idiots." When this conduct of hers came to be known, members of the Legislature, before indifferent to the school, became interested in it, and one of them, who had been converted from infidelity to some faith in God by reading one of Theodore Parker's books, led the way in securing a good appropriation for the school. So these two friends, Dr. Howe and Theodore Parker, reached hands to each other in Ohio, and, ignorant of it themselves, kindled a flame of generous faith in God and man in that region.

> " How far that little candle sends its beams!
> So shines a good deed in this naughty world."

In this church, at Dr. Howe's funeral, last Thursday, was Laura Bridgman, mourning him who had come to her, when she, poor child, was shut into that dismal prison of fourfold darkness, to bring her into the light of knowledge. There she sat, with wisdom at five entrances quite shut out — eyes, ears, taste, smell, speech, all paralyzed. What courage it required to attack such a problem! What faith, what hope, what confidence in the powers of the soul ready to coöperate with his efforts; what patience, what ingenuity, what untiring industry! Tell me, wise man of this world! learned doctor of social science! what was the use of it all? Would it not have been better to expend the same time and toil on some healthy soul in a healthy body, giving a grand education to a perfectly developed genius? Leave out the principle of Christianity, which makes one brotherhood of us all, and it was a great mistake to squander this high art on such poor material. But no! it was an immortal soul, sitting in that shadow of death, and when he lifted her up and showed to her a little of the wonder and beauty of God's world, and gave her language, and brought her into communion with her race, he had done enough to make his life noble.

Dickens, in his "American Notes," quotes largely from Howe's account of this case, and says: —

"Well may this gentleman call that a delightful moment, in which some distant promise of her present state gleamed upon the darkened mind of Laura Bridgman. Throughout his life the recollection of that moment will be to him a source of pure, unfailing happiness; nor will it shine less brightly on the evening of his days of noble usefulness.

"Ye who have eyes and see not, ears and hear not; ye who are the hypocrites of sad countenances, learn healthy cheerfulness and mild contentment from the deaf and dumb and blind. Self-elected saints with gloomy brows, this sightless, earless, voiceless child may teach you lessons you will do well to follow. Let that poor hand of hers lie gently on your hearts, for there may be something in its healing akin to that of the great Master."

I have received the following account of the last visit made by Dr. Howe, a few weeks since, to the pupils of the School for the Feeble Minded. The teacher of the female department thus writes : —

"At his last visit to the school, on Sunday afternoon, about four weeks ago, the doctor seemed more genial and interested than I had seen him before. As he entered the school-room his face was radiant with smiles. The girls were singing a Sunday-school song, and had commenced the chorus, ' Hallelujah, thine be the glory, Revive us again ! ' Surprised at his sudden appearance, I was about to rise and welcome him, but he motioned me to continue playing, and he joined his voice with those of the children, beating time with his uplifted hand until the close of the strain. Then, turning to the children, he spoke these words in a pleasant but pathetic voice: ' I am glad to see you all, looking so well and happy. I hope you will be good children. Learn all you can.' Then, raising his right hand, and waving it towards them and over them, he said, ' Goodby, God bless you, good-by.' These were his last words to the school."

The teacher adds : —

"The scene was strangely significant and touching. The intense earnestness of his manner, the moment of entrance, as the children were singing the appeal, ' Revive us again,' his joining in the singing, his final benediction, all seemed prophetic, and we felt that this was the last visit to the school."

The teacher of the boys says : —

"He came in so quietly that I was not aware of his presence till he stood among us. Then, after his usual kind word to myself, came that tone of voice and expression of eye we have all learned to know so well, with which he said, 'Are you good children?' I told him we all missed him very much, and his lips quivered as he said softly, as if to himself, 'Poor children, it is little I can do for you.' Then, going suddenly amongst them, he patted the heads and cheeks of the little ones, and stretched out his hand over them as a benediction, feebly uttering the words, 'Be good children, be good.' This was our last remembrance of Dr. Howe. The children were silent; but in that deep hush there came an awe, as though they had looked upon the face of the dead. We realized that this was his final farewell. It was very sad and solemn, but very sweet. There can be no monument raised to his memory more lasting than will be his remembrance in the hearts of these children."

It was a great instance of courage, of chivalric courage, to go from Massachusetts in his youth to join in the terrible fight for Greece against the Turkish barbarians, where the mountains looked on Marathon, and Marathon looked on the sea. Surrounded by memories of old heroic days, amid classic scenes, under the shadow of Parnassus, amid the hum of Hyblean bees, this young medical student from Boston threw his arm and life into the arena. It was noble to carry help to the starving Poles in their desperate struggle against

the gigantic power of Russia. The same spirit
led him in after days to go again, to carry help
to the Isle of Crete, and to take part in the attempt to lift the people of San Domingo to better
fortunes. But was the courage less, or was it
greater, which devoted itself to the rescue of the
soul of Laura Bridgman and Oliver Caswell;
which plunged into the darkness of the mind of
the poor idiots to seek to give them light, and
which led the blind by a way they knew not into
intelligence and a happy future? To me it seems
that his last work was far greater than his first,
and that the chivalry of his youth was crowned by
the diviner and more gallant endeavors and suc-
cesses of his manhood and age.

> " Would'st know him now ? Behold him
>   The Cadmus of the blind,
> Giving the dumb lip language,
>   The idiot clay a mind.
> Walking his round of duty
>   Serenely, day by day,
> With the strong man's hand of labor,
>   And childhood's heart of play."

So active, energetic, industrious was this man,
that he made a part in all the best activities of
his time. He was intimately associated with La
Fayette and Lamartine in European republican-
ism, with Florence Nightingale in the care for the
sick, with Charles Sumner in the reform of pris-
ons, with Horace Mann in education, with John

Andrew in the war, with Dr. Cabot in helping
Kansas, with Henry Wilson in organizing the free
soil party, with John Brown in hostility to slavery,
with Dr. Bellows in the sanitary commission, with
Owen and McKaye in labor for the freedmen.
And when he was seventy years old, he went to
San Domingo as a commissioner, to examine the
condition of that island, and the expediency of
annexing the Republic to the United States.
There, for three months, he endured fatigues
which would have exhausted younger men, and
nothing could exceed the energy and judgment
shown by him in his extensive tours to obtain
information.

The lesson of this life is for us all. It may not
be given to us to fight for Greece, or Poland, or
France; to help Crete or San Domingo; to origi-
nate and carry on the education of the blind, or
that of the idiots, or to be the inspiration of a
sleeping soul, wakening it to life and light. But
the spirit in which he lived we all can have. We
also can do with our might whatever we find to
do. We can find our Greece close by — wherever
any man, or woman, or child, or lower animal is
oppressed by superior force. Near to each of us
are those who need our aid, as Laura Bridgman
needed his, and whom we can help by opening
the blind eyes, and leading the captive soul out
of its prison house. We may not have that lion

mood, that iron will, that fearless blood, that intense eye, that unmeasured power; but we also may be brethren and sisters of this fellowship of the brave and true, if we do in our way what he did in his.

VI.

WILLIAM ELLERY CHANNING.

WILLIAM ELLERY CHANNING.[1]

WHEN, twenty-five years ago to-day, the hills
of Berkshire stood solemn watchers while Channing breathed his last breath on earth, the hearts
of all noble men were moved, and two of our best
poets laid laurel-wreaths on his tomb.   From one
of them we take these lines : —

> " Thou livest in the life of all good things ;
>   The words thou spak'st for freedom shall not die.
> Thou sleepest not, for now thy Love hath wings
>   To soar where hence thy Hope could hardly fly.

> " And often, from that other world, on this
>   Some gleams, from great souls gone before, may shine,
> To shed on struggling hearts a clearer bliss,
>   And clothe the Right with lustre more divine."

It is twenty-five years since Channing died ;
but, during all this time, his spirit has been working in the Church and in the nation.   His faith
in man, in progress, in freedom, has been more
and more widely felt and received ; and were he

---

[1] Address, October 6, 1867, at services held in Arlington
Church, Boston, on the twenty-fifth anniversary of Dr. Channing's death.

to look upon us now, as perhaps he does, he would
see that his ideas are becoming the commanding
opinions of the land and time, — the " master-lights
of all our being."

Twenty-five years have already brought a new
generation on the stage, — one which did not know
him. Were he here, he would be eighty-seven
years old. I am glad to have the opportunity
to tell those younger than myself of what Channing was to my generation, — first, by his writings, and then by his character.

At the time when Channing began to preach, a
certain lethargy prevailed in the Church. A
sleepy orthodoxy and a drowsy liberalism stood
side by side in our pulpits. The letter, which
kills, had destroyed the living spirit. " The word
of the Lord was precious in those days ; there was
no open vision." I have heard my grandfather,
Dr. Freeman, describe the electric effect produced,
first by Buckminster, and then by Channing.
Dr. Freeman belonged himself to the old school
of Unitarians ; he was a scholar of Priestley and
Belsham ; but he had the head and the heart to
see and love the genius of a man like Channing.
He spoke of him as the greatest of thinkers, when
as yet he was not widely known to fame. Channing rose out of the region of opinions into that
of ideas. The ideas of human nature, of freedom,
of reason, and of progress, filled him with prophetic enthusiasm, and caused him to speak with

the tongue of men and of angels. Who that ever
heard him can forget that solemn fire of his eye,
that profound earnestness of tone, which took and
held captive all minds, from the beginning to the
end of his discourse? There was nothing like it,
nor second to it, in any pulpit of America. It was
not oratory, it was not rhetoric: it was pure soul,
uttering itself in thoughts clear and strong as the
current of a mighty stream. As we listened, we
forgot the weak tabernacle : we were mastered by
the thought of that mighty soul, which

> " Fretted the pigmy body to decay,
> And o'erinformed its tenement of clay."

The earth seemed good to live in, while we listened to him. It was a great thing to be a human
being. Life was too short for what we wished to
do in it. Christianity was such a holy gift that
to serve it was joy sufficient for this world. I
know at least one who never would have been a
Christian minister if he had not heard Channing ;
who blesses him to this hour for having directed
his steps into so noble a field of duty. The writings of Channing went through America and over
Europe, and filled millions of readers with admiration and love. I heard of a man in Wisconsin,
who, unable to buy the volume, copied with his
pen the whole of it from beginning to end. When
Dr. Channing wrote his book on slavery, I was
living in Kentucky, and reprinted several chapters
in a monthly journal I edited there ; and they

were read with interest by thousands. I knew a
Kentucky planter, to whom I gave his letter to
Henry Clay, who had it bound up with blank
leaves, took it in his pocket as he rode through
his fields, and filled it full of notes made during
his leisure moments. His son afterwards became
attorney-general under Abraham Lincoln, and one
of the strongest supporters of emancipation. Who
can tell how far Channing's thought has gone, and
how much of it was seed which grew up and bore
a hundred fold in the emancipation of a race in
America?

But it was not merely the great thought of
Channing, but his pure character, which has borne
this fruit. He gave an example of personal nobleness in all his life. He was the most accessible
of men. Young men, poor men, unknown men,
could visit him, and find him as ready to talk with
them as with the European *savans* and British
noblemen, who, as soon as they landed in Boston,
would find their way to the study of Dr. Channing
on Mount Vernon Street.

I owe a great debt of gratitude to Dr. Channing for his kindness to me, when, comparatively
a young man, I gathered a church in this city, —
in some respects differing from those then established. He sent for me to come and see him,
gave me invaluable advice and .encouragement,
and even came himself, evening after evening, to
the hall where we worshiped, and took a chair

near the pulpit. Before that, when I edited the "Western Messenger," he wrote for it a long and very valuable article on Catholicism, which any of the great reviews in England or America would have thankfully received, but which he gave to this obscure Western periodical. His kindness to all young men, to all struggling enterprises, his sympathy with every attempt to improve the age, came from his generous interest in truth, and his large expectation. When Mr. Garrison was the most unpopular man in Boston, and himself the most admired, Dr. Channing took him by the hand. When Abolition and Abolitionists were odious, Dr. Channing laid the weight of his great character in this scale. Of all the events of his life, there are few finer than that which was described afterwards by Miss Martineau. She says that, when a committee of the Massachusetts Legislature was in session to inquire whether some bill should not be enacted, making it a penal offense to publish, here in Massachusetts, anything against Southern slavery; and Mr. Garrison and his friends came before that committee to protest against any such law being passed, the door of the committee-room opened, and there stood Dr. Channing. He was invited by the committee to come and sit with them: but he walked across the room, came up to Garrison, took him by the hand, and sat down by his side; thus showing his determination, as he did on all occasions, to stand by any one whom it was attempted to oppress, no matter what was the weight of power against him.

In one of the last conversations I had with him, he told me that the wish of his life had been to write a work which should embody his views on the Philosophy of Man and on General Theology; "but," said he, "the cause of freedom demands all the little strength I have. I am continually called upon, by the occasions of the hour, to write pamphlets, which task all my strength; and I shall never be able, I foresee, to do the work which I had hoped was to be the work of my life."

Among all his noble traits, this ceaseless expectation, this undying hope, this sympathy with every new person who had anything to say for himself, every new movement which promised anything for itself, — this expectation, so tranquil and calm, but so ready, was one of the noblest.

Some men live always on the plane of what is common : they live in averages, and take life at low-water mark. Others rise and fall again, sometimes having a moment of enthusiasm, a sparkle of generosity, and then subsiding into their old routine. But Dr. Channing was always breathing the pure air of the mountain-top. Whenever you went into his room, he would begin some strain of a higher mood, some theme of pure religion, something which would lift you into the realm of eternal truths, something which would make you better and happier during the whole day. In this, he reminded me of what Goethe wrote concerning Schiller, in the service of commemoration after his death : —

> " For he was *ours;* and may this word of pride
> Drown with its lofty tone pain's bitter cry!
> With us, the fierce storm over, he could ride
> At anchor, in safe harbor, quietly.
> Yet onward did his mighty spirit stride,
> To beauty, goodness, truth, eternally ;
> And far behind, in mists dissolved away,
> That which confines us all, — the Common, — lay."

I remember Dr. Channing once telling me, that, of all the words of Jesus, nothing struck him more than his saying to the Jews around him, " Be perfect, as your Father in heaven is perfect." " Why," said he, " when I consider what kind of people they were ; when I consider the hardness of their hearts, the barrenness of their minds, — the faith in humanity which could inspire such a saying as that, seems to me a marvel of the love of Jesus. You or I," said he, " would just as soon have thought of saying to these chairs and tables, ' Be ye perfect, as your Father in heaven is perfect,' as to those men."

I recall a day in October spent at his house in Newport, during the whole of which he talked of the need of more spiritual life. The topic of that long conversation was *life:* that we might have more life ; that we might have it more abun-

dantly; that we might have it in the nation; that
we might have it in the churches; that we might
find it in our own souls. It was like one of the
Dialogues of Plato; it was like the " Phædo;" it
was like the apology.of Socrates before his judges.
It was a strain, all through the day, of aspiration,
expectation, hope.

I quoted two verses from Lowell, written after
Dr. Channing's death, in commencing these remarks; and now, in closing them, I will quote
some lines, written at the same time, by our other
great American poet, Whittier : —

> " Not vainly did old poets tell,
>   Nor vainly did old genius paint,
>   God's great and crowning miracle, —
>   The hero and the saint.
>
> " For, even in a faithless day,
>   Can we our sainted ones discern
>   And feel, while with them on the way,
>   Our hearts within us burn.
>
> " And thus the common tongue and pen,
>   Which, world-wide, echo Channing's fame,
>   As one of Heaven's anointed men,
>   Have sanctified his name.
>
> " In vain shall Rome her portals bar,
>   And shut from him her saintly prize,
>   Whom, in the world's great calendar,
>   All men shall canonize.
>
> " How echoes yet each Western hill
>   And vale with Channing's dying word !
>   How are the hearts of freemen still
>   By that great warning stirred !

" Swart smiters of the glowing steel,
  Dark feeders of the forge's flame,
Pale watchers at the loom and wheel,
  Repeat his honored name.

" Where is the victory of the grave ?
  What dust upon the spirit lies ?
God keeps the sacred life he gave :
  The prophet never dies."

VII.

WALTER CHANNING

AND SOME OF HIS CONTEMPORARIES.

WALTER CHANNING AND SOME OF HIS CONTEMPORARIES.[1]

A GOOD physician has a hard life in many ways. His work is on the shady side of life, by the bed of sickness and pain — sickness which he often cannot cure, pain which he is sometimes unable to alleviate. He has great responsibilities, involving grave anxieties. The life, health, happiness of others depend much on his wisdom, attention, promptness, fidelity. Most of us do our day's work and then go home to rest or to amuse ourselves, to turn to favorite studies or go into pleasant society. The work of the physician never ends. He never can rest without the possibility of being suddenly summoned back to his duties. If he is not actually called he is always in expectation of being called, and that interferes with perfect rest. He is a sentinel who cannot sleep on his post. His work continues through night and day, through storm and shine, through heat and cold, through summer and winter. Other men may take their vacation, but wherever he goes,

[1] A sermon preached after Dr. Channing's death.

the lightning message follows after and asks, " Where are you ? "   At home, he is the slave of the door-bell ; abroad, of the telegraph.

Yet, with all this labor, care, anxiety, a physician's life has many compensations ; compensations so great that, when a person is able to fulfill its duties aright, it is one of the happiest of all professions.   The good physician has the consciousness of usefulness in his work.   The family physician studies the constitutions of the members of a household ; he is able to advise them in regard to . diet, air, exercise, work, and recreation.   He foresees danger before it comes, and shows them how to avoid it.   If prevention is better than cure, modern medical science which tends that way, is certainly better than that of our fathers.   But when the inevitable disease arrives, then the use of the physician appears in alleviations of pain, in taking charge of the case and so relieving the anxieties of the patient and his friends.   When we have confided our beloved ones to the care of the wise and faithful physician, we have a sense of reposing trust.   If all drugs were abolished, I do not think the need and use of a physician could be sensibly diminished — perhaps it would be increased.   All this is compensation for his toil and anxiety, but more still is the affection which gathers around him.   The apostle has indicated this reward of the profession in one striking epithet, " Luke, the *beloved* physician."   He does

not say " the wise," " the learned," " the celebrated," physician, but the " beloved." The good
physician becomes a friend in many homes. Grateful love attends his footsteps. As his life ad-
vances, there grows up around him a neighborhood filled with friends. He is the friend of old
and young, for all need his care, and depend on
his counsel. He becomes intimately acquainted
with the interior life of many families; but you
will notice that a physician is very seldom a gos-
sip. He no more thinks of speaking abroad of
what is confided to him, than if he were a father-
confessor ; as, indeed, he often is. And he who
is able to inspire confidence in another helps
the body through the mind, as daily experience
teaches. We all feel the truth of what Walter Scott
says : —

> I have lain on the sick man's bed,
> Watching for hours for the leech's tread,
> As if I deemed that his presence alone
> Had power to bid my pains begone.
> I have listed his words of comfort given
> As if to oracles from Heaven,
> I have counted his steps from my chamber door,
> And blessed them when they were heard no more.

I have made these remarks in reference to the
recent death of one who has had a long career as
a physician in this city, and has been connected
with most important persons and events in Boston
during more than half a century. Dr. Walter
Channing was appointed a medical professor in

Harvard University sixty-one years ago, and physician in the Massachusetts General Hospital at its very commencement, fifty-five years ago. He was one of the Boston Society of Natural History, and took part in most of the movements which have identified Boston with philanthropic reform, educational progress, and an advanced civilization. As he grew older, he did not, like many men, refuse to admit new discoveries and improvements. At the age of fifty-nine he fought actively for the introduction of pure water into Boston. When he was sixty-two he took the lead in introducing the use of ether into medical practice as a means of alleviating pain. When he was seventy-one he published a work on "Reform in Medical Science," and when seventy-two, became consulting physician to the New England Hospital for Women and Children. He was a true child of Boston, in always loving to tell or hear some new thing. This is a habit of Boston people, whence, perhaps, our city has been called the modern Athens. I have been told that in Dr. Channing's lectures he could easily be diverted from his main subject, and use up his time in speaking of some recent theory. But I have also been assured by one of his oldest students that when his notice was called to any important question, or any serious case, his whole attention was given to the matter before him. In such instances his patience and devotion never failed. To help the youngest physician who asked his aid, or to visit the poorest patient that needed his presence, he would go at any time of the day or the night. All *real* physicians, I know, do this ; but physicians themselves have spoken to me of Dr. Channing's loyalty to such calls as something to be specially noticed. How often, in observing these conscientious, unselfish services of medical men, services which bring to them neither renown nor pecuniary reward, I have thought of the touching lines of Dr. Johnson to his poor old friend Dr. Levett : —

> In misery's darkest cavern known
>   His useful care was ever nigh,
> When fainting anguish poured her groan,
>   And lonely want retired to die.
> No summons, mocked by chill delay ;
>   No petty gain, disdained by pride ;
> The modest wants of every day
>   The toil of every day supplied.

That medical men are often wanting in religious convictions and religious sentiment is an old charge, mentioned by Sir Thomas Browne in his " Religion of a Physician." That the study of natural causes disinclines to the belief in supernatural ones is certain ; and hence the remark, that " where there are three physicians there are two atheists." But there is no such opposition between the large and profound study of nature and a reasonable form of religious faith. Two of the wisest physicians whom Boston has had and lost in my day, Dr. James Jackson and Dr. John

Ware, were religious men in the noblest sense. Both of them told me that they considered it an advantage to have their patients visited by a sensible minister, who should come not to agitate, but to give calmness, hope, and courage. Such physicians are themselves gospel ministers. When Jesus compared himself to a physician, he accepted this work as in the same line with his own; certainly not in opposition to it. He who makes the soul sound helps the body; he who makes the body sound helps the soul. Maladies of the body affect the soul; a diseased soul reacts on the body.

In Walter Channing, belief and sentiment both ran together in a common religious channel. At least it was so when I knew him. When the Church of the Disciples was founded in Boston, he became a member at the first. He took part in our meetings, and often presided over the Bible class, which then consisted of fifty to a hundred men and women, meeting on Sunday afternoon. In that early day, when I was absent, laymen belonging to the church would also conduct the service and preach a sermon, and this Walter Channing would do, in his turn. He was glad to visit the poorest member in the church; and, though in full practice, would give them a generous portion of his time. I once called to see a lady who was an invalid, a devout and refined person, and she told me she had received a delightful visit from Dr. Channing. After he had prescribed for her malady, she asked him if he could tell her anything comforting, and he said " Yes ; the most comforting thing ever spoken ; " and then repeated a large part of the chapters in John, beginning " Let not your heart be troubled."

Generations are bonded together, like bricks in a well-laid wall where the joints are broken, or like shingles on a roof : each generation overlapping the two which follow it, and underlapping the two which precede it. Thus there are always three generations in a community at the same time, and every long-lived man transmits the knowledge, manners, and moral life of his parents and grandparents to his children and grandchildren. This preserves the character of a community amid the continual arrival and departure of individuals, as the identity of the human body remains amid a perpetual flux of all its atoms. I recollect, some years ago, hearing the late John G. King of Salem say that, when he was a child, his grandmother had told him that her grandmother had told her how she had gone with her mother to a witch trial in Salem, and that the trial was in a church with high backed pews, and how her mother wore a red cloak, as was not unusual then ; and that one of the witnesses cried out that " the little woman in the red cloak was sticking pins in her," and that her mother, terribly frightened, had crouched down behind the pew. This little piece

of life had thus come to me by only three steps
from that time, nearly two centuries ago. Thus a
single long life is a telegraphic wire from one age
to another, transmitting its thoughts and its spirit.

Dr. Channing began to practice medicine in
Boston in 1812, — sixty-four years ago. From a
copy of the Massachusetts Register of that year I
learn these facts : In that year Elbridge Gerry,
one of the signers of the Declaration of Independence, was Governor of Massachusetts. So near
were they then to the Revolution. William Gray,
the greatest ship-owner in America, was Lieutenant-
governor. In the Senate, as a member from Boston, was Harrison Gray Otis, and the speaker of
the House was Joseph Story of Salem, afterwards
Judge Story. Among the members of the House
from Boston were William Sullivan, that courteous and stately gentleman whom many yet well
remember ; Benjamin Russell, for many years the
leading Federal editor in Boston ; Lemuel Shaw,
afterwards Chief Justice, and James Savage, the
historian and genealogist. The whole of Maine
was then a part of Massachusetts ; consequently
we find in this Legislature members not only from
Portland, Bath, and Augusta, but from Mount
Desert, Castine, Eastport, and Calais. Boston, the Register tells us, had then only 33,000
inhabitants. The Irish population of Boston to-
day are twice as numerous as the whole population
then. It was not a city till long after ; the whole

people met in Faneuil Hall for town-meeting, and
voted money to lay out streets and pave them. It
was governed by nine selectmen, — among whom
I find the names of Charles Bulfinch, the architect
who built the State-house, and Ebenezer Oliver,
whom I remember seeing, when I was a boy, in
his pew in King's Chapel. Among the overseers
of the poor were Joseph Coolidge, Jr., another
King's Chapel gentleman, and Jonathan Phillips,
the friend of William Ellery Channing. William
E. Channing, then a young minister not much
known to fame, was on the school committee with
another young minister already very famous,
Joseph Stevens Buckminster, and still another
young minister, whom many of us remember well,
Charles Lowell.

In this year, 1812, when Walter Channing
opened his office, there were only forty-six physicians in Boston, among whom were some well-
remembered names, as Dr. Danforth, rough in his
ways but sagacious, and Dr. Dexter, much beloved in families ; and Drs. Spooner, Ingalls, Dix-
well, Shurtleff, and Gorman ; Dr. John C. War-
ren, the famous surgeon living at 7 Park Street,
Dr. Randall on Winter Street, Dr. Shattuck on
Cambridge Street, — where they continued to live
and practice for long years. Out of the whole
list of forty-six who were here in 1812, only one
remains, honored and beloved, the last survivor of
that race of good physicians, Jacob Bigelow.

There were only twenty-nine churches in Boston in 1812. Wm. E. Channing was minister of Federal Street; Horace Holley, a famous orator in his day, drawing crowds to hear him, thought to be somewhat of a heretic, was at Hollis Street; Charles Lowell at the West Church; John Murray, founder of Universalism in America, was in Bennet Street; Thatcher at the New South Church; James Freeman and Samuel Cary at King's Chapel; Buckminster, that soul of fire, at Brattle Street; and the good Catholic Bishop Cheverus, whom all men loved, was in Franklin Street. There was one Methodist church and five Baptist churches.

Among the lawyers of Boston, in 1812, were Samuel Dexter, Harrison Gray Otis, Timothy Fuller (father of Margaret Fuller), William Minot (whose venerable and benign countenance has only lately disappeared from our midst), James Savage (the antiquarian), William Sullivan and his brother George, Samuel F. McCleary, Benjamin Guild, and David S. Greenough. The descendants of these men who helped to form the institutions of our city are still among us.

Dr. Kirkland was president of Harvard College in 1812, and of the corporation, overseers, and twenty professors and tutors, not one remains. Professor Farrar, a man of genius, taught mathematics then, as he did in my time. The library, which now contains 155,000 volumes, had then

'17,000. There were only twenty officers and teachers then; now there are 145. Among the names of the corporation and overseers I find those of John Lothrop, Abiel Holmes, William E. Channing, Joseph Stevens Buckminster, Horace Holley, Governor Gore, Judge Dawes, Samuel Dexter, Josiah Quincy, Nathaniel Bowditch, Theophilus Parsons, Oliver Wendell, and John Lowell.

Boston was then a small town, but a very pleasant one. There was no gas, nor Cochituate water; no railroads, steamboats, or telegraphs. There were large gardens in different parts of the town, and the cows fed on the Common and were driven home at night. The great merchants, like Joseph Coolidge, Samuel Parkman, Theodore Lyman, Thomas H. Perkins, Israel Thorndike, William Gray, Governor Phillips, and Henderson Inches, lived in large, square, comfortable brick houses, with gardens behind and spacious areas in front. The houses of Governor Phillips and Gardner Greene occupied, when I went to the Latin School, nearly the whole space in Tremont Street from School Street round to Court Street, including Pemberton Square. One old black-looking house, with diamond window-glass set in lead, stood opposite to our present Museum. It was the house in which Sir Harry Vane had lived, which had remained down to that time.

I have mentioned among the merchants of that day Thomas H. Perkins. He was a type of the

large-minded, generous, and princely merchants
of Boston, who early set the example of using
their wealth for public ends. These were the
men who endowed Harvard College and founded
the Massachusetts Hospital and the Athenæum,
and gave liberally to all good objects. Colonel
Perkins, as is well known, was the great benefac-
tor to the blind asylum which bears his name.
The charities of Boston, in fact, date far back. In
this Register of 1812 I find a large number already established — such as the Boston Dispensary;
the Massachusetts Charitable Society ; the Irish,
Scotch, Episcopal, and Congregational Charitable
Societies; the Charitable Fire Society ; the Charitable Mechanic Association ; the Female Asylum ;
the Boylston and Franklin Donations ; the Humane Society ; and many missionary and educational associations. Wealth in Boston has always
tended toward such good objects as these.

Those who grow up among good institutions, institutions of education, of religion — who live in
a city like Boston, with its beautiful common, its
public library, its churches and schools, its hospitals and charities, are apt to think that these
things come of themselves, by some natural process of evolution. They forget the wisdom, the
energy, the generosity, the high ideal aims, which
have combined to produce them. These institutions, our noble heritage, are the gifts of those who
have gone before us. They were built up by men

inspired by a liberal Christianity, — for Boston has always been the home of liberal Christianity. They are legacies left us by large-souled men and women, who have walked these streets before us with minds meditating good works. They have not come of themselves. All such institutions had to be fought for, prayed for, worked for. They were resisted then, as they are resisted now, by the dead weight of indifference, by the active opposition of combined selfishness, by personal interest and blind prejudice. And this is why we ought to remember those who, amid bitter opposition, held on and conquered, and left us these fair results. "Other men labored ; ye have entered into their labors."

In that company was the wise physician, James Jackson. He stood at the head of his profession, unequaled in his sagacious, clear judgments, his benign good-will, his unspotted Christian character. He also left his stamp on his time, a stamp not to be effaced. The whole medical profession in Boston occupies a higher position of honor and usefulness because of this one life.

Nor can we forget the upright statesman, magistrate, and scholar, — who led a life of such varied usefulness, as member of Congress, mayor of Boston, president of Harvard College, — Josiah Quincy. He stood among us as one of the solid pillars of our social edifice. Boston rested on him, and felt safe. He was embodied integrity ; not to be touched by anything low, anything mean. We may apply the Scripture blessing to any community where such men live, and say: "Happy the people that are in such a case." Through such honorable citizens, such pure lives, religion becomes incarnate as goodness. Christianity, too often deemed only a creed or a profession, is seen as a living, working power to sustain the whole of society in right-doing.

In the letters of John Adams to his wife, we learn that the people of Massachusetts, as late as a hundred years ago, had a prejudice against lawyers, and thought them not safe or useful citizens. The lawyers of Dr. Channing's generation, and those who have succeeded them, have left a record which has effaced all such prejudices. The judges in our courts, from the days of Theophilus Parsons until now — the bar of Suffolk, illustrated by such upright, pure, and useful men, have raised the standard of intelligence, refinement, and character in this community. I will not stop to repeat names familiar to all of you.

The year 1812, when Walter Channing commenced practice in Boston, was the beginning of what we call the last war with Great Britain. May it always bear that name! Madison was President; George Clinton, Vice-president; Henry Clay, speaker of the House of Representatives. The naval force of the United States in commission consisted of six frigates and a few brigs. With this lilliputian fleet, we went out to attack Great

Britain, ruler of the seas. It was like little David
going to fight Goliath. But what events have
intervened since the day when Walter Channing
began his modest practice in Boston till the day
he was carried to his grave! How this nation
has extended from sea to sea! How it has developed art, literature, agriculture, commerce, manu-
factures! What difficulties it has surmounted,
what sufferings borne! And when we look back
on what has occurred in the course of a single
human life, can we help thanking God and taking
courage? Thanking God, — for if there is a
Providence in human affairs we must see it in
ours. If God led the Israelites through the Red
Sea and the wilderness to the promised land,
surely he has guided our feet through the terrible
trials of civil war to universal freedom and national integrity. And shall we not take courage
in looking back over the past ninety years? We
have still, no doubt, many evils to contend with,
many trials to encounter. Folly and corruption
are to be found among us still; many reforms are
still needed; but the God of our fathers is ours,
and the plant they planted and watered — the
plant of a liberal and practical Christianity, of
freedom joined with order, of liberty guided by
justice, that plant is still to grow and spread and
bear fruit for the healing of the nations and the
blessing of mankind. Looking back, then, on our
fathers' honorable and useful lives, let us manfully

take their places and do their work. Grateful for
the institutions they founded, let us cherish and
improve them. We are not here for our sakes
alone. We are members of a great body; we
belong to the past and to the future. If we were
only here to make money for ourselves, to get
position and reputation for ourselves, and then
die, that would be a small affair. But we are
here as the representatives of all who have gone
before us; taking their places when they go, accepting their responsibilities. We are here to
support and elevate the schools, the churches, all
the good methods which they initiated. If we
abdicate this position, selfishly indifferent to the
mother-land which has cherished us, cynically
despising the human life around us, thinking it
a fine thing to neglect doing anything for society,
while we criticise what is done by others, we
are degenerate sons of Boston. But let us rather
gladly take our part in all that will lift and help
others, so that when we shall follow this "innumerable caravan" to the mysterious Beyond, and
meet our fathers there, we shall not hear from
their lips the sad rebuke: "O negligent children!
we labored and toiled that you might be born
amid the influences of religion, education, and good
manners, and you have hidden your talent in a
napkin. When your brothers were marching to
battle, you have stepped out of the ranks and gone

to the rear. O degenerate children, why have you thus dishonored our names?"

Let it not be so with us; but, while we remain, let us each do with our might what our hands find to do, for truth and humanity, for God and for man.

VIII.

EZRA STILES GANNETT.

EZRA STILES GANNETT.

———

ONCE, after a long and severe illness, I was walking on Boston Common, and met Dr. James Jackson. The wise and kind old man took my arm and went a little way with me, while he made these remarks: "I will say to you what I once said to Henry Ware. Let us estimate a man's usefulness in a community at some number — say ten. If the man continues to live in the place ten years, then, though he may only do just as much work as he did at first, his influence is no longer ten but twenty. Simply by continuing to work, his usefulness is doubled, because each year he is extending his acquaintance and becoming better known. But if, by inattention to his health and by neglecting the laws of his physical nature, he becomes an invalid, he never reaches that point of influence represented by twenty. Good morning, sir."

Dr. Gannett, long before his death, had become such an influence in Boston. We all felt a little better and happier for knowing that he was living

among us. He was one of the men who gave
character to the city. Wherever he was seen
passing with his rapid step, jumping along on his
two canes, men felt the presence of the Sense of
Duty. Conscience was incarnate before their
eyes. The Moral Sense was made flesh, and dwelt
among them. Such a man, by continuing to live,
does more for a city than half a dozen banks,
and is a greater power than the whole Common
Council.

In Dr. Gannett we have lost, I fear, the last
man in our circle who had a full sense of ministerial brotherhood. He believed, with all his heart,
in the brotherhood of the clergy. No man ever
stood by his order as heartily as he. How he
loved the meeting of ministers — how he welcomed them to his hospitable table — what loyalty he manifested to all his brethren! He never
could think ill of a brother minister. He always
gave to them " the benefit of clergy." When a
young man passed from the ranks of the divinity
students into that of the ministers, he felt himself
welcomed by that cordial hand to a new sphere.
No matter who gave the formal " right hand " at
his ordination, that pressure of Dr. Gannett's was
the real " right hand of fellowship." It almost
seemed as if he regarded ordination in the Catholic sense, as a sacrament communicating some
new spiritual quality to him who received it. To
him all his ministerial brethren were sacred and

sanctified. Brother A. might seem to others dull, brother B. a bigot, brother C. too self-indulgent, brother D. a cold, dry man. Not so to him. He refused to recognize anything but good in them. He himself, the very opposite to them in all these things, never seemed to have the sense of their defects. Or, if his sharp eye could not help noticing them, he spoke of them with a smile, as one notices a trifling blemish on some great work of art. He was " The Last of the Brethren."

It was among the mountains that I heard of the terrible disaster which desolated so many homes, and took from us our father and friend. When my first shock of surprise and grief was over, I said, "What does it matter to him how he went? " Death fell on him suddenly, unexpectedly, but it did not find him unprepared. The Litany of the Episcopal Church deprecates " sudden death." The improved form of it, as used in the King's Chapel service, prays to be delivered, not from " sudden death," but from " death unprepared for," which is a better prayer. All of Dr. Gannett's life was a preparation for death. I think he was the most conscientious man I ever knew. He was even *too* conscientious. His conscience was often a morbid one, or rather a tyrannical one, and ruled him too despotically. He never seemed to forgive in himself what he willingly forgave in others. He went mourning all his days because he could not attain his own lofty ideal of duty. He was only contented when he could be making sacrifices, renouncing comfort, giving up something to some one else, denying himself and taking up his cross. That, to him, was the chief command of Christ, and he lived a life of perpetual, remorseless self-denial and labor. He ought to have been an anchorite — a hermit, living on herbs, in a cave, in order to be satisfied. And certainly, when we think how our life runs to luxury and self-indulgence, it was a great thing to have among us one man who never indulged himself, but always longed to bear hardship as a good soldier of Christ. I do not think he ever quite saw that side of the Gospel which brings pardon and peace to the soul, and makes us feel as safe in the love of God as the little child feels safe, sleeping in its small crib by the side of its mother. I often longed that he should see more of this part of Christianity, and thought what immense power he would have to shake society, and pour into it a new revival of faith and love, if to all his other gifts he could have added a fuller faith in the pardoning love of God. I do not mean that he doubted or denied it, but he never seemed to me wholly to realize it. He could believe that God would pardon the sins of others, but not his own. This deprived him of a portion of the power he would otherwise have had, and threw a certain austerity into his services, which made them too severe for young and sensitive natures. His young

people sometimes left him for churches where
there was more comfort and hope, and then he
blamed himself for it, as he did for every trial
that befell him. But it was no fault of his — he
was made so; his conscience was too strong for
him, and, as I said, too despotic.

And yet how sweet he was! What a lovely
smile of affection played on his lips as he met
you! how warm and generous his greeting! how
glad he was to do full justice to the work of
others! how tender his sympathies! and how his
sense of justice flamed against evil and wrong
everywhere.

Here let me relate a little anecdote. I once
went into Theodore Parker's study, just after Dr.
Gannet had preached a sermon in which he maintained it to be our duty, under the Constitution, to
return fugitives to slavery. For no man had more
the courage of his opinions than he; what his
mind thought, that his tongue uttered. His truthfulness was perfect. He was perhaps often a little too subtle in his reasonings, and so seemed
to argue like a lawyer, with special pleading.
But this was merely because his mind was naturally very quick, very acute, and keen rather than
broad. But he was always the incarnation of
truthfulness; and if he believed a thing, no mortal
power could keep him from expressing it. So,
against his sympathies, which were always with
the unhappy, he had preached his sermon, taking

13

what was called conservative ground. When I
went into Theodore Parker's study, he was reading this sermon, and expressed his indignation
strongly against Gannett. I said : " Theodore,
I wish to tell you a story which I lately heard
about Gannett." So I told him of a case of a
poor, wretched, despised character, whom Gannett had devoted himself to helping and saving.
I told, as I had heard it, how he spared himself
no time, labor, nor reproach, to save this one
brand from the burning. When I finished, Parker's eyes were full of tears, and he said, " Well,
he is a dear, good old soul after all."

And the other day, looking over some old letters,
I found one relating to the time when Parker was
most offensive to the conservatives, and it was
proposed to put him out of the Boston Association. Dr. Gannett and John Pierpont were
among the few of the older members who opposed
it. He disliked and feared Parker's views, but
he would not consent to the spirit of exclusion or
persecution, and he resisted it with all the fire
and ardor of his eloquence ; and it was so resisted
by him and by others that every such attempt was
defeated.

For he was one to whom that often used, much
abused, word, eloquence, might justly be applied.
When he kindled into flame, his words had a
singular power, which pervaded and charmed an
audience. I never have known a greater mag-

netism than they exercised at such moments. His
power of language was so great, he was so fluent
and affluent in his expression, and so inspired by
his passion, that he swept away all our coldness,
and was almost sure of carrying his cause, whatever it was, right or wrong. To him his opinion
was not only right, but absolutely right; and his
smallest judgment seemed to him to be freighted
with immense consequences; and this sincerity of
passion was very apt to make even a poor argument triumphant.

In regard to all matters of this world, Gannett was the most disinterested of men. It was
impossible to make him accept a favor, or allow
anything to be done for him which he could do
himself. Once his congregation voted an increase
of salary. He refused to accept it. They paid
no attention to his refusal, and when quarter-day
came the treasurer paid him according to the new
tariff. He sent back the surplus. The treasurer
returned it, saying he had no right *not* to pay it.
Gannett sent it back again, and became so indig-
nant at their persisting to pay him that at last
they could merely lay it aidse and let it accumulate till they could do something with it for his
benefit. Whether they succeeded in this I have
never learned. When I heard the story, their
failure was a decided one.

He is happy now. Now he is able to see that
side of the gospel which, during life, was too

much hidden from his eyes. At last he has entered into his rest. Peaceful close of a tumultuous and laborious day — sweet sense of calm after many a storm. I grieve not for his death. I thank God for what he has been, and for what he has done; and I am grateful for that noble, generous, never-resting, always-aspiring and struggling soul, which one day we shall meet again, in a state where, all his limitations removed, he will be an angel both of power and of peace in the many mansions of the Heavenly Father.

IX.

SAMUEL JOSEPH MAY.

SAMUEL JOSEPH MAY.

I HAVE just been reading, with much interest, the biography of this remarkable man. I am glad that the work fell into the hands of one who has made of it a labor of love. The writer was one of Mr. May's " children " — one of the many drawn into the ministry by the encouragement and welcome which he always gave to young men of promise. In fact, the view of the ministry taken by Mr. May was so cheerful, hopeful, practical, that its work, as illustrated by himself, was attractive. In the ministry he knew no constraint. He was free as air. All trammels of custom, all formalities of the profession, dropped away from him. He was free, and made others free, wherever he came. And this he did without complaint, railing, or dispute. Some men are born free ; others have liberty thrust upon them ; and some gain it through a bitter conflict, which leaves them a little sour and cynical. Mr. May's freedom was of the first sort.

I also received, from some kind friend, a pamphlet containing the services, in Syracuse, at the funeral of this good man. All in the book is good, except the black lines of mourning around the pages. Such emblems of sorrow, at the birth into a higher state of a Christian soul, are seldom appropriate, and never less so than at the departure of such a man as Samuel J. May. If the Republican journals in Illinois had been draped in mourning when Abraham Lincoln was chosen President, because he was about to leave the State and reside in Washington, it would not have been more inappropriate than to do this on the occasion of the departure of Samuel Joseph May to a higher work and a serener joy.

Mr. May's father, Colonel Joseph May, was one of those striking figures not easily forgotten. As a boy attending King's Chapel, I recollect him passing our pew every Sunday morning, on his way from the vestry to his own seat; his sharp, clear eye, firm step, knee-breeches, and shoe-buckles giving the impression of a noticeable character. From his distant pew, his voice, in response to the minister, came louder than that of the clerk close by. That clerk was, in those days, Mr. Joseph T. Buckingham, who rather slighted his responses, as it seemed to us young folks. However that may be, Colonel May's responses made an essential part of the service to our minds, and we should have regarded the ceremonies as incomplete without them.

Colonel May was an upright, intelligent, determined character; universally respected, and one of the earliest and firmest supporters of Dr. Freeman in his movement in behalf of a reformed liturgy and a Liberal Christianity. Between the two, as long as both lived, there was an indissoluble friendship, — such an one as exists between those who have fought side by side in the same battle for truth and freedom.

A graduate of Harvard University, both in its Academic Department and its Divinity School, Samuel J. May began life under conditions which might have made him conservative in politics and morals. But it was otherwise determined; and his first step in radicalism he took at the Divinity School, under the guidance of that good man, Dr. Henry Ware, the elder.

Down to the time of his entering the Divinity School, Mr. May had never thought much on theological questions, but had reverently received the instructions of his father and pastor. But now he had great questions laid before him, and was told to look at both sides faithfully. He was too honest to pretend to look at both sides while he only saw the reasons for one, and not those in favor of the other. Being honest, he honestly weighed the arguments in favor of opposing opinions, and soon found himself in a condition of doubt. One by one, every belief he had been taught to revere became uncertain. He had become a skeptic, so it seemed to him, in regard to all the main doctrines which he was expecting by and by to preach. Under these circumstances there was only one thing for him to do. It was a hard thing to disappoint his father's hopes and his own, and renounce the ministry, but he must do it. So he went to see Dr. Ware, the head of the Divinity School, and mustered courage to tell him that he must quit the school and give up his profession. He then described the state of mind into which he had fallen. When he had finished, and was waiting, expecting to be rebuked for his skepticism, Dr. Ware looked at him from under his bushy eyebrows, and over his large spectacles, and said, quietly, "I am very glad to hear all this." Struck dumb with astonishment, the youth could only stare in silence. The good man proceeded: "Yes, I am very glad to hear it. It shows you have begun to think. To doubt is the beginning of belief. Go on thinking. Do not be afraid — you will come out all right. You are doing what you came to this place for — you are really thinking. It is an excellent sign."

This lesson was never lost on Mr. May. He continued all his life to think for himself on all subjects, and advised all others to do the same. He was hospitable to all honest thought. The following anecdote was told me, many years ago, by the gentleman who is its subject : —

A youth in Brooklyn, Conn., a farmer's son,

was seized with a desire to study for the ministry. So he went to Mr. May, told him his wishes, said he had only received a common-school education, and asked what he should study. Mr. May gave him "Locke on the Understanding," and told him to read it through carefully. Some two or three months after, meeting the young man, he asked him how he got on with the book. "Rather slowly," replied the student. Nothing further occurred until a year had passed. At the end of that time the young man returned the book, and said, "It is of no use, Mr. May, for me to try to be a student. You see it has taken me a whole year to read one book." "But let us see," said Mr. May, "what you know about it." On examination, it appeared that the youth knew everything in these volumes. There was not a point made anywhere but he knew all about it. He had mastered the whole argument. Whereupon Mr. May assured him that a year spent in this way in studying one work was itself a liberal education. He encouraged him to pursue his studies. I afterward met, in the West, this *" homo unius libri,"* and found him a most intelligent and able man ; and he told me he owed to the encouragement and good advice of Mr. May his success in life.

It was while Mr. May was preaching to the society in Brooklyn, Conn., that he became the champion of an oppressed woman, Miss Prudence

Crandall. This lady was guilty of the grave offense of opening a school for colored young women, in the adjoining town of Canterbury. The Legislature of Connecticut passed an act forbidding any teaching, within that State, of colored youth from other States. She continued to teach; her school was broken up by a mob, and she herself imprisoned. Mr. May stood by her side and advocated her cause in the meetings called to denounce her and to put her down. This excited opposition to him in his own society, and one man, a neighbor, was especially abusive in his language concerning Mr. May. Mr. May took no notice of this at the time, made no reply to the attacks, and would not allow his friends to reply to them. Some time after, driving past his neighbor's garden, he saw him at work there. He stopped his horse, and said, in those pleasant tones which no one will forget who ever heard them, "My dear sir, what fine melons you have there! I wish you would give me one for my wife; she is very fond of melons, and I have seen none as good as yours this summer." Nothing which could have been said or done could have convinced the man so entirely that Mr. May cherished no ill-will toward his assailant. So — confused, joyful, and grateful — he cried out, " A dozen, Mr. May, let me give you a dozen. I will bring them myself to your house." Mr. May at first declined this abundant civility, but as the man insisted, he allowed him to do so. From that hour the opponent became his devoted friend, and when Mr. May left Brooklyn this man took leave of him with tears.

Mr. May was one of the earliest friends and fellow-workers with Mr. Garrison in the antislavery cause. It is a great thing for a young man or woman to be taken hold of by some generous idea or great truth. It transforms, renews, transfigures life. Mr. May was not by nature a man of genius. He had in him good blood, and came of a good stock, — of an honest, patriotic, truth-loving race. He was early convinced of the truth of the antislavery doctrine, and was so honest that he at once gave his adherence to it ; and that made him a man of power. In those days it was exceedingly unpopular, even in Boston. One can hardly believe, what yet is a fact, that Mr. May, having arranged to preach in Hollis Street for John Pierpont, was besought by men in that society, who afterwards were distinguished for their antislavery convictions, *not to do so*, because it would occasion such dissatisfaction to have him in the pulpit. But, more than any man I ever knew, Samuel Joseph May combined the two elements of courage and gentleness. He was a gentle knight — a knight as brave as Launcelot, and as courteous as Calidore. His Christianity was aggressive, and yet liberal, generous, and kind. His influence was like that of a June Sunday — a perpetual breath of summer and Sabbath-days.

A leading peculiarity of our friend was the combination of traits usually disjoined. One of the most serious of Christians in his earnestness of purpose, he was also one of the most cheerful. Looking continually with a tender pity upon the woes and wrongs of men, he was full of a glad hope concerning the issues of human destiny. One of the most practical of men in his habits of thought, and always aiming at definite results, he yet would never sacrifice a principle or surrender abstract right to any apparent expediency. A peace man and non-resistant, both by disposition and conviction, he was a born belligerent, and his life was one long battle against falsehoods and wrongs. He united a courage which never feared the face of man and shrunk from no opposition in expressing his convictions, with an almost unequaled modesty and a genuine respect for views differing from his own, no matter by whom those views were maintained. A democrat in all his convictions and feelings, he nevertheless had an unfeigned reverence for all superiority of genius and of character. This manly modesty, this combative peacefulness, this reverential independence, this practical idealism, this sympathetic self-reliance, this entire toleration of the opinions of others joined to clear and confident assertion of his own, gave to our friend an extraordinary influence everywhere. His love had edge to it, his kindness was not "a mush of concession." A strong

man on whom many leaned, he was a sweet man
whom every one loved. His disposition was fortunate, for it was full of the spirit of content. He
seemed, more than most men, at home in this
world. He found, or made, opportunities of usefulness wherever he went. He sympathized so
heartily with all about him, such glad interest in
their affairs beamed from his eyes, that he walked
through the world attended by hosts of friends.
His enemies were always at a distance, for no
man could come near him without being instantly
changed into a friend. Always interested in some
good cause "not his own," he was lifted up by
the greatness of the subject, and walked with
larger steps in the transfiguration of that idea.
He devoted himself through life to the cause of
the slave, of peace, of education, of the Christian
church, of Unitarian Christianity, of temperance,
of the emancipation of woman, — and carried into
all the same wise and courageous activity; always
ready to speak the truth, and always speaking it
in love.

Mr. May arrived one afternoon at the house of
Mr. Henry Colman, at Deerfield, where he was to
pass the night. It was in the height and bitterness of the antislavery conflict. Mr. Colman met
him at the door, and said, " Oh, Mr. May, I hope
you will not speak about slavery to-day. We
have a Southerner staying here, who is very irritable; and it would be extremely disagreeable to

have a dispute." Mr. May replied, "I shall not introduce the subject, but if my opinion is asked I must give it, you know." He had scarcely entered, and taken his seat next to the Southern gentleman, when a lady on the other side, who knew that Mr. May had just come from an anti-slavery meeting, asked him some question about it. "I was glad," said he, "of the opportunity to let the slaveholder know what our objects really were, and so I told the lady what we had been doing and what we meant to do." The Southerner was evidently becoming more and more excited every moment, and at last, unable to control himself any longer, he cried out, "And what business is it of yours, I should like to know, what is to be done about slavery? It is our affair, not yours." Whereupon Mr. May turned toward him, and asked the Southerner whether he thought it right to hold a man as a slave. As, in those days, slaveholders had not yet been taught by Christian divines to defend slavery on principle, he replied, "No. I don't believe in slavery in the abstract. But you have no right to interfere in the matter." On this Mr. May proceeded to explain that the abolitionists did not propose to interfere in any other way than by reason and argument, and *that* addressed to the mind and conscience of the masters, not of the slave. He added that it was not only every man's right but also his duty to take an interest in the sufferings and wrongs and sins of his fellow-men — no matter where they might live, or how far off they might be. In fact, he communicated so many new ideas to the mind of the Southerner, and did it with so much good-temper, and such respect for the opinions of the other, that at last the man was quite overcome. He rose from his chair, walked up and down the room, much excited; and then, turning to Mr. May, said, "You must not think as badly of us slaveholders as if we had been brought up at the North, where slavery does not exist, and had not become accustomed to it." "Oh, no!" answered Mr. May, "I certainly can make great allowance for your situation. I do not think as badly of you as if you had always breathed an atmosphere of freedom; but I should think very badly of myself if I, who have been always taught to believe in liberty, did not do all I could to promote it, here and everywhere else."

At another time Mr. May sent a note to his friend, Rev. Thomas K. Beecher, of Elmira, N. Y., telling him that he knew the Beechers were afraid of nothing, but that now he could give the Beecher courage a severe trial. "I write you," said he, "to exchange pulpits with me, who am a Unitarian, a non-resistant, a woman's rights man, an anti-capital punishment man, and a Garrisonian abolitionist." To this Mr. Beecher replied: "Pooh, pooh! that is nothing. Come and

14

exchange." Mr. May went to Elmira and preached, avoiding, however, the questions on which he might be supposed to differ from Mr. Beecher.

Such anecdotes as these, which might be indefinitely multiplied, will, perhaps, give a better idea than any mere description of the charm of his character. But, in truth, no words can adequately describe it. Fortunate are those who knew him. They will never cease to recall that wonderful union of qualities which gave him such power and made him so great an influence wherever he was known. It was this harmony of truth and love, manly courage and a womanly gentleness, magnanimity and modesty, which gave to his character the quality of greatness. Because of this, the people of the city where he lived were dissolved in tears at his departure. Well might they mourn for him; not soon shall such another man be found. Persons gifted with more splendid talents are not very rare; men of more extensive attainments are not infrequent. But he is to be congratulated who once in his life comes to know a man like Samuel Joseph May, who was a conservative without bigotry and a radical without narrowness; who felt all wrong done to others as a personal injury, and yet could pardon the offender; who was full of sunshine, radiant with hope, trusting always in God, and believing always in man.

X.

SUSAN DIMOCK.

SUSAN DIMOCK.

WHEN a person so highly gifted and accomplished is taken away, it is well to think of what she has been, and what we have lost.

One of our eminent surgeons, Samuel Cabot, said to me yesterday: " This community will never know what a loss it has had in Dr. Dimock. It was not merely her skill, though that was remarkable, considering her youth and limited experience, but also her *nerve*, that qualified her to become a great surgeon. I have seldom known one at once so determined and so self-possessed. Skill is a quality much more easily found than this self-control that nothing can flurry. She had *that* in an eminent degree ; and, had she lived, she would have been sure to stand, in time, among those at the head of her profession. The usual weapons of ridicule would have been impotent against a woman who had reached that high position which Susan Dimock would certainly have attained."

The striking fact about Dr. Dimock was that

she combined energetic determination and firmness with extreme feminine gentleness. Her voice was soft and low, her manners refined and modest in the highest degree. In speaking of her we can reverse the riddle of Samson, and say: " Out of sweetness came forth strength." These qualities made her services invaluable to her patients. In lecturing to her students she said: " If I were obliged in my practice to do without sympathy or medicine, I should say, do without medicine." She did not care to have any woman study medicine who was naturally unsympathetic. One student having said: " I have not much pity for hysteric patients," Dr. Dimock remarked: " If medical science is not yet so far advanced as to discover any lesion in what we call ' hysteria,' this is no reason why we should have no sympathy with those thus afflicted, for they suffer severely."

Born in North Carolina in 1847, she early saw the evils of the institution of slavery. She once said to her mother, " I am slow to take an idea, and always have been. I was eight years old before I realized the injustice of slavery." Most of her fellow-citizens were much older than that before they realized it. At twelve years she told her father that she wished to study medicine and become a physician. As her family were then in easy circumstances, and lived in a community where no woman ever worked except from necessity, this was regarded as an eccentricity.

But she had formed her purpose, and adhered to it. When about thirteen or fourteen, being at a watering-place, she was observed to be absorbed in a book; and continued sitting in the corner of the piazza reading for an hour or more. " What interesting story has Susie got ? " asked one. An old physician, standing by, replied : " It is one of my medical books, which I have lent her; and one of the driest, too."

After her family had come to the North during the rebellion, she pursued her studies here, and finally applied for admission into the Medical School of Harvard University, preferring, if possible, to take a degree in an American college. Twice she applied, and was twice refused. Hearing that the University of Zurich was open to women, she went to that institution, and was received with a hospitality which the institutions of her own country did not offer. She pursued her medical studies there, and graduated with honor. A number of the " Revue des Deux Mondes " for August 1, 1872, contains an article called " Les Femmes à l'Université de Zurich," which speaks very favorably of the success of the women students in that place.

The first to take a degree as doctor of medicine was a young Russian lady, in 1867. Between 1867 and 1872, five others had taken this degree, and the article speaks of them as all successfully practicing their profession. Among these

was Susan Dimock It adds : " It will be seen
that the attempt made in Switzerland, by men
emancipated from prejudice, has been crowned
with a striking and well-deserved success. It had
been feared that the promiscuous character of an
audience composed of both sexes would be an
embarrassment to the professors, or even occasion
disagreeable scenes. Nothing of the sort has occurred. The modest and serious attitude of the
young women has, on the contrary, exercised a
happy influence on the tone and behavior of the
other students. At the examinations the women
have obtained high marks, and in hospital practice they have manifested remarkable aptitude for
their work."

From the medical school at Zurich, she went
to that at Vienna ; and of her appearance there
we have this record : A distinguished German
physician remarked to a friend of mine residing
in Germany, that he had always been opposed to
women as physicians — but that he had met a
young American lady studying at Vienna, whose
intelligence, modesty, and devotion to her work
was such as almost to convince him that he was
wrong. A comparison of dates shows that this
American student must have been Dr. Dimock.

On her return to the United States, Susan Dim-
ock took the position of resident physician at
" The Hospital for Women and Children," on
Codman Avenue, in Boston. Both the students of

medicine, and the patients became devotedly attached to her. They were fascinated by her remarkable union of tenderness, firmness, and skill. The secret of her influence was in part told by what she said in one of her lectures in the training-school for nurses connected with the woman's hospital: " I wish you, of all my instructions, especially to remember this. When you go to nurse a patient imagine that it is *your own sister* before you in that bed ; and treat her, in every respect, as you would wish your own sister to be treated." While at this hospital she was also able to carry out a principle in which she firmly believed ; namely, that the rights of every patient, poor and rich, should be sacredly regarded, and never be sacrificed to the supposed interests of medical students. Except with the consent of the patient, no students were allowed to be present at any operation, except so far as the comfort and safety of the patient rendered their presence desirable. They were not admitted as mere spectators, and she applied this rule to the patients who were received gratuitously as well as to those who paid their board. She was satisfied that this system worked well, and had been perfectly successful, and that the students were more thoroughly taught by being admitted for practical services than by being frequently present only as spectators.

Her interest in the New England Hospital was very great. She was in the habit, at the beginning of each year, of writing and sealing up her wishes for the coming year. Since her death her mother has opened the envelope of January 1, 1875, and found it to contain a prayer for a blessing on " my dear hospital."

And now, this young, strong soul, so ardent in the pursuit of knowledge, so filled with a desire to help her suffering sisters, has been taken by the remorseless deep.

> It was that fatal and perfidious bark
> Built in the eclipse, and rigged with curses dark,
> That sunk so low that sacred head of thine.

But we must believe that there is some higher purpose in such events than we can see. No accident of a fog or a low tide explains adequately the departure of such heroic souls as these. We cannot doubt that there is as good work for them to do in the unknown beyond as that they have left here. We thank God for all we have had from such a presence among us, and trust in his perfect providence in regard to what we cannot understand or explain.

XI.

GEORGE KEATS.

GEORGE KEATS.[1]

To the Editor of "The Dial":—

Dear Sir, — When last at your house I mentioned to you that I had in my possession a copy of some interesting remarks upon Milton, hitherto unpublished, by John Keats the poet. According to your wish I have copied them for your periodical. But I wish, with your permission, to say how they came into my possession; and in doing this I shall have an opportunity of giving the imperfect tribute of a few words of remembrance to a noble-minded man and a dear friend.

Several years ago I went to Louisville, Ky., to take charge of the Unitarian church in that city. I was told that among those who attended the church was a brother of the poet Keats, an English gentleman, who had resided for many years in Louisville as a merchant. His appearance and the shape of his head arrested my attention. The heavy bar of observation over his eyes indicated

[1] First published in *The Dial*, then edited by R. W. Emerson.

the strong perceptive faculties of a business man,
while the striking height of the head, in the region
assigned by phrenology to veneration, was a sign
of nobility of sentiment, and the full development
behind marked firmness and practical energy. All
these traits were equally prominent in his character. He was one of the most intellectual men I
ever knew. I never saw him when his mind was
inactive. I seldom knew him to acquiesce in the
thought of another. It was a necessity of his
nature to have his own thought on every subject;
and when he assented to your opinion, it was not
acquiescence but agreement. Joined with this
energy of intellect was a profound intellectual
modesty. He considered himself deficient in the
higher reflective faculties, especially in that of a
philosophical method. But his keen insight enabled him fully to appreciate what he did not himself possess. Though the tendency of his intellect
was critical, he was without dogmatism, and full of
reverence for the creative faculties. He was well
versed in English literature, especially in that of
the Elizabethan period; a taste for which he had
probably imbibed from his brother and other literary friends, among whom Leigh Hunt was prominent. This taste he preserved for years in a region where few could be found who had so much
as heard the names of his favorite authors. The
society of such a man was invaluable, if only as intellectual stimulus. It was strange to find, in those

days, on the banks of the Ohio, one who had successfully devoted himself to active pursuits, and
yet retained so fine a sensibility for the rarest and
most evanescent beauties of early song.

The intellectual man was that which you first
discovered in George Keats. It needed a longer
acquaintance before you could perceive, beneath
the veil of a high-bred English reserve, that profound sentiment of manly honor, that reverence
for all truth, loftiness, and purity, that ineffaceable
desire for spiritual sympathy, which are the birth-
right of those in whose veins flows the blood of a
poetic race. George Keats was the most manly
and self-possessed of men — yet full of inward aspiration and conscious of spiritual needs. There
was no hardness in his strong heart, no dogmatism in his energetic intellect, no pride in his self-
reliance. Thus he was essentially a religious man.
He shrunk from pietism, but revered piety.

The incidents of his life bore the mark of his
character. His mind, stronger than circumstances,
gave them its own stamp, instead of receiving
theirs. George Keats, with his two younger
brothers, Thomas and John, were left orphans at
an early age. They were placed by their guardian
at a private boarding school, where the impetuosity
of the young poet frequently brought him into
difficulties in which he needed the brotherly aid
of George. John was very apt to get into a fight
with boys much bigger than himself, and George,

who seldom fought on his own account, often got into a battle to protect his brother. These early adventures helped to bind their hearts in a close and lasting affection.

After leaving school, George was taken into his guardian's counting-room, where he stayed a little while, but left it, because he did not choose to submit to the domineering behavior of one of the partners. Yet he preferred to bear the accusation of being unreasonable rather than to explain the cause, which might have made difficulty. He lived at home, keeping house with his two brothers, and doing nothing for some time, waiting till he should be of age, and should receive his small inheritance. Many said he was an idle fellow, who would never come to any good; but he felt within himself a conviction that he could make his way successfully through the world. His guardian, a wise old London merchant, shared this opinion, and always predicted that George would turn out well.

His first act on coming of age did not seem, to the worldly wise, to favor this view. He married a very young lady, without fortune, the daughter of a British colonel, and came with her to America. They did not, however, act without reflection. George had only a few thousand dollars, and knew that if he remained in London he could not be married for years.* Nor would he be able to support his wife in any of the Atlantic cities, in the society to which they had been accustomed. But by going at once to a western State, they might live, without much society to be sure, but yet with comfort and the prospect of improving their condition. Therefore this boy and girl, he twenty-one and she sixteen, left their home and friends and went away to be content in each other's love in the wild regions beyond the Alleghanies. Happy is he whose first great step in the world is the result, not of outward influences, but of his own well-considered purpose. Such a step seems to make him free for the rest of his life.

Journeys were not made in those days as they are now. Mr. Keats bought a carriage and horses in Philadelphia, with which he traveled to Pittsburg, and thence descended the Ohio in a keel-boat. This voyage of six hundred miles down the river was full of romance to these young people. No steamboat then disturbed, with its hoarse pantings, the sleep of those beautiful shores. Day after day they floated tranquilly on, as through a succession of fairy lakes, sometimes in the shadow of the lofty and wooded bluff, sometimes by the side of wide-spread meadows, or beneath the graceful overhanging branches of the cotton-wood and sycamore. At times, while the boat floated lazily along, the young people would go ashore and walk through the woods across a point around which the river made a bend. All uncertain as

15

their prospects were, they could easily, amid the luxuriance of nature, abandon themselves to the enjoyment of the hour.

Mr. Keats stayed some months in Henderson, Ky., where he resided in the same house with Audubon, the naturalist. He was still undetermined what to do. One day he was trying to chop a log, and Audubon, who had watched him for some time, at last said, " I am sure you will do well in this country, Keats. A man who will persist, as you have been doing, in chopping that log, though it has taken you an hour to do what I could do in ten minutes, will certainly get along here." Mr. Keats said that he accepted the omen, and felt encouraged by it.

After investing a large part of his money in a boat, and losing it, he took charge of a flour mill, and worked night and day with such untiring energy that he soon found himself making progress. After a while he left this business and engaged in the lumber trade, by which in a few years he accumulated a handsome fortune. In the course of this business he was obliged to make visits to the lumberers, which often led him into wild scenes and adventures. Once, when he was taking a journey on horseback, to visit some friends on the British Prairie, in Illinois, he approached the Wabash in the afternoon, at a time when the river had overflowed its banks. Following the horse path, for there was no carriage road,

he came to a succession of little lakes, which he
was obliged to ford. But when he reached the
other side it was impossible to find the path again,
and equally difficult to regain it by recrossing
The path here went through a cane-brake, and
the cane grew so close together that the track
could only be distinguished when you were actually upon it. What was to be done? There
was no human being for miles around, and no one
might pass that way for weeks. To stop or to go
on seemed equally dangerous. But at last Mr.
Keats discovered the following expedient, the only
one, perhaps, that could have saved him. The
direction of the path he had been traveling was
east and west. He turned and rode toward the
south until he was sure that he was to the south
of the track. He then returned slowly to the
north, carefully examining the ground as he passed
along, until at last he found himself crossing the
path, which he took, and reached the river in
safety.

George Keats not only loved his brother John,
but reverenced his genius and enjoyed his poetry,
believing him to belong to the front rank of English bards. Modern criticism concurs with this
judgment. A genuine and discriminating appreciation of his brother's poetry, from any one, gave
him great pleasure. He preserved and highly
prized John's letters and unpublished verses, the
copy of John's Spenser filled with his marks,

which he had read when a boy, and which had
been to him a very valuable source of poetic inspiration, and a Milton in which were preserved
in a like manner John's notes and comments,
which appear to me among the most striking criticisms we possess upon this great author.   That
the love of the brothers was mutual, appears from
the following lines from one of John's poems, in-
scribed "To my brother George : " —

> " As to my sonnets, though none else should heed them,
> I feel delighted, still, that you should read them.
> Of late, too, I have had much calm enjoyment,
> Stretched on the grass, at my best loved employment,
> Of scribbling lines to you " —

In the prime of life and the midst of usefulness,
George Keats passed into the spiritual world.
The city of Louisville lost in him one of its most
public-spirited and conscientious citizens.   The
Unitarian society of that place lost one who,
though he had been confirmed by the Archbishop
of Canterbury, was too honest not to leave the
popular and fashionable church for an unpopular
faith, since this was more of a home to his mind.
For myself, I have ever thought that it was quite
worth my while to have lived in Louisville, even if
I had gained thereby nothing but the knowledge
and friendship of such a man.   I did not see him
in his last days.   I was already in a distant region.
But when he died I felt that I had indeed lost a
friend.   We cannot hope to find many such in this

world. We are fortunate if we find any. Yet I could not but believe that he had gone to find his brother again among

> " The spirits and intelligences fair,
> And angels waiting on the Almighty's chair."

The love for his brother, which continued through his life to be among the deepest affections of his soul, was a pledge of their reunion again in another world.

Perhaps I have spoken too much of one who was necessarily a stranger to most of your readers. But I could not bear that he should pass away and nothing be said to tell the world how much went with him. And " The Dial," which he always read, and in whose aims he felt a deep interest, though not always approving its methods, seems not an improper place, nor this a wholly unsuitable occasion, for thus much to be said concerning GEORGE KEATS.

XII.

ROBERT J. BRECKINRIDGE.

ROBERT JEFFERSON BRECKINRIDGE.

WHEN, in 1836, Robert J. Breckinridge preached
in Louisville, Kentucky, I thought him the best
extempore preacher I had ever heard. Matter
and manner were both simple and strong. It was
like the direct, earnest conversation which one
holds with you, on a subject of which his mind
and heart are full. He never hesitated for a
word, never repeated himself, but went on rapidly and easily from point to point, like Goethe's
star, "without haste and without rest." There
was little or no metaphor, few illustrations, and
nothing of the ornate style and oratorical delivery
which were very popular then in the West. Two
favorite speakers, Mr. Maffitt and Mr. Bascom,
had lately been preaching in the city, and drawing large crowds of admirers. Nothing could be
more opposed to their florid style than his severe
simplicity. It was a delight to me to listen to
him, notwithstanding the vigor of his orthodoxy;
and I thought it showed the good sense of the
Kentuckians, that, though caught by the flowery

grandiloquence of the others, they yet regarded Mr. Breckinridge as one of their finest orators. It is evidence of good taste when one prefers the early English pointed architecture to the flamboyant style of later centuries.

And the Kentuckians in those days *were* good judges of public speaking. They did not read books, and had very little of the culture which derives from literature — but they were passionately fond of good speech. They assembled in great numbers at the political barbecues, where, under the shadows of the majestic beeches and tulip trees of the Kentucky forest, they spent long summer days in hearing Whig and Democratic speakers discuss questions of public polity. They then had an opportunity of hearing both sides ; and speakers of both parties spoke to both parties. Members of Congress were called upon to explain to their constituents their course in Congress, and must answer on the spot the most trying questions. This educated a race of stump-speakers, of whom the tradition long lingered in Kentucky, — men like the famous Joseph Hamilton Daviess, prompt, clear, and confident, — who could

> "Bend, like perfect steel, to spring again and thrust."

And, among these ready speakers of his own day, Robert J. Breckinridge stood easily the chief, and was accounted the best stump-speaker in Kentucky.

Mr. Breckinridge and his brothers, John and William L., were all originally lawyers, and all afterward became Presbyterian ministers. The gift of fine extemporaneous speech belonged to all three. In John there was perhaps more of illustration and more appearance of emotion than Robert. Both were full of fire, but in John it appeared in lambent flames, while in Robert it was a central force, on which his whole nature rested. I once was listening to John Breckinridge, and as I sat directly in front of the pulpit he could not help seeing me, and, knowing me no doubt as the Unitarian minister of the place, he took occasion to denounce all those who taught Unitarian doctrines as men " dripping with the blood of souls." No doubt he believed it, and he, like his brothers, always had " the courage of his opinions." But afterward, in New Orleans, visiting a dying lady, a relative of his own, and a warm Unitarian, finding that, notwithstanding her heresy, her faith in Christ was sincere and strong, the good man forgot his theology, and said, " If you feel so, cousin, I have nothing to say against your faith." Robert J. Breckinridge was as brave as a lion, and his chivalric nature led him always to take part with the oppressed. A relative of his, an older man, told me this anecdote, which belongs to the period before he became a preacher. They were riding together, on horseback, on their way to Frankfort, Ken-

tucky, and as they approached the city they came
up with a wagoner who was cruelly abusing a
negro boy. Mr. Breckinridge rode up to him,
and asked him why he treated the boy in that
way. The wagoner replied by a curse and
threat, which, however, were no sooner out of his
mouth than Mr. Breckinridge responded by ad-
ministering to him a severe beating, cutting him
about the face with his riding-whip, so that the
ruffian ran, got on one of his horses, and rode
away. Then my friend said to Mr. Breckinridge,
"The fellow has got what he deserved, but it becomes us to go into Frankfort as soon as possible,
for he has gone back to get that party of wagoners whom we passed half a mile back." So they
rode on toward Frankfort — but as they descended
the long hills which surround the place, fast riding was difficult, for these hills are of limestone,
lying in horizontal strata, which crop out, making
the descent like a flight of steps. When about
half-way down they heard a loud noise behind,
and found that half a dozen wagoners were coming on after them, full speed, in one of their wag-
ons. Dangerous or not, they were obliged to ride
down the hill at the same pace, and just succeeded in escaping their pursuers.

The same courage and energy were shown by
Mr. Breckinridge, afterward, on a more important
field. He, with Drs. Junkin, Plumer, Baxter,
and others, led the Old School party in the Gen-

eral Assembly when they cut off four Synods, containing some forty thousand members — a step which caused the disruption of the church. The pretext for cutting off these Synods was some alleged unconstitutionality in their original union. But as they had remained in the church without objection for thirty-seven years, it is not likely they would have been removed if they had been considered as orthodox. But these New York and Ohio Synods were tainted with New School heresies. So Mr. Breckinridge, a Calvinist genuine and sincere, if there ever was one, considered it necessary to save the church at all hazards from the poison of these heresies. Under his splendid captaincy the deed was done, and the victory was gained for Calvinism pure and simple.

But another generation has now come, which knows not Joseph. The interest in those severe discussions has died away, and many will wonder why such a vehement controversy should have raged around such abstract and purely metaphysical questions. The principal " error " of the New School men, and one which was denounced as being equivalent to " another gospel," was this : —

" That God *would* have prevented the existence of sin in our world, but was not able, without destroying the moral agency of man; or, that for aught that appears in the Bible to the contrary, sin is incidental to any wise moral system."

The substance of the dispute was just at this point. The New School divines said that God *would* have prevented sin, but could not do it. The Old School said He *could* have prevented sin, but would not. But when the latter were asked *why* God *would* not, they gave the same answer as their opponents — " Because God chose that man should be a free agent." The only difference between the " Could nots " and " Would nots," therefore, was as to which phrase should come first in the statement. And on this point the church was divided.

But give due credit even to bigotry. These excommunicating chiefs were narrow, were one-sided, were intolerant, but they were logical and sincere. When you once adopt the principle that any theological statement is essential to salvation, it is difficult to know where to stop. To draw the line between essentials and non-essentials is difficult; for to a logical mind every part of a system is essential to the integrity of the whole.

No doubt R. J. Breckinridge was a born fighter, — a man of war from his youth. He snuffed the battle afar off, and rejoiced in the conflict. A sincere antislavery man, though born and raised in the midst of slave-holders, he remained true to his convictions when other men fell away, and the love of many waxed cold. I remember the time when all the leading men in Kentucky, Whigs and Democrats, with few exceptions, were op-

posed to slavery, and declared themselves in favor
of amending the State Constitution by inserting
an antislavery clause. But when a convention
was called in the State to form a new Constitution,
the great majority of these theoretical antislavery
men were afraid to act. Not so Robert J. Breckinridge. During three long summer days he
stood in front of the court house in Lexington,
maintaining against all opponents that the interests of Kentucky, no less than its conscience, required the abolition of slavery. It was like a
knightly tournament, only in a nobler cause, and
fought with better weapons. He wrestled not
against flesh and blood, but against the rulers of
the darkness of this world, and spiritual wickedness in high places. Well would it have been for
Kentucky if she had listened to that manly voice,
and been led by that commanding eloquence. She
then would have been the advanced fortress of the
Free States during the war, and would not have
been ravaged alternately by the opposing armies.
She would not have seen her families divided,
son against father, and brother fighting against
brother. She would not have had that still worse
record, that in the greatest conflict of the age for
truth and freedom, she alone of all the States preferred to remain neutral.

In that great conflict, also, Robert J. Breckinridge was true to himself and his ideas. Amid
the falling away on all sides, of those most near

and dear, the old man stood by the flag of the Union. He saw his fields and home repeatedly ravaged by the rebel troops ; he saw disaster after disaster fall on the Union arms; he saw his old friends leaving him, but he remained firm and true to the end.

> ' Among innumerable false, unmoved,
> Unshaken, unseduced, unterrified,
> His loyalty he kept, his love, his zeal ;
> Nor number, nor example, with him wrought
> To swerve from truth, or change his constant mind
> Though single. From amidst them forth he passed,
> Long way through hostile scorn, which he sustained,
> Superior, nor of violence feared aught ;
> And with retorted scorn, his back he turned
> On those proud towers to swift destruction doomed."

Mr. Breckinridge was, as we have said, in some things narrow and intolerant. But he had a candid mind, and if convinced of an error was willing to acknowledge it — if he saw good in an opponent, was glad to admit it. In a journey through Europe, about the year 1836–7, he came to Geneva, and there became acquainted with the Venerable Company of Pastors, and heard them preach in the cathedral. He frankly confessed his "great surprise and sincere delight" in hearing the Scripture expounded "with clearness, truth, and fervor." "I had, also," he says, "the pleasure to make the acquaintance of two of the Venerable Company of Pastors, whose kindness deserved my thanks, as much as their intelligence excited my interest. And, in general, I think the lives of that body are, in private, blameless to a degree not common either in most established churches or decided errorists."

One more little anecdote, which we heard in Western Pennsylvania. An elder of the Presbyterian church, in the town of Butler, wished one Saturday to go to Pittsburg on business of importance. The stage from Erie came through so full that he could get no seat, but presently there followed an extra stage, containing only one gentleman and two ladies. He asked permission of the gentleman to take a seat and was permitted to do so. As he rode on, he allowed his hand carelessly to drop on some flowers belonging to the ladies, which were in a pot beside him. This happened once or twice, notwithstanding the request of the original traveler to the church elder, to be more cautious. At last he said: "Sir! I have permitted you to take a seat with us because you said you were anxious to reach Pittsburg, but you shall leave the stage if you touch those flowers again, even if I have to put you out myself." This made a little "unpleasantness" for the rest of the journey. The elder did his business and then went to a friend's house, who said: "It is fortunate that you came to-day, for to-morrow we have the celebrated Robert J. Breckinridge to preach for us." The elder went to church, and saw in the pulpit his stage-coach com-

panion, and found that he had used his excellent
opportunity for becoming well acquainted with
Robert J. Breckinridge by making himself specially disagreeable to him.

Sleep peacefully in thy grave, good soldier of
the cross. We who are fighting in another camp,
to which thou wert not very friendly, can see and
admire generous, brave, and honest qualities, and
force of intellect and character, even in an opponent; and we lay this tribute on thy coffin : *Sit
tibi terra levis!*

XIII.

GEORGE DENISON PRENTICE.

GEORGE DENISON PRENTICE AND KENTUCKY FORTY YEARS AGO.

It was in the summer of 1833, being then a youth fresh from the divinity school, that I first saw the Ohio River at Wheeling — a river which afterwards became as familiar to me in its quiet beauty as the hills of my native New England. The journey from Boston to Cincinnati occupied a week. Most of it then, and during many years after, had to be performed by the stage-coach, the usual rate of travel being only three or four miles an hour. The roads were horrible — on the sides of the hills cut into deep gullies by the rain, and on the level surface frequently made almost impassable by mud and pools of water. The rich, black soil which was a blessing to farmers, was a curse to travelers. In order to arrive at our journey's end in any reasonable period, it was necessary to travel all night as well as all day; and I have sometimes ridden in this way five days and nights, only stopping for meals. In the night time the dangers of the road were aggravated by the darkness. It was not the custom to carry lamps, and the tall forests rising close to the road on either side would, especially in a rainy night, create an impenetrable darkness. Then, if the wheel sank suddenly into a hole, or ran over a stump, the stage would be overturned, and it would take a long time to get it up again. Once, in the middle of Ohio, at midnight, the stage was thus overturned into a deep mud-hole in the midst of pitchy darkness; and the passengers, men and women, were pulled from the inside through the door which was uppermost. Nothing could be done but to sit on the side of the coach in the rain, and wait, while the driver went for help to the nearest house. On another occasion the darkness was so profound that the horses wandered away into the woods, the driver being unable to see which way they were going. At last they stopped, and would go no farther. Then a light was procured, and it was found that the coach and horses were standing on the top of a little hill in the middle of the woods, at a considerable distance from the road. At another time the stage overturned at noon-day, when the horses were slowly walking down a hill. The road had been so gullied by the rain that there was absolutely no place left where the coach could stand upright. Sometimes, in crossing the mountains, the passengers would get out and walk, and they would walk so much faster than the horses that it would often be an hour or two before they were overtaken.

On my first visit to the West I went over the old Cumberland road to Wheeling. The present generation is ignorant of the controversy which raged in regard to this avenue between the East and the West. The vast subsidies in land and money which have since that time been made to railroads by the United States government, make the grants to the Cumberland road seem quite insignificant. But this was a project of Henry Clay and the Whig party, and so was violently opposed by the Democrats. It was simply a macadamized road running from Cumberland in Maryland to Columbus in Ohio. At the time I passed over it, it was in a terrible state, the large stones from beneath having worked up, and the small ones worked down, so that it seemed uncertain to the traveler whether he was riding in a coach or being tossed in a blanket.

The Ohio River, as is well known, is apt to be very low in summer. According to John Randolph's saying, it is "frozen up during half the year, and dried up during the other half." In descending the river, therefore, we continually struck on sand-bars. In order to get off, the first effort was to reverse the wheels and try to back off. That failing, a strong rope was carried to the shore, made fast to a tree there, and to the windlass on board, and attempts were thus made to pull the boat off. If these, also, were fruitless, they put spars from the bow against the bottom of the river, and, by means of tackle, tried to lift the vessel backward into the water. But if nothing else would answer they were obliged at last to bring flat-boats to the side and take out the cargo. All this, of course, caused great delay and protracted the voyage. But the river was so lovely, with the high bluffs on one side, covered with unbroken forests, and the broad meadows on the other, covered with farms and fields, with its long reaches of blue water, like a succession of quiet lakes, that one could well be content to loiter for a long period upon its bewitching, quiet current.

When I first reached Louisville, George D. Prentice had been editing the " Louisville Journal " for about two years. This was a Whig paper, and constantly engaged in fierce conflict with its Democratic rival, the " Advertiser," edited by Shadrach Penn. The bitterness of newspaper strife in those days was fearful. The last Whig editor had been driven from the town by the violent assaults of his opponents. Mr. Prentice, when he arrived, was only known as a young man from Connecticut, who had written some pretty poems of the sentimental order. Mr. Penn no doubt supposed that it would be very easy to crush him. Then commenced an editorial warfare, which was in full operation when I arrived. Every morning each newspaper would contain a leading article devoted to the destruction of the antagonist editor. They accused each other, mutually, of the blackest crimes. If we were to believe their statements, both of them should be sent to the penitentiary for life. Each had swindled his creditors, committed manifold breaches of trust, deserted his family, slandered the good, lived a life of drunkenness and debauchery, and probably committed many murders. Each was declared to be black with falsehood, corrupted by a life of infamy, and without a single decent associate or friend. The Dictionary was searched to find abusive epithets, nor was it searched in vain. This was the entertainment which during a year or two was served up at every breakfast table in the city, with the coffee and rolls. The question was, which would hold out the longest. And that question was finally decided in favor of Prentice. He did not exceed Penn in virulence or violence, but he had more imagination. He could invent more libels and tell more astonishing stories about Penn than Penn could about him. The poetic faculty, hitherto occupied in writing newspaper stanzas, was now employed to invent new stories of infamous rascality about his rival. So Shadrach came one day to see Prentice, and proposed that they should stop abusing each other; to which Prentice agreed, and the city had rest from their billingsgate.

As the Democratic leaders found that this brilliant Whig editor was not to be silenced by denunciation and abuse, they tried to put him down by terror. He was only a Yankee, and Yankees were supposed not to fight duels ; nor are Yankees accustomed to street fights. He was known chiefly as a writer of sentimental verses in the style of Nathaniel Willis. They thought he would be an easy victim. By no means. He was more than a match for them at their own favorite weapons. He was perfectly willing to fight, and after one or two duels and a few street fights, in which his opponents generally got the worst, they decided to let him alone. Once I saw a great crowd rushing together on Jefferson Street, and running up, found that a man, after meeting Prentice, had turned around and fired a pistol at his back. But, with his usual good luck, Prentice happened to turn round at the moment the pistol was discharged, and so escaped the ball. He ran upon the assassin, knocked him down, jumped on him, took out his knife and seemed inclined to stab him, but when the crowd shouted : " Kill him, Prentice ! " he changed his mind, and let the man go. The angry crowd, who were all fond of Prentice, pursued the terrified wretch with yells, and he only escaped by jumping, head-foremost, like a harlequin, through a glass window.

A man named Moore, living in Harrodsburg, was running for Congress on the Democratic ticket. Prentice vilified him every day in the " Journal " until it made his life a burden. So he came down to Louisville, and challenged Prentice to fight a duel. Prentice readily accepted the challenge, and proposed to fight with rifles at thirty yards. Moore replied that as his arm was lame he could not support the weight of a rifle unless he was allowed a rest. Prentice responded that if he let him rest his gun on a tree he would be sure to hide behind the trunk, which was not to be allowed ; but he would propose the following terms : Two posts should be driven into the ground a few feet apart, in front of each combatant, and a strong cord fastened from pole to pole, at the proper height, to serve for a rest. Each man should be placed behind this cord, with his rifle at his left side, with its but on the ground. When the word " Fire " was given, he should raise his rifle and fire, either from the rest or otherwise, as he should prefer. After firing the rifle, each might take a double-barrelled gun, which should be lying on the ground by his side, the barrels loaded with fifteen slugs each, and fire it when and as he chose. They should then close with bowie-knives. This terrific programme had the effect which was probably intended — Mr. Moore went back to Harrodsburg, and said no more about fighting.

In those days street fights and duels were normal facts of Kentucky life. By preaching a sermon against duelling I excited much wonder among the solid and serious citizens. Old Judge Rowan, the famous advocate and senator, expressed his astonishment that I should speak against duels. "He might just as well preach against courage," said he. Judge Rowan was a good friend of mine, used to come to church, and talk to me often about Lactantius and other Latin writers, whom he was fond of reading. The judge was also fond of high play, and many stories were told of his exploits in that direction. The people's consciences were not disturbed by what would seem grave delinquencies to Eastern men. Many respectable people never thought of paying their debts. It did not seem to them worth while to do so. Others, very estimable in other ways, would win or lose a fortune at brag or poker, with a charming feeling of innocence in regard to such transactions. To have a *spree*, or fit of drunkenness of two or three days' duration, did not disqualify a man from moving in good society. Some Mississippi gentlemen on a visit to Louisville attacked and slew two or three tailors in the bar-room of the Galt House, in a quarrel about a badly-cut coat. This murder was utterly unprovoked and barbarous, but the murderers were so well defended by Judge Rowan that they escaped unpunished, although the prosecuting officer was assisted by the equally celebrated Ben Hardin. But public sentiment was wholly in favor of the Mississippi murderers. What would the world come to if a Mississippi slave-holder was not allowed to murder a tailor or two, once in a while? The most fashionable ladies sent flowers and pleasant little dinners to these persecuted gentlemen while in prison, and crowded the court-room on the day of trial. In the face of so much beauty, desiring their acquittal, what chivalric Kentucky jury would venture to convict them? The Mississippians went home in triumph, prepared to kill more tailors if they should find it expedient to do so. But I was not sorry to hear that Judge Rowan never received from them the large fee which they had promised to him before the trial.

One morning John Howard Payne, who was traveling through the West, and had brought me a letter, came to my room and said: "I have seen a great variety of life, but never anything exactly like this society in Louisville. I was last night at a ball at the house of Judge Rowan. In the same cotillion were dancing a son of the judge, Mr. Thomas F. Marshall, and two ladies to whom these gentlemen are said to be respectively engaged. Every one in the room knew that Rowan and Marshall were to fight a duel in the course of a week, which would probably result in the death of one or both; but no one showed any surprise, and all was pleasant on the surface."

The story of this duel illustrates the features of society at that period. The judges of the courts were paid such small salaries that no good lawyer would accept the position; consequently the judges had little influence, and were treated with small respect by the bar. One day the judge of the Jefferson county district, considering himself insulted by a lawyer, one Colonel Robertson from Virginia, committed him to the county jail for twenty-four hours. The bar, thereupon, agreed to go to jail, too, and have a supper. At this supper a slight quarrel occurred between two gentlemen, Mr. Thomas F. Marshall and a younger man named Garnet Howell. A glass of wine was thrown by one in the face of the other, and a duel was the result. Shots were exchanged without effect, and the honor of both parties were satisfied. Then Tom Marshall took his remaining pistol and fired it at a small tree at some distance, and the bark flew from the sapling. This he did in order to show that he had purposely spared the life of his opponent. Mr. John Rowan, Jr., who was Howell's second, and no friend of Marshall, thereupon remarked : "It is singular, Mr. Marshall, that you cannot hit a man, since you can hit a tree so easily." To this sarcasm Marshall replied : "If *you* were the man, Mr. Rowan, I should not have missed you." Rowan responded : "I will give you an opportunity to try, Mr. Marshall." So a duel was thereupon arranged, which was likely to be much more serious than the first, as both parties were first-rate shots. In this duel Marshall was wounded in the leg and lamed for life.

Mr. Prentice's wit was inexhaustible. Each

morning's paper contained half a dozen epigrammatic sentences, one or two of which were usually good enough to be remembered and preserved. They sparkled with puns, antitheses, and happy illustrations. His opponents often seemed to say things as if to give him an opportunity for a fine retort. Thus, a Democratic paper having mentioned that a jackass had fallen from a precipice and broken its neck, added : " That the jackass, which turned such a somerset, must have been a Whig." To which Prentice rejoined : " No Whig, who was *not* a jackass, would turn a somerset in times like these — when the Whigs are carrying everything before them."

In those days General Jackson was very obnoxious to the Whig party, and Prentice steadily abused him every day. " The stinging, hissing bolts of scorn," as Bryant calls them, flew from his typographical weapon in each morning edition, in the direction of the Hermitage. At last it was reported that General Jackson had become a member of the Presbyterian Church. People asked each other : " What will Prentice say now ? He cannot ridicule General Jackson for that. The " Journal " has too many subscribers among the Presbyterians, who would be offended if he blamed General Jackson for joining their church. Yet, he will have to say something about it. What will it be ? " The morning " Journal " appeared. In it Prentice mentioned the fact that

General Jackson had joined the church, and merely added two lines from Dr. Watts — which no pious Presbyterian could object to : —

> " While the lamp holds out to burn
> The vilest sinner may return!"

Still, it may be doubted whether Prentice, with all his wit, materially aided the cause of his party in Kentucky. He was only a politician, not a statesman. He found the State of Kentucky a Whig State, and an antislavery State. He left it Democratic and proslavery. He had no fixed convictions, no leading principles, but drifted in any way that the current went. He allowed the State to fall into the proslavery ranks, because he had not the moral courage to take, openly, an antislavery position. No doubt he would have lost many subscribers at first, but he would have gained more in the end. Public sentiment in Kentucky, in 1835, was almost unanimous against the continuance of this system in the State. I frequently heard leading public men declare themselves abolitionists. All agreed that the State would be much better off if slavery were at an end. A newspaper, like that of Prentice, ought to have concentrated and guided this sentiment and directed it wisely toward some practical measures. If Prentice himself had any opinions on this question, they were opposed to slavery. But he never took this ground plainly and strongly, though he would allow communications in this sense to be inserted in his paper. He permitted me, for example, to reply in his columns to a certain physician, Dr. M'Dowell, who maintained that the African was little better than a monkey, and that slavery is in accordance with Christianity. Mr. Prentice was perfectly willing to allow such opinions to be contradicted in his paper, though he did not care to do it himself.

Mr. Prentice was perhaps as fair as most political editors in his treatment of his opponents. But this is not saying much. He would seldom correct any statement which had once appeared in his paper, even though convinced that it was false. I once succeeded in inducing him to do this, but was obliged to use a stratagem for that purpose. The case was this: In a controversy between the professors in the Medical School in Louisville, the " Journal " had taken sides with one party, and had brought some unjust charges against a young man, a graduate of the institution. The young man being absent from the city, I laid before Mr. Prentice proofs that the charges were false, and asked him to retract them ; but he refused to do it. I then said: " Will you, then, Mr. Prentice, allow me to have half a column of to-morrow's paper in which to reply? " and he consented. I then said: " Will you promise to insert *anything* which I will write? " to which he also agreed. I then wrote an article of such a kind that I knew

17

that Prentice would be extremely reluctant to insert it. In fact, I made it as disagreeable to him as possible. When I took it to him, and he read it, his face grew as black as night. "I can't print this," said he.

"You promised to print whatever I should write," I replied.

"I did not think you would write such an article as this. I do not like to print it."

"Nor do I wish to have it published, Mr. Prentice. I should much prefer to have you retract your charge against Mr. H."

"What do you wish me to say?"

"Not much. Just say that you are glad to find that you were mistaken in bringing the accusation, and that, seeing it to be unfounded, you willingly retract it. Say that, and you need not publish my communication." So Prentice sat down and wrote such a statement, which appeared in the next paper.

In those days, habits of intemperance were not uncommon, even in the best society. I knew, indeed, many pure and virtuous Kentuckians who were wholly free from any intemperance. But the habit was very common, and no one was ashamed of it. Mr. Prentice was often much the worse for liquor. I once saw him at a party, sitting on a sofa, with a gentleman sitting on each side, keeping him from falling over. Afterward he took the pledge, and joined a temperance society. How it was in the last years of his life I never knew, but it is certain that a cloud rested over his later days. He lost the commanding position which he once occupied. He tried to maintain slavery and yet oppose the rebellion; but his position was not logical, and was necessarily a failure. The man who once seemed to direct the destinies of Kentucky with his pen, the leading journalist of the West, was at last only retained as a subordinate in the office which had been the scene of his great triumphs. So passes away the influence of any mind, however brilliant, which clings to no convictions, and holds to no universal ideas.

XIV.

JUNIUS BRUTUS BOOTH,

THE ELDER.

AN INCIDENT IN HIS LIFE.

JUNIUS BRUTUS BOOTH.

AN INCIDENT IN HIS LIFE.

———◆———

MORE than twenty years ago,[1] being pastor of a
church in Louisville, Kentucky, I was sitting one
evening meditating over my coal fire, which was
cheerfully blazing up and gloomily subsiding again,
in the way that Western coal fires in Western coal
grates were then very much in the habit of doing.
I was a young and inexperienced minister. I had
come to the West fresh from a New England
divinity school, with magnificent ideas of the vast
work which was to be done, and with rather a
vague notion of the way in which I was to do it.
My views of the West were chiefly derived from
two books, both of which are now obsolete. When
a child, with the omnivorous reading propensity
of children, I had perused a thin, pale octavo,
which stood on the shelves of our library, containing the record of a journey by the Rev. Thaddeus
Mason Harris, of Dorchester, from Massachusetts
to Marietta, Ohio. Allibone, whom nothing es-

[1] Written in 1861.

capes, gives the title of the book, "Journal of a Tour into the Territory Northwest of the Alleghany Mountains in 1803, Boston, 1805." That a man should write an octavo volume about a journey to Marietta now strikes us as rather absurd, but in those days the journey to Ohio was more difficult than that to Japan is now. The other book was a more important one, being Timothy Flint's "Ten Years' Recollections of the Mississippi Valley," published in 1826. Mr. Flint was a man of sensibility and fancy, a sharp observer, and an interesting writer. His book first taught us to know the West in its scenery and in its human interest.

I was sitting in my somewhat lonely position, watching my coal fire, and thinking of the friends I had left on the other side of the mountains. I had not succeeded as I had hoped in my work. I came to the West expecting to meet with opposition, and I found only indifference. I expected infidelity, and found worldliness. I had around me a company of good Christian friends, but they were no converts of mine; they were from New England, like myself, and brought their religion with them. Upon the real Western people I had made no impression, and could not see how I should make any. Those who were religious seemed to be bigots; those who were not religious cared apparently more for making money, for politics, for horse-racing, for dueling, than for the

difference between Homoousians and Homoiousi-
ans. They were very fond of good preaching, but
their standard was a little different from that I had
been accustomed to. A solid, meditative, carefully written sermon had few attractions for them.
They would go to hear our great New England
divines on account of their reputation, but they
would run in crowds to listen to John Newland
Maffit. What they wanted, as one of them expressed it, was " an eloquent divine, and no common orator." They liked sentiment run out into
sentimentalism, fluency, point, plenty of illustration and knock-down argument. How could a poor
boy, fresh from the groves of our Academy, where
good taste reigned supreme, and where to learn
how to manage one's voice was regarded as a sin
against sincerity, how could he meet such demands
as these?

I was more discouraged than I need to have
been, for, after all, the resemblances in human beings are more than their differences. The differences are superficial, the resemblances radical.
Everywhere men like, in a Christian minister, the
same things, — sincerity, earnestness, and living
Christianity. Mere words may please, but not
long. Men differ in taste about the form of the
cup out of which they drink this wine of Divine
Truth, but they agree in their thirst for the same
wine.

But to my story.

I was sitting, as I said, meditating somewhat sadly, when a knock came at the door. On opening it, a negro boy, with grinning face, presented himself, holding a note. The great fund of good-humor which God has bestowed on the African race often makes them laugh when we see no occasion for laughter. Any event, no matter what it is, seems to them amusing. So this boy laughed merely because he had brought me a note, and not because there was anything peculiarly amusing in the message which the note contained. It is true that you sometimes meet a melancholy negro. But such, I fancy, have some foreign blood in them; they are not Africans *pur sang.* The race is so essentially joyful that centuries of oppression and hardship could not depress its good spirits. It was cheerful in spite of slavery, and in spite of cruel prejudice.

The note the boy brought me was as follows :—

" UNITED STATES HOTEL, *January* 4, 1834.

"SIR,— I hope you will excuse the liberty of a stranger addressing you on a subject he feels great interest in. It is to require a place of interment for his friend[s] in the church-yard and also the expense attendant on the purchase of such place of temporary repose.

"Your communication on this matter will greatly oblige, sir, your respectful and obedient servant,

"J. B. BOOTH."

It will be observed that after the word "friend" an [s] follows in brackets. In the original the word was followed by a small mark which might or might not give it the plural form. It could be read either " friend " or friends," but as we do not usually find ourselves called upon to bury more than one friend at a time, the hasty reader would not notice the mark, but would read it " friend." So did I ; and only afterward, in consequence of the *dénoument,* did I notice that it might be read in the other way.

Taking my hat, I stepped into the street. Gas in those days was not ; an occasional lantern, swung on a wire across the intersection of the streets, reminded us that the city was once French, and suggested the French Revolution and the cry, *" A la lanterne ! "* First I went to my neighbor, the mayor of the city, in pursuit of the desired information. A jolly mayor was he, — a Yankee melted down into a Western man, thoroughly Westernized by a rough-and-tumble life in Kentucky during many years. Being obliged to hold a mayor's court every day, and knowing very little of law, his chief study was, as he expressed it, " how to choke off the Kentucky lawyers." Mr. Mayor not being at home, I turned next to the office of another naturalized Yankee, — a Yankee naturalized, but not Westernized. He was one of those who do not change their mind with their sky, who, exiled from the dear hills of New England, can never be otherwise than the inborn, inherent Yankee. He was a Plymouth man, and religiously preserved every opinion, habit, and accent which he had brought from Plymouth Rock. When Kentucky was madly Democratic, and wept over the dead Jefferson as over her saint, he publicly expressed the opinion that it would have been well for the country if he had died long before, — for which expression he came near being lynched. He was the most unpopular and the most indispensable man in the city, — they could live neither with him nor without him. He founded and organized the insurance companies, the public schools, the charitable associations, the great canal, the banking system; in short, all Yankee institutions. The city was indebted to him for much of its prosperity, but disliked him while it respected him. For he spared no Western prejudice; he remorselessly criticised everything that was not done as Yankees do it; and the most provoking thing of all was that he seldom made a mistake; he was very apt to be right.

Finding neither of these men at home, and so not being able to learn about the price of lots in the church-yard, I walked on to the hotel, and asked to see Mr. J. B. Booth. I was shown into a private parlor, where he and another gentleman were sitting by a table. On the table were candles, a decanter of wine and glasses, a plate of bread, cigars, and a book. Mr. Booth rose when I announced myself, and I at once recognized the distinguished actor. I had met him once before,

and traveled with him for part of a day. He was
a short man, but one of those who seem tall when
under excitement. He had a clear blue eye and
fair complexion. In repose there was nothing to
attract attention to him, but when excited, his
expression was so animated, his eye was so brilliant, and his figure so full of life, that he became
another man.

Having told him that I had not been successful
in procuring the information he desired, but would
bring it to him on the following morning, he
thanked me, and asked me to sit down. It passed
through my mind, that, as he had lost a friend
and was a stranger in the place, I might be of use
to him. Perhaps he needed consolation, and it
was my office to sympathize with the bereaved.
So I sat down. But it did not appear that he
was disposed to seek for such comfort, or engage
in such discourse. Once or twice I endeavored,
but without success, to turn the conversation to
his presumed loss. I asked him if the death of
his friend was sudden.

" Very," he replied.

" Was he a relative ? "

" Distant," said he, and changed the subject.

It is so long since these events took place that I
do not pretend to give the conversation accurately,
but what occurred was much like this. It was a
dialogue between Booth and myself, the third person saying not a word during the evening. Mr.

Booth first asked me to take a glass of wine, or a cigar, both of which I declined.

"Well," said he, "let me try to entertain you in another way. When you came in, I was reading aloud to my friend. Perhaps you would like to hear me read."

"I certainly should," said I.

"What shall I read?"

"Whatever you like best. What you like to read I shall like to hear."

"Then suppose I attempt Coleridge's 'Ancient Mariner'? Have you time for it? It is long."

"Yes, I should like it much."

So he read aloud the whole of this magnificent poem. I have listened to many eminent readers and actors, but none of them affected me as I was moved by this reading. I forgot the place where I was, the motive of my coming, the reader himself. I knew the poem almost by heart, yet I seemed never to have heard it before. I was by the side of the doomed mariner. I was the wedding-guest, listening to his story, held by his glittering eye. I was with him in the storm, among the ice, beneath the hot and copper sky. Booth became so absorbed in his reading, so identified with the poem, that his tone and manner were saturated with a feeling of reality. He actually thought himself the mariner, — so I am persuaded, — while he was reading. As the poem proceeded, and we plunged deeper and deeper into its mystic horrors, the actual world receded into a dim, indefinable distance. The magnetism of this marvelous interpreter had caught up himself and me with him, into Dreamland, from which we gently descended at the end of Part VI., and "the spell was snapt."

> "And now, all in my own countree,
> I stood on the firm land," —

returned from a voyage into the inane. Again I found myself sitting in the little hotel parlor, by the side of a man with glittering eye, with a third somebody on the other side of the table.

I drew a long breath.

Booth turned over the leaves of the volume. It contained the collected works of Coleridge, Shelley, and Keats.

"Did you ever read," said he, "Shelley's argument against the use of animal food, at the end of 'Queen Mab'?"

"Yes, I have read it."

"And what do you think of the argument?"

"Ingenious, but not satisfactory."

"To me it *is* satisfactory. I have long been convinced that it is wrong to take the life of an animal for our pleasure. I eat no animal food. There is my supper," — pointing to the plate of bread. "And, indeed," continued he, "I think the Bible favors this view. Have you a Bible with you?"

I had not furnished myself with a Bible.

Booth rang the bell, and when the boy presented himself called for one. Garçon disappeared, and came back soon with a Bible on a tray.

Our tragedian took the book, and proceeded to argue his point by means of texts selected skillfully here and there from Genesis to Revelation. He referred to the fact that it was not till after the Deluge men were allowed, "for the hardness of their hearts," as he maintained, to eat meat. But in the beginning it was not so; only herbs were given to man, at first, for food. He quoted the Psalmist (Psalm civ. 14) to show that man's food came from the earth, and was the green herb; and contended that the reason why Daniel and his friends were fairer and fatter than the children who ate their portion of meat was, that they ate only pulse (Daniel i. 12–15). These are all of his Scriptural arguments which I now recall; but I thought them rather ingenious at the time.

The argument took some time. Then he recited one or two pieces bearing on the same subject, closing with Byron's lines to his Newfoundland dog.

"In connection with that poem," he continued, "a singular event once happened to me. I was acting in Petersburg, Virginia. My theatrical engagement was just concluded, and I dined with a party of friends one afternoon before going away. We sat, after dinner, singing songs, reciting poetry, and relating anecdotes. At last I recited those lines of Byron on his dog. I was sitting by the fire-place, my feet resting against the jamb, and a single candle was burning on the mantel. It had become dark. Just as I came to the end of the poem, —

> " ' To mark a friend's remains these stones arise,
>   I never knew but one, and here he lies,' —

my foot slipped down the jamb, and struck a *dog*, who was lying beneath. The dog sprang up, howled, and ran out of the room, and at the same moment the candle went out. I asked whose dog it was. No one knew. No one had seen the dog till that moment. Perhaps you may smile at me, sir, and think me superstitious, — but I could not but think that the animal was brought there by some *occult sympathy*."

Having uttered these oracular words in a very solemn tone, Booth rose, and, taking one of the candles, said to me, " Would you like to look at the remains ? "

I assented. Asking our silent friend to excuse us, he led me into an adjoining chamber. I looked toward a bed in the corner of the room, but saw nothing there. Booth went to another corner of the room, where, spread out upon a large sheet, I beheld to my surprise, *about a bushel of wild pigeons!*

Booth knelt down by the side of the birds, and

18

with evidence of sincere affliction began to mourn
over them. He took them up in his hands tenderly, and pressed them to his heart. For a few
moments he seemed to forget my presence. For
this I was glad, for it gave me a little time to
recover from my astonishment, and to consider
rapidly what it might mean. As I look back now,
and think of the oddity of the situation, I rather
wonder at my own self-possession. It was a sufficiently trying position. At first I thought it was
a hoax, an intentional piece of practical fun, of
which I was to be the object. But even in the
moment allowed me to think, I decided that this
could not be. For I recalled the long and elaborate Bible argument against taking the life of animals, which could hardly have been got up for the
occasion. I considered also that as a joke it would
be too poor in itself, and too unworthy a man like
Booth. So I decided that it was a sincere conviction, — an idea, exaggerated perhaps to the bor-
ders of monomania, of the sacredness of all life.
And I determined to treat the conviction with
respect, as all sincere and religious convictions
deserve to be treated.

I also saw the motive for this particular course
of action. During the week immense quantities
of the wild pigeon (Passenger Pigeon, *Columba
migratoria*) had been flying over the city, in their
way to and from a *roost* in the neighborhood.
These birds had been slaughtered by myriads, and

were for sale by the bushel at the corners of every
street in the city. Although all the birds which
could be killed by man made the smallest impression on the vast multitude contained in one of
these flocks, — computed by Wilson to consist
sometimes of more than twenty-two hundred millions, — yet to Booth the destruction seemed
wasteful, wanton, and, from his point of view, was
a willful and barbarous murder.

I could not but feel a certain sympathy with his
humanity. It was an error in a good direction.
If an insanity, it was better than the cold, heart-
less sanity of most men. By the time, therefore,
that Booth was ready to speak, I was prepared to
answer.

"You see," said he, "these innocent victims of
man's barbarity. I wish to testify, in some public way, against this wanton destruction of life.
And I wish you to help me. Will you?"

"Hardly," I replied. "I expected something
very different from this, when I received your
note. I did not come to see you, expecting to be
called to assist at the funeral solemnities of birds."

"Nor did I send for you," he answered. "I
merely wrote to ask about the lot in the grave-
yard. But now you are here, why not help me?
Do you fear the laugh of man?"

"No," I returned. "If I agreed with you in
regard to this subject, I might, perhaps, have the
courage to act out my convictions. But I do not

look at it as you do. There is no reason, then, why I should have anything to do with it. I respect your convictions, but do not share them."

"That is fair," he said. "I cannot ask anything more. I am obliged to you for coming to see me. My intention was to purchase a place in the burial-ground and have them put into a coffin and carried in a hearse. I might do it without any one's knowing that it was not a human body. Would you assist me, then?"

"But if no one *knew* it," I said, "how would it be a public testimony against the destruction of life?"

"True, it would not. Well, I will consider what to do. Perhaps I may wish to bury them privately in some garden."

"In that case," said I, "I will find you a place in the grounds of some of my friends."

He thanked me, and I took my leave, exceedingly astonished by the incident, but also interested in the earnestness of conviction of the man.

I heard, in a day or two, that he actually purchased a lot in the cemetery, two or three miles below the city, had a coffin made, hired a hearse and carriage, and had gone through all the solemnity of a regular funeral. For several days he continued to visit the grave of his little friends, and mourned over them with a grief which did not seem at all theatrical.

Meantime he acted every night at the theatre,

and my friends told me that his acting was of unsurpassed excellence. A vein of insanity began, however, to mingle in his conduct. His fellow-actors were afraid of him. He looked terribly in earnest on the stage; and when he went behind the scenes, he spoke to no one, but sat still, looking sternly at the ground. During the day he walked about town, giving apples to the horses, and talking with the drivers, urging them to treat their animals with kindness.

An incident happened, one day, which illustrated still further his sympathy with the humbler races of animals. One of the sudden freshets which come to the Ohio, caused commonly by heavy rains melting the snow in the valleys of its tributary streams, had raised the river to an unusual height. The yellow torrent rushed along its channel, bearing on its surface logs, boards, and the débris of fences, shanties, and lumber-yards. A steamboat, forced by the rapid current against the stone landing, had been stove, and lay a wreck on the bottom, with the water rising rapidly around it. A horse had been left fastened on the boat, and it looked as if he would be drowned. Booth was on the landing, and he took from his pocket twenty dollars, and offered it to any one who would get to the boat and cut the halter, so that the horse might swim ashore. Some one was found to do it, and the horse's life was saved.

So this golden thread of human sympathy with

all creatures whom God had made ran through the darkening moods of his genius. He had well laid to heart the fine moral of his favorite poem, that

" He prayeth well, who loveth well
　　Both man, and bird, and beast.

" He prayeth best, who loveth best
　　All things, both great and small ;
　　For the dear God, who loveth us,
　　He made and loveth all."

In a week or less the tendency to derangement in Booth became more developed. One night, when he was to act, he did not appear ; nor was he found at his lodgings. He did not come home that night. Next morning he was found in the woods, several miles from the city, wandering through the snow. He was taken care of. His derangement proved to be temporary, and his reason returned in a few days. He soon left the city. But before he went away he sent me the following note, which I copy from the original faded paper now lying before me : —

　　　　　　" LOUISVILLE THEATRE, *January* 13, 1834.

" MY DEAR SIR, — Allow me to return you my grateful acknowledgments for your prompt and benevolent attention to my request last Wednesday night. Although I am convinced *your* ideas and *mine* thoroughly coincide as to the *real* cause of Man's bitter degradation, yet I fear human means to redeem him are now fruitless. The fire must burn, and Prometheus endure his agony. The Pestilence of Asia must come again, ere the savage will be taught humanity. May *you* escape! God bless you, sir! J. B. BOOTH."

Though this was an odd adventure for a young minister, less than six months in his profession, it left in my mind a very pleasant impression of this great tragedian. It may be asked why he came to me, the youngest clergyman in the place. He himself gave me the reason. I was a Unitarian. He said he had more sympathy with me on that account, as he was of Jewish descent, and a Monotheist.

XV.

WASHINGTON

AND THE SECRET OF HIS INFLUENCE.

WASHINGTON, HIS ADVICE AND EXAMPLE.

———◆———

IT is not my purpose to-day to deliver an oration on the character and life of Washington. This has been done too often, and too ably; and it is not the hour or place for such an oration. But I cannot help remembering that to-morrow is the birthday of the great man whom we have agreed to call the Father of our Country, and now, when the building he founded and helped to finish is nearly one hundred years old,[1] we may invoke his spirit to preserve that which his spirit gave. His example is very precious at the present hour. Let us see what we can learn from it — what it can do for us.

The four greatest men this country has produced are, I think, Washington, Franklin, Jefferson, and Abraham Lincoln. Of these, Jefferson was the greatest genius, Franklin the greatest intellect, Lincoln the most marked product of American institutions, and Washington the greatest character.

[1] This address was spoken February 21, 1875.

In regard to intellect merely, we may distinguish two classes of minds. It is the province of one to *manage the present;* of the other, to *introduce the future.* Jefferson belonged to the latter class, Washington to the former, Franklin and Lincoln to both. Franklin was, perhaps, the greatest intellect of all, for he combined the genius of Jefferson, the wisdom of Washington, and the American sagacity of Lincoln. But the peculiarity of Washington was the weight of his character. Never has there been, in modern times, a similar example of the influence of personality. Washington, while he lived, was the only man in the nation whom the people trusted, the only man who had that wonderful power of supporting a nation in its greatest crisis by the strength of his single arm. While he lived there was one man who could save his country. When he died, it was thrown on its own resources — it was obliged to save itself.

It was this which justified the epithet applied to Washington by Southey : " *Awful !*" We are filled with awe in contemplating one so separated from common men as to be the equipoise for all other living men ; to weigh as much, morally, as all of them together. Jupiter, in Homer, tells the gods to take hold at one end of the golden chain which holds the earth in its place, and he will take hold of the other, and draw them all up, gods, goddesses, earth and ocean. It is sometimes granted to a single man, in whom a perfect loyalty to right is joined to an iron inflexibility of will, to do the same thing in the moral world. If the whole American people inclined in one direction, and Washington in the opposite direction, it was in the power of Washington to hold the whole nation back, and arrest it in its course. He did this more than once. His firmness of purpose saved us in the Revolution. It held the nation back from despair in its darkest hours. His firmness of purpose, after the Revolution, enabled the nation to form the Federal Union. His great name, great influence, and perfect conviction brought them up to the point they might not otherwise have reached, — of accepting a constitution which was unquestionably unpalatable to the great majority. He lost more battles than he won, and he often lost them from the want of a military genius. But, after a defeat, the nation continued to trust him more than Marlborough or Napoleon were trusted after a victory. Three times his character saved the country ; once, by keeping up the courage of the nation till the Revolutionary War was ended ; then by uniting the nation in the acceptance of the Federal Constitution ; thirdly, by saving it from being swept away into anarchy and civil war during the immense excitements of the French Revolution. Such was the greatness of Washington, — a gift of God to this nation as far beyond any other of God's gifts as virtue is more than genius, as character is more than intellect, as wise conduct is better than outward prosperity.

Washington, in his portraits, and in history, seems a perfectly calm and self-possessed man, of imperturbable coolness, and, to the superficial observer, even wanting in passion. But Taylor, in his " Van Artevelde," paints a portrait which describes him better.

> " An equal nature, and an ample soul,
> Rockbound and fortified against the assaults
> Of momentary passion ; but beneath
> Built on a surging, subterraneous fire,
> Which stirred and lifted him to great attempts."

When the steam-engine is out of order it may make a noise and shake violently, and the steam escaping through the cracks may hiss; but all this is a sign of weakness, not of power. The engine which works without jar and without noise, sending its piston easily to and fro, and turning its shaft quietly round and round, this is the strong engine. Its power is all restrained, guided, and made to do the will of the master. So it is with the fire in the souls of great men. It is the deep lying fire — the tide of fire below, which slowly lifts the whole continent — not the ebullition of fire which wastes itself at the orifice of a volcano. The passion in the soul of Washington helped to raise our American continent.

Such was our Washington, — self-possessed, in perfect equipoise of soul, with no unbalanced tendencies, with no loose, undirected powers, with conscience always in command, with wisdom always as the counselor — a perfectly disinterested patriot, into whose soul the thought of a private end could not enter; brave without bravado, and a gentleman by the threefold right of birth, education, and character. So there came to him at last, by virtue of his perfect fidelity, this miraculous accumulation of reverence. He seemed superior to all human weakness — his life was one

> " That dare send
>   A challenge to its end,
>   And when it comes, say, ' Welcome, Friend.' "

Such being the position of Washington to this nation, we can appeal to his great spirit to-day; we, who are not men worshipers; we, who do not idolize saints and martyrs, we can appeal to his spirit to look from its high sphere, and counsel the land he loved in every situation.

Instead of eulogizing again what has so often been the subject of eulogy, — the character of Washington, — let us ask how he would advise us if he were to be able to address the American nation to-day. There are not many men whose advice we should care to have. Most of our great statesmen were too deeply immersed in the politics of their time. Jefferson and Hamilton, Andrew Jackson, Calhoun, Webster, Clay may have been intellectually greater than Washington, but they were not so wise. They were all ardent partisans, champions of partial interests; but the unselfish conscience of Washington raised him to a higher plane of principles, gave him a judgment undistorted by partiality. He could overlook the whole ground; he could see the value of opposing interests; the simplicity and honesty of his thought raised it to the level of wisdom. Talent alone, knowledge alone, the most brilliant imagination, the most penetrating insight, the most comprehensive and exact perceiving faculty — these do not make the wise man. Wisdom is born, not from the head, but from the upright conscience and the pure heart. Singleness of purpose and honesty of intention eliminate all the sources of error arising from personal feeling, from party spirit, from local interests, from individual prejudices; and so they leave the judgment free to act on the practical question without bias. In calculating the most complex movements of the heavenly bodies, the simple rules of mathematics will bring out an accurate result, provided every source of error is carefully removed. In practical life, these sources of error are oftenest found to be in the feelings. That is why purity of heart opens the way to truth, and why things hidden from the learned and the brilliant are revealed to babes. This was the commanding power of Washington's mind. Of the first American Congress, meeting in Philadelphia in September, 1774, Patrick Henry said that its best orator was Rutledge of South Carolina, but for solid information and sound judgment, Washington was the greatest of all.

The paper of Washington which contains his most carefully expressed opinions in regard to our national affairs is his parting address. Studiously reserved on most occasions, the silent man opened his mouth and became almost expressive. As Paul once said, when his feelings overflowed in words of fire, so Washington, in writing this address, might have exclaimed: " O Americans! my mouth is open unto you; my heart is enlarged!" After forty-five years of public service he was about to leave public life forever; and, as a father on his death-bed will give advice to his children on subjects to which he has never before alluded, so Washington, in this address, freed his heart and uttered his whole thought for the benefit of the nation.

The great danger at that time was to the Union. The centrifugal force was stronger than the centripetal. Washington, therefore, urges most strongly, at the opening of his remarks, loyalty to the Union, fidelity to the central government, opposition to local and sectional prejudices. He exhorts the North and the South, the East and the West, to regard themselves as one. Since our great and terrible civil war has restored the Union, and made the central government so strong, it may be thought that his advice is not now so very much required. Yet I believe this counsel is never quite unnecessary. Before the Rebellion the South governed the North — now, the North governs the South. A triumphant political party, representing union, freedom for all, and the rights of the North, has now, during fourteen years, governed the nation. It does not mean to be a sectional party, but there is great danger of its becoming so. I think that, if George Washington could speak, he would say, "You have fought and labored to give freedom to Southern black men, and you have done well. But remember that Southern white men have rights also; do not make slaves of them while freeing the blacks. They also are your brethren. The evil influence which corrupted them — Slavery — has come to an end. The passions excited by the war and its results have had nearly ten years wherein to cool. The interests of North and South, before hostile, are now the same. Recognize their rights, and give real peace to the nation."

The habit which has grown up since the war, of the interference by the general government in the local politics of the reconstructed States, was for a time, perhaps, excusable, because possibly unavoidable. But it has evidently become very dangerous.

Recent grave events in Louisiana have called the attention of all thoughtful persons to this subject. An officer of the United States army, with a file of soldiers, entered the hall where the Legislature of the State was in session and removed five members; thus taking the majority from one political party and giving it to another. The action of the general government in approving this proceeding seemed to me so serious, that I signed a call for a meeting in Faneuil Hall to consider it. I have been frequently asked why I did so, since so many good men and women thought the action of the President right. Perfectly willing to admit that the intentions of all concerned were good, I think the act a dangerous one.

Louisiana has been readmitted into the Union as a sovereign State. If so, she has all the rights which Massachusetts has. In Massachusetts we have a Democratic governor and a Republican Legislature. Suppose the governor should request the United States military commandant of this district to go to the state house and remove Republican members from the senate chamber, so as to give a Democratic majority to that body. If he should do so, and a Democratic President and Cabinet should approve the action, would those who defend his action in Louisiana approve of it in Massachusetts? and if not, why not?

It will be said in reply that the cases are different; that the people of Louisiana are rebels, and that they must be held down by military power. This is a very good reason for putting the State back into the condition of a territory and giving it a military government, but not for violating all its constitutional rights while it remains one of the States of the Union.

It may be said that the representatives removed had no right to be there, and that the Legislature was not properly organized. One famous orator has declared that the Louisiana Legislature was not properly organized, and therefore was not a legislature, but a mob. But who is to decide whether it was properly organized or not? Shall the governor of Louisiana decide it? He had no more right to decide it than you or I have. The Constitution of Louisiana declares that " each house of the General Assembly shall judge of the qualifications, elections, and returns of its members." So the Constitution of Massachusetts declares that the Senate and the House shall each be the final judge of the elections, returns, and qualifications of its members. Each house, also, by the Constitution, adopts its own rule of proceedings. If it chooses to have a motion put by its clerk, it may ; if it allows a motion to be put by one of its own members, it may. But, at all events, right or wrong, the question of its organization belongs to itself, not to the executive. Allow the governor of the State to decide whether a certain body is the Legislature or only a mob, and the independence of the Legislature is at end. Listen to George Washington's opinion on this subject. If he had foreseen this very case, he could not have expressed himself more plainly : —

" It is important," he says, in his Farewell Address, " that the habits of thinking, in a free country, should inspire caution in those intrusted with its administration, to confine themselves within their respective constitutional spheres, avoiding, in the exercise of the powers of one department, to encroach upon another. The spirit of encroachment tends to consolidate the powers of all the departments in one, and thus to create, whatever the form of government, a real despotism. . . . . If, in the opinion of the people, the distribution or modification of the constitutional pow-. ers be in any particular wrong, let it be corrected by an amendment in the way which the Constitution designates. But let there be no change by usurpation ; for though this, in one instance, may be the instrument of good, it is the customary weapon by which free governments are destroyed. The precedent must always greatly overbalance in permanent evil any partial or transient benefit which the use can at any time yield."

Many good people think that the rights of the colored people require such acts of military interference on the part of the United States. If this be so, then, I repeat, reduce the Southern States to Territories, and keep them so for a generation.

But do not, in the fancied interests of the colored people, destroy, one by one, all the guarantees of constitutional liberty.

Perhaps I may be considered as one not wholly indifferent to the rights of the colored people of the South. But I do not think that their safety, peace, happiness, rights will be best secured by such gross violations of the rights of the white people of the South. By persecuting the white people in the interests of the blacks, you are intensifying and perpetuating the hatred of one race to another. Their mutual interests are now the same. The prosperity of the whites, who are owners of the soil, depends on the good will of the laborers who cultivate it. This is a much better security for their good treatment than a military force. What John A. Andrew saw and said nine years ago is still the only true method. He proposed to reconstruct the South, "not by its ignorance, but by its intelligence." Governor Andrew said, in *his* farewell address to the Legislature: "We ought to demand, and to secure, the coöperation of the strongest and ablest minds and natural leaders of opinion in the South. If we cannot gain their support of the just measures needful for the work of safe reorganization, reorganization will be delusive and full of danger. It would be idle to reorganize those States by the colored vote. I would not consent, having rescued those States by arms from secession and re-

bellion, to turn them over to anarchy and chaos."
Nothing can be wiser, nothing more true, than
this.

The danger pointed out by George Washington,
of the arrival of despotism by the encroachment
of one department of government on the constitutional rights of another, is not confined to Louisiana. It has already reached Washington. A
bill has been prepared in a Republican caucus,
with the intention of forcing it through Congress
by the Republican majority, to give to the President the power, according to his own discretion,
of suspending the bill of Habeas Corpus throughout the Union. The first article of the Constitution designates the powers of Congress; and in the
ninth section of this article the power of suspending the act of Habeas Corpus, but only in times of
rebellion or invasion, is committed to Congress,
and to Congress only. It has been solemnly decided by the courts that only to the Legislature
belongs the power of suspending the operation of
this great writ, which protects the personal freedom of us all. Personal liberty is safe, and is only
safe, so long as this writ is in force.

The power of party has shown itself in nothing
more than in this attempt to transfer to the President what belongs to Congress. I have always
been a Republican since the Republican party was
first formed. I have never voted any other ticket.
But I shall feel bound, with thousands of others,

to resist to the last such encroachments on human liberty, such rash defiance of all the guarantees of personal rights, as is here attempted. The foundation of Saxon liberty was laid here. The chief point in Magna Charta is giving the protection of each man's freedom to the national legislature. It is now proposed to put this great and terrible power, which in a moment may deprive every man in the land of all his civil rights, into the hands of the President, to be exercised at his own discretion. The mere suggestion of such a surrender of the great guarantee of freedom ought to have aroused the nation. But the fact that it is proposed illustrates the tyranny of party and of party allegiance. When a party caucus has decided on a course, any politician is a brave man who ventures to dissent. "The caucus" is a power not mentioned in the Constitution; but, with "the ring" and "the lobby," it is seeking to take possession of the whole government. The tyranny of party has resulted, as all tyranny does, in making the tyrant a slave. The tyrant, Party, has become the slave of the despot, Caucus.

What George Washington would say on this subject may be easily known from his advice in regard to the power of party and party allegiance. He declares it to be a "fatal tendency" which "puts the will of a party in the place of the delegated will of the nation." He wisely says that most parties are a "small but artful and enterprising minority of the community," and that "the alternate triumphs of different parties will make the public administration the mission of the ill-concerted and incongruous projects of faction, rather than the organ of consistent and wholesome plans, digested by common councils, and modified by mutual interests." Washington gives us a solemn warning against the spirit of party, and declares that there is great danger to our institutions in that direction.

We may be sure, then, that Washington would have favored the plan, now proposed, which will give to minorities their due share of representation. According to our present methods, minorities have little or no influence in legislation. In South Carolina, where the colored vote is about fifty-four per cent. of the whole, the colored people hold all the power. In Georgia, where the white vote has a small majority, the white people hold all the power. It would be better, in both cases, that the minority should be adequately represented. According to our present system, minorities have no rights which a triumphant party is bound to respect.

Another point on which Washington dwells in his address is general education. He urges us to promote, as an object of primary importance, the general diffusion of knowledge. Since public opinion, in this country, governs all things, it is absolutely necessary that public opinion should be enlightened. Such is the distinct declaration of Washington. He founds the necessity and duty of public free schools on the fact that the whole government of the country is in the hands of the whole people. Our lives, our fortunes, our liberties, are at the mercy of the majority. If the people are instructed, they will see that their own interests require just and equal laws. If they are ignorant, they can be led by demagogues, by priests, by selfish politicians. Free institutions rest on common schools.

The only danger to common schools in this country is from the Roman Catholic Church. Since the declaration of Papal Infallibility, the Catholics in this, and in every other country, are bound to obey the decisions of the Roman court, and that is in the hands, as the most distinguished Roman Catholic in England, Dr. Newman, informs us, of a small coterie of Jesuits. The public school system of the United States is in danger from this source, and from this source only. I regard this as the chief danger of the present time. It is to be met fairly, justly, and courageously. Under no circumstances whatever must we allow the sectarian school system of Europe to be substituted for the public, unsectarian school system of America.

Perhaps it may be thought that I have gone out of my sphere as a Christian minister, in discussing in the pulpit, and on the Lord's day, questions belonging to national affairs. I have, indeed, been discussing national politics; but not party politics. I have been criticising the party to which I myself belong. These matters concern the rights, the freedom, the safety of the nation; they concern the permanency of republican institutions. If there be any matters in which Christianity is and ought to be interested, anything for which Christian men and women ought to care, anything about which Christian ministers ought to speak, it is the political movements and acts which involve the rights and duties of the whole people. Such has always been my own opinion; such has always been my own course. During many years, during the long antislavery struggle, I was frequently accused of bringing politics into the pulpit. But I have never spoken of politics unless when politics concerned humanity. I am sorry when my friends differ from me, or when I differ from my friends; but I am afraid I am too old now to change my course in this matter, unless I see stronger reasons for doing so than I now perceive. I claim no authority to dictate to any one; others have a right to their opinions, and they may be more sound than mine; but I must hold my own, and utter them when it seems necessary.

In the great storm which drove the vessel containing the Apostle Paul on the shore of Malta, we are told that the mariners "cast four anchors out of the stern, and wished for day." *Our* four anchors, holding us fast from behind, are the examples and teachings of Washington, Franklin, Jefferson, and Abraham Lincoln. The first represents *virtue* in politics; the second, *good sense* in politics; the third, *democracy* in politics; the fourth, *humanity* in politics. Let us reverence these great examples holding us firm to a noble Past, and so saving us for a better Future. With four such illustrious lives as these to reverence, to study, and to follow, we may feel that in the most stormy hours, and the darkest nights, we may hold safe by these anchors " and wish for day."

XVI.

SHAKSPEARE.

SHAKSPEARE.[1]

WE meet to-day, my friends, as members of the
great family which speaks the English tongue, to
commemorate the three hundredth birthday of the
man who, in pure intellect, stands at the head of
the human race. But how little do we know of
Shakspeare, except in his works! We do not
know how to spell his name correctly. We cannot tell the day he was born, but are obliged to
assume this on probable grounds. Whether he
went to school, or not, is uncertain. The business of his father is uncertain. His life, till he
was married, is a blank. After that date, we only
know that he had three children; that he went
to London, became an actor, then a writer of plays,
then a joint proprietor of the theatre; that he
was comparatively wealthy; returned to Stratford, and died at the age of fifty-two.

If, therefore, it should be thought desirable, by

---

[1] Address before the New England Historic-Genealogical Society
on the ter-centenary celebration of the birth of Shakspeare, April
23, 1864.

the critics of the twentieth century, to treat Shakspeare as certain critics have treated Homer, Moses, and Christ, and deny his existence, they have
an excellent opportunity and ample means for
their destructive analysis. As they have proved
to their satisfaction that the books of Moses are
composed of innumerable independent historical
fragments carefully joined together, and so are a
Mosaic work only in the artistic sense; as they
have taken away Homer, and left in his place a
company of anonymous ballad-singers, so that we
are able to settle the dispute between the seven
cities which claimed to be his birthplace, by giving them a Homer apiece, and having several
Homers left; as these able chemical critics have
analyzed the Gospels, reducing them to their elements of legend, myth, and falsehood, with the
smallest residuum of actual history : so much
more easily can they dispose of the historic Shakspeare.

See, for example, how they might proceed.
They might say: "How can Shakspeare have
been a real person, when his very name is spelled
at least in two different ways, in manuscripts professing to be his own autograph ; and when it is
found in the manuscripts of the period spelled in
every form, and with every combination of letters
which express its sound or the semblance thereof ?
One writer of his time calls him 'Shake-scene;'
showing plainly the mythical origin of the word.

He is said to have married, at eighteen, a woman of twenty-six — which is not likely; and her name also has a mythical character, — 'Anne Hathaway,' — and was probably derived from a Shakspeare song addressed to a lady named Anne, the first line of which is 'Anne hath a way, Anne hath a way.' If he were a real person, living in London in the midst of writers, poets, actors, and eminent men, is it credible that no allusion should be made to him by most of them? He was contemporary with Sir Walter Raleigh, Edmund Spenser, Lord Bacon, Coke, Cecil Lord Burleigh, Hooker, Queen Elizabeth, Henry IV. of France, Montaigne, Tasso, Cervantes, Galileo, Grotius; and not one of these, though so many of them were voluminous writers, refers to any such person, and no allusion to any of them appears in all his plays. He is referred to, to be sure, with excessive admiration, by the group of play-writers among whom he is supposed to move; but as there is not, in all his works, the least allusion in return to any of them, we may presume that the name Shakspeare was a sort of *nom de plume* to which was referred all anonymous plays. If such a man existed, why did not others, out of this circle, say something about his circumstances and life? Milton was eight years old when Shakspeare died, and might have seen him, as he took pains to go and see Galileo, who was born in the same year with Shakspeare. Oliver Cromwell

20

was seventeen years old when Shakspeare died ; Descartes, twenty years old ; Rubens, the artist, thirty-nine years old. None of them had heard of him ; though Rubens resided in England, and painted numerous portraits there. Spenser, it is true, has two stanzas, in one of his poems, that seem undoubtedly to refer ·to this mythological person : —

> "' He, the man whom Nature's self had made
> To mock herself, and Truth to imitate,
> With kindly counter under mimick shade, —
> Our pleasant Willy, ah ! is dead of late ;
> With whom all joy and jolly merriment
> Is also deaded, and in dolour drent.'

" But this only proves more clearly the mythical character of Shakspeare ; since the poem, in which he is said to be ' lately dead,' was published by Spenser in 1591, when Shakspeare is stated to have been twenty-seven, — twenty-five years before the date given for his death. The believers in a personal Shakspeare say, indeed, that Spenser means that he is dead to literature, having left off writing ; and quote the following stanza to support this view, in which Spenser thus continues : —

> "' But that same gentle spirit, from whose pen
> Large streams of honey and sweet nectar flow,
> Scorning the boldness of such base-born men
> Which dare their follies forth so rashly throw,
> Doth rather choose *to sit in idle cell,*
> Than so himself to mockery to sell.'

" But, unfortunately for this theory, so far from leaving off writing, Shakspeare had hardly begun to write then, and did not print his first work till two years after."

In this way the critic might argue to prove the non-existence of any personal Shakspeare. He might add that there is something quite suspicious in his being said to have been born and to have died on the same day of the month — April 23; and in the fact that Cervantes was said to die the same day as Shakspeare — April 23, 1616; and Michael Angelo in the same year. The year of his birth, he might add, seems to have some mythical significance; since Calvin is said to have died, and Galileo to have been born, each in 1564. The critic might add that many great events occurred in his supposed lifetime, to none of which he has alluded, — as the battle of Lepanto; the Bartholomew Massacre; the defeat of the Spanish Armada; the first circumnavigation of the world; the Gunpowder Plot; the deliverance of Holland from Spain; the invention of the telescope, and the discovery therewith of Jupiter's satellites. In an era of great controversy between the Roman Catholics and Protestants, no one can tell from his works whether he was Catholic or Protestant. " Unlike Dante, Milton, and Goethe, he left no trace on the political or even social life of his time." And, finally, our twentieth-century critic may say, that already, in 1857 and 1866, two

American writers (Miss Delia Bacon and Judge
Holmes) published books to show that Shakspeare's plays were not written by Shakspeare,
but by Lord Bacon.

So little has been learned in the last three
centuries concerning this miracle of the human
mind.   A whole pack of Shakspeare scholars have
been on his track with the sagacity and persever-
ance of sleuth hounds.   Every trace of Shakspeare
has been examined with microscopic care ; every
muniment-room, with its mound of musty paper,
has been dug over and sifted, as men sift the sands
of Australian rivers in search of gold ; and with
what result ?   Two or three autographs of his
name, spelt in two or three different ways ; and
half a dozen allusions to him by his contemporaries.   It has been discovered that his father was
named John, and was either a glover, a farmer, a
butcher, or a dealer in wool ; that his father married a daughter of the gentry, — Mary Arden, —
and lost his property in his latter days ; that there
is good reason for thinking that Shakspeare himself was well acquainted with Latin, Greek, Italian,
and French ; good reason also for thinking that he
was not.   The story of his stealing the deer of Sir
Thomas Lucy is believed by Richard Grant White ;
who, however, says that " we know nothing positively of Shakspeare from his birth till his marriage ; and, from that date, nothing until we find
him an actor in London about the year 1589, he

being then twenty-five years of age. Here he became actor, afterwards dramatic writer, and finally also proprietor of one of the theatres. The success of his plays was immediate and great : they filled the theatres, — 'cockpit, galleries, boxes,' says a contemporary. In 1597, when thirty-three years old, he was able to purchase the finest house in Stratford ; and, in the same year, invested in the securities of his town a sum equal to about thirteen thousand dollars." [1] Nothing is

---

[1] "But Shakspeare continued to hold his property in the theatre. In 1608 the corporation of London again attempted to interfere with the actors of the Blackfriars ; and, there being little chance of ejecting them despotically, a negotiation was set on foot for the purchase of their property. A document found by Mr. Collier amongst the Egerton Papers at once determined Shakspeare's position in regard to his theatrical proprietorship. It is a valuation, containing the following item : —

"'*Item.* — W. Shakspeare asketh, for the wardrobe and properties of the same playhouse, £500 : and for his four shares, the same as his fellows Burbidge and Fletcher ; viz., £933 6s. 8d. £1,433 6s. 8d.'

"With this document was found another, unquestionably the most interesting paper ever published relating to Shakspeare. It is a letter from Lord Southampton to Lord Ellesmere, the lord chancellor ; and it contains the following passage : —

"'These bearers are two of the chief of the company ; one of them by name Richard Burbidge, who humbly sueth for ·your lordship's kind help ; for that he is a man famous as our English Roscius, one who fitteth the action to the word, and the word to the action, most admirably. By the exercise of his quality, industry, and good behavior, he hath become possessed of the Blackfriars Playhouse, which hath been employed for plays since it was built by his father, now near fifty years ago. The other is a man no whit less deserving favor, and my especial friend, till

known of his intercourse with actors, or men of letters, except the admiration expressed for him by Ben Jonson, the praise of Chettle, and a few vague rumors. He gave up the stage about 1604, when forty years old, and returned to Stratford to live when about forty-six. He was said to have been "a handsome, well-shaped man." From all the portraits, and the bust, it is evident that his head, like those of Homer, Plato, Napoleon, and Goethe, was fully developed, and a fit dome of thought; probably the noblest head, in its shape, of which we have any artistic record.

But, though the Shakspeare scholars do not furnish us with much beside this "tombstone information," they have helped us to form a picture of his life by showing the character of the times.

of late an actor of good account in the company, now a sharer in the same, and writer of some of our best English plays, which, as your lordship knoweth, were most singularly liked of Queen Elizabeth, when the company was called upon to perform before her majesty at court at Christmas and Shrovetide.

"'His most gracious majesty King James also, since his coming to the crown, hath extended his royal favor to the company in divers ways and at sundry times.

"'This other hath to name William Shakspeare: and they are both of one county, and indeed almost of one town; both are right famous in their qualities, though it longeth not to your lordship's gravity and wisdom to resort unto the places where they are wont to delight the public ear. Their trust and suit now is, not to be molested in their way of life whereby they maintain themselves and their wives and families (being both married and of good reputation), as well as the widows and orphans of some of their dead fellows.'"—*Knight's English Cyclopædia*, art. SHAKSPEARE.

Shakspeare lived in that period known as the Renaissance, — the new birth of the human intellect. The great wave of mental life which rolled over Italy in the previous century at last reached the shores of England. Europe had discovered that there was knowledge outside of the Church formulas. The literatures of Greece and Rome had been unlocked ; and, instead of a barren theology and a dead philosophy, the intellect of mankind bathed in the pure waters of Hellenic and Latin knowledge. It was the fashion with men and women to read Homer and Plato, Sophocles and Euripides, Virgil, Tacitus, and Cicero. In England, at this time, the drama was the vehicle of instruction and entertainment. It took the place now occupied by newspaper and novel. The land swarmed with strolling players. Every great nobleman had his private company of actors. In London, in spite of the opposition of the corporation and the Puritans, several theatres had been opened. Fourteen of them we find existing at the same time, in and near London, during Shakspeare's life. They were named the Theatre, the Curtain, the Globe, Blackfriars, Paris Garden, Whitefriars, Salisbury Court, the Fortune, the Rose, Hope, the Swan, Newington, the Red Bull, Cockpit, and Phenix. The top was open to the sun and rain : the people stood in the pit, and sat on benches in the rooms and boxes, and also on the stage itself. There were few properties, and little scenery: sometimes they had to hang up a placard, on which was written, in large letters, " A Castle," " A Country House," " A Temple," " A Ship ; " and the audience were thus requested to imagine themselves in the presence of these objects. The dining-hour in London being twelve, the plays began at three, and lasted two hours: admission at first, a penny ; by and by, sixpence. Those who sat on the stage had a three-legged stool, and paid a shilling. The rage for new plays was great. Every theatre had authors at work, writing new plays. Thomas Heywood says he wrote part or the whole of two hundred and twenty. Philip Henslowe, whose diary has been recently discovered, a proprietor or manager of one of the theatres, states that he purchased a hundred and ten new plays between 1591 and 1597 ; and, in the next five years, a hundred and sixty more. People wanted a new play then, just as they now wish for a fresh newspaper or novel : the old ones did for yesterday ; but others are needed to-day. The prices paid for them varied from five pounds to twelve. Before 1600, eight pounds was the highest ; which would be equal to about two hundred and fifty dollars at this time. When plays had been thus purchased, they became the property of the theatre, and the authors abandoned all care of them. As there was no copyright to be had, the theatre could only keep them by not printing them. Even then, they were sometimes printed by emissaries from rival theatres, who "copied by the ear." Thomas Heywood says, "Though some have used a double sale of their labors,—first to the stage, and after to the press,—I here proclaim myself faithful to the first, and never guilty of the last."

We see how it was that Shakspeare did not print his plays himself in his life-time. It was not because of any ostrich-like indifference to them, but simply that they did not belong to him. He had sold them to the theatre. We see also one reason of the corruptions of the text,—many of them had been pirated, and were printed from copies taken by the ear, and, as Heywood says of his, were "so corrupt and mangled, that I have been as unable to know them as ashamed to challenge them."

That Shakspeare knew the worth of his plays, we cannot doubt. He must have been intensely conscious of their vast superiority. But literary fame, in the common sense, they did not bring at first. His literary works were "Venus and Adonis" and "Lucrece." Plays, as yet, had not become a part of literature. After this Ben Jonson was universally ridiculed for calling a collection of his dramas his "Works." When genius flows into any new channel, and appears in a new form, it takes some half century before it can be recognized. But at last its day comes, certainly and inevitably, though mysteriously; and the

world learns to love a great poet, much as Shakspeare himself describes the growth of a youthful
affection : —

> "The idea of his life shall sweetly creep
> Into its study of imagination ;
> And every lovely organ of his mind
> Shall come appareled in more precious habit,
> More moving, delicate, and full of life,
> Into the eye and prospect of its soul."

In this deficiency of information concerning the
life of the great Poet of Humanity, recourse has
been had to his sonnets, which have been thought
to be a journal of his inmost soul. Some persons,
indeed, think these wonderful poems to be the
mere play of fancy; but others believe them to
be, as Wordsworth says, "the key with which he
unlocked his heart." There can be no doubt that
the last view is the true one. It has been no unusual thing for poets to put their deepest life into
their poems, and keep a private journal in verse.
Horace says of Lucilius, "that he committed the
secrets of his soul to his books, as to faithful
friends; going to confide in them his joy and his
grief : so that the whole life of the old man appears painted in his poems as in votive pictures."
Goethe also says of himself, that, " in prose, no
one willingly confesses himself; but in poetry we
trust ourself *sub rosâ*, as in a true confessional.

> " Youthful grief and riper wrong
> In my stanzas echo long :
> Joy and pain both turn to song."

So, when we read these sonnets, we seem to stand by the door of the confessional, and listen to the most secret secrets of the heart of Shakspeare. These mysteries are veiled in a language so wonderfully delicate, that it at once tells all, and tells nothing. Shakspeare, so wholly objective in his dramas; with such absolute impersonality passing into one and another of his characters; so impartial, so inclusive, giving every side of life its due; ranging through such a compass of notes, from the deep organ diapason of " King Lear " to the wild melody of " The Tempest " and airy carols of " Midsummer Night's Dream," — here, in his sonnets, comes to himself; is all personality; is wholly subjective. As no writer who ever lived left himself so entirely out of his works as Shakspeare does in his plays, so no writer ever gave us himself so purely and personally as Shakspeare does in his sonnets.

In saying this we have not forgotten the sonnets of Petrarch. The difference between these and Shakspeare's comes from the circumstance that Petrarch's give us the picture of a lover possessed by his love. It is the agitated surface of a mind swept by winter storms of passion, or sleeping in the summer calms of purely emotional repose. But from how much deeper depth does the life of Shakspeare flow into *his!* It is not passion, but active devotion. It is love, so purified by truth from merely selfish emotion, that it might be felt in one angel in heaven for another. Somehow it is perfectly real yet ideal too. It seeks no earthly gratification ; there is no jealous monopoly in it, no self-delusion. He sees all the faults of his friend ; he tells him of his vices. His love does not claim any return : it is sufficient for itself. We may all agree with Mr. Alger that these sonnets mainly describe the friendship of Shakspeare for a noble and wonderful young man, — perhaps William Herbert, or perhaps the Earl of Southampton. Some lines of Ben Jonson describe well the character of this friendship of Shakspeare : —

> " 'Tis not a passion's first access,
>   Ready to multiply ;
> But, like Love's calmest state, it is
>   Possessed with victory :

> " It is like Love to truth reduced,
>   All the false values gone
> Which were created or induced
>   By fond imagination."

A friendship something like this was felt by Goethe and Schiller ; and, in our time, we have a parallel to the hundred and twenty-six sonnets addressed by Shakspeare to his boy friend in the hundred and twenty-nine poems addressed by Tennyson to *his* lost friend, Arthur Hallam. Allowing for the difference of times and customs, the tone and spirit of these two collections are strikingly the same.

The history of opinion in regard to Shakspeare is one of the most interesting records of the progress of human ideas. He stands in the flowing current of thought, as the Nilometer in the Nile; and the level of taste and intelligence at any time is shown by its relation to him. As far up as it reaches on the mind of Shakspeare, so high is the rise of human thought. In his own day he was the most popular of writers. " The common people heard him gladly." Whenever his plays were performed, the Globe Theatre was full, — in the pit, box-rooms, galleries. But the literary men, though they liked him, rather treated him *de haut en bas.* His immense popularity with the people they could not ignore: and Meres, in 1598, when Shakspeare was thirty-six years old, mentions twelve of his plays by name; compares him with Ovid; calls him " honey-tongued Shakspeare;" speaks of " his sugared sonnets among his private friends;" and concludes, that, if the Muses spoke English, they would use his " finefiled phrase." [1]

[1] " As the Greek tongue is made famous and eloquent by Homer, Hesiod, Euripides, Æschylus, Sophocles, Pindarus, Phocylides, and Aristophanes; and the Latin tongue by Virgil, Ovid, Horace, Silius Italicus, Lucanus, Lucretius, Ausonius, and Claudianus: so the English tongue is mightily enriched, and gorgeously invested in rare ornaments and resplendent habiliments, by Sir Philip Sidney, Spenser, Daniel, Drayton, Warner, Shakspeare, Marlow, and Chapman.

" As the soul of Euphorbus was thought to live in Pythagoras, so the sweet, witty soul of Ovid lives in mellifluous and honey-

That King James liked Shakspeare was then counted to Shakspeare's honor: now it is a great thing for King James, and saves him from being thought only a pedant. Always those who believed they were judging Shakspeare, were, in fact, only judging themselves.

In truth, these plays were not thought at first to belong to literature at all. The drama, in England, was a newly created form of art. Every new form of art is first enjoyed without being admired; afterwards it is admired without being enjoyed. It comes up to meet a popular desire or a real want; comes to be used, not to be looked at. Literary criticism has not reached it; considers it, in fact, below its level. Shakspeare himself appears to have thought his " Venus and Adonis " and " Lucrece " his first-written literary works; though, when these were published, he

tongued Shakspeare: witness his ' Venus and Adonis,' his ' Lucrece,' his sugared sonnets among his private friends, etc.

" As Plautus and Seneca are accounted the best for comedy and tragedy among the Latins; so Shakspeare, among the English, is the most excellent in both kinds for the stage: for comedy, witness his ' Gentleman of Verona,' his ' Errors,' his ' Love's Labor 's Lost,' his ' Love's Labor 's Won,' his ' Midsummer Night's Dream,' and his ' Merchant of Venice ;' for tragedy, his ' Richard II.,' ' Richard III.,' ' Henry IV.,' ' King John,' ' Titus Andronicus,' and his ' Romeo and Juliet.'

" As Epius Stola said that the Muses would speak with Plautus's tongue if they would speak Latin, so I say that the Muses would speak with Shakspeare's fine-filed phrase if they would speak English."

had already composed many of his dramatic masterpieces. So Shakspeare's contemporaries loved him very tenderly, — " this side idolatry," says Ben Jonson. They called him " pleasant Willy," and other endearing epithets. They very much enjoyed his plays; but as works of art — no, they were too *irregular* for that.

So, all through the next century, Shakspeare was regarded as a wild, irregular genius, — very agreeable, but not very authentic in a literary point of view. Even Milton's best allusion to him says : —

" Sweetest Shakspeare, Fancy's child,
Warbles his native wood-notes *wild*."

William Bosse, in 1621, requests Spenser, Chaucer, and Beaumont to lie a little nearer to each other in their graves, to make room for the " rare tragedian, Shakspeare." And, in the same style, Holland and Digges and Jasper Mayne, Davenant and Shirley, and the like, eulogize his wild fancy and irregular genius; till good Dr. Johnson comes and gives us the picture of " Time " toiling after him, and losing his breath trying to overtake him. Pope informs us that Shakspeare wrote for gain, and " became immortal in his own despite." Gray calls him " Nature's darling." Churchill says that " a noble wildness flashes from his eyes; " and at last Voltaire arrives, and gives us the *ultimatum* of this sort of criticism in his famous account of Hamlet : —

" It is a gross and barbarous piece, which would not be endured by the vilest populace of France or Italy. Hamlet goes crazy in the second act; his mistress goes crazy in the third. The prince kills the father of his mistress, pretending to kill a rat. They dig a grave on the stage. The grave-diggers say abominably gross things, holding the skulls of the dead in their hands. Hamlet replies in answers no less disgusting and silly than theirs. During this time, Poland is conquered by one of the actors. Hamlet, his mother and father-in-law, drink together on the stage: they sing, quarrel, fight, and kill each other. One would think this play the work of the imagination of a drunken savage."

Shakspeare may be said to have been rediscovered in Germany, — first by Lessing, afterward by Goethe and his friends. Gervinus, whose work, lately translated, gives us the whole literature of the matter in two large volumes of exhaustive criticism, says that Lessing was the man who first valued Shakspeare according to his true desert, and Goethe the first who gave an example of the true method of criticism. Then Schlegel and Tieck in Germany, Coleridge and Lamb in England, assisted in the rehabilitation of Shakspeare. They proved that he was as much of an artist as of a genius; that he is as full of wisdom as of fancy; that his supposed faults are often his greatest merits; and that no one is quite great enough yet fully to know him.

The effect on literature of this new-born love

for Shakspeare was most beneficial. The dead, dry literature of the eighteenth century came to life when the body of Shakspeare touched it, as the corpse revived, and stood on its feet, when it touched the bones of Elisha. Thus the course of thought in regard to our poet has been like the course of his own brook, — falling at one time over rough pebbles and hard critical rocks, but again resuming its sweet and placid course with an ever-deepening, ever-enlarging volume of water: —

> " The current that with gentle murmur glides,
> Thou knowest, being stopt, impatiently doth rage;
> But, when his fair course is not hindered,
> He makes sweet music with the enameled stones,
> Giving a gentle kiss to every sedge
> He overtaketh in his pilgrimage:
> And so, by many winding nooks, he strays,
> With willing course, to the wild ocean."

Thus the opinion of the world, under the guidance of the greatest thinkers, has tended more and more to this result, — that WILLIAM SHAKSPEARE stands at the summit of human intelligence; that of all mankind, since creation, his is the supreme intellect. But, if so, this conclusion follows, — that the imagination is the highest intellectual faculty; for, in him, all others were subordinate to that. That power of creation, almost divine, which most likens man to God, was supreme in him. Compare him with other thinkers; with great metaphysicians, like Plato, Aristotle, Descartes, Spinoza, Bacon; and how poor

21

does their analysis seem by the side of his majestic synthesis! They can take a man to pieces: he can create new men. Consider great mathematicians and naturalists, like Newton, Galileo, Leibnitz, Pascal: they can observe the laws of Nature which are the skeleton of the universe; but Shakspeare brings before us the universe itself, vitalized and harmonious in every part. All master intellects make use of the imagination: nothing can be done in the world without it. Imagination is the most practical of all the intellectual faculties: it collects all the broken and scattered knowledges of the mind into one complete picture. But in most thinkers, even in great thinkers, it is the servant of other faculties. The one distinction between Shakspeare and all others is this, — that in him all other faculties were subordinated to this: he was, as he describes his poet, " of imagination all compact." Observation, reason, memory, wit, humor, the analytic judgment, the critical understanding, — all were its willing servants; all brought their gifts of gold and silver, iron and stone, gems and pearls, to be used by this imperial faculty. No matter what is the special theme and spirit of his subject: it comes immediately and submissively under the rule of its king and chief. In his historic plays, or histories, memory is the chief servant of the imagination. It brings the characters, events, costume, and tone of a past age, taken bodily out of books or previous plays;

but they are all immediately harmonized and vitalized by the creative idea. We are carried back to
the streets of Rome in the days of Cæsar. Faithfully taking his facts from Plutarch in Thomas
North's translation (1579), he places us behind
the scenes; shows us Rome as it looked to the
eyes and mind, first of Brutus, then of Cæsar, then
of Antony. All the minutest details he accepts
from Plutarch: he copies the text with a ser-
vile fidelity, and then, by this wonderful power,
breathes life into this dry dust of history. If we
had been in Rome at the time of Cæsar's death,
we should not have known as much of it as we can
now know through the mediation of Shakspeare.

In these histories his imagination is served by
memory; but in such dramas as the " Tempest "
and the " Midsummer Night's Dream," another
faculty, — namely, FANCY — is called up to show
its loyalty to the same chief. As memory, uncontrolled by imagination, gives only dry and dead
facts, showing the mere outside of things, details
unconnected by any law; so fancy, uncontrolled
by imagination, gives no clear picture, but only
kaleidoscopic changes. We have enough of wild
fantastic fairy tales, extravaganzas where no law
restrains the willfulness of fancy; but Shakspeare's
fairies — like Ariel, like Puck, like Oberon, like
Titania — are persons. Though the whole scene
is in Dreamland, yet here Dreamland becomes a
reality, has laws of its own, a unity pervading and

restraining all its wildest variety; showing that
one idea is steadily in the master's mind, polar-
izing all details toward itself.

Then take another class of plays, — the reflective dramas, like " Hamlet," like " Lear," or
" Othello." Here the characteristic faculty at
work throughout is reason, — and analytic reason. These masterpieces are strictly philosophic
studies of human nature. The human mind is
searched to the core, tried by every test and re-
agent, — shocked by terror, melted by passion,
dissolved in grief and pity, put into the fiery
crucible of terrible anguish, subjected to the question by torture, till every element of human nature
is disclosed. And yet, during all this most destructive analysis, the central life of each person
remains : the personal identity is not reached.
Hamlet, Lear, Othello, do not fall apart into ab-
stractions of jealousy, rage, misanthropy : they
remain persons, and their lives are the real lives
of men.

Then there are the social dramas, — charming
scenes of daily life. Refined social intercourse ;
brilliant dialogue ; development of character by
conversation, not by events, in the absence of any
story, — make the staple. The faculty which pre-
vails in these plays is that which we call *wit*,
especially that more refined order of wit which
appears in the conversation of brilliant women.
" Much Ado about Nothing," " The Two Gentle-

men of Verona," " Twelfth Night " are dialogue
plays of this sort. The main element in all is dialogue. " As You Like It," " The Winter's Tale,"
and " Love's Labor 's Lost " differ from these only
in having more of nature. In the first, the out-
door life of the woods, inhabited by dukes and
lords, gives a picnic tone to the conversation. In
the " Winter's Tale," a more rustic and wilder
rural society of shepherds and clowns, and the air
of the hills, cause nature to predominate over man.
But in each of these pieces the ideal power masters the subject-matter ; and we may say of each
and every play, as Ovid says of the golden palace
of the gods : —

" Materiam superabat opus."

To each there is one tone, one spirit, one life.
Some of the plays are so purely poetical as to be
almost lyrics, as " Romeo and Juliet " and the
" Midsummer Night's Dream." Some are saturated with humor, as the " Merry Wives of Wind-
sor," the " Comedy of Errors," and " Twelfth
Night." But whether the element of the piece is
comedy, is poetry, is philosophy, is fancy, is history, is outward nature, each one has its own pervading life, is a unit, is a whole, because of the
steady mastery of that grand imaginative faculty
which always keeps one idea supreme, and sub-
ordinates to that all details.

This creative, unifying power of imagination
causes Shakspeare's characters to become so many

real human beings added to mankind. We refer to them as illustrations of human nature, as examples of human conduct, just as we should to real beings. In one sense he has created another world, and peopled it with another race of men and women. Were Shakspeare's characters obliterated we should lose about as much as if so many of Plutarch's heroes were annihilated.

It is not so with the creations of other writers. Take the characters of Scott, of Schiller, of Goethe : they are not quite persons. They owe something to costume, to circumstances. Take an every-day man, and educate him in the Middle Ages as a knight, and you have Ivanhoe; take the same man, and let him be brought up in Scotland in the days of John Knox, and you have Halbert Glendinning. In Goethe's characters you get a glimpse of Goethe himself ; in Scott's, you catch the twinkle of the sheriff's eye. " Tasso " is only Goethe as he might have been if he had been an Italian in his Werther-period. So it is with the dramatists of Shakspeare's own day. Massinger's villains only pretend to be villains : the nobleness of Philip Massinger shines out of their generous faces presently. Ben Jonson's *dramatis personæ* are variations of that sturdy, hard-working, crabbed, poetic, prosaic, ill-adjusted great man. But each one of Shakspeare's men and women is as distinctly, though often as slightly, individualized as the leaves of neighboring trees, — almost the

same, yet forever immutably different. Especially
does this appear in his women. Read Mrs. Jameson's work on his female characters, and notice
how each of the lovely creatures is her own sweet
self, though like enough to the others to be their
sister : —

> " Facies non omnibus una,
>   Nec diversa tamen, qualis decet esse sororum."

Thus there is something of the lay figure in the
work of other authors, even the greatest. They
are built up from without. Take away what is
due to the times, to their situation, to their education, and to certain external habits, and they
lose all individuality. But Shakspeare's grow
from within. Shylock is not merely a Jewish
miser, embittered against Christians by ill usage :
he is, first of all, Shylock himself. Falstaff is not
merely a glutton, a drunkard, a buffoon : back of
all these habits is the individual man. Othello
is not a picture of jealousy only ; Iago of cruel
intellectual malice ; they are persons with these
habits of mind and states of feeling.

And consider the most marvelous of them all,
— Hamlet ; the most wonderful, because in this
the artist has gone wholly out of his own age and
century, and come down to ours. Hamlet belongs,
not to the sixteenth-century period of vernal and
luxuriant growth, but rather to an epoch in which
reflection often outweighs action. Hamlet is a

man sick of life before he has begun to live; to
whom "all the uses of the world seem stale, flat,
and unprofitable;" "sicklied o'er with the pale
cast of thought." Overthought has paralyzed the
will-power in Hamlet. He is in a condition of
moral catalepsy; seeing and knowing everything,
but incapable of motion, — staying in any position
in which he happens to be. This moral torpor
of Hamlet gives its gray tone to the whole play.
How different is the character of Macbeth! Here,
Shakspeare, instead of throwing himself forward
three centuries, has gone back five. Macbeth hes-
itates over his deeds, as Hamlet does, but not
from the same cause. His indecision comes from
too little power of reflection, not from too much.
Hamlet is like a man dazzled by too much light;
Macbeth, like one groping in the dark. A wild,
rude, half savage stream of life rushes like a
mountain torrent through one play; a languid
stream, half hidden with fogs, creeps through the
other.

The conclusion to which we are brought by
these studies of Shakspeare's genius is, that man
is really what the ancients called him, — a micro-
cosm, a little world. Though it is evident that
the powers of observation in our poet were extraordinary, yet observation could never have given
him this knowledge of man and life. The soul
of man has unexplored depths of latent knowledge, which the imagination uses in these crea-

tions. Look at the figures in the Sistine Chapel, hundreds of human forms in every position and attitude, of human faces with every expression of thought and feeling, all drawn in two years by Michael Angelo. Does any one pretend that he had observed the human face in all these states; that he had noticed the human figure in all these attitudes; and so only copied what he had seen? No; but he, the Shakspeare of art, created new men and women as Nature herself would have created them. He did not remember how they had been; he created them as they ought to be. And so Shakspeare created his hundreds of persons, each such an individual soul as Nature would herself have created, if she had reason for it; not by putting together this trait and that which he had noticed in men and women, but out of some " pattern shown him in the mount," some instinctive inborn familiarity with Mother Nature's original types and methods.

No doubt the imagination, in its full activity, kindles the memory. We see examples of this in our dreams, where this creative spirit prepares a stage, scenery, actors, and introduces us as one of the persons in a tragedy or comedy in which we take a part, without knowing beforehand what the *dénoûement* is to be. Awaking from such a dream, we have noticed that the characters in it were well preserved throughout, and that it had a plot of its own, though we did not ourselves know

what it was to be; and yet we had arranged it
ourselves. And how perfect the pictures of persons and places, how exact the scenery, which our
sleeping memory had furnished to our imagination! No such vivid pictures could we create
by any effort of our waking memory. Coleridge
says that in his dream every man is a Shakspeare. At all events, we see by our dreams
something of the nature of that commanding faculty, in its unconscious action, which in Shakspeare worked consciously, in full harmony with
all the other powers of thought, and which every
other power of that kingly intellect served with a
most loyal allegiance.

Mr. Emerson, in his wise and charming Essay
on Shakspeare, qualifies him as " THE POET."
Shakspeare is, emphatically, THE poet, — the poet
of mankind, — poet in the highest sense, combin-
ing both classic and romantic definitions, — ποιητής,
or " maker; " Trovatore, or " finder." He is the
great MAKER, the master-artist, who forms men
and women of the clay. He is also the *Trou-
badour*, " the finder; " the soul to which every-
thing·comes; who discovers as well as forms. In
a word, he is both purely passive, and open to
the universe to receive; wholly active, self-possessed, and diligent to use what he sees. He
is, therefore, the perfect synthesis of the classic
and the romantic school; the Persian Gulf, into
which these twin rivers of thought, this Tigris

and Euphrates, running so long side by side, at last mingle their waters in a sweet consent. He disregarded the unities, did he? — therefore was not classic? But what is the unity of all unities in art but the bringing into harmony the wildest variety, the most antagonistic forms? It is the unity of the spirit, not of the letter. The narrow and limited genius, whether in poetry, architecture, or painting, seeks unity through dilution and emptiness. Let your picture contain only a single figure; let there be no contrasts of color, no accidental lights, no long-reaching perspectives, no gradation of tints; certainly you attain a sort of unity; notably that of monotony. So in architecture: you may have a symmetrical unity just as monotonous, — three windows on one side, and three on the other; but who does not prefer the unity born of infinite variety in the groupings of a Gothic minster or the spire of Strasburg? The perfect unity of each Shakspearian drama is that it has its own tone, spirit, life, all through, amid its wildest freedom and extremest contrasts of incident and character.

And, in that other charm of poetry which consists in music and melody, our great master is still unsurpassed. We have had other exquisite lyrical writers, but no such lyrics as his. Whoever has had the pleasure of hearing Mrs. Kemble read these perfect gems of song, knows that nothing else resembles them. There is no such music, no such language: —

> " When he speaks,
> The air, a chartered libertine, is still,
> And the mute wonder lurketh in men's ears
> To steal his sweet and honeyed sentences."

If the primal, central element of every poem is its Idea, which gives it its unity, that in which it ultimates itself is the Word. Language is fluent with Shakspeare. Words cease to have any arbitrary or conventional character; they take the meaning he chooses to give them. There are no *phrases* in his writing; no conventionalisms; no words obdurate to the fiery faculty which fuses them all, and then gives them new forms and uses. It may, perhaps, be said, that all his language is suggestive and figurative. There is no mathematical or logical use of words, — no use which allows them to retain a definite sense. Every word is vital, and therefore capable of a new expression in every new position which it may occupy. This alone gives the absolute mastery of language to the creative faculty; and thus Shakspeare, among all writers, is never the servant of his own words.

To illustrate my meaning here, I will take the first example that comes : —

> "There are a kind of men whose visages
> Do cream and mantle like the standing pool."

The rigid, self-satisfied stupidity in the face of the pompous blockhead first *creams*, then *mantles*. The interior self-complacency comes to the surface in a standing smile like cream. But it is a mantle too. It does not express thought; it merely hides the absence of all thought. And then it is "like the standing pool,"—at once you see the green surface of the pool, with no ripple, no flow. A second-rate genius, having hit on such a simile, would have spent twenty lines in elaborating it. Shakspeare touches it, and passes on. He gives in two lines three distinct pictures, yet all in harmony, and each carrying farther the thought suggested by the other. Thus words become vital in his treatment.

When we speak of the great MORAL influence of Shakspeare, we do not intend any Puritanic, scholastic, or pedantic morality. We do not mean morality after the letter, but after the spirit. We do not mean that his plays wind up with a moral, that each one teaches a distinct ethical proposition, or that they are constructed on the plan sometimes called *moral*,—of rewarding the good by earthly success, and punishing the wicked with temporal losses. Shakspeare's moral influence is of a far higher order than this. It lies in his firm persuasion that this world is God's world; that all things, therefore, have a divine and sacred meaning; that nobleness tends upward, and sin downward. *That* influence is most moral which most inspires us with love for goodness; which makes faith, integrity, generosity, purity, seem infinitely charming and lovely; and shows sin, however successful in appearance, to be a miserable failure. Whatever makes us love goodness, and hate sin, is most moral; and this is what Shakspeare always does.

There is another important element of morality in literature. Goethe says that the only kind of moral tale is that which shows us that, beside appetite and passion, there is a power within us able to deny and control them; that we need not be conquered by our lower nature, but can always conquer it. Those books are the most immoral books, therefore, which (like Balzac's novels, for example) assume that it is a matter of course for people to go wrong, to follow usage, to yield to temptation. A man who tries to *persuade* you to do wrong is not so much of a Satan as the man who assumes, as a matter of course, that you are going to do wrong. For the first admits that there is another way, by trying to induce you to go his way: by urging you to go wrong, he admits that there are motives which may lead you to go right. But the most dangerous, subtle, and successful of all tempters is he who ignores the existence of any other way than the wrong one; or who treats wrong-doing as a merry joke, that it would be silly and ridiculous to consider seriously. Just so Shylock persuades Antonio to consent to his frightful proposition by treating it as a jest: —

> " Go with me to a notary; seal me there
> Your single bond; and in a merry sport,

> If you repay me not on such a day,
> In such a place, such sum or sums as are
> Expressed in the condition, let the forfeit
> Be nominated for an equal pound
> Of your fair flesh, to be cut off and taken
> In what part of your body pleaseth me."

Nothing could be more unnatural than for Antonio to consent to such a proposal, if made seriously, — nothing more likely (if put in the offhand way, as a mere joke, — to be consented to, of course) than for him to say as he does, —

> " Content, in faith: I 'll seal to such a bond,
> And say, There is much kindness in the Jew."

Considered in this light, Shakspeare's writings have a high moral influence. He never makes evil fascinating. His villains are often sagacious, and highly intellectual, like Iago ; often very droll and witty, like Falstaff : but they are *never* made attractive ; we never like them, nor what they do. Did ever any temperance orator hold up such a picture of the evils of a debauched life as we have in the last days of Sir John Falstaff, driveling, silly, fallen from the society of princes into that of Pistol, Dame Quickly, and Doll Tearsheet? The successful ambition of Macbeth, forcing its way up to the royalty of Scotland, might seem, if wicked, yet full of energy and courage. But Shakspeare withdraws the veil, and shows us how weak, vacillating, cowardly, and empty is such ambition and such success. Not a word of moralizing meantime : he shows us the moral; he does not tell us of it.

So the substance of his works is eminently moral; for it is reality, truth, beauty, love. If these are moral, he is so.

> "Fair, kind, and true is all my argument, —
> Fair, kind, and true, varying to other words;
> And in this change is my invention spent, —
> Three themes in one, which wondrous scope affords."

Perhaps the one feature of Shakspeare which gives most purity to his works is his real respect for woman. He had seen bad women; there is reason to think that he was not happy in his own marriage; some of his sonnets are addressed to a woman, whose thousand errors he notes, but says that his five senses, seeing those errors, cannot " dissuade his one foolish heart from serving her." Yet whoever knows the corrupt, cynical tone in which woman and love were spoken of by Shakspeare's predecessors and successors, must wonder at his perception of woman's purity, truth, and nobleness. He *could* paint wicked women, like Lady Macbeth; frail women, like Cressida; unpoetic women, like Mrs. Page and Mrs. Ford; vulgar women, like Dame Quickly; and a fine lady, like Beatrice. But he most loved to draw, with delicate pencil dipped in celestial tints, characters of the snowy purity of Imogen, the saintly grace of Isabella, the brilliant intelligence of Portia, the poetic soul of Miranda, the devoted tenderness of

Desdemona. Never was such an offering of reverence laid at the feet of woman as Shakspeare has presented in characters like these. And, to complete the expression of his admiration and homage, he has selected his most satanic creation, — the one who neither believed in God nor man, — and put into his mouth that kind of contempt toward the whole sex which folly and wickedness have in every age hastened to utter, thereby pronouncing their own condemnation. It is Iago, the bitter cynic, the man who has no faith in virtue; the cold materialist; the man to whom a ruined character seems a less evil than a broken head, — this is the one whom Shakspeare has selected to utter the stock satires, the regulation witticisms, against woman; and he could not show his reverence for woman more than by thus making Iago her libeler. Therefore, if the happiness and virtue of the world, and the progress of society, depend, as they do, on the position which woman occupies, and the esteem in which she is held, Shakspeare's influence may be considered as one of the motors in Christian civilization.

This being his view of woman, his idea of love is high and noble. Coleridge says, " There is not a vicious passage in Shakspeare, though many gross ones, for grossness belongs to the age ; " the age of such writers as Beaumont and Fletcher; and afterward of Dryden.

Shakspeare's drama, amid such associates, was

22

like the Lady in "Comus" among the obscene and
riotous company around her. The love he described was of the soul. The reasons his heroes
give for loving are such as these : —

> " For she is wise, if I can judge of her ;
> And fair she is, if that mine eyes be true ;
> And true she is, as she hath proved herself :
> And therefore like herself, wise, fair, and true,
> Shall she be placèd in my constant soul."

The lower fascination of love he describes thus,
in lines which do not contain one feeling which is
not spiritual and refined : —

> "Except I be by Silvia in the night,
> There is no music in the nightingale ;
> Unless I look on Silvia in the day,
> There is no day for me to look upon.
> She is my essence ; and I leave to be
> If I be not by her fair influence
> Fostered, illumined, cherished, kept alive."

And how noble is Portia's confession of her affection for Bassanio, and the pure womanly surrender of herself, her possessions, her high position, as the princely heiress of Belmont! Mrs.
Jameson, quoting the passage, says it has a consciousness and tender seriousness approaching to
solemnity : —

> "You see me, Lord Bassanio, where I stand,
> Such as I am. But the full sum of me
> Is an unlessoned girl, unschooled, unpracticed ;
> Happy in this, — she is not yet so old
> But she may learn ; and happier than this,

She is not bred so dull but she may learn ;
Happiest of all is, that her gentle spirit
Commits itself to yours, to be directed
As from her lord, her governor, her king."

But that for which, most of all, we remember Shakspeare's birth with gratitude to-day is his wisdom. He saw the laws which govern the world. "He is inconceivably wise," says Mr. Emerson; "the others conceivably." The follow, ing passage in Ben Jonson's "Poetaster" seems to me to describe Shakspeare, though professing to refer to Virgil : —

" That which he hath writ
Is with such judgment labored and distilled
Through all the needful uses of our lives,
That, could a man remember but his lines,
He should not touch at any serious point
But he might breathe his spirit out of him."

And again, —

"And for his poesy, 't is so rammed with life,
That it shall gather strength of life with being,
And live hereafter more admired than now."

His wisdom is for all times. He possessed knowledge of man, in each of its three forms, more than any other writer. He knew *human nature*, or the common soul with its depths and heights, — those universal principles the same in all. Then he knew man as an *individual*, — not the same, but various ; each one himself, no one like another. And, thirdly, he knew *mankind*, —

man in action, the social man; that is, he knew
man in repose, man in personal development, and
man in society.

This last knowledge is what we name Wisdom,
as the first is Philosophy, and the second is Dramatic Genius. The wisdom of life, the same in all
ages; the proverbial wisdom of Solomon, of Saadi,
of Æsop, of Dr. Franklin; the sayings which guide
men in all affairs great and small, — this is what
makes him our teacher, the common teacher of all
thinking men in all ages. England and America
especially, whose tongue he speaks, have both been
taught by him. Perhaps they never needed his
teachings more than now.

Three hundred years have passed since Shakspeare was born; and he is still the educator of the
English, German, and American intellect. His
works are the university where the teachers of our
land are themselves taught. The great inventions
which have come since his time, and have revolu-
tionized England and America, are of trivial importance compared with his thought and speech.
Coleridge says of him, " I have been almost daily
reading him since I was ten years old. The thirty
intervening years have been unintermittingly and
not fruitlessly employed in the study of the Greek,
Latin, English, Italian, Spanish, and German
belles-lettrists; and the last fifteen years, in addition, far more intensely in the analysis of the laws
of life and reason as they exist in man: and upon

every step I have made forward in taste, in acquisition of facts from history or my own observation, and in knowledge of the different laws of being, and their apparent exceptions from accidental collision of disturbing forces, — at every new accession of information, after every successful exercise of meditation and every fresh presentation of experience, I have unfailingly discovered a proportionate increase of wisdom and intuition in Shakspeare."

And Mr. Emerson, whose essay resumes in itself most of our best thoughts concerning this great master, says: " He wrote the airs for all our modern music; he wrote the text of modern life, — the text of manners; he drew the man of England and Europe; the father of the man in America; he read the hearts of men and women, their probity and second thought and wiles, — the wiles of innocence, and the transitions by which virtues and vices slide into their contraries; he drew the fine demarcations of freedom and fate; he knew the laws of repression which make the police of nature; and all the sweets and terrors of human lot lay in his mind as truly, but as softly, as the landscape lies in the eye."

XVII.

JEAN JACQUES ROUSSEAU.

JEAN JACQUES ROUSSEAU.[1]

THIS book, published some years since, contains
interesting matter for any new biography of the
great, sad, prose-poet of France.   It contains rem-
iniscences concerning him from simple, honest,
Christian men, — his fellow-townsmen, who knew
him well.   They do not think of him as the
great philosopher and marvelous writer, who set
the French language on fire, and turned its cold
phrases into burning eloquence.   They think of
him only as one whom they could not quite understand, or quite approve ; but whom they could
not help loving.   It has also contributions from
many citizens of Geneva and the neighboring
towns, and shows us Rousseau as he was, when
his unquiet heart and sensitive nature found peace
for a time among his simple fellow-citizens.   The
period, perhaps, has hardly yet arrived for writing
the biography of this great soul ; but, when it
comes, this unpretending volume will be one of its

[1] Article in *The Christian Examiner*, on " Rousseau et les
Génevois.   Par M. J. Gaberel, ancien pasteur."

" Memoires pour servir." It informs us, too, that there is a collection of nearly two thousand inedited letters of Rousseau in the Library of Neufchâtel, classified by the librarian, M. Bovet. It also mentions that M. le docteur Coindet, grand-nephew of Rousseau's friend of that name, has a voluminous collection of notes and letters addressed to his uncle by the philosopher. It contains many interesting anecdotes, all tending to show that, in the opinion of these good men, who knew Rousseau in his private life, he was a religious man ; a truth-seeking, truth-loving man ; and one who desired human love rather than fame.

Perhaps the present century may be able to do justice to Rousseau. I have long desired to utter a protest against the wide-spread opinion, held by the Christian public, of his infidelity in opinion and his immorality of character. The common view of Rousseau is unjust to his belief and his life. Unfortunate and unhappy in a thousand ways, he is not that ogre of evil which his name represents to so many minds.

Rousseau was a phenomenon, unintelligible to his own time, and not yet understood by ours. To his contemporaries he was the object of immense admiration and odium ; and to our age he stands as a misty representative of sophistry and unbelief. He is classed with Hume and Voltaire, though radically opposed to them in his ideas, and antipathic in the tendencies of his nature.

When his works first appeared they electrified France and Europe. Hume writes from Paris in 1765 : " It is impossible to express or imagine the enthusiasm of this nation in his favor ; no person ever so much engaged their attention as Rousseau. Voltaire and everybody else are quite eclipsed by him." When " La Nouvelle Héloïse " appeared, the libraries could not answer the calls made for it from all classes. The book was let by the day and by the hour. But this universal admiration was attended or immediately followed by a terrible persecution. Banished from Paris for the publication of " Émile," a work which contains the germs of our modern improvements in education, he went to Geneva ; threatened with imprisonment there, he fled to Neufchâtel ; driven from that place, he lived on an island in the Lake of Bienne, from which he was again expelled by the Canton of Berne. Longing for repose, he was a perpetual wanderer ; thirsting for sympathy, he was in constant warfare. The one literary man of his time and land who was sincerely religious, he passed then, and has passed ever since, as an example of unbelief. A singular character, certainly, and well deserving of our study. Lord Holland tells us that Napoleon said of Rousseau, that "without him there would have been no French Revolution." The historian Schlosser speaks of his " bringing forward an entirely new system of absolute democracy." Von Raumer, in his history of education, gives Rousseau a high place as the founder and inspirer of this modern science. Sismondi says, " Rousseau in his writings went to the foundations of human society." Buckle remarks that he has not found a single instance of an attack on Christianity in all Rousseau's writings; and that in this respect he was entirely distinguished from the other writers of his day. Louis Blanc declares that Rousseau alone withstood the movement headed by Voltaire and all the philosophers, resisting by himself the whole spirit of his time. " The age exalted reason ; he preached sentiment. Among the prophets of individualism he alone taught the Christian doctrine of brotherhood. The mission of Jean Jacques, in a society which was in a state of disintegration, was to oppose to the exaggerated worship of reason the worship of sentiment." M. Villemain, one of the foremost among the historians of French literature, considers him " the successor of Montesquieu in political science," " the sincere friend of morality and justice," " magical in his talent," " with a soul of fire ; " and agrees with those who ascribe to his genius an immense influence over the future. He was, says he, " the Bible of his time ; and there was not an act in the French Revolution in which you do not find his good or evil influence." But, as regards religion, Villemain declares that, " at a period when the old religious beliefs had faded away from the public mind, no better and no more useful book than 'Émile' could have been offered to it." Rousseau, he adds, " was the religious teacher of his age, inspiring a faith in God, in the soul, in goodness here and immortality hereafter, which was not taught then, even in the Christian pulpits. For the Catholic pulpit of France then preached mere moral discourses on ' Affability,' on 'Equanimity of Temper,' or 'The Love of Order ;' and sought to be pardoned its sacred mission by affecting a kind of judicious worldliness." The school of sensation ruled in philosophy ; and to the school of sensation Rousseau uttered these words : " Judgment and sensation are not the same thing : I am not merely a sensitive and passive being, but also an active and intelligent being; and, whatever philosophy may say about it, I shall venture to claim the honor of being able to think." In reply to Diderot, D'Holbach, and Helvetius, and to the Atheism which they taught, he inferred an intelligent supreme being from the very existence of matter. To the Encyclopædists he replies : " Philosophy can do nothing which religion cannot do better than she ; and religion can do a great many other things which philosophy cannot do at all."

These facts indicate, that down to the present time Rousseau has not been generally understood, and that he deserves a further and more impartial study.

Jean Jacques Rousseau was born at Geneva in 1712, and died near Paris in 1778, at the age of 66. He was a contemporary, during most of his life, with Swedenborg, Kant, Voltaire, John Wesley, Benjamin Franklin, Linnæus, Dr. Johnson, Hume, and Burke. How different were these men from each other! how hard for them to understand each other! How hard for the practical Benjamin Franklin, the tory Samuel Johnson, the pious Wesley, the philosophic Kant, or the mystical Swedenborg, to find any meaning in such a man as Rousseau! But posterity, looking backward, can recognize the good which all have done by their different methods. " There are so many voices in the world, and none without its own signification."

The family of Rousseau was French; and though he was fond of calling himself a citizen of Geneva, he belonged altogether in his soul, as in literature, to France. His ancestors were Huguenots, who had gone to Switzerland to secure liberty of conscience. His father was a watchmaker. His mother died when he was born; and he never knew a mother's care. He was a sickly child; and his father, to amuse him, would sit up all night reading novels to him. But when he was ten years old he lost his father also, who went into exile in consequence of fighting a duel, and abandoned his child to the care of his uncle, who placed him at school in the town of Bossey. At twelve years he was put as an apprentice with an engraver, who was a harsh employer; and when Rousseau was sixteen he ran away and took refuge with a Catholic curate in Savoy, who, instead of sending him back to his family, preferred to keep him, that he might convert him to the Catholic Church. For this purpose he sent him to live with Madame Warens, a lady who figures largely in his memoirs. She was a recent convert to the Catholic Church. She had deserted her husband, with whom she did not live happily. Protected by the King of Sardinia, and living on a small pension; a pretty woman, kind-hearted, but without principle, — she persuaded Rousseau to abjure Protestantism, which he did in the city of Turin in 1728. Here, as before, the boy was left without friends or protectors. He lived at service, and received good advice from a deistical abbé, who taught him at the same time morality and deism. From Turin he returned to Madame Warens, who was still living at Annecy. He studied music and gave music lessons, by which he gained a partial support. After some wanderings and changes of fortune, at the age of twenty-one he received an office from the King of Sardinia, through the influence of his old friend, Madame Warens. In 1736 he went to live with her at Charmettes, in the country, where he passed some happy years in work, in study, and in the enjoyment of nature.

In 1741, at the age of twenty-nine, Rousseau

went to Paris in order to exhibit a new method of musical notation. He carried in his pocket fifteen pieces of silver and his comedy of "Narcissus." His musical notation did not succeed; but he obtained introductions to different persons of distinction, and through one of them received the office of Secretary of Legation to the French embassy at Venice, where he distinguished himself by his fidelity and energy. Returning to Paris, he became acquainted with Thérèse le Vasseur. She was a laundress, three and twenty years old, ignorant, and incapable of being educated. She never could learn the names of the months, nor how to count. But she was lively, gentle, and kind. With her Rousseau lived many years, and finally married her. His father dying about this time, Rousseau secured his share of his mother's inheritance, the life interest of which he had allowed his father to enjoy. But all his means were wanted to help his friend, Madame Warens, who had become poor, and the relations of Thérèse, who were very greedy.

In 1750, when thirty-eight years old, he wrote the work which introduced him to the public, which was a short treatise for a prize proposed by the Academy of Dijon, on the question whether the revival of learning has contributed to the improvement of morals. He took the negative side, and here began the career of thought which gave him all his distinction. His doctrine was that man was only good and only happy while following nature, and that the arts and sciences are the children of a corrupt civilization. His treatise received the prize. It was followed by a successful opera, a letter on French music, and, in 1753, a Treatise on the Origin of Inequality among Mankind. In this he carried still farther his favorite doctrine of the fall of man through civilization.

He had before him the terrible inequalities which then existed in France. He wished to attack despotism, and he attacked all society. He desired to assail the enormous distinctions of property, and he assailed property itself.

"The first man," said he, "who, having inclosed a piece of ground, said, 'It belongs to me,' and found people simple enough to believe him, was the true founder of civil society. How many crimes, wars, and murders would not *he* have spared to the human race who should have plucked up the fence, and said to his companions, 'Beware of listening to this impostor : you are lost if you forget that the fruits of the earth belong to everybody, and that the earth itself belongs to nobody.' "

This treatise produced great excitement, and of course much opposition as well as admiration. Voltaire, thanking Rousseau for his work, wrote to him, "One feels a desire to go on all fours while reading your essay." Buffon made some serious objections, founded on the physical nature

23

of man, which demanded society to protect the feeble age of childhood.

From this time it was evident that there was a breach between Rousseau and the French philosophers Diderot, Grimm, and Holbach. His ideas and theirs were radically opposed. He believed in God, in Immortality, and Retribution: they believed in this present world and the five senses. He believed in the brotherhood of man: they believed in every one for himself. He was the champion of Equality: they were the friends and *protégés* of the Aristocrats. They looked down upon him with an air of patronage and of contemptuous superiority. The blame for these difficulties long rested on Rousseau, and was attributed to his morbid jealousy. But M. Villemain says that now, when so many correspondences have been published, we must confess that these friends of Rousseau were very hard upon him.

In 1754 Rousseau took possession of a cottage at Montmorency, about four miles from Paris, called the Hermitage. It was a present from Mme. d'Épinay, who owned the estate. Walking with her one day in this pleasant valley, he cried out, " What an asylum for me! " She made no reply, but rebuilt the house, and the next time they visited the place playfully said, " My bear, behold your asylum! " In this happy retirement he wrote the " Nouvelle Héloïse " and most of the "Émile." What an active employment of his

time during the six years which he passed here
and at the village of Montmorency afterward!
For, beside the "Héloïse" and "Émile," he wrote
the letter to D'Alembert and the "Social Contract;" and, when driven from his asylum, during
his flight, "The Levite of Ephraim." It was the
most fruitful period of his life, — the happy au-
tumn in which the long, cold spring-time of his
struggling youth and the passionate heats of his
summer bore the rich fruits of thought and labor.
It was his only really happy time, — the little interval of sunshine in the midst of a stormy day.
The rest of his years — persecuted at once by Catholic and Protestant bigots and by philosophical un-
believers; driven in exile from France into Switzerland, from Switzerland into Prussia, and from
Prussia into England; half crazy with suspicion
and jealousy; the object at the same moment of
fanatical hatred, extravagant admiration, and bitter ridicule — he never knew a quiet hour till he
dropped exhausted into his grave. And, as if the
same fate which pursued him in life was to follow
him into his tomb, he was not allowed to sleep
peacefully on the island in the little lake, shaded
with poplars, but was carried, in 1791, with Voltaire, to the Pantheon, and placed in a kind of
stone cellar below the church, in a wooden sar-
cophagus, *en attendant* something better.

What, then, was the religious belief or unbelief
of Rousseau?

First : in an age in which atheism was the fashion he believed firmly in God.

For, in the period preceding the French Revolution, philosophy in France had sunk into the grossest materialism. De la Mettrie gave himself all possible trouble to deny to man a soul and immortality, and to prove him an automaton, or at most a vegetable. He was a decided materialist and atheist. He wrote one book called " The Man-Machine ; " and another called " The Man-Plant." Him followed Denis Diderot and Jean d'Alembert, hating not only Christianity but all religion, — philosophers of matter, believers in sensation alone, preaching the gospel of the five senses. They were the chief editors of the " French Encyclopædia," the object of which was to revolutionize all belief on the basis of atheism. To them associated himself Baron d'Holbach, author of " The System of Nature ; " and Helvetius, writer of two shallow books on " Man " and " The Mind." Of all this party only Voltaire was a theist. Voltaire was by no means an atheist. On the contrary, he wrote a story called " Cosi-Sancta," containing one of the best arguments from the evidences of design in nature for the existence of Deity. But Voltaire's theism was purely intellectual, and not, like Rousseau's, a sentiment, a feeling, a love. Rousseau believed in God with his whole heart : not merely as a law or an order of the universe ; but as a personal God and friend

to the human race, especially to the poor and
wretched. The philosophers pardoned Voltaire
his theism, for it was a mere speculation; but
they could never forgive Rousseau, for his was
faith — and faith in a living God.

Take, as one proof of this, not any single passage from his own writings which might be suspected of not giving his average belief, but an
account given by his friend and protector, Mme.
d'Épinay, of a conversation in which he took part
in her house. There can be no doubt that this
expresses his real conviction, since he could not
have thought that it would ever be preserved. It
was the overflow of his mind at the hour. Rousseau here maintains, in private and in difficult
circumstances, the same positive religious convictions which he always announces in his works: —

"Mlle. Quinault said that in religious matters every
one was right; but that each should remain in the religion in which he was born.

"'Not so,' replied Rousseau, warmly; 'not if it is a
bad religion, for then it could only do one harm.'

"I then said that religion often did much good; that
it was a restraint for the lower classes, who had no other.
Every one cried out against me, and overwhelmed me
with objections; they said that for the lower classes the
fear of being hung was a much better restraint than the
fear of being damned. So they went on, till I, fearing
they would destroy all religion, begged for mercy, at
least, for natural religion. 'Not more for that than for

the rest,' said St. Lambert. Rousseau said, ' I don't go
with you. I say with Horace, " I am more infirm." '

" Then St. Lambert and others attacked with bitterness all belief, even in God. Rousseau muttered something between his teeth: they laughed at him.

ROUSSEAU. " ' If it is a baseness to hear one's friend
abused in his absence, I consider it a crime to listen to
things said against one's God, who is here. For myself,
gentlemen, I believe in God.'

" They went on, however, in the same way, till Rousseau said, ' If you say another word of this sort I shall
retire.'

" Afterward, being seated near Rousseau, I said, ' It
troubles me that St. Lambert, so intelligent a man,
should not believe in God.' ' I cannot bear,' answered
Rousseau, ' this rage for pulling down everything, and
never building up anything.' ' Still,' said I, ' his arguments are very strong.' ' What! are you going to be
convinced by his atheism? Don't say that, madame;
for I could not help hating you. Besides, the idea of
God is necessary for our happiness; and I wish you to
be happy.'

" A few days after, as we were walking together out
of doors, I confessed to him that I had been disturbed
by St. Lambert's arguments.

" ' I think,' said Rousseau, ' that there are some convictions so rooted in our nature, so universally received,
so efficaciously preached, not by men only, but by the
phenomena of nature, always renewed around us, that
we cannot resist such concurrent proofs. The animals,
the plants, the fruits of the earth, the rain, the seasons
of the year.' ' Yet,' said I, ' what St. Lambert said was

very strong.' 'Madame,' replied he, 'sometimes I am of
his opinion: in my shut-up study, with my two fists in
my eyes, or in the darkness of the night. But look at
that' (said he, lifting his hand to the sky, like one inspired): 'the sunrise, sweeping away the vapors, and re-
vealing the magnificence of nature, sweeps away at the
same time these dark vapors from my soul. I recover
my faith in God; I reverence and adore him; I bow in
his presence.'"

In 1756 Rousseau published a letter addressed
to Voltaire in defense of Providence. In it he
says:—

"No: I have suffered too much in this world to be
content to relinquish the hope of another. All the sub-
tleties of metaphysics never induce me to waver for a
moment in my faith in the Immortality of the Soul, and
in a beneficent Providence. I feel it to be true; I believe it to be true; and I long to have it true."

The theism of Rousseau was not the common
deism of his time, which was a negation. His was
positive, full, warm. His God was with him in
all his sorrows as a comforter. No pious Christian
was more constant in his devout habits than this
so-called philosopher of unbelief. He read the
Bible every day, not as a critic, but exactly as
the humblest Christian reads it, — for comfort,
strength, and inspiration. One anecdote has come
up among the recent memoirs, which gives us a
little picture of Rousseau, with the " Imitation of

Christ" in his hand as his companion, wandering among the fields and gathering flowers. It is from the "Memoires d'un Bibliophile, par M. Tenant de Latour, Paris, 1861."

M. Latour one day picked up at a book-stall in Paris a copy of Thomas à Kempis' "De Imitatione Christi," with the autograph of Jean J. Rousseau on the title-page. It had been evidently read with great care, and more than half the book was underlined with the pencil. It bore marks also of having been the constant pocket companion of Rousseau. It had been read in the evening, for there were drops of grease from the candle on its pages; and it had accompanied him in his country walks, for there were dried flowers stuck here and there between the leaves. Now a letter of Rousseau to a Paris bookseller is extant, dated 1763, containing the following sentence: "Voici des articles que je vous prie de joindre à votre premier envoi, 'Pensées de Pascal, Œuvres de la Bruyère, Imitation de Jésus Christ, Latin.'" It may be added, also, that this volume contained a dried and pressed periwinkle; and that, just a year after the date of this order for the purchase of the book, occurred the event recorded in his "Confessions," of his finding a periwinkle in one of his walks near Crozier, and the pleasure it gave him.

Such being the character of his theism, what were his views concerning Christianity? Here it will be supposed that he was, of course, an entire infidel. But the whole amount of his infidelity was a skepticism concerning the miracles of the New Testament. He does not profess to disbelieve them: he thinks them doubtful. He questions them, and leaves them. He asserts everywhere that he believes Christianity, but he believes it on the ground of its own sublime truth, beauty, and usefulness, and because of the holiness of Christ's character. His belief here, also, is no cold assent. So far as he does believe, it is with the passionate faith of an admiring and loving heart.

It is well known that the book in which his infidelity is supposed to be taught, and for printing which he was driven from France, from Geneva, from Neufchâtel, and from the little island of St. Peters in the Lake of Bienne, is his "Émile." In this book, which is a work on education, an ideal view of the education of a young man is presented — as in the "Cyropædia" of Xenophon. In the course of it he gives the profession of faith of a vicar of Savoy; and as this contains the chief offense of Rousseau against Christianity it must not be omitted : —

"In regard to revelation," says the vicar, "if I were a better reasoner, or better taught, I might perhaps be sure of its truth. But if I see in its favor proofs which I cannot refute, I see against it objections to which I cannot reply. There are so many solid reasons for and against, that, not knowing what to determine, I neither

admit nor reject it. I only reject the obligation to believe it, because this pretended obligation is incompatible
with the justice of God. I remain in a state of respectful doubt. I am not so presumptuous as to believe myself infallible. I reason for myself, not for others. I
neither blame nor imitate them. Their judgment may
be better than mine : it is not my fault that it is *not*
mine.

"I also confess to you that the majesty of the Scriptures astonishes me: the holiness of the gospel is an
argument which speaks to my heart, and which I should
be sorry to be able to answer. Read the books of the
philosophers with all their pomp: how petty they are
beside this! Is a book at once so sublime and so simple
the work of man? Can it be that he whose history it
relates was himself a mere man? Is this the tone of
an enthusiast, or of a mere sectary? What sweetness,
what purity in his manners! what touching grace in his
instructions! what elevation in his maxims! what profound wisdom in his discourses! what presence of mind,
what acuteness, what justness in his replies! what empire
over his passions! Where is the man, where the sage,
who knows in this way how to act, suffer, and die, without weakness and without ostentation? When Plato
describes his imaginary good man, covered with the
opprobrium of crime, yet meriting the rewards of virtue,
he paints, trait by trait, Jesus Christ. . . . . What prejudice, blindness, or· bad faith does it not require to
compare the son of Sophroniscus with the son of Mary!
What a distance between the two! Socrates dies without pain, without ignominy; he sustains his character
easily to the end. If he had not honored his life with

such a death, we should have thought him a sophist. They say Socrates invented ethics; but others practised morality before he taught it. Aristides was just before Socrates described justice ; Leonidas died for his country before Socrates taught the duty of patriotism. Sparta was temperate before Socrates praised sobriety; Greece abounded in virtuous men before he defined what virtue is. But Jesus, — where did he find the lofty morality, of which he alone gave both the lesson and the example? From the midst of a furious fanaticism proceeds the purest wisdom; among the vilest of people appears the most heroic and virtuous simplicity. The death of Socrates, tranquilly philosophizing among his friends, is the sweetest one could desire; that of Jesus, expiring amid torments, abused, ridiculed, cursed by a whole people, is the most horrible which one could fear. . . . . Yes: if Socrates lives and dies like a philosopher, Jesus lives and dies like a God!

" Will you say that the history of Jesus is an invention ! My friend, people do not invent in this way; and the actions of Socrates, which no one doubts, are less strongly attested than those of Jesus Christ. Besides, you thus merely remove the difficulty farther backward, without overthrowing it. It would be more inconceivable that four men should have agreed to invent this story than that one should have furnished its subject. No Jewish authors could ever have found out this tone, or such a morality; and the gospel has traits of truth so imposing, so perfectly inimitable, that its inventor would be more astonishing than its hero. And yet this same gospel is full of incredible things, of things opposed to reason, and which it is impossible for a sensible man to

conceive or to admit.   What shall I do amid such con-
tradictions ?   Remain modest and circumspect, my child;
respect in silence what we can neither reject nor com-
prehend, and be humble before the Great Being who
alone knows the truth."

It was for saying this that a storm of persecution arose against Rousseau.   All united against
him, — the Catholics, because he preached toler-
ance toward all churches ; the Protestants, because
he preached indifference of dogmas ; the atheists
because he believed in God ; the deists, because
he gave such praise to Christ and to Christianity.
Voltaire was so incensed with him for this reverence toward Jesus, that he cried out, " The Judas !
he deserts us when we are just about to triumph."
Beaumont, Archbishop of Paris, issued a manda-
mus condemning " Émile " as containing abomi-
nable and pernicious doctrine.   The Parliament of
Paris issued a decree to seize the book and its
author.   " Thus," says Rousseau, " the fanaticism
of atheism and that of Jesuitism, meeting in their
common intolerance, united against me."   He was
quietly and happily living at Montmorency, under
the protection of the Marshal of Luxembourg,
when the news came.   He had a habit of reading
in bed every night till he became sleepy.   His
usual reading at night was in the Bible ; and he
had read it thus through in course five or six times.
How many of those who have denounced his in-

fidelity can say as much! That night he had been
reading in the Book of Judges; and the painful
story of the Levite of Mount Ephraim was in his
mind when the news came that he was to be arrested and sent to prison the next day. At first,
he determined to remain; but in those days one
went to the Bastile without examination or trial,
and remained there during life, without the power
of communicating with the world. By the advice of all his friends he fled; and on the way
to Geneva wrote out as an idyl, in the style of
Gessner, the story he had been reading from the
Bible.

How he was driven from Geneva and from
Switzerland we will not stop to say; but that the
doubts expressed by the Savoyard vicar went beyond his own degree of unbelief is probable. He
wrote in the midst of a circle of atheists and deists
who mocked at Christianity and all religion; he
wrote for people under their influence; and he
thought it best to put less of faith in the mouth
of his vicar than he had himself. Two terrible
answers to his opponents he wrote: one to the
Archbishop of Paris; the other to the Council of
State at Geneva. There is no finer specimen of
polemical writing in any literature than these.
In eloquence they compare with Milton's "Defense of the People of England;" in keenness of
satire they rival Voltaire; in compact logic, wit,
and terrible invective they remind us of Pascal.

As a dialectician, Rousseau is unrivaled. He is arguing for toleration, and his theme is a noble one. If one remembers that, while men and women were gayly supping in the skeptical saloons of Paris, heretics were being punished all over France;[1] that, for example, in 1746 forty Protestant gentlemen were condemned to death in a French province for having been present at a religious service in the night-time,—one can see the need of Rousseau's arguments. Consider his position. On one side the great hierarchy, still supported by the whole power of the state; on the other, Rousseau, a fugitive, pursued by a parliamentary decree, supporting himself by his books and his music, defended by no one, condemned also by the magistrates of Geneva, and then turning on both Catholic and Protestant, citing both before the bar of European Reason, and delivering battle against both for freedom of conscience. He shows easily that he is more religious than his age and his opponents; he stands as defender of the cause of God; he tears in pieces, by his ardent logic, the archiepiscopal mandate; and these writings, says Villemain, constitute a great social event in the age.

In his " Letters from the Mountains," addressed to the people of Geneva, he maintains the proposition, that a belief in miracles is not essential to a belief in Christianity; and for this reason, that

[1] Villemain.

Christianity has a variety of proofs, of which miracles are only one. Thus it is proved by the nature of its doctrine, its sublimity, beauty, holiness; it is also proved by the character of its founder and of his apostles, by their purity, simplicity, and self-denying goodness; and also, in the third place, it may be proved by miracles.

" Now," says he, " I declare myself a Christian. My persecutors say that I am not. They prove that I am not, because I reject Révelation ; and they prove that I reject Revelation because I do not believe in Miracles.

" But in order that this inference should be correct one of two things must be assumed, — either that Miracles are the only proof of Revelation or that I also reject the other proofs of it. Now it is not true that Miracles are the only proof of Revelation; and it is not true that I reject the other proofs of it.

" This, then, is our position. These gentlemen, determined to make me reject Revelation in spite of myself, count for nothing that I receive it on grounds satisfactory to my own mind unless I also receive it on grounds which are not so. Because I cannot do that they say that I reject it. Can anything be more extravagant than this? "

" I do not deny the miracles of the New Testament," says Rousseau, in this same writing: " I suspend my faith in regard to them. I also contend that it is not essential to Christianity to believe them."

" The Savoyard vicar brings forward objections to miracles. But objections are not negations. As for myself, I see miracles attested in the Scriptures : that is

enough to arrest my judgment. If I did not see them
there I should reject them at once, or not call them
miracles; but since they are there I do not reject them,
nor do I admit them, because my reason refuses to do
so, and because I do not consider it necessary to do so./
I can believe Christianity without them.

"I might go farther. I have proved that no one can
be sure that any particular fact is a miraculous fact;
. . . . for since a miracle is an exception to the laws of
nature, to decide that a fact is miraculous we must be
acquainted with *all* the laws of nature. For a single
law which we do *not* know, might, in certain cases unknown to us, change the effect of the laws which we *do*
know. Whoever, therefore, declares that any particular
fact is a miracle, declares that he knows all the laws of
nature, and that this one fact is an exception to all." "I
might therefore admit all the facts contained in the
Bible, and yet, without impiety, deny that they are miraculous. But I do not go so far as this. I do not
deny: I suspend my judgment."

This seems clearly enough to define Rousseau's
position in regard to Christian belief. He believed in Christ as a revelation of the divine will,
accepted his truth as divine truth, called him his
Master, wished to belong to his Church, and studied his words with reverence; but hesitated upon
miracles. Here is a little scene which shows still
further his *feelings* on the subject of Christianity: —

"After my solemn return into the Protestant Church,
living in a Protestant country, I could not, without failing

in my engagements and in duty as a citizen, neglect the public profession of the worship to which I had returned. I attended, therefore, public worship. But I was afraid, if I presented myself at the communion table, of being repulsed. I therefore wrote to the clergyman to say to him that I was in heart a Protestant, but that I did not wish to discuss dogmas. To my surprise and pleasure he came to tell me that he would willingly admit me to the communion with this understanding; and that both himself and his elders would be pleased to have me in their flock. I have seldom had so agreeable and consoling a surprise. To live always alone in the world was to me a very sad fate. In the midst of so many persecutions it was very sweet to be able to say, 'At last I am among brethren.' I went to the communion with emotions of tenderness in my heart that were perhaps the best preparation I could make in the eyes of Heaven." [1]

Accordingly, Rousseau, so far from being an infidel, was a Christian who had his doubts about miracles. In this age we should call him, on the side of his unbelief, a rationalist, or a naturalist, — nothing harder. Why, then, it may be said, was he thus fiercely pursued by all parties?

The answer to this throws light on the age, the man, and the subject.

The explanation of Rousseau is given in a single word. He was a man of genius, — that is, a man of ideas; but the ideas which possessed him were

---

[1] *Confessions,* Book xii.

24

not those of the eighteenth century, but those of
the nineteenth. He was before his time in everything, and as much before himself as he was before his time. He could no more realize his ideas
in his own life than he could realize them in the
belief of his contemporaries. His startling originality, his fiery eloquence, interested, beyond all
example, the nation, but gave him no disciples, no
associates, no converts, no friends. He stood always alone. What was there in common between
him and those he called his friends, — a sneering
Diderot, a worldly-minded Grimm, a frivolous
race of fine ladies, a good-natured and commonplace Madame Warens, or a poor Thérèse le Vasseur? What did the great noblemen, the Prince
of Conti, the Marshal Luxembourg, who were entertained by his flashing genius, care for his ideas?
They did not understand that a whole revolution
lay hidden in them. Possessed, driven, devoured
by his thoughts, he could not carry them out in
his own life. With a whole modern science of
education teeming in his brain, — a science which
was to rescue children from many false fetters, —
he deposited his own children in the Foundling
Hospital. With pure ideas of love, like those de-
picted in the "Héloïse," which among the novels of his day is like Milton's Lady among the
jabbering satyrs of "Comus," his own intercourse
with women was unworthy. He was not a licen-
tious man; but neither had he a single experience

of a truly noble love. With a thirst for society, and convictions of what true society is, with a feeling of brotherly love toward men of all classes, and a grand democratic socialism, he fled, tormented, even from those who really wished him well. The mean and selfish actions and unworthy loves, which he faithfully records in his "Confessions," filled him with remorse all his days. He was an Orestes pursued by the Furies. His abandonment of his children was contemplated by him, all his life after, with horror; and he wrote "Émile" as his only way of making reparation to society for this great wrong. So we say that his ideas were as far above his own conduct as they were before the opinions of his contemporaries. His belief came to him from a better future; his life flowed into him from the corrupt channels of the miserable eighteenth century.

Still there were many noble actions in Rousseau's life. The strain and tendency of his soul was toward whatsoever things were true, just, and generous. He was no flatterer of the powerful; he would not eat the bread of idleness; he refused the pension offered him, and supported himself by copying music.

Mme. de Pompadour, the king's mistress, secured the services of Voltaire, Duclos, Crébillon, and Marmontel. They were all willing to write to her verses of adulation for the sake of her patronage. Not so Rousseau. She made him all kinds of handsome offers of money, place, position, if he would write a few lines in her favor. Rousseau for a time simply ignored these proposals. At last, as they were continued, he wrote to her, " Madame, the wife of a collier is more respectable in my eyes than the mistress of a prince." Mme. de Pompadour did not resent this boldness, but simply said he was an owl. " Yes, madame," replied one of her friends, " but the owl of Minerva."

M. Gaberel, the Genevese pastor, tells us that Rousseau was offered the place of librarian in Geneva in order to give him a support. He writes in reply, that it is just what he should like best to do, but that he has not the requisite knowledge. " I do not know," says he, " a single book as a librarian ought to know them. I cannot tell which is the best edition of an author ; I am ignorant of Greek ; I am very imperfectly acquainted with Latin ; and I have not the least particle of memory ! God forbid that I should introduce into this country the habit of accepting duties which one is not able to perform, and taking offices which one cannot properly fill."

Rousseau was a man of ideas. This is his merit, this is his mission. He was a prophet in the eighteenth century preparing the way of the nineteenth. In our time, how much more sympathy would his ideas receive ! But *then* he went " in the heat and bitterness of his spirit ; " his work was "a burden;" he was obliged to make his face like a flint, and lift up his voice, whether men would hear, or whether they would forbear.

What, then, were his ideas? These will best be seen by quoting a few passages from his "Émile," which seems to us his master-piece.

Its subject is education. Rousseau had faith in nature everywhere. He wished to follow the method of nature in education, and to throw off the shackles of system. The following are some passages from this work, now half forgotten: —

All is good, coming from the hands of God. All degenerates in the hands of man.

The man of society is born, lives, and dies in slavery. At his birth he is wrapt in swaddling-bands; at his death nailed in a coffin; all his life between, he is fettered by our institutions.

The man who has lived the most is not he who has counted most years, but he who has felt most of life.

It is of less importance to prevent one from dying than it is to cause him to live. To live is not merely to breathe: it is to act.

The earliest education is the most important; and this belongs unquestionably to woman. Speak, then, to women in your treatises of education.

The laws are always occupied too much with property, and too little with persons, because their object is peace, and not virtue; and therefore they do not give enough of authority to mothers.

All that which we do not possess at our birth, and which we need when we are grown, comes from education.

Education comes from nature, from man, or from things. Nature develops our faculties, man teaches us to use this development, and things give us personal experience.

Distrust the cosmopolites who seek in books far off the duties which they disdain to fulfill to those near at hand. They love the Tartars, but not their own neighbors.

The trade I desire to teach is life. I wish to make my pupil neither magistrate, priest, nor soldier, but man.

True education consists less in precepts than in exercises.

Expose your pupil to physical evil to save him from moral evil. One does not kill one's self because of the sufferings of the gout; only those of the soul produce despair.

Zeal may take the place of talent; but talent cannot take the place of zeal.

The humanity of Rousseau appears, in this work, in his care for the little infant. He uses all the resources of his logic and eloquence to procure for him the freedom of his limbs and the food of his mother's bosom. He drives away from the child the potions and medicines of which he himself had so often been the victim. Tenderness for their infants, it is said, became at once *à la mode* among the great ladies of Paris, and from being only half-mothers, they became whole-mothers of their children. Rousseau uses and improves the ideas of Locke. As the child grows up, he does not allow of emulation, he de-

presses vanity; and he substitutes for these conscience and the love of doing good. More salu-
tary counsels on the' chaste employment of youth
were never given from the pulpit. The moral enthusiasm of the work is a kind of religion throughout its pages; and if Rousseau had done only this
he would have deserved well of his race.

But he wrote also the " Héloïse; " he wrote the
" Social Contract; " both of them books in which
the same lofty ideas of the destiny of man to rise
above a degraded society bear full sway, — books
belonging to a better age, and meant to bring it
nearer.

No doubt these works contain many errors;
how could it be otherwise? Such a love as that
described in' the " Héloïse " may not be possible
to man; one cannot tread safely in such a narrow
way. But the *idea* of a holy, chaste, respectful
love, which does not seek its own gratification, but
the highest good of its object, is certainly as true
as it was certainly then unusual in all French literature. How much higher, indeed, is it, and how
much purer, than the " Sorrows of Werther," or
the selfish passion of Byron!

There never was such a thing as the " Social
Contract." True; but the fundamental *ideas* of
the book, — that government is for the good of
the people, and that their consent is necessary to
make it legitimate, — these are the foundations
of all modern political liberty. Yet not liberty

only, but fraternity, was in the mind of Rousseau, as the object of society. Man was to respect and love man. All aristocracy, all monopoly, all class privileges, were false and evil. This thought, at least, we in America can accept.

Pure love, born of Christian thought, — love whose object is the soul, and not mere personal charms, — was put into words on the shores of the lake of Geneva. The place where the scene is laid has become holy ground. Even Byron, whose idea of love was so much meaner, could reverence the noble muse of Rousseau, and not pass near Clarens or the rocks of Meillerie without offering his homage in his own inimitably sweet and flowing verse : —

" Clarens, sweet Clarens, birthplace of deep Love,
    Thine air is the young breath of passionate thought ;
  Thy trees take root in Love ; the snows above
    The very glaciers have his colors caught,
    And sunset into rose-hues sees them wrought
  By rays which sleep there lovingly : the rocks,
    The permanent crags, tell here of Love, who sought
  In them a refuge from the worldly shocks
  Which stir and sting the soul with hope that woos, then mocks."

As a writer, Rousseau still stands at the summit of French literature. M. Sainte-Beuve says that Rousseau is " the swallow which announces a new spring for the French language." His patience in correcting his sentences was extraordinary. He did not attain to his perfect mastery of language without the greatest labor. Here is a specimen of the way in which a sentence was brought to perfection. He first wrote, "Devant moi s'étalait l'or du superbe genêt, et la pourpre de la modeste bruyère." He then corrected it thus : " Le splendide genêt doré, et la bruyère éclatante." He then again altered it to " L'or du genêt sauvage, et la pourpre des steriles bruyères." And finally he left it, " Devant moi s'étalait l'or des genêts et la pourpre des bruyères."

Yet this perfect writer and man filled with ideas was at first thought an idiot. When he was twenty years old, M. D'Aubonne, cousin of Mme. Warens, said, " Rousseau est un garçon sans idées, très borné, s'il n'est pas tout-a-fait inepte."

The life of Rousseau was, unhappily for him, in an age in which Dogmatism and Formalism had resulted in Skepticism. The Church was dead in routine and in doctrinal orthodoxy ; and an inevitable reaction drove men into unbelief. Catholic formalism in France, Protestant formalism in Geneva, resulted, — in the one place, in the atheism of the Encyclopædists ; in the other, in the milder skepticism of Rousseau. When we make religion to consist in ecclesiastical forms or in stern dogmas we are preparing the way for rebellion and revolution. The infidelity of France did not come from the philosophers ; it came from the bigotry of the Jesuits who guided Louis XIV. in his persecution of the Huguenots. The skepticism of Rousseau was the child of Calvin's bitter theology ; and we think that Rousseau's warm-hearted and loving skepticism was preferable to that ferocious, though honest Christianity. If the one had more of truth, the other had more of love.

The misery of Rousseau's life came partly from himself. He violated great and sacred laws which cannot be broken with impunity. He wasted the precious hours of his youth in weak enjoyment of the leisure provided for him by Madame Warens, — without any healthy labor or any manly aim. He left her, not from conscience, but from irritated vanity and self-love. He took to his home another woman, no way suited to him, and lived as a husband with her — not really loving her, but making her half-companion, half-housekeeper — for long years. The same weak self-indulgence led him to renounce the charge of his children. All through life, he followed feeling and sentiment rather than any intelligent law of duty. His ideas were noble, his practices were inferior and commonplace. As a man of thought he has done a great work in the world by leading the way toward something higher : as a man of action he has served the world as a warning to be shunned. His teaching is like the pure and heavenly light of the stars, pointing mariners on their way ; his conduct, the light-house set among roaring breakers and over perilous rocks, showing them what they ought to avoid.

But let us have pity for him, remembering his long sorrows and bitter sufferings. Worn with severe and chronic disease during the most of his life; undoubtedly insane in his later years; never understood; having no real friends; a forlorn wanderer, an exile, a banished man, the object of alternate enthusiasm and abuse; having known no mother's love nor father's care in childhood, no wise counsel in youth; thrown on his own resources for support all his life long; never meeting a single noble-hearted and wise friend or adviser; having never the happiness of real domestic joy; tormented with jealous suspicions; longing for love and never finding it, — there has not wandered on this earth a more unhappy man, nor one who deserved more truly to be called the apostle of affliction.

M. Villemain — one of the best of French critics, worthy compeer of Guizot and Cousin, of whose lectures on the eighteenth century we have made frequent use in this essay — thus concludes his remarks on Jean Jacques : —

"When I speak of Rousseau, and mingle with my sincere criticisms the admiration which it is impossible to refuse him, I am publicly reproached with having made an apotheosis of that 'vile,' that 'infamous' Rousseau. I will stop speaking of him, and then will grow tiresome, since that is more orthodox. And yet, gentlemen, you know with what conscience I have told both the good and the evil; how I have dwelt long on the

errors which obscured in Rousseau the brilliancy of his
strong imagination, and of the soul which rose naturally
toward noble objects.   I have explained his errors, but
not justified them, out of the history of his time.   Well,
this, it seems, is not enough.   But it is not my fault if
his words, descending like a sword or like fire, have agitated the souls of his contemporaries.   I do not belong to that age.   I am not M. Malesherbes, the Minister of State, who, in his enthusiasm, privately corrected
the proofs of the ' Émile.'   I am not the Duke of Luxembourg or the Prince of Conti.   I did not, in opposition to the prejudices of my rank and the scruples of my
faith, welcome, as they did, to my castle, Jean Jacques,
democratic philosopher and free-thinker.   It is after
sixty years have passed that, led by curiosity, in the
course of study, opening a book whose pages are still
glowing with an eloquence which can never pass away,
I merely give you an account of the impressions of enthusiasm, of astonishment, of doubt, of blame, which this
book occasions within me.   These I communicate without art; judge them for yourselves : I neither impose on
you my admiration, nor forbid you to censure.   I have
only told you the truth, — it is the truth which they
accuse."

He loved much ; perhaps he has been forgiven
much.   He suffered much ; perhaps his faults have
been enough punished.   *His* faults were those of
éclat ; those which it is easy for all men to condemn.   Dr. Johnson, denouncing pensioners in
his Dictionary as those who sold themselves for a
bribe to betray their country, and then accepting

a pension himself from a Whig king; poured contempt on Rousseau, who preferred copying music to taking a pension from the King of Prussia. Rousseau had an upright soul, and a truth-loving soul: he was faithful to his light; or, if led astray, openly confessed and bewailed his sin. We forgive David his murder because he repented. We forgive Peter his repeated lies because he repented. Shall we not forgive Rousseau his chief sin, of abandoning his children, when he bitterly bewailed it ever after, and made an expiation in his " Émile," devoted to saving little children from the sufferings and cruelty they endured in his time?

We cannot better close this study of Rousseau's life than with the words of Thomas Carlyle: —

" Hovering in the distance, with woe-struck, minatory air, stern-beckoning, comes Rousseau. Poor Jean Jacques! Alternately deified and cast to the dogs; a deep-minded, high-minded, even noble, yet wofully misarranged mortal, with all misformations of Nature intensated to the verge of madness by unfavorable fortune. A lonely man; his life a long soliloquy! The wandering Tiresias of the time, — in whom, however, did lie prophetic meaning, such as none of the others offer. Whereby, indeed, it might partly be that the world went to such extremes about him; that, long after his departure, we have seen one whole nation worship him; and a Burke, in the name of another, class him with the offscourings of the earth. His true character, with its lofty aspirings and poor performings, — and how the spirit of the man worked so wildly, with celestial fire in a thick, dark element of chaos, and shot forth ethereal radiance, all-piercing lightning, yet could not illuminate, was quenched and did not conquer : — this, with what lies in it, may now be pretty accurately appreciated. Let his history teach all whom it concerns to '*harden* themselves against the ills which Mother Nature will try them with ; ' to seek within their own soul what the world must forever deny them ; and say composedly to the Prince of the Power of this lower Earth and Air, ' Go thou thy way : I go mine.' "

XVIII.

THE HEROES OF ONE COUNTRY TOWN.

THE HEROES OF ONE COUNTRY TOWN.[1]

MEETING to dedicate these stones to the memory of the brave men of this place who gave their lives in the cause of Union and Freedom, our minds are carried back to the time when they went from among us. Who can forget those dark hours at the commencement of the war? The long struggle between Liberty and Slavery had brought face to face two gigantic foes. One was the slave-power, — an oligarchy of about four hundred thousand slave-holders, owning some four millions of slaves, worth three thousand millions of dollars. Intermarrying among themselves, holding the chief political offices in the South, the slave-holders were an aristocracy as proud, exclusive, and domineering as that of Venice or Poland. United by common interests, — pecuniary, social, and political, — with the single paramount purpose of maintaining and extending slavery, it ruled the South with a rod of iron, allowing no freedom of

---

[1] An address delivered to the people of West Roxbury, Mass., on the dedication of a monument to the soldiers of that town.

speech, of the press, or of the pulpit. By means of this perfect union it obtained the control of the national government, and, before 1860, had taken possession of the whole national organization. It annexed Texas in 1845, defeated the Wilmot Proviso in 1846, passed the Fugitive Slave Bill in 1850, repealed the Missouri Compromise in 1854, obtained the Dred Scott Decision in 1857. It controlled both houses of Congress, possessed the executive, and directed the decisions of the judiciary; so holding in its hand the army and navy of the Union.

But, on the other side, there had grown up, with wonderful rapidity, a mighty opposing force. It was unorganized; it was invisible. Its weapons were not carnal; its missiles were the imponderables of the soul. It had neither fleets nor armies, neither judges nor presidents; but it was a terrible power, ominous of coming change. It was the antislavery opinion of the North, which had been opposed first by mobs, then by ridicule, lastly by arguments, but had conquered them all. As Herod the king, in the midst of his power and glory, feared John the Baptist, " knowing that he was a just man," so the slave-power, which feared nothing else, feared the antislavery platform. William Lloyd Garrison might have used the words of Pope, and said, —

> " Yes, I *am* proud; I must be proud, to see
> Men, not afraid of God, afraid of me."

Both the great parties, Democratic and Whig, united in 1850 to put down the antislavery agitation. For a few months there was a lull in the storm. Then a woman's pen, inspired by genius and profound conviction, broke the silence. "Uncle Tom's Cabin" was published. Five hundred thousand copies were sold before the end of the year, — a million in England. It was translated into nineteen languages, and the whole world was again discussing the great theme.

At last the "irrepressible conflict" of tongue and pen — as Mr. Seward happily termed it at Rochester in 1858 — drew to its close, and a sterner strife became imminent. Abraham Lincoln was chosen President in November, 1860. Seven States seceded from the Union. Southern Senators resigned their seats in Congress. The seceding States seized on the forts and other public property of the United States in their neighborhood. Finally, April 12, 1861, fire was opened on Fort Sumter, and the war began.

And here let me stop a moment to see how the Providence of God had prepared the way for a successful defense of the Union against its foes. The North had been educated for years by two great political parties : by the Republican, whose war-cry was *Freedom;* and the Democratic, whose watchword was *Union.* Secession struck at both. It defied Freedom, by its purpose of maintaining and extending slavery ; it struck at Union, by its purpose of establishing a Southern Confederacy. It therefore united against itself all that was honest and true in the two great Northern parties. Those who had been educated by the Democrats to believe in Union, those who had been educated by the Republicans to believe in Freedom, joined hands to defend both when threatened by secession. Let us remember this, and always maintain Freedom and Union, one and inseparable.

Again, consider how fortunate we were in the President chosen for the hour. He seems to have been the very man to unite the North. Had he been more of an abolitionist he would not have carried with him the conservatives; had he been more of a conservative, he would not have had the support of the reformers. Moving slowly, but always moving; cautious, but determined; surrounding himself with the best and wisest advisers, but at last deciding all great questions himself; bearing the malignant assaults of foes and the impatience of friends with imperturbable good temper, — he gained and held the confidence of the people. Remembering all this, let us also bless God for having sent us, in our hour of need, the great and good Abraham Lincoln.

And once again, a good Providence had prepared the nation for this terrific struggle when the Fathers of our State established the system of free schools. Without these we never could have conquered the rebellion. The government could have done nothing if it had not been supported always by the determined will of the nation. That will was the result of conviction, and that conviction was born of intelligence. Every man at the North knew that his prosperity and security, his present comforts and his hope for the future, depended on putting down the rebellion. That knowledge alone enabled the people to make the efforts, meet the dangers, and bear the privations of the long war. Without the free-school system, the people could never have attained that knowledge. The common schools saved the nation. Therefore let the nation always maintain the common school, — the best democratic institution in the land, where the sons of the richest and poorest man sit side by side, — the unsectarian school, whose doors are open to all the children of the State.

But still another element was needed to organize these convictions, and to apply them to the work in hand ; and that also was providentially provided by our plan of local self-government. The people, accustomed from the first to assemble in town meetings, did not wait to be called upon from Washington, but came together in their townships, chose committees to raise men, voted money for immediate wants, and proceeded to discipline troops. Let us maintain the townships and the primary meetings, and resist all excessive centralization.

Lastly, there was the preparation made by the Northern church in giving a religious education to the conscience. When the general in command went into Faneuil Hall to see the troops who passed the night there before marching to relieve Washington, he found them singing psalms, and is reported to have said: " Good heavens! have the Southerners got to fight men who sing psalms ?" — remembering, perhaps, Cromwell's iron-clad regiments. The New England churches differ on many points, but in one they agree; they all teach that religion consists in obedience to God's moral laws, and not merely in the belief of creeds. Religion at the South is often a belief, a ceremony, or an emotion; religion at the North has been, in the main, an attempt to do justly, love mercy, and walk humbly with God.

The nerve of our army was in its religious convictions. The true leader of our nation's armies was that stern old man, possessed by the sense of justice, — a fanatic if you will, but a fanatic for humanity and right; awful in his purpose as an old Jewish prophet; the incarnation of Puritanism as applied to the nineteenth century. Wherever our armies marched, John Brown's soul marched before them, making them feel that theirs was the cause of God, and that the Lord was on their side, so that they were sure of ultimate success. In that faith Shaw fell at Wagner, and Putnam at Ball's Bluff. In that faith these

our noble sons and brothers were sanctified, and
the war became a holy war. The battle-hymn of
the republic was inspired by this idea, for

"Their eyes had seen the glory of the coming of the Lord."

So it came to pass, by means of our free schools
and our other Northern institutions, that when the
hurricane of secession burst on the land the country was prepared to resist and conquer it. Then
it was seen that the cold, hard North was built on
a " surging, subterranean fire," which lifted it to
the height of the solemn hour. Then, when the
awful storm of secession swept like a tropical cy-
clone over the South ; black with thunder, red with
forked lightning ; it was answered by a Northern
earthquake which shook the land from Maine to
Minnesota, and poured out its volcanic fires of patriotism from the pine forests of Katahdn to the
snowy peaks of Colorado. Then one great impulse united all hearts and hands in the determined purpose to save the country. Then we
knew no longer any distinction of Republican or
Democrat, foreign citizen or native American,
Catholic or Protestant, capitalist or day-laborer.
Then the hardy German and the warm-hearted
Irishman joined with the Puritan and Yankee to
save the country, the dear, common mother of all.
Then the fair-haired boy — the support of his
aged father, the joy of his mother's heart, the
ripe fruit of our best culture — said, " Father,

mother, it is my duty to go ; let me go and die, if it must be, for my country ; " and they laid their hands on his young head, and answered, " Go, my boy ; go and die ! "   Then from all the towns of Massachusetts came one voice, — from her farms and her manufactories, from her fisher-men and her sailors : —

> " From her rough coasts and isles, which hungry ocean
>   Gnaws with his surges ; from her fisher's skiff,
>   With white sail swaying to the breezes' motion
>   Round rock and cliff ;

> " From the free fireside of her unbought farmer ;
>   From her free laborer, at his loom and wheel ;
>   From her brown smithshop, where, beneath the hammer,
>   Rings the red steel," —

From each and all, — one grand impulse of con-science, courage, and patriotism hurried the young and old forward to imitate their fathers, and offer in the holy cause " their lives, their fortunes, and their sacred honor."

Our rulers at Washington, far behind the peo-ple in their appreciation of the situation, were alarmed at the magnitude of the popular move-ment, and tried to check it.   May 15, 1861, Secretary Cameron positively refused to accept from Governor Andrew more than six regiments of three months' volunteers, and said, in his letter to our Governor, " it is important to *reduce* rather than to enlarge this number (of six regiments), and in no event to exceed it.   Let me earnestly recommend to you, therefore, to call for no more than eight regiments, of which six only are to serve for three years ; and if more are already called for, to reduce the number by discharge."

But before the end of the war Massachusetts sent to the front sixty-one regiments of infantry, besides artillery and cavalry; furnished, out of a population of one million two hundred thousand one hundred and fifty-nine thousand soldiers and sailors to the army and navy of the United States, and raised and expended $42,000,000. At the end of the war it appeared that every city and town had filled its quota upon every call for troops ; and all, except twelve, had furnished a surplus over all demands, the aggregate of which surplus was over fifteen thousand men. These facts have been furnished me by one of our townsmen, General Schouler, whose services during the war, as Adjutant-general, were of the greatest value to the State and nation.

In all this work our town took an ample share. Our first town meeting in relation to the war was held May 20, 1861, and its chairman was a man who devoted his time, thought, and means, during the whole war, to his country and its cause. In 1863 the town voted him its thanks for his services in procuring volunteers. But no formal vote of thanks can express what we all owe to the energy, patriotism, and devotion of our loved, revered, and lamented fellow-citizen, STEPHEN M. WELD.

At a meeting in 1862, it being proposed to lay out a new road, it was resolved, on motion of John C. Pratt, "that the only road desirable to be opened at the present time is the road to Richmond."

West Roxbury furnished seven hundred and twenty men to the war, a surplus of twenty-six over and above all demands, and appropriated $86,000 to war purposes, besides $22,000 from private subscriptions.

The women of West Roxbury, at the beginning of the struggle, formed a Soldiers' Aid Society, which raised over $8,000, and furnished our soldiers with more than eight thousand articles of clothing and comfort. I may be allowed here to name the president and active promoter of that Society, Mrs. GEORGE W. COFFIN.

In this town was recruited and drilled one of the finest of the Massachusetts regiments. I happened to be the owner of Brook Farm in 1861; and when the Second Massachusetts was about to be organized, I offered it to my friend, Morris Copeland, Quartermaster of that regiment, and it was accepted. Before I had the farm it had been the scene of a famous social experiment not eminently successful. I never raised much of a crop upon it before; but in 1861 it bore the greatest crop of any farm in Massachusetts, in the courage, devotion, and military renown of the officers and men of that noble regiment.

And now we are here to do honor to the brave
men who went from among us to give themselves
to this great struggle for Union and Freedom.
We have welcomed back, with tears and praises
and thanks to God, those whom the cruel horrors
of war spared to return. We welcome to-day,
with tears and praises, those immortal souls whose
mortal bodies could not return alive. They sleep
on many fields, — in the lovely valleys of Virginia,
on the pestilential plains of North and South Carolina, on the shores of Texas, on the bluffs of the
Mississippi, in the far South, and in the cemetery
of Gettysburg amidst the smiling valleys of Pennsylvania. Of our forty-six West Roxbury soldiers
who died in the war for Union and Freedom,
one was killed at Bull Run, in the first battle of
the war; nine fell in 1862, seven in 1863, nine in
1864, three in 1865, and seven at times unknown.
Would that the time would allow us to speak of
each separately. But one or two cases of special
interest I may be permitted to dwell upon for a
moment.

General THOMAS J. C. AMORY, who died of
yellow fever at Beaufort, North Carolina, October
7, 1864, four days after the death of his wife of
the same disease, was the first officer of the regular
army who became an officer of volunteers in Massachusetts; and the first officer of the regular army
who received a military commission from Governor Andrew, who appointed him to the command

of the Seventeenth Massachusetts. He assisted Governor Andrew greatly at the beginning of the war by his military knowledge in forming regiments and dispatching troops; and the high position taken by our State at that critical hour is to be attributed in part to his efforts. In command of his regiment, he proceeded to Washington; and then, with Burnside's expedition, to North Carolina; and there remained, till his death, in a most important outpost, where his judgment was shown in many services, and his courage tested in many serious engagements. He died honored and loved by all who knew him, and after his death his commission of Brigadier-general was received from the War Office, on the back of which is this indorsement in the writing of Governor Andrew : —

"These papers are forwarded through Colonel Henry Lee, Jr., to the father and family of the late Thomas J. C. Amory, for their information of the fact that the records of the Department of War show that his devoted and meritorious services and character obtained (though too late for his own enjoyment of the honor) the recognition of a brevet promotion to the rank of Brigadier-general of Volunteers.

"JOHN A. ANDREW,
"*Governor of Massachusetts.*"

Lieutenant-colonel LUCIUS MANLIUS SARGENT was the son of one of our worthy fellow-citizens and the son-in-law of another. He entered the army as surgeon, but soon became captain in the

First Massachusetts Cavalry; and for his energy, courage, and skill was promoted to the rank he held at his death. He fell near Belfield, Virginia, sword in hand, in the presence of the enemy. His fighting comrades called him a "man of iron:" those who had seen him in his home knew that to this iron strength was added much of culture, taste, tenderness, and Christian faith.

Would that I might speak fully and in detail of all the noble men whose names are before us. But I must at least mention Captain WILLIAM B. WILLIAMS, who, when he entered the service, said, "I am young and unmarried, and am just the one to go." He fell in the terrible battle of Cedar Mountain, where the Second Regiment, out of twenty-two officers, brought out only eight uninjured. With him, at the same time, fell CARY, GOODWIN, ABBOTT, and PERKINS. "It was splendid," says their comrade, ROBERT SHAW, "to see those fellows, some sick, walk straight up into the shower of bullets, as if it were so much rain, — men who, until this year, had lived lives of perfect ease and luxury. It is hard to believe we shall never see them again, after having been constantly together for more than a year. I do not remember a single quarrel of importance among all our officers at that time."

He who wrote these words to his mother in August, 1862, himself, in less than a year, fell gloriously on the parapet of Fort Wagner, calling to his regiment to follow him. By his side fell another of our brave boys of West Roxbury — Captain WILLIAM H. SIMPKINS. His friend and comrade, CABOT RUSSELL, had been struck by a ball, and fell. Captain Simpkins offered to carry him off. " No," replied the brave boy, " but you may straighten me out." As Simpkins stooped to perform this service, a bullet pierced his breast, and he fell dead on his friend's dying body. Captain Simpkins entered the Fifty-fourth Regiment of colored soldiers, not from enthusiasm, but from a solemn sense of duty, and he died nobly on one of the noblest fields of battle in the war.

And another name stands on that stone, — the name of one, the child of a dear friend of mine, — one whose purity of heart, sincerity, tenderness, and conscience endeared him to all who knew him. Like Captain Simpkins, HENRY MAY BOND went to the war, and returned to it again, from a pure sense of duty. He had no taste for military life; in his modesty he distrusted his own fitness for the service; but he thought it his duty, having served his time, to reënlist and go again; and he went. In a letter to a brother officer he says: " In the hour of personal danger I am strong and courageous only in the faith that, should it please God to take my life while in the discharge of what I deem to be my highest duty, all will be well with me. I should be worth nothing to my friends or my country without that faith in God." So the good, brave boy lived cheerfully and patiently; so, cheerfully and patiently, he died.

In speaking of the officers who were more conspicuous, let us not forget that the services of those who enlisted, fought, and died as private soldiers were at least as honorable and deserving of our gratitude. The private surrendered his liberty, he encountered more hardships, he was often exposed to greater danger, he had fewer of the compensations and little of the glory. Let us, then, give him as full a measure of our gratitude and our love. Among the names of the private soldiers on our monument are those of two brothers, CHARLES H. HARPER and JOSEPH HARPER, whose father and mother are with us. They gave their two boys to their country, and it was a greater gift than the whole fortune of an Astor or a Vanderbilt.

On the tomb of Sir Christopher Wren, in the crypt of St. Paul's, in commemoration of this great architect who filled London with his churches, are the simple words, *Si monumentum quæris, circumspice,* — "If you ask for his monument, look around you." So we may say of those who fell in defense of our common country, — "If you ask for their monument, look around you." The country itself, saved by their devotion, is their true monument. Not for their sakes, then, but for our own, do we erect this monument. They do not need it, but we do.

The whole land, redeemed, regenerated, and disenthralled, is the only adequate monument to their heroism. But, in the hurry of our busy life, in the pressure of our multitudinous cares, we need to be reminded, by the sight of this simple structure, by the letters of these noble names, that we are bound to keep the country pure which they made safe.

There are some, I believe, who object to such monuments, on the ground that they tend to keep alive the memory of civil warfare, which had better be forgotten. But this is a mistake. If I were in a Southern State, and stood by a memorial erected there in love and gratitude to the soldiers of their lost cause, would it excite any feeling of hostility in my mind? Rather, I should say, "They died in a bad cause; but if they believed they were right, I can respect their self-devotion." Such monuments would impress on me the conviction that *they believed* in their cause and were sincere, and so would lead me to respect them. But if Southerners, traveling through the North, should see no testimony on our part to our heroes and martyrs, they might justly infer that we did *not* believe in *our* cause. But wherever the eye falls on such memorials as this, it is at once felt that we were in solemn earnest; that we considered the war for Union a holy one, and all who fell in it heroes and martyrs. These stones will say to every citizen of the South, "We did not fight you in anger or from selfishness, but in pure love of Union and Freedom. It is because we believe Union and Freedom as good for you as for ourselves. It was no battle of North against South, but of right against wrong; and when we won the victory, we won it for you as well as for ourselves. The country these brave men saved is your country as well as ours. We can all be proud in the triumph of our common land."

To our heroes and martyrs we erect these stones, — not so much for their sake as for our own. They, being dead, still speak. They speak, to teach us never to despair of the country. They tell us that, though the times may be bad, there are yet many noble souls; that patriotism, courage, conscience, and devotion do not die out of human hearts; that though there may be robbers who plunder the country, and demagogues who deceive the people; though evil abounds, and the love of many waxes cold, — there is yet a power to redeem and to save. In the darkest hour of our nation's night there flamed up this great spirit of generous courage in the souls of our boys, and turned the darkness into day. Let us remember this, and never despair.

And when we pass this monument, when our eyes fall on these names, let us remember that what they saved we are bound to keep safe. Therefore let me close by adopting the sublime words

26

of Abraham Lincoln at the dedication of the Cemetery at Gettysburg : " In a larger sense we cannot dedicate, we cannot consecrate, we cannot hallow this ground.   These brave men, living and dead, have consecrated it far above our power to add or detract.   The world will little note nor long remember what we say here, but it can never forget what they did. It is for us, the living, rather to be dedicated here to their unfinished work, — to be here dedicated to the great task remaining before us, — that from these honored dead we take increased devotion to the cause for which they gave the last full measure of devotion ; that we here highly resolve that the dead shall not have died in vain ; that the nation shall, under God, have a new birth of freedom, and that the government *of* the people, *by* the people, and *for* the people, shall not perish from the earth."

XIX.

WILLIAM HULL.

WILLIAM HULL.

Among the beautiful situations which abound in the vicinity of Boston, that in Newton, now occupied as the residence of Governor Claflin, is very attractive. The house stands on an elevation above an extensive lawn, through which winds a large brook, and where groups of graceful elms throw their shadows along the soft grass in the summer afternoons. In my childhood this was the home of my grandfather, William Hull; and one to which all the grandchildren loved to go. He had been an officer in the American army during the whole Revolution; had known Washington, Lafayette, and other leaders; had been for many years Governor of Michigan Territory, and could tell numerous anecdotes of his early days, to entertain the children who collected around his hospitable hearth. He would narrate to us stories of the sufferings and exploits of the Revolutionary troops; of the terrors of the French Revolution which he saw in Paris in 1798; and of the wild Indians among whom he lived in Michigan. A kind and genial old man, disposed to be a friend to every one, his house was a rendezvous for many sorts of people, who made themselves at home in its parlors or its kitchen. After a youth of adventure and a manhood which had brought many distinctions and honors, his age had been clouded by unmerited disgrace. Put in a position of command where success was impossible, deserted by his government and betrayed by his colleagues, he had been made the scapegoat of a blundering administration, and of other commanders who knew how to throw on him the blame of their own mistakes. But his sweet temper remained unimbittered by this ill-treatment; he was always cheerful; he was never heard to complain; and was sure that his character would be finally vindicated. And thus he spent his last peaceful years in the pursuits of agriculture, on the farm which his wife had inherited from her ancestors, and which supplied the modest expenses of his household.

This farm, of about three hundred acres, came into his possession through his marriage with Sarah Fuller, only daughter of Abraham Fuller, who was a conspicuous character about the period of the Revolution. His record illustrates the position which might be reached in those days in the country towns by an intelligent farmer of Massachusetts. Having only had a common school education, he held the offices of selectman, town clerk, and treasurer, representative to the general court, delegate to the provincial congress, state senator, state councilor, and judge of the court of common pleas. He was an ardent patriot during the Revolution. He was celebrated for four things: his remarkable honesty; his determined patriotism; his very loud voice, which could be heard a mile; and the fact that after he died his body remained undecayed for a long period. Nine years after his death, the tomb in Newton being opened, his features were found nearly the same as when alive. Thirty-six years after his death, in 1830, I myself visited my great-grandfather's tomb, and found the body shrunk away indeed, and changed in color, but resembling leather in color and firmness. He inherited his farm from his great-grand-fathers, John Fuller and Edward Jackson. John Fuller, in 1658, bought seven hundred and fifty acres on Charles River for £150. Edward Jackson, in 1646, bought for £140 five hundred acres, covering what is now called Newtonville, but which ought perhaps to be named Jackson. From these two ancestors Judge Fuller inherited the estate where his son-in-law, General Hull, spent the last years of his life.

In 1848, long after the death of General Hull and his wife, and when the last of his family had moved from the homestead and left it unoccupied, I penetrated one summer afternoon into the old upper garret of the house, seeking for papers to help me in my task of writing a book on the campaign of 1812. I found there a trunk which had evidently not been opened or examined for many years. It was filled with files of letters, closely packed together, many of which had been received by my grandfather during the War of Independence. There were four letters from General Washington himself, and numerous others from Lincoln, Knox, Steuben, George Clinton, Lord Stirling, Jefferson, Madison, Monroe, Robert Morris, Aaron Burr, General Heath; with military commissions, and passports for traveling in Europe, from Governors Hancock and Samuel Adams. Some of these I took, to aid me in my work; but, being too absurdly conscientious, I left the rest, and they were afterward carried away by some unknown persons. Let us hope that, since they cannot be in my collection of autographs, they may adorn that of some other more enthusiastic collector.

William Hull was born in Derby, Conn., in 1753. His ancestor, Richard Hull, made freeman in Massachusetts in 1634, removed to New Haven, Conn., in 1639. His son John removed to Derby, Conn.; and his grandson, Joseph, was the grandfather of William. William's father, Joseph Hull, was a farmer. His eldest brother, the father of Isaac Hull, who commanded the frigate *Constitution* in its battle with the *Guerriere*, became, like William, an officer in the Revolutionary army.

Among his exploits was that of taking a British armed schooner in Long Island Sound. He went out of Derby in a boat in the night-time with twenty men, boarded the schooner, and took her into port with her crew. Another brother was also an officer in the Revolution.

William Hull, the fourth son, graduated at Yale College with honors; afterward entered the law school at Litchfield, Conn., and was admitted to the bar in 1775.

When the news of the battle of Lexington reached Derby a company of soldiers was raised there, and William Hull was chosen their captain, very unexpectedly to himself. But, full of the enthusiasm of the hour, he at once accepted the appointment, and joining Colonel Webb's regiment, of which his company made a part, marched to Cambridge to join the army of Washington. His father dying at this time, he resigned his share of the inheritance, saying, " I only want my sword and my uniform." From that time till the end of the American war he continued in the army, being present in many of the most important operations and engagements, such as Dorchester Heights, White Plains, Trenton, Princeton, Ticonderoga, the surrender of Burgoyne, Fort Stanwix, Monmouth, Stony Point, and Morrisania. He was inspector under Baron Steuben, lieutenant-colonel in 1779, and commanded the escort of Washington when he bade farewell to the army.

His commander, Colonel Brooks (afterwards
Governor of Massachusetts), wrote a letter in
1814, in which he says, " In September, 1776, at
White Plains, General Hull (then captain) acted
under my immediate orders, and was detached
from the line to oppose a body of Light Infantry
and Yagers advancing on the left flank of the
American army. His orders were executed with
promptitude, gallantry, and effect. Though more
than double his number, the enemy was compelled
to retreat, and the left of the American line enabled to pass the Bronx."

He was then hardly more than a boy, twenty-
three years old, fresh from college and the study
of law. In the brief memoirs he has left of his
Revolutionary life, he mentions this action in the
abstract and dignified manner which was then
supposed to be the proper style for history. In
fact, had it not been for Colonel Brooks, we
should not have known that he commanded this
body, for he does not even mention himself. O,
if he, and the other young heroes of that time had
only told us of their feelings on being suddenly
called to such important duties ; if they had only
relinquished the abstract formal narrative and
given us pictures of the looks, dress, behavior of
the soldiers ; had only condescended to paint the
details and add the color which so enliven modern
history ! But such was not the style of writing
they had learned at college from Hume and Lord

Kames. This was the first time that he had stood with his regiment to see a British army marching to attack them, and his MSS. glow for a moment with the admiration he felt as a young soldier for the splendid military equipments and discipline of the enemy. He speaks of "the magnificent appearance" of the British troops, of the glitter of their polished arms under the bright autumnal sun; of their rich uniforms and equipage. So the boy captain stood with his poorly dressed provincials to receive the volleys of grape and chain shot from the advancing foe, looking down on them from Chatterton's hill, till he was called to lead the body which was to oppose the force trying to turn the American left. All he says of this is: "It was promptly done, with much order and regularity; and, after a sharp conflict, the object was completely attained;" merely adding that "his regiment had the honor of receiving the personal thanks of Washington after the engagement." But of the glow of satisfaction and pride which he must have felt in listening to those words of praise from his great commander he carefully says nothing.[1]

The next little touch of reality which breaks out from his memoir is concerning the fatigues of the soldiers at Trenton and Princeton. He was one of

---

[1] Nor does he mention his first wound, received in this engagement. That would be quite contrary to good writing, according to the rhetoric of his day.

those commanders who made the sufferings of his soldiers his own. On leaving the Highlands of New York to join General Washington in Pennsylvania, he says he found that his company, then reduced to fifty men, had only one poor blanket to two men ; many had no shoes or stockings ; those which were in the company were nearly worn out ; their clothes were wretched ; they had not been paid ; yet they were patient, patriotic, and willing to serve on without compensation. During their march they slept on the cold ground, though it was December, and that without covering. It was a bitterly cold Christmas night when Washington crossed the Delaware to Trenton. There was a driving storm of snow and sleet, and the ice was running in the river. The storm continued all night, and when the troops were halted they were so fatigued that they fell asleep as they stood in their ranks, and could with difficulty be awakened. In the action which followed, Captain Hull acted as Lieutenant-colonel. As soon as the battle had been fought and won, the army marched back with their prisoners and the artillery and military stores they had taken. Nearly all that night was spent in recrossing the Delaware. After gaining the other side, our young captain marched his troops to a farmer's house to get them some refreshment and rest. " After my men had been accommodated," says he, " I went into a room where a number of officers were sitting round a table, with a large dish of hasty-pudding in its centre. I sat down, procured a spoon, and began to eat. While eating I fell from my chair to the floor, overcome with sleep; and in the morning, when I awoke, the spoon was fast clinched in my hand." Happy days of youth, when no hardship nor fatigue can prevent blessed sleep from coming to seal up the eye and give rest to the brain!

The waking of the boy-soldier from this sleep on the floor was followed two days after by an agreeable incident. Washington, whose eye was everywhere, had probably noticed Hull's good behavior in this action.

The day before the march to Princeton, one of General Washington's aids came to Captain Hull's tent, and said, " Captain, the Commander-in-chief wishes to see you."

The young soldier went, we may suppose, with some trepidation, to the General's quarters. Washington looked at him, and said, " Captain Hull, you are an officer, I believe, in the Connecticut line."

Hull bowed, and General Washington went on. " I wish to promote you and I have the power to do so. But for that purpose I must transfer you to the Massachusetts line, since there is no vacancy in yours. If you are willing, I will appoint you major in the Eighth Massachusetts."

Hull thanked his general warmly for this mark of favor, and said, " All I wish, General, is to serve my country where I can do it best; and I accept the promotion gratefully."

He was then appointed to command a detachment to watch the approach of Cornwallis, and to detain him as long as possible while Washington was fortifying himself beyond the little creek, behind which he concealed his rapid night march upon Princeton. After serving in these two battles he was sent to Massachusetts to recruit his regiment. Having recruited three hundred men, he was then ordered to join General St. Clair's army at Ticonderoga. When General St. Clair evacuated that post an outcry of reproach went up against him from all quarters, though this event probably caused the final surrender of Burgoyne. Major Hull, satisfied of the injustice of these censures on his commander, wrote a letter to a friend in Connecticut during the retreat — the stump of a tree serving him for a table — defending the course of St. Clair. Major Hull was then sent with his regiment under General Arnold to relieve Fort Stanwix on the Mohawk River. After this work had been accomplished, Arnold and his troops rejoined the army of Gates at Saratoga, and Major Hull commanded detachments in the battles which compelled the surrender of Burgoyne. In one of these battles, when he drove the enemy from their post with the bayonet, his detachment lost one hundred and fifty men out of three hundred. He commanded the rear guard in

Schuyler's retreat from Fort Edward, and was constantly engaged with the advanced troops of Burgoyne. He commanded a volunteer corps on the 19th September. His detachment, by charging the enemy with the bayonet at a critical moment, aided in the repulse of Burgoyne on that day. In the battle of the 7th of October Major Hull commanded the advanced guard. At the final surrender of Burgoyne, he says, " I was present when they marched into our camp, and no words can express the deep interest felt by every American heart. Nor could we help feeling sympathy for those who had so bravely opposed us."

The Massachusetts regiment of which young Hull was major had now earned the right to some short period of rest. It had marched from Boston to Ticonderoga ; had retreated through the wilderness to Saratoga ; had thence marched to Fort Stanwix on the Mohawk and back ; and had been engaged in all the battles with Burgoyne. But it was now ordered to Pennsylvania to join the army of Washington, and was in the winter-quarters during the cruel winter passed at Valley Forge. Major Hull and Lieutenant-colonel Brooks had a hut together. It contained but one room, with shelves on one side for books, and on the other for a row of Derby cheeses sent to Hull by his mother. Here they passed the dreary days of the winter. The men wanted provisions, blankets, and shoes. The officers were scarcely better off than the men. Discontent, approaching to mutiny, was the natural result. Terrible diseases broke out in the camp. Long years after these trials had passed by, my grandfather Hull could scarcely allude to them without emotion.

The army was fading away by disease and desertion, and by the expiration of the term of enlistment. A little vigor on the part of indolent Sir William Howe would have driven this shadow of an army back into the mountains of Pennsylvania. Fortunately for Washington, General Howe was incapable of any such enterprise. He preferred feasts and games in Philadelphia.

One attempt, however, he made. He tried to surround a detachment of twenty-five hundred men under Lafayette, but failed in this from the superior alertness and vigor of the young French general. Hull was with the body sent to meet and assist Lafayette on this occasion. Years after, on Lafayette's visit to Boston in 1824, he came to visit General Hull, who had collected his grandchildren around him that they might see his old friend. I recollect the affectionate manner in which these two aged men took each other by the hand, and the kind interest which Lafayette manifested in the grandchildren of his comrade in the Revolution.

After the battle of Monmouth, in which Major Hull served under Lord Stirling, taking part in the successful resistance to the attack of the right

wing of the British, he was ordered to march his
regiment to Poughkeepsie, and then to Kingsbridge, in front of the enemy's lines near New
York. Hull had the command of the corps of observation at this place, which faced the whole
British army, and was eighteen miles in advance
of any other body of American troops. Great
circumspection and constant watchfulness was
necessary. He moved his troops from spot to
spot, about White Plains, above and below Dobbs
Ferry, patrolling to the right and left, and watching every movement of the British army. This
was the region ravaged by the Cow-boys and Skinners, and is the scene of Cooper's novel, " The
Spy." Major Hull commanded here during three
winters, trying to repress the cruelty of these law-
less marauders, so far as his small force would allow. He was then about twenty-five years old,
and in excellent health. " In a command so responsible," says he, " I adopted a system to which
I steadfastly adhered ; nor did storms, cold, or the
darkness of the night ever interfere with its per-
formance. Early in the evening, without taking
off my clothes, with my arms by my side, I lay
down before the fire, wrapped in my blanket, and
gave directions to the sentinel to awaken me at
one in the morning. My adjutant, or some other
officer, was with me, and one or two of the faithful guides from among the loyal inhabitants of
the region. The troops were ordered to be paraded

27

at the same hour, and to remain on parade until
my return.   After the whole were assembled, one
half were allowed to go to rest, and the other half
were formed into strong guards, which patrolled
in front and on the flanks of the detachment until
sunrise.   This force was in addition to the small
parties which were constantly patrolling with the
guides.   After making this arrangement, I rode
with my adjutant and one or two guides across to
the North River, and then back, on the line of
my patrols, toward the East River, and rode thus
in different directions until sunrise.   I commonly
rode about twenty miles at night, and as many
during the day.   I was directed to preserve peace
and good order among the inhabitants, and cau-
tioned not to allow supplies to be carried to the
enemy.   The enemy made many attempts to surprise and destroy my detachment; but, by the
precautions taken, his plans were invariably defeated.   I selected a number of families on whose
fidelity I could rely, and formed a line of them,
extending from Kingsbridge to my most advanced
guards.   I requested them to come to me at night,
and gave them my instructions.   The man who
lived nearest to Kingsbridge, whenever he noticed
any extraordinary movement among the enemy,
was to take a mug or pitcher in his hand, and in
a careless manner go to his next neighbor on this
line for some cider, beer, or milk, give him notice,
and return home.   His neighbor was to do the

same, and so on, until the information reached my station. Thus the enemy could make no movement without my being informed of it. I rewarded these good people for their services, which they could not perform without much personal risk. Not one was faithless to his trust, though surrounded by hardship and danger. The State of New York required them to take the oath of fidelity, and if they refused their property might be confiscated. Those who did not take the oath were plundered by the Skinners, and those who did, by the Cow-boys."

About the end of May, 1779, Sir Henry Clinton moved up the Hudson from New York, the American army retreating before him. The British troops took possession of the two strong positions of Stony Point and Verplanck's Point, and put garrisons in them. Major Hull was ordered to West Point, where his detachment erected a fort overlooking and commanding the other works at that place.

Stony Point and Verplanck's Point were the keys of the Highlands, and formed the eastern and western termini of King's Ferry, an important line of communication. They were just at the head of the Tappan Sea. General Washington, whose head-quarters were just above West Point, determined to attack Stony Point and retake it. He intrusted the enterprise to General Wayne. On this occasion Major Hull commanded a column, and received the commendation of his commander for his conduct. His name having been accidentally left out in General Wayne's first letter to the President of Congress, General Wayne, in a subsequent letter to Congress expressed his great regret at this omission. Major Hull thereupon wrote a letter to General Wayne, expressing his entire satisfaction with this act of justice. This letter is preserved in Dawson's account of the assault on Stony Point, and Wayne's reply is in my possession in the original autograph, and is as follows : —

"LIGHT INFANTRY CAMP, 25 *August*, 1779.

"DEAR SIR, — The Candor with which you have delivered your sentiments, gives a sensation much better felt than expressed. My highest ambition is to merit the Esteem and Confidence of the Light Corps — conscious of the Rectitude of my own Conduct, I feel doubly happy in your approbation of it, and have the most happy presages, that by mutual Confidence. and a strict Observance of Orders and Discipline, we shall produce a Conviction to the World that the sons of America deserve to be free.

"I am, with true esteem, yours most sincerely,

"ANT'Y. WAYNE.

"MAJOR HULL."

Major Hull, in his account of the attack, gives a vivid picture of the troops marching all day over the rugged mountains which lay between West Point and Stony Point, and of their silent advance through the midnight darkness to the attack. He describes the columns, who had strict orders not to load a single gun, but to do everything with the bayonet, feeling their way across the marsh and over the beach in silence. The column led by Wayne himself, together with that of Hull, crossed the beach on which was two feet of water. Some outlying guards perceived or heard the advancing body and fired, and the fort was alarmed, and immediately opened fire on the Americans who were silently struggling up the very steep hill, which was also protected by a strong abattis of trees, and strong pickets. While tearing these away, under a heavy fire of artillery and musketry, Wayne having just passed the abattis received a musket-ball, and was stunned for a moment. His soldiers rushed on, and the two columns entered the fort nearly at once. Then the mountains "found a tongue" and echoed back the loud cheers of the victors. Hull had two narrow escapes, one ball passing through the crown of his hat, and another striking his boot.

For his conduct on this occasion Major Hull received promotion, and was made a lieutenant-colonel. He was also much gratified by an invitation from General Washington to enter his family as one of his aids. But he was obliged to decline this, as General Steuben, who was introducing a new system of discipline into the army, was very desirous to have Hull as one of his assistants, as inspector, in which position he remained for some

time.   He was afterward ordered to West Chester to his old position before New York, where he
commanded a detachment of four hundred troops.
In this position he offered to make an attack on
the British post of Morrisania, which was gar-
risoned by a partisan corps who were constantly
plundering in the neutral ground and in the State
of Connecticut.   General Washington gave his
permission rather reluctantly, in a letter, printed
by Sparks, and dated January 7, 1781.   Washington doubted of the success of the enterprise, on
account of the long distance the Americans would
have to march to attack fresh troops, and because
they would leave fortified British posts in their
rear.   He added that " success depends absolutely
upon the secrecy and rapidity of the movement."
Hull was accustomed to this watchfulness and
caution from his long command in this exposed
vicinity.   He marched past the enemy's posts
unperceived, with six hundred troops, and succeeded in dispersing the enemy, taking prisoners
and cattle and the horses of the British cavalry.
They then burned the barracks and stores, and he
returned without rest, and amid frequent attacks
on the rear from an ever-increasing foe, and at
last brought off his prisoners and his troops in
safety.   He received the thanks of Washington
and Congress for this service.   Having served six
years without having asked for leave of absence,
he now obtained permission to spend the rest of

the winter in Boston, where he was married to the only child of Judge Fuller, at her father's house in Newton.

At the close of the war, William Hull, then thirty years old, having all this experience behind him — full of energy, health, and talent, began to practice law in Newton. He must have been successful, for, during the next twenty years he built a large house at Newton Corner, traveled extensively in America and Europe, and engaged in various kinds of business speculations. He bought and sold lands in Georgia, Ohio, Vermont, and elsewhere. He went to France during the French Revolution, and, I believe, took a cargo of some sort to England.

Meantime he was very happy when at home in Newton, where he had a large family growing up around him. Of his eight children, seven were daughters, all lively and agreeable, and drawing many visitors to the hospitable house. It must have been a very pleasant place to visit; at least, so I was told by Governor Levi Lincoln, who, when ninety years old, still remembered the gayeties of the place, where he and others had visited seventy years before. All the seven daughters were married; one going to live in New York, two to Georgia, one to Michigan, one to Maine, and two making their homes in Boston.

During these years he was a leading man in the State, and was frequently elected to the Massachusetts Legislature. In Shays' insurrection he commanded a column of Lincoln's force, which surprised and dispersed the insurgents. He was made major-general of militia in 1796. In 1793 he was commissioner to Canada to treat with the Indians.

In 1805 William Hull received from Thomas Jefferson the appointment of Governor of Michigan Territory, and also that of Indian agent. All the white inhabitants of the territory amounted to less than five thousand, but the Indian tribes were numerous, warlike, and needed to be treated with much wisdom. The object of Governor Hull was to civilize them and gradually extinguish their title, and to turn them, if possible, into citizens.

Detroit, where the Governor lived during his seven years' administration of the territory, was then more difficult to reach from New York than it is now to go to China. It was necessary to traverse Lake Ontario and Lake Erie on small sailing vessels, which only sailed occasionally from Buffalo and from the other ports. Here, however, he remained until 1812. He was asked, as war with England and with the Indians around Detroit seemed imminent, to accept a commission of brigadier-general in the United States army, and lead a body of troops to Detroit to protect the inhabitants. He refused the commission, and Colonel Kingsbury was appointed in his place; but this officer falling sick, Hull at last consented to take the command. He collected his troops in Ohio, and cut a military road through the wilderness, and on reaching Detroit found that war had been declared against Great Britain. Everything had been mismanaged at Washington. So tardy were they in sending him notice, that the British at Malden heard of it first, and captured a vessel in which he had sent his stores. General Dearborn, who was to have coöperated with him by invading Canada from the east, instead of doing this had made an armistice with the British commander, which allowed him to send all his troops against Detroit. Although General Hull had, during several years, urged again and again on the government the importance of building a fleet on Lake Erie, nothing had been done, and it was in the possession of the British fleet. Provisions soon became scarce ; the woods were filled with hostile Indians, his supplies were stopped, his communications cut off. Under these conditions his post became not tenable, and he surrendered, — for the same reasons which had compelled Burgoyne to surrender at Saratoga and Cornwallis at Yorktown. But these two British generals had put themselves voluntarily into a position, where they were surrounded and cut off from their supplies. General Hull went, in obedience to orders, to Detroit, depending on the support which had been promised him by his government, and which was never given.

Burgoyne and Cornwallis returned to England, and instead of being condemned for their surrender were rewarded with other and higher positions. General Hull was punished by the government which had deserted and betrayed him by being made the scapegoat for their own mistakes and their own incapacity. A victim was necessary to appease the disappointed hopes of the nation, which had been taught to believe that Canada was to fall an easy prey to our arms.[1] The anger of the people must be diverted from the government which had plunged into the war without preparation. At this juncture they found a serviceable tool in Colonel Cass. He went directly to Washington after the surrender of Detroit, and wrote a letter September 10, 1812, in which he threw all the blame of the disaster on his general. In this letter he informed the government, " that if Malden had been immediately attacked it would have fallen an easy victory." But Colonel Cass himself had voted in a council of war, with a majority of officers, *against* such an attack. In this letter he states that there was no difficulty in procuring provisions for the army. But a month before this was written, and four days before the

---

1 Henry Clay said in 1812: " We can take Canada without soldiers. . . . . I would take the whole continent from the British. I wish never to see peace till we do so." Better advised in 1814, he himself signed the treaty of peace at Ghent, which left Canada where it was before.

surrender, this same Colonel Cass wrote to the Governor of Ohio that the communication with Ohio must be kept open, as the very existence of the army depended upon it, and that supplies must come from that State. And on August 3d he wrote to his brother-in-law that "both men and provisions were wanted for the very existence of the troops." Yet Cass' letter and testimony was what diverted the anger of the people from the government upon General Hull. It was published as an official account of the surrender in all the newspapers of the Union. Its author, Colonel Cass, was immediately rewarded for this service (for he had performed no other which could excuse such advancement), by being promoted from his position of colonel in the Ohio militia to that of brigadier-general in the army of the United States. He also was appointed Governor of Michigan in place of his old commander; on the principle, apparently, that to the victor belong the spoils.

At the time when General Hull surrendered Detroit, the condition of affairs was as follows: His provisions were nearly exhausted. Communication by the lake was impossible, that being in the hands of the British, and remaining so until Perry's victory. His communications through the woods by land were entirely cut off, and two efforts to reopen them, made by strong detachments, had failed. The territory itself could furnish no supplies, as it depended on Ohio and Indiana for its own. By the fall of the American forts on the upper lakes all the hostile Indians were set free to attack Detroit. Brock had more troops, numerous Indian allies, ample supplies behind him, and the lake in his possession. Hull might have fought a battle, but if he had won it his position would have remained nearly the same. A victory would not have opened the woods or given him the lake ; but a defeat would have caused the massacre by the Indians of the white inhabitants of the territory. General Harrison, well acquainted with the country, foresaw and foretold the coming disaster. That it was inevitable that Detroit must belong to whichever nation held the command of the lake, appears from the fact that General Harrison, after the surrender, advanced to within a short distance of Detroit and was obliged to remain there a whole year, unable to move upon that place till Perry's victory gave the lake to the Americans, when the British commander evacuated at once both Detroit and Malden, without waiting for the American forces to appear.

When the court martial was summoned to try General Hull, the officer whose neglect of orders had caused the whole disaster was appointed its president. This was General Dearborn, who was to have coöperated with General Hull by invading Canada on the east ; and who, instead of this, had

signed an armistice which allowed the British
troops to be sent against General Hull.   The acquittal of Hull would have been the condemnation
of Dearborn.   And thus a man was made a judge
of the case who had a personal interest in the conviction of the prisoner.

The charge of treason was abandoned by the
court as being wholly untenable.   They found
that General Hull was guilty of cowardice in sur-
rendering Detroit, sentenced him to be shot, and
told him to go home from Albany to Boston, and
wait there for the execution of the sentence.   Of
course it was not intended that the sentence should
be inflicted.   All they wanted was a victim, and
to put him to death might make him a martyr.

Public opinion has long since reversed this sentence.   The charge of cowardice has been abandoned by all well informed writers.   It was
indeed absurd in itself.   Physical courage, in a
soldier, is very much a matter of habit.   Most
soldiers are alarmed in their first battle; few but
show courage in their tenth.   Now General Hull
was the only man in the army who was accustomed to war.   He had been in the thick of numerous battles, had led charges at the point of the
bayonet, had received again and again the thanks
of Congress and of Washington for his bravery.
Against this man's courage evidence was received
on his trial from militia officers who had never
heard a gun fired in anger, and who testified, *as*

their opinion, that his looks seemed to show anxiety and fear.

Since this charge has been given up, some writers have fallen back on another position. " He was an old man," say they, " and wanted *moral* courage. He was afraid to take responsibility." At the time of the surrender he was fifty-nine, an age at which many commanders have won great victories. There is therefore no reason to ascribe this cause for his conduct, if it is sufficiently justified by military considerations. And it certainly is so, unless we are to condemn all the other commanders who have surrendered when their provisions were exhausted and their supplies cut off.

History has at last reached the position in which its final verdict for William Hull is entire acquittal. His condemnation still stands on the records of our army ; but it was the nation which was condemned by that sentence, and not Hull. His reward for having given the strength of his youth and the vigor of his manhood to his country's service was the termination in obscurity and disgrace of a career before prosperous, brilliant, and full of hope.

But he had the one never-failing support — the consciousness of having done his duty ; on this point he never expressed a doubt. He maintained to the last, and repeated on his death-bed, his conviction that he had done right in this act, which had brought upon him so much unmerited misfortune. As a boy I used often to visit his home, and nothing could be more cheerful, kindly, and attractive than his whole manner. I never saw a cloud on his brow, I never heard a harsh word from his lips. All his grandchildren loved him, and it was a holiday when they could go to the old place in Newton, row in his boat on the pond, or try with his old carbine to shoot a rabbit in his woods. Nothing in his whole manner indicated that there was any cloud on his mind or heart.

Before his death there came a little sunshine from without also, in addition to the peace which reigned within. In 1824, by the kindness of Mr. Calhoun, then the secretary of war, he was able to procure documents from Washington, by the help of which he wrote an appeal to the people of the United States from the sentence of the court martial. This series of letters, in the "Boston Statesman," were read with interest all over the country. Public testimonials of esteem were offered to him by men of all parties; and a marked change took place from that time in the opinion of the community concerning his character and conduct.

This favorable opinion has been more and more confirmed by the conclusions of the best historians. The latest of these, who has written the most exhaustive account of the War of 1812, completely justifies General Hull's conduct. Benson

J. Lossing, in a monograph published on the surrender of Detroit in " Potter's American Monthly " for August, 1875, calls the trial a disgraceful one, its sentence unjust, and says that the court was evidently constituted in order to offer Hull as a sacrifice to appease public indignation and to preserve the administration from disgrace and contempt. " The conception of the campaign against Canada," says Lossing, " was a huge blunder. Hull saw it, and protested against it. The failure to put in vigorous motion for his support auxiliary and coöperative forces was criminal neglect." Lossing adds, that in choosing to surrender Detroit Hull " bravely determined to choose the most courageous and humane course ; and so he faced the taunts of his soldiers and the expected scorn of his countrymen rather than fill the beautiful land of the Ohio and the young settlements of Michigan with mourning. To one of his aids he said : ' You return to your family without a stain ; as for myself, I have sacrificed a reputation dearer to me than life, but I have saved the inhabitants of Detroit, and my heart approves the deed.' "

General Hull, as we have said, spent his last days at Newton, on his wife's farm, in the peaceful pursuits of agriculture. His means were very limited, and he was often in quite straightened circumstances, when he was supposed by the ignorant to be reveling with " British gold," for which he had sold his country. A large part of his support he derived from the produce of his farm. And none of his grandchildren will ever forget the happy hours spent at his house in the Thanksgiving holidays, or the dances in his hall in the evening to old Tillo's fiddle. Tillo, a negro retainer, whose father had been rescued from the ill-treatment of the Cow-boys in West Chester by Major Hull, during his command in that region, considered the old place as much belonging to himself as to his master, and regarded it as his chief duty "to fiddle for the childers." Nor can we ever cease to remember the bounteous Thanksgiving dinner, nor the long table around which the company assembled, nor the satisfaction of our grandfather, when, at the commencement of the feast, he spread his hands above the board and said, "All that you see on this table, my children, is the produce of my own farm."

There is something instructive in the story of such a life. It is one of the lessons which will always bear repeating, which show us that the peace and joy of the heart come from a consciousness of right-doing rather than from outward circumstances. It is probable that General Hull, fallen on evil days and tongues, was quite as happy, fully as contented, as when his life led from one success to another. The "stupid starers and the loud huzzas" were gone, but the self-approval remained. Cast down but not destroyed, persecuted but not forsaken, he realized the description of the poet, —

> " Thou hast been
> As one, in suffering all, that suffers nothing,
> A man that fortune's buffets and rewards
> Hast taken with equal thanks."

www.ingramcontent.com/pod-product-compliance
Lightning Source LLC
Chambersburg PA
CBHW020900130726
47900CB00014B/1165